· *Wimbledon 2000* ·

Dawson sank down onto the bedside chair. 'So give me back the money,' he suggested sarcastically.

'I can't,' she conceded.

'Then give me the kids.'

'I can't do that either.'

'Whatever else happens you're going to have to give me one. Think of the boys, Grace. Think of their future. It'd be a crime to separate them.'

'One of them is mine,' the emotion of the moment was proving too much for her. 'I'm never going to let him go. You can never make me. I'd rather die, I promise you.'

Over in the cot one of the boys began to cry. The noise woke up the other, so now they both were screaming.

'Which one will it be, Grace?' he demanded in a final act of provocation, realising that she meant business.

Feeling like a child herself, isolated and vulnerable and alone in her narrow bed, she turned away from him and buried her head deep into the pillows. 'You decide,' she said.

Iain Johnstone is a tennis enthusiast and a member of Queen's Club. Research for *Wimbledon 2000* took him round the world from Flinders Park in Melbourne to Roland Garros in Paris, from the Florida tennis academies to behind-the-scenes Wimbledon. He is the film critic for the *Sunday Times* and a frequent broadcaster on radio and television. His previous books include biographies of Clint Eastwood and Dustin Hoffman, and the bestselling *Cannes: The Novel*. He is married with three children and lives in Fulham, London.

IAIN JOHNSTONE

· *Wimbledon 2000* ·

A Novel

Mandarin

A Mandarin Paperback

WIMBLEDON 2000

First published in Great Britain 1992
by William Heinemann Ltd
This edition published 1993
by Mandarin Paperbacks
an imprint of Reed Consumer Books Limited
Michelin House, 81 Fulham Road, London SW3 6RB
and Auckland, Melbourne, Singapore and Toronto

Reprinted 1993 (twice), 1995

Copyright © Iain Johnstone 1992
The author has asserted his moral rights

A CIP catalogue record for this title
is available from the British Library

ISBN 0 7493 1013 8

Printed and bound in Great Britain
by HarperCollins Manufacturing, Glasgow

• For Mo •

The scene should be laid on a well-kept garden lawn. There should be a bright warm sun overhead and just sufficient breeze whispering through the trees and stirring the petals to prevent the day being sultry. Near at hand, under the cool shade of a tree, there should be strawberries and cream, iced claret mug and a few spectators who do not want to play but are lovers of the game, intelligent and appreciative. If all these conditions are present, an afternoon spent at lawn tennis is a highly Christian and beneficient pastime.

Lawn Tennis by Lt.-Col. R.D. Osborn, 1881

· One ·

Left shoe first. Some superstitions never change; once they're in the bloodstream nothing can eradicate them. Stronger than religion, Winston reflected, as he idled with his lace. Moses always used to say that people only really believed in things that couldn't be proved. There was no religious faith based on the fact that the sun would rise the next morning, because everybody knew it would. So it was with superstitions: even when the magic didn't work you still stuck to them, hoping that it was only some contrary combination of circumstances that had temporarily lost the luck on that occasion.

The atmosphere in the dressing room had dramatically changed from earlier in the week. It was as if there had been a death in the family. No buzz or banter, none of that carefree whistling that masked every care in the world, nor loudly called congratulations, as shrill as they were insincere. No noise at all, really. Just the sound of outside – an unbroken murmur, rising and falling like a threatening ocean or the growl of a gathering storm.

He wondered what effect, if any, it was having on Shimizu. There had been an exchange of nods when his opponent arrived – much later than him – but that had remained the extent of their communication. Although he was with his coach, Okamoto, the two Japanese had remained out of sight and curiously quiet on the other side of the sturdy central row of mahogany lockers, a traditional frontier between men who wanted to avoid each other. Winston wished they would talk; he was beginning to find the silence unnerving. Why didn't they discuss last-minute tactics, they must know he couldn't understand Japanese? Maybe they didn't need to. Maybe they wanted him to think they didn't need to.

Moses had decided not to come to the locker room. He considered it would look too conspiratorial. Winston had thought he would arouse just as many suspicions – maybe more – by staying away, but had held his peace. There was enough pressure on him without the coach ticking off every niggling detail. He needed time to work out things in his own mind. This was the moment to purify it of extraneous worries, no simple task.

Right shoe now. He drew the fresh white lace up through the five pairs of holes, making a slow knot just below the sixth. Not a double knot. Keep it single, Mo always insisted, the foot expands and you may need to make adjustments. And don't forget a loose lace is another way of buying you time.

He had no idea he would feel so suicidally alone. There was an aching need to discuss things one final time: the plan and its execution and, above all, its implications. Who was he doing it for? He wished Phoebe were with him. Even if she didn't understand his anxieties at least she would be prepared to listen to them. But he doubted if women would be allowed in by this stuffy old . . .

'Gentlemen, if you're ready.'

And even if we're not, Winston thought as he zipped up his tracksuit. It was so very British to make a command sound like a request. The hangman probably used these very words to summon his victims to the gallows. The tournament referee, his hands on his hips and the symbols of some fashionable regiment gleaming from his blazer buttons, smilingly transferred his weight from his heels to his toes like an enthusiastic sports master. Most of the officials of the All England Club were keen amateur tennis players.

'No need to carry your racquets.' The referee motioned to the man in the long white overall beside him. 'Ted does that today. Our little treat. Takes the weight off your mind.'

It was a joke of sorts, completely lost on Shimizu who watched suspiciously as the short, stooped changing-room attendant came over and gathered up the racquets.

'Right,' smiled the referee holding the door open and continuing his light-hearted patter. 'A few people turned up to watch you play. Hope you don't mind.'

The sound of the fifteen thousand souls outside grew in rumbling intensity as the four men reached the end of the landing and descended the stairs. For many years the finalists had been closeted together in a claustrophobic players' box before the match but the Association had put an end to that.

'Kipling.' The official jabbed his right forefinger peremptorily into the air.

It wasn't the first time that Winston had observed the famous couplet from 'If' above the entrance to the Centre Court. 'If you can meet with triumph and disaster and treat those two impostors just the same.' Only when he had been shown it before, the word 'impostor' had not imparted the same sense of unease as it did today.

However, this discomforting emotion was swiftly swept away by a cascading waterfall of sound. The crowd was undoubtedly cheering him for being there but also, in some tribal fashion, they were cheering themselves for being there as well.

'Do it for England,' the referee murmured quietly to him, just before they rounded the back-stop onto the court. 'Sixty-four years since Fred. It's been a long wait.'

Winston affected not to hear him, trying to clear his mind of all such irrelevancies – just as Mo had taught him – in order to address his thoughts with uninterrupted single-mindedness to the game.

Shimizu was walking beside him now and raised his arm in acknowledgement of the unbroken applause.

'Boo,' he called across in a stage whisper.

The Englishman eyed him warily. They had never played before but Winston had studied innumerable videos of his matches – especially his last two victories in 1998 and 1999 – and he had not been aware of the Japanese attempting any pre-match intimidation.

'Boo,' he called again, more emphatically.

This time Winston understood. He stopped and nodded and together they turned back to the Royal Box. As he lowered his head he could see, out of the corner of his eye, his opponent fold his body almost to the ground in a deep, imperial bow.

They posed amicably for photographs together, no animus between them save the shared knowledge that there were few crueller sporting crosses to bear than that of forgotten finalist.

The umpire summoned them to the net. 'You call,' insisted Shimizu, seizing the initiative by a whisker.

'Heads.' Winston uttered his choice automatically and then

glanced down to see a bronze portcullis, like a prison gate, nestling in the compact grass, cut as close as cashmere.

'You serve,' smiled his opponent. 'Serve your country.'

'We didn't need to toss; I'd have chosen that anyway,' Winston retorted as they moved back to their chairs.

Notions of patriotism couldn't have been further from his mind as his eyes travelled up to the Royal Box. Take a minute to look around, Moses had instructed. See where everybody is. Don't let anything come as a surprise later that might break your concentration. The king was sitting pensively in the front row, his fingers forming a pyramid in front of him, as the chairman of the club fed respectful information into his left ear. He nodded graciously and gravely with the burdened expression that had accompanied him since the abdication.

His eye panned left from the Royal Box and up to the area reserved for the friends and family of those on court. The Japanese had colonised the front row and the camera company that paid Shimizu two million dollars a year to wear its logo had been quick to supply his relations with an array of long-lensed equipment. Behind them Moses Hoffman was nestling in the corner, skimpy and skinny, his familiar black tracksuit gleaming like a newly waxed car and his deeply peaked truck driver's cap bearing the personalised name-plate: 'Mo'.

He could see Winston looking at him and gestured with a thumbs-up towards the scoreboard where an illuminated dot by the player's name indicated that he would serve first. He doesn't know I lost the toss, Winston reflected.

Moses kept up a running commentary, like an individual radio station, for the benefit of the thickset figure in dark glasses beside him. Despite the humid, overcast afternoon, Dawson Silver was garbed in the strict city ensemble of chalk-striped suit, white shirt and silver-grey tie as if he had been called away from an investment meeting to attend the game. He held his head very still, the better to concentrate on Hoffman's monologue, seeming almost entranced as he gazed into the space straight ahead of him.

The dark-haired girl on his other side was, in contrast, alive with animation. Phoebe Carter had been attempting to attract Winston's attention since the moment he had reached the net, gesticulating with her almond arms. Now she had it. She tapped the left side of her chest with her right hand in a Napoleonic gesture and then pointed to him.

He smiled back as he stood up to take off his tracksuit top but she responded by shaking her head and repeating the gesture, more emphatically this time. Her hair, usually swept back in a severe pony-tail when she was on court herself, settled with natural grace on her shoulders, their deep tan exhibited and offset by her slight primrose singlet. And her darting dark eyes sparkled like spring water.

Winston got the message and searched in the breast pocket of his jacket before hanging it on the back of his chair. His hand touched on a swatch of material which she must have secreted there. It was lace, from Chantilly. He unfolded it on his lap and a note fell out. 'Ospreys can fly as well as storks,' it read enigmatically. Searching for her expectant eye again, he signalled his receipt of the communication with a nod and the flicker of a grin.

He slipped the piece of paper into the pocket of his shorts as he walked to the back of the court, an armoury of television cameras trained on him like border guards. Shimizu had chosen the Royal Box end, evidently intending that his opponent should face the intimidating panoply of his support as they knocked up.

Winston accepted the fresh, chilled ball from the Indian boy clad in the understated, regal colours of the All England Club, and drove a lazy backhand down the centre of the court to Shimizu. The game has already begun — Mo's voice came like an irremovable tape-recorder in his brain — you're not playing for points but for psychological position. Drop your first six shots in the knock-up on exactly the same spot on the baseline, just to let him know you can do it.

Shimizu interrupted his rhythm by catching the fourth ball and advancing agitatedly towards the umpire's chair.

'Those cameras,' remonstrated the man with the photographic logo on his sleeve, 'they must sit down.'

'They will when the game begins,' the official assured him.

Winston's attention was caught by the tousled blonde, dressed in khaki as if for combat, who was the most obvious offender. Brandi de Soto, how the hell did she get accreditation? He thought she was back in Boston. The girl gave no indication that she had been spotted as she ruefully resumed her position.

The knock-up's a nonsense, Mo always said. It's the opposite of tennis. You keep hitting the ball to the other guy whereas the object of the game is to hit it where he's not. You can see people in the park who've spent their lives knocking up, afraid to hit a drop shot or an angle, just wanting to send the ball back to their friend.

'One minute, gentlemen.'

Shimizu needed no further encouragement to stop returning the ball and start practising his serves, targeting on the inner tramline. Winston held out his hands to the two ball-boys behind him and assembled four balls in his palm. He cannoned them fast and hard, one rapidly after another, down the centre line.

Now was the time to do it – for Mo, for Grace, for Dawson, for William Tatem, for Phoebe, for himself.

The umpire tapped his microphone. 'Mr Shimizu has won the toss and elected to receive. Mr Winston to serve. Play.'

· Two ·

'Winston, Winston . . . comme la cigarette . . . Winston.'

Winter had made an untimely entry to the Château Benoît on the borders of Bergerac. The proprietor paid little attention to the agitated tones of the man with the megaphone as he cast his eye over the several hundred men and women, most of whom were now stripped down to their shorts and singlets with Bergerac '74 pinned to their chests, moving restlessly in the cobbled courtyard. His concern was less with their welfare than that of his vines which had been unexpectedly assaulted by the early December frost.

'Nous avons Grace Winston, d'Angleterre, quatre-vingt huit . . . number eighty-eight?'

The starter switched to English with emphatic irritation, something that was certainly spreading to the ranks of the runners, attempting to keep warm and anxious to get going.

'Oui, she's here. Winston ici.'

The Frenchman threw an exasperated glance in the direction of the voice and then continued to tick off the last few names on his list.

'Why did you do that?' Grace muttered acidly to Alice. 'I told you I wasn't going to go.'

'You have to.' The New Zealand girl, lean and limber in her all-black kit, angled her body forward against an invisible wall in order to stretch her Achilles tendon. 'You have no option.'

'I'm not ready,' Grace complained. 'I don't feel right.'

'Nobody ever feels right. If you waited until you felt right you'd never run. If you want to get to Boston, go now.'

'You're a bully.' Grace reluctantly pulled her windcheater over her short-cropped dark hair. 'A nasty antipodean insect-woman. I'm putting your name down for the Da Nang marathon.'

'You can do it,' Alice ignored the insult. 'Just remember you've got to keep it under three hours thirty or Boston won't want to know you. Stay with me until we get to Boisse, you'll know by then what you've got left.'

The starter's pistol cut through the French countryside like a hunting rifle, causing the front of the field to sprint hungrily off.

'How will I know when it's Boisse?' Grace shouted at the dark figure rapidly moving away from her.

'Two windmills,' Alice twisted her fingers above her head in a victory sign, 'on the top of a hill, like twins.'

Grace Winston picked up the pace and fell in behind her friend, still unsure whether she was right to run or not. Her weight was wrong, her training schedule had been disrupted in recent weeks and her emotions seemed equally out of control. Ever since she had begun the affair with Lenny she wondered whether her reason for entering the Bergerac marathon was a love of running or merely a love of him.

She had never been a natural athlete. At school she was a chubby child – the kind who was stuck in goal for hockey by an unthinking games mistress. And at university, in the sixties, nobody knew where the sports fields were. It had been a time of boys and Beatles and embattled causes. Athleticism took second place to idealism as she and her fellow students gave peace a chance and revelled in a new morality, or a new immorality as it was perceived by their parents' austere generation.

Grace had duly made a sixties marriage – but, like many of these matches, it proved as evanescent as the times. People who had enjoyed the exciting freedom of shifting from partner to partner often found the first stab at stability uncomfortable and unnatural. It was as if they were conceding that their parents had been right all along. There was a perverse need to wave one final fist at the older order, to present their mothers with a divorce to distress them rather than a grandchild to cuddle.

So Grace Winston – she reverted to her maiden name – became single once more, and somewhat solitary. She lived in London but wasn't really of London. Her work as a teacher might have given her some status in a small town or village, but in Shepherd's Bush in the west of the city it just made her another statistic in the crowd – a poorly paid statistic, at that.

From time to time she would come across someone she had known at school or university and the inevitable supper ensued, but usually only one. An evening spent disinterring the pleasures of the past nearly always ended with plans for future meals to come but they were rarely followed through. Most of her contemporaries were concerned about house prices and careers and children, and someone who floated on as a piece of driftwood from the sixties did not sit comfortably in the reformed and changing order.

She bought a heavily mortgaged flat near the school in Askew Road, not leaving herself enough money to pay for the double glazing that might have ensured her a peaceful night's sleep. It was equidistant from a Malayan and an Indonesian restaurant and Grace frequently availed herself of takeaway meals from both. Where once she had been well-built, she now became solidly rounded. Her social agenda was set by the television schedules. The high point of her week was *Kojak*: she was drawn by the tenderness with which the detective treated the underdog, perhaps because he seemed so vulnerable himself with his bald head and missing finger. Sometimes she only washed her thick dark hair once a week; some weeks she didn't wash it at all.

Then, on 8 April 1974 – Grace's thirty-first birthday, Alice Walker arrived at the school to teach mathematics. She knew no one in London, save a rich cousin from Auckland whom she would go to considerable lengths to avoid. Ignoring Grace's idle protestations, Alice adamantly forced her out of her shell. They went to theatre matinées and movies and museums and ate out, when they could afford it, in nearby wine bars.

Alice had no sooner touched down at Gatwick than she joined an athletics club which met in Battersea Park and which had an affiliation with the one she belonged to in Wellington. As soon as she was well established there she blackmailed Grace into coming to a visitors' night, insisting that the English girl would forfeit her friendship if she didn't try it just once.

It was a Wednesday evening in early June. The air was heavy with the sticky city heat and it seemed an act of madness to Grace to take any form of exercise when all she wanted to do was flop in front of a fan. Reassuringly not all the other guests were svelt and muscled as she feared they might be.

She was resentful to begin with. Having gone to such lengths over the past years to preserve the citadel of her own individuality, the notion of being part of a group and joining in had become repugnant to her. At the same time she didn't want to let her friend down and, clad in an aggressive 'Impeach the Bastard' T-shirt and borrowed shorts, submitted herself to a routine of arm swings, trunk rotations, gluteal stretches and deep knee-bends with minimal complaint.

'Why are we doing this?' she whispered to Alice.

'To warm up.'

'But I'm sweltering already.'

'To show you how to warm up.' The man in charge of the class had overheard their conversation. 'Gotta wake up the old muscles. They go to sleep if they haven't been used for the past week or two – or year or two.'

Grace flushed with embarrassment, resolving never to set sneaker inside Battersea Park again.

'I spent ten years of my life sinking ten pints a night,' their leader continued, deflecting the slur back on himself. 'Drinking away the worries of the day. Now I run them off instead. Cheaper. Let's try a circuit.'

Grace had taken an instinctive dislike to the man – as she did to most – and obtained a slightly perverse satisfaction in having her judgement confirmed by this smugness. But she still followed on at the back of the pack, not wishing to draw attention to herself by refusing to join in.

'Feel good?' Alice enquired as they lay exhausted on the welcome blanket of newly-mown grass afterwards.

'Fucking awful,' Grace replied.

The following day she had a phone call from her tormentor. He introduced himself as Lenny and, before she could inform him of her intention never to move faster than a slow walk in her life again, he asked her to the movies.

'Which film?' she demanded testily.

'I've no idea what's showing,' he confessed, 'I haven't been to anything since *The Sound of Music*.'

'I thought you might be a nun-fancier,' she couldn't help herself saying.

He ignored the remark – or, at least, affected to. 'What about the one with those guys who were in *Butch Cassidy*? They've made a sort of sequel.'

'They died at the end of that.' She was prevaricating to buy time although she knew she would go. 'Is it set in heaven?'

'No, Philadelphia, I think.'

'I thought you hadn't seen a film since *The Sound of Music*?' she countered.

They went to *The Sting* the following Sunday at the Odeon Kensington. Grace insisted that she pay her own way, a precondition which she also set before she would go to Jimmy's Wine Bar for a meal afterwards. They had been late for the film and barely spoken so it was with mutual unease that they settled themselves at a table.

Assertively Lenny suggested the lamb chops and jacket potatoes from the menu chalked on the blackboard on the wall and Grace was glad to have her mind made up for her. Without even asking, he ordered a bottle of red Bergerac.

'It's got a good nose,' he smiled when the waitress poured him a little to taste.

'You've used that line before,' said Grace.

'To better effect,' he acknowledged.

The fact that she hadn't been out on a date with a man for so long made her barbed and defensive so she resolved to control herself and merely listen. It was what he wanted.

He pointed to a small map on the label of the bottle. 'There's going to be a race there just before Christmas. A crowd of us from the Badgers are intending to enter – Alice, too, I think. If you get a good enough time at Bergerac, you can qualify for Boston. Collect some sponsorship, as well, with any luck.'

'Boston what?'

'The Boston Marathon. The oldest one in the world. Been going since 1897.'

'I thought there was one in Greece the year before. Baron de Coubertin?'

Lenny gave her a wary glance, unused perhaps to being contradicted. 'Sure, the first Olympics. Founded on the myth that some guy ran back to Athens from Marathon with news about the invading Romans and then dropped dead.'

'He was called Philippides,' the teacher in her could no longer restrain herself. 'And they were invading Persians. It may be a myth but it's in Herodotus.'

Grace could see that she had impressed him and rather liked the fact. Until that moment she hadn't realised quite how coiled up she was inside. Now she found herself able to look at Lenny more directly. There was a lean, almost mean aspect to him that was icily attractive.

'History,' she shrugged with a grin. 'School swot.'

'Well, maybe you should have swotted up on the Boston Marathon,' he countered. 'It's a vital part of the social history of women's liberation in sport. I'm surprised that feminists like you don't know about it.'

'I'm not a feminist,' Grace said. 'Just a woman. But I would like to learn about it anyway.'

It was a concession to his superior knowledge which he accepted without hesitation. 'You know there's no female marathon in the Olympics. The International Committee thinks they aren't tough enough. But one day there will be and that'll be thanks to the women who inflitrated Boston.'

'Infiltrated?' Her interest was genuinely awakened.

'Exactly that. For the first seventy-five years the Boston Athletic Association didn't acknowledge the existence of women athletes. And they probably never would have if a girl called Roberta Kidd hadn't disguised herself as a man in a hooded sweatshirt and run it in three hours twenty-one. With that time she'd actually have won the St Louis Olympics. That was in 1965. Two years later Kathrine Switzer entered Boston as K.V. Switzer and managed to get an official starting number. They tried to stop her when they found out she was a girl but she still ran. And after that women just kept joining in. Sarah Berman – a mother of two – won in '69 and '70 and '71 although you won't find her in the record books because she wasn't a recognised runner. But she paved the way. A couple of years ago they let women enter officially. So, as I said, I'm sure the Olympics will come round to it eventually. Like you.'

Grace was taken aback. 'What do you mean?'

'You should run,' said Lenny, tipping the remains of the Bergerac into her glass. 'You owe it to the Boston pioneers. Besides, it gives you a sense of belonging – and a satisfaction in yourself.'

She looked accusingly into his eyes. 'Did Alice put you up to this?'

'No,' he assured her, taking a hasty sip of his own wine. 'Well, in part I suppose. I asked her if you'd mind if I rang you. And she said she thought you'd get a lot out of running. No more than that.'

'I'm too old,' Grace sighed. 'And too fat.'

'There's a chap in Greece who's ninety-five and still runs marathons. Slowly, mind you. He could have competed in the first marathon in 1896. He'd have been eighteen.'

Grace regarded him patronisingly. 'It's another myth. Beware of Greeks, remember?'

'It's not, I promise you. Look, I'll make a wager. If I can prove Dimitris exists, will you come down to Battersea and at least train?'

'Sure,' she smiled. 'That's a fair bet.'

She reached in her purse and put four pounds on the table. 'That's for my share of the meal.'

He tried to push it back to her, but she returned it with a tenacious look that let him know this was not a mere gesture.

'Why do you run, Lenny?' she asked him, as they stepped out into Kensington Church Street, still sultry with the heat of the day.

'Away from things, I suppose, to begin with.' He stopped for a moment to digest the question, as if he had never faced it before. 'And then towards them.'

She felt emboldened by the wine. 'Away from life? A wife?'

He stifled a dry laugh. 'Yep. And a job and a couple of kids.'

The newspaper cutting arrived in her post the next morning. He must have mailed it on Saturday in anticipation of the bargain he intended to strike. Grace felt her pulse beat perceptibly faster as she tore the end off the brown envelope; this was one bet she intended to lose.

There was even a photograph of the old stager: 'Dimitris Iordanidis, 96, holder of the fastest time for anyone over 90 from Marathon to Athens – 6 hours 42 minutes.'

'I bet you send him to all the girls,' she chided Lenny when she turned up at Battersea Park the following Wednesday evening.

'Only those who are going to make it,' he grinned back.

Or those you hope to make, she thought comfortingly.

'You've left it a bit late,' he warned her. 'We normally say that thirty-nine weeks is the absolute minimum training time for a novice, slightly longer than a pregnancy. But we're going to have to take some short cuts with you. Talking of which – your hair.'

She decided against having it cut immediately: that would have been too obvious a response. Instead, at the next training session, she pushed it under a baseball cap that the owner of the athletics store had presented her with when she bought two pairs of expensive running shoes at the same time. It had the team name 'Red Sox' written above the peak, although she had no idea who they were.

In most other respects she was more compliant. Alice was already well ahead of her in terms of training and, delighted that Grace had joined in so readily, counselled her to put up a wall chart and follow it religiously.

As the weeks wore on, the mileages required for each day assumed a more significant reality than the date. By the end of term she was up to twenty miles a week. Sunday: six miles, slow and steady all the way. Monday: rest. Tuesday: interval training; four miles with 300-metre fast bursts. Wednesday: rest. Thursday: five miles steady road run round the park, no pressure. Friday: rest. Saturday: Go For It. One mile warm-up followed by four miles flat out.

She was was surprised by how quickly she began to lose weight. Her stomach flattened and the excess around her hips seemed imperceptibly to melt away. It was not that she was eating any less. The club diet sheet insisted that you ate plenty of carbohydrates on the rest days before training. Grace consumed potatoes, pasta, cakes, cereals and rice with a freedom of guilt unknown to her since she was a child. The equation became part of the blackmail: if you didn't run, you couldn't eat; and to eat like that you had to keep running.

As her body changed, her being changed. She had the sense of becoming somebody else – someone who appealed to her infinitely more than the old Grace Winston. During the school holidays the rest days from training became onerous and hard to fill. She had intended to work on a research project for her class about the history of Shepherd's Bush. Who was the shepherd? Where was the bush? But it had always been a half-hearted endeavour. At the local library her attention was drawn to a section on athletics and she began to divert her research towards marathon runners, finding a kinship with those who had bitten on the same opiate as she had.

These figures became her daytime companions. Ionni Vanoulis, the Greek, who competed in the first ever marathon but was disqualified for taking a lift in a cart. The Japanese twins, Shigeru and Takeshi Soh, who were fast becoming as inseparable on the road as they had been in the womb. Takeshi had been born five minutes before his brother but, according to Japanese custom, the first-born was considered the younger. The great Jim Peters who entered the stadium twenty minutes ahead of his nearest rival in the 1954 Vancouver Commonwealth Games but collapsed before he could reach the tape. He didn't regain consciousness until the following day. Francisco Lazaro, the Portuguese champion, who suffered a similar fate in the 1912 Stockholm Olympics but, unlike his namesake, didn't return from the dead. He was only twenty.

Grace comforted herself with the thought of some happy Valhalla where people like young Lazaro were still scampering through distant Elysian fields. Or was that a mixed metaphor, she wondered? She asked herself why she was doing all this. But that question was easier to answer, if she took the time to be honest with herself. For Lenny.

'Don't get too close,' Alice had warned. 'He's a runner. He doesn't stand still. Wait for someone who'll wait for you.'

The advice came too late. Lenny was the agent of her renewed lease on life and, for that alone, the focus for the release of all the emotion that had become pent up in her over her recent past. Empirically, she tried to argue with herself, he was not a handsome man. There was too little of him: his arms were waif-like, his chest was bony and his hair fast receding. But he had a confident, toothy grin that managed to light up her day like a new-found tonic.

One Tuesday evening towards the end of the summer she went down to Battersea. It was a rest day but she had nothing else to do and Alice was away for a fortnight in France.

Lenny was there, in his tracksuit as always, sitting on the steps of the clubhouse filling in forms on a clip-board.

He motioned her to join him. 'Not trying to cheat, are you?'

Grace felt she had been caught out. 'No,' she replied, thinking quickly. 'I thought I left a jersey here last night. I was just on my way somewhere . . . you know.'

He didn't look up at her but merely continued with his neat civil servant's writing. 'You weren't wearing a jersey last night.'

Her lie was detected and she didn't care. She didn't offer any alternative explanation but just smiled at him, a genuine open smile, her sallow skin tight across her upper lip and her brown eyes cheekily unapologetic.

They sat together in silence for a while watching a lone runner circumnavigate the track. His feet moved in a splayed fashion that made his balance all the more remarkable and he threw his elbows out at frequent intervals, as if trying to dislodge invisible competitors. All the time he kept up an incessant and incomprehensible chatter to himself.

'Poor Ron,' Lenny observed. 'Not in this world. Not in our world, anyway.'

'Did the training drive him mad?' Grace asked innocently.

Lenny capped his pen and stood up. 'No. Ron's always been like that. Born in Battersea. Something hereditary apparently. They say his father roamed this park as well, like a stray cat. At least he's getting an endorphin high, he deserves some pleasure.'

Grace was anxious to slow his departure. 'Endorphins. I looked those up. That's where the feeling of euphoria comes from, isn't it? As if your body was manufacturing some illegal drug while you run.'

'I don't know that it's illegal. At least I don't think they can arrest you for it. Sometimes we experience emotions that come from other places than the brain. Like being in love.'

Grace got up so that she could look him directly in the eyes. 'Am I on target for Bergerac?' she asked.

'Oh yes,' said Lenny. 'Bang on target.'

The sleet cut into her body like shrapnel. A cruel wind carried it low over the Dordogne, salting the hedges and driving the cattle into sheltering huddles. No such luxury was afforded the competitors. Grace sought out a secure footing on the slippery path. No one else was in sight. She wondered if she was even on the right road, the last checkpoint had been more than twenty minutes ago. Perhaps she was just running aimlessly into the French countryside, as lost as the people she had read about in the 1900 Olympic marathon in the Bois de Boulogne. Perhaps she would end up as a foolish footnote in the future edition of one of the books she had borrowed.

'Who loves ya, baby?'

Kojak's reassuring greeting came out of the spray behind her. It was Alice.

'Thank God,' breathed Grace. 'Have you come to find me?'

'I've had enough difficulty trying to catch up with you. Are you trying to sprint the whole way?'

Grace gulped for air. 'I've lost all sense of pace. I followed some Belgian guys for a while but then they took off. I keep looking for the windmills. When do we get to the windmills?'

'You passed them forty minutes ago. You're on your way home, kid. Take it easy. Arrive in style.'

'How did you know I'd let you in?' she demanded as Lenny climbed into bed beside her. He was naked and she could feel him erect against her cotton nightdress.

'The hair,' he said. 'I knew when you cut your hair you'd be ready for me. You look like a boy – a principal boy, anyway.'

'I did it for the race,' she insisted.

'Exactly. Nice time incidentally. Start a little more slowly at Boston though, it makes for a better . . .'

'Climax?' she suggested.

'Have you noticed how running makes you randy?' he laughed. 'People always assume you're exhausted after a race. Anyway, my wife does, thank goodness.'

Grace felt a moment of unease but it passed as he took the shoulder straps of her nightdress in his thumbs and skilfully peeled it off her body. She grabbed him round the shoulders and held him tight against her breasts, tearful with pleasure and relief.

'You did know I was married,' Lenny continued casually.

'Love is blind,' she whispered to herself.

· Three ·

'I'm going to go blind. That's what you mean, isn't it?'

'I didn't say that. I said you were suffering from retinitis pigmentosa.'

'You doctors always hide behind Latin phrases when you want to keep the facts from the patients.' Dawson Silver tried to make light of it but the information had settled on the bottom of his stomach like a fatal potion. 'How long have I got?'

Edmund Michaels took out a well-chewed pencil and sketched casually on the pad in front of him. 'Look, this is the retina, the coating of the eye that receives light and converts it into chemical energy. It's actually part of the brain and that's its gift and its failing. It only has a limited capacity for repairing damaged tissue.'

'Mine's damaged?' Silver wanted to get to the point.

'Well, it's deteriorating. But the cause isn't what you think. It has nothing to do with dealing with figures all day. You could have been an astronaut instead of an actuary and the same thing would have happened to your sight.'

'Except if I were an astronaut I'd have had more expert check-ups and I wouldn't have had to wait till I was forty-seven to find this out.'

'There's nothing anybody could have done,' the doctor assured him. 'Your tests were carried out by the best ophthalmologist in Harvard and they don't come better equipped than that. It's a hereditary disease. It's in your genes. What about your parents? Grandparents?'

Dawson shrugged. 'My mother's sight was fine. My father didn't live to find out what his was like.'

Dr Michaels looked at him through his grey-filtered spectacles with an unspoken interrogative.

'Arnhem,' Silver explained. '82nd Airborne under Jumping Jim Gavin. The Germans picked them off like clay pigeons.'

'I'm sorry, I remember now. Well, he undoubtedly suffered from it as well. Sometimes in childhood it begins as a night blindness, the eye isn't strong enough to discern things in a dim light. And then – and this is what's happening to you – the peripheral parts of the retina start to atrophy and while the central tubular vision may remain good, over the years your field of sight will gradually narrow.'

'So how long?' Dawson repeated.

Michaels pushed back his chair and removed a Tareyton cigarette from the pack in the breast pocket of his shirt. He blinked at regular intervals, like a warning light on a hazard, as if trying to rid his own alert eyes of some continuing irritant. 'No need to worry too much. You'll probably be able to watch them nailing the lid down on your coffin from the inside. Only it might be a bit fuzzy.'

'That's the optimistic prognosis, isn't it?'

The doctor flicked open a Zippo lighter, put the flame to the cigarette in his mouth and nodded. 'There's actually nothing we can do. You could lose your sight before you're fifty. But you could also be hit by a tram on Storrow Drive tomorrow.'

Dawson Silver looked out of the window of the cold consulting room down to the River Charles which broadened into a bend far beneath them. The waters were trying their best to reflect the thin rays of the dim December sun. Or was it his eyes that were putting a gauze over the sparkle? He focused deliberately on a rowing eight that was carving a lone passage back upstream towards the boat houses.

'Boston University,' he announced with pride.

'What?' enquired the doctor.

'Down there. BU. I can actually make it out on the vest of the stroke.'

Michaels pushed his glasses back up onto his forehead. 'Very good. More than I can. You see, your central vision has a fair chance of remaining reasonably good – though they'll certainly need to alter the prescription on your glasses from time to time. It's just the sight at the side, like the edges of a cinema screen, that's likely to degenerate.'

'Genes.' Silver spat out the word. A lifetime of attempting to seem authoritative had made him look older than his forty-seven years. His sparse remaining hair was prematurely grey and his square head sat on a correspondingly squat body that even the expensive tailoring of his city suit could do little to enhance.

'Something that should interest an actuary,' said Michaels, scribbling on his pad again. 'Essentially it's just playing the numbers game. Gregor Mendel, the father of genetics. He worked his theory out with garden peas. What he did was to fertilise short plants with pollen from tall plants and found that the offspring were uniformly tall. Then he got plants of this generation to self-pollinate – you know, fertilise themselves – and the offspring exhibited the characteristics of their grandparents: three tall to one short. Do you follow me? And he subsequently found that if the short plants alone were allowed to self-pollinate they only produced short plants.'

Silver rose from his chair and cleared his teeth with his tongue. 'I don't really get it. Actuaries aren't concerned with peas. I can knock up a nice pension fund for you. Cheaper than most – doctors have a shorter life expectancy than other professions. Longer than some people though.'

Edmund could sense from the reflective nature of this last remark the direction of Dawson's thoughts. He adjusted his Hawkes Club bow-tie uneasily. 'How's Bunny?' he casually enquired.

'I thought you were meant to know that.' The reply was unexpectedly sour.

'She hasn't consulted me in ages. She called me up. She said she had another doctor out on the Cape.'

'Dr Jack Daniels, to be precise.' Dawson wearily picked up his black velvet-collared coat from the chair beside him.

'No change?'

'No change. We all have our ways of dealing with this thing. Whiskey's as good as any, I suppose. Better than living with it. Or me, apparently. She hasn't been back to Marlborough Street since the day of the funeral.'

'Listen,' Michaels leant intently across the desk, 'we should talk further. Nothing to do with your eyes. Let me buy you lunch on

Saturday. You know the Orson Welles cinema by MIT? It's got a restaurant. Twelve thirty. There's something I want to show you.'

Silver's chauffeur leapt smartly out of the Lincoln when he saw him emerge from the front door. The temperature was still well below freezing and the steps might be slippery. He ran forward to offer assistance but Dawson waved him gruffly away.

'I won't need you any more this afternoon, Doherty. Seven sharp tomorrow. And don't forget the *Wall Street Journal*.'

The driver acknowledged the reprimand by touching the peak of his cap. 'Yes, sir. Mary has prepared dinner. Fresh stuffed lobster, bought it myself at the market.'

The portly actuary ignored the remark, and the man, and began to make his way down Revere Street. Somebody had thrown fresh grit on the sidewalk and he followed the trail, as a runner might follow a paperchase, only more cautiously. The lamps of Beacon Hill cast their superior light onto the low heaped wall of snow by the side of the road.

Although Dawson lived in the area, he was aware that he would never really belong there. He had known the district from his wedding day when Bunny's father had quoted the immortal verse from the Holy Cross Alumni Dinner of 1910.

> And this is good old Boston
> The home of the bean and the cod,
> Where the Lowells talk to the Cabots
> And the Cabots talk only to God.

His god had been the wrong one for an established Catholic family such as the Mahoneys. A child of Seventh Avenue immigrants in New York, Dawson had seen the style of old New England while he was at Temple University, where Bunny had been in his economics class, and decided it was right for him. But he soon discovered that marrying into a family was a far remove from belonging to it. The Mahoneys had not built up generations of wealth for it to be shared by those who did not share their blood.

However, he loved Boston – the town, they proudly insisted locally, where the Charles and Mystic Rivers converged to form the Atlantic Ocean. There was no history of huddled masses here; this was where the Yankees threw mud in the face of the British and their taxable tea to the bottom of the harbour. This was old America at its most arrogant, rich with Boston Brahmins. 'The hub of the solar system,' Oliver Wendell Holmes had once called the city and 'the hub' it was still known as throughout the country.

The proudly swelling red-brick homes of Beacon Hill – themselves symbols of cash and class and culture – made their way up to the gold-domed State House, Charles Bulfinch's architectural celebration of confidence and independence. Beneath them lay the stone-built solidity of Back Bay where Dawson occupied the former Mahoney family home, one of the few houses that had not been subdivided into apartments. He still obtained a comforting satisfaction from the fact that some erstwhile city father, with a mind not unlike his own, had named the cross-streets in alphabetical order: Arlington, Berkeley, Clarendon, Dartmouth, Exeter, Fairfield, Gloucester, Hereford. Most American cities gave their streets numbers; Boston gave hers style.

He decided not to return to the office – he had left his diary deliberately empty, anticipating worse news than Michaels had actually delivered – nor to go straight home, although Marlborough Street was within easy walking distance. Instead he headed for the Common – the oldest public park in the United States.

He needed to clear his mind and try to clear his conscience. Not that he had much confidence in achieving the latter. Involuntarily he kept giving himself eyesight tests, fixing on buildings in the distance and closing first one eye and then the other. To begin with he feared his vision had taken a dangerous turn for the worse but then he realised that his glasses were flecked with the light snow that had begun to fall. When he wiped them clean he could see quite clearly. Dawson blamed himself for ever agreeing to the damn test in the first place. He, above all people, could have arranged to increase his insurance cover without further medical examinations.

'Rockfeller sworn in as vice-president.' 'Support for Carter candidature grows.' The billboards were insufficiently appetising to tempt him to buy an evening paper. Massachusetts might have been the only state not to vote for Nixon but Dawson Silver had supported him wholeheartedly. The man had been a weak-kneed idiot to resign. What could be worse than the left-wing media running the country? Who on earth wanted a peanut farmer from Georgia?

Last night's snow lay largely undisturbed over much of the Common save for the beaten tracks where government workers had made their daily way to the State House. Around the periphery of the park, dark muffled figures on cross-country skis made steady, joyless circuits. Dawson headed for the lake in the centre – more of a pond, really. It was frozen over and the covering of snow made it hard to discern the edges, were it not for the fierce notices enjoining people not to skate on it. Forty years ago it would have been alive with local citizens, he thought, gliding along with their hands behind their backs like characters on the Thames in a London lithograph. But in the age of the insurance claim, pleasure took second place to public parsimony.

But it wasn't skaters that he visualised as he stared at the unbroken snow: it was the Swan Boats. In the summer they would circle the lake with their carefree cargo of children, rich and poor, white and black, privileged and underprivileged, all equal immigrants to the less innocent world of adulthood. Simon had loved to go on those boats again and again and again.

'But they don't take you anywhere,' his father would protest.

'They bring you back,' the boy insisted, 'they bring you back to where you started.'

Nothing would bring him back now, no Swan Boat, no act of atonement. Only memory. Dawson wondered, not for the first time, why he had been dogged by such unforgivingly cruel luck. Was there some divine division of fortune that spread the load in deliberately uneven shares? Did the equation balance after death, with all those golden people who had lived blissful lives paying the actuarial price for their temporal happiness? Would it have helped if he had been less ambitious and more humble? Should he have fought to bring his son up in the faith?

'No,' he found himself saying out loud. He glanced around but fortunately no one was in earshot. The boy's mother was a Catholic. More than that, a Boston Catholic. Such a devout religion was clearly dominant over Judaism, any all-seeing God would grant you that. In the few days immediately after their son's death she had found some solace in her faith. The priest had come round and explained that it wasn't God's intention just to have heaven full of old people. So some were summoned early. True belief required you to see things from God's point of view. But it had provided her with infirm support after the event. To his knowledge, Bunny had never been to church again since the day of Simon's funeral. Their estate at Chatham on Cape Cod had closed its gates to prelates of every rank: indeed to visitors of any kind, save the delivery boy from the liquor store.

She blamed herself. The boy had played in the waves a hundred times before and would have done so a hundred times again if the surf board hadn't caught the side of his head. Did he cry out? Should she have heard him? Would she have heard him if her attention had not been absorbed by her book and her glass of wine? Only Bunny knew. She had grown up on Harding beach as a child herself and, even in her fifties, was still a strong swimmer. But Simon wasn't granted the chance of a last-minute reprieve. His fate was swift and irrevocable. The current carried him several hundred yards down the shore. He would have been ten the following week. Dawson had already bought him the promised go-kart and hidden it above the lawn-mowers in the loft of the garage at Chatham.

He often wished he had shown it to his son. Instead he had kept up the pretence that he couldn't afford so expensive a gift. Did the child have one last shaft of consciousness when he cursed his father for his lack of generosity, lack of love? Or, if he had seen it, would the thought that he would never live to drive it have made his final moments even more cruel?

School was out. The sound of youthful voices across the Common made him turn and head for home. Snow offered children such instant pleasure, he thought, as if it were some magic dust sent to entertain them. It was falling more densely now and he could see the top-hatted doormen of the Ritz-Carlton Hotel opening their umbrellas to shelter the arriving guests. He crossed over Arlington to where the gas-lights of Marlborough Street marked his path home. A group of student carol singers, entrenched in mufflers, had assembled on the corner with Berkeley. 'God rest ye merry, gentlemen, let nothing you dismay.' One of them was jingling a collecting box but Silver used the cover of the thickening snow to avoid them.

Edmund Michaels was already at a table in the cinema restaurant when Dawson made his way in past the box-office, shaking the sleet off his umbrella. The doctor was wearing his weekend casual regalia: a vertically striped rugby shirt with blue jeans and sneakers. Were it not for his thatch of greying hair, he could be taken for one of the city's half a million students – although he was, in fact, two years older than his lunch guest. In his tie and sports jacket Dawson felt out of place and somewhat overdressed.

Michaels rose to greet him, proudly brandishing the menu as if he had just been awarded it. 'Ever been here before? Neat, isn't it? Get a load of some of these – Kane Pie, Rochester Roast, Ambersonburger, Rosebud Stew. Kinda cute, no?'

The actuary hung his dripping coat over the back of a cheap wooden chair and perched himself on the one beside it. Removing a handkerchief from his breast pocket to wipe his glasses, he repeated: 'Cute?'

'The menu – it's all from his movies.'

'Whose movies?'

'Orson Welles. Who did you think, Desi Arnaz?'

'I don't think I've ever seen either of their films. I've watched Welles advertising stuff on television. Can't think what it was now. Some drink – or maybe a country.'

The doctor was genuinely suprised. 'You must have seen one. Everybody's seen *Citizen Kane*. Even on television.'

'Everybody except me,' Dawson retorted gruffly. 'I only use television for news and sport. The rest is garbage.'

'You amaze me. Well, what are you going to have? My treat.'

'A salad will do' – Dawson rarely ate much during the day – 'chicken or beef or something.'

'Shanghai salad,' Edmund pointed to the menu with satisfaction.

'No, nothing Chinese. My stomach. You should know.'

His doctor smiled. 'It's not Chinese, it's chicken. *The Lady from Shanghai*. Remember the Hall of Mirrors. Rita Hayworth and her crippled husband – they're trying to shoot each other but they see these multiple reflections and they don't know which one is real.'

Silver took a sip of water. 'Did you bring me here to recite the plots of bygone movies? I hope you don't charge your usual rates for that.'

Michaels ignored the half-hearted insult. 'Have you spoken to Bunny, by the way?'

'The lady from Chatham? Well, I haven't attempted to shoot her recently, if that's what you were thinking.'

'You mentioned she was drinking. Have you tried to get help?'

Dawson glanced around the restaurant. They were the only people there. 'I'm not trying to get help, Edmund. I'm trying to get out. We stayed together for Simon. Now, well . . . what?'

'The money?' Michaels wondered whether he knew him well enough to venture such an impertinent remark, but Silver didn't seem offended.

'That's not so important any more. I guess I can remain in Marlborough Street, as long as we're formally married. Chatham was always the place her family thought of as home. Simon loved it there. That kid . . . you saw him . . . no fear. He and I used to agree he was going to be either a downhill racer or a Grand Prix driver. Not sit behind a desk like his old fart of a father. We had it all planned. I'd even taken out policies that would mature at regular intervals and see him on his way. Worthless now – I never calculated he might die. He gave me fresh life, Edmund. It wasn't just Simon died there out on the Cape.'

'I think I knew that.' Michaels dropped his voice. A group of students, noisy with good-natured banter, had now occupied the corner table. 'It's what I wanted to talk to you about. Ever think of having another child?'

'Bunny's fifty-two. Even her money can't buy miracles. And we're hardly the ideal couple to adopt.'

'By someone else?'

'Anyone I know?' the actuary asked superciliously.

'Not necessarily,' Edmund responded.

The waitress – dressed as an old-fashioned usherette – arrived to take their order. 'Don Quixote gazpacho's finished,' she announced.

'How can it be finished?' demanded Silver exasperatedly. 'We're the first people here.'

'Welles never finished *Don Quixote*,' Michaels tried to make light of his companion's short fuse. 'Some people think he never will. There's a psychological barrier. Better not to complete it and avoid being judged by it. Ever since *Citizen Kane* he's always been searching for perfection, but that's not something men can achieve. That's for God.'

'Where are we going?' Silver found he had to break into an intermittent jog to keep up with the doctor's eager pace.

'I told you at lunch,' Michaels reminded him. 'My inheritance. I wanted you to be the first to see it.'

'Put half in C/Ds at the bank and the other half in an overseas managed fund,' shouted the actuary over the swish of traffic. 'Stay out of stocks. There's no confidence in this country at the moment. Remember, we've got a Ford not a Lincoln.'

'It's not money,' Michaels called over his shoulder. 'In fact I'm not quite sure yet what it is.'

They turned off Massachusetts Avenue and came to a halt outside a small terraced house a third of the way down Castor Street. Silver stepped back to appraise it. 'Ninety thousand, maybe a hundred if you did it up.'

Michaels struggled with the key. 'It's rented I'm afraid. I think the lease runs out at Christmas. I'll give some of my students a couple of dollars an hour to clean it out – once I've taken what I want.'

They climbed the uncarpeted staircase to a compact kitchen on the first floor. It was antiquated but clean, with each drawer and cupboard labelled in a methodical fashion.

'Coffee?' Michaels enquired, lighting the smallest gas ring on the cooker from a book of matches he had picked up at the restaurant.

Dawson nodded. 'Who did you say this guy was – cheeseburger or something?'

'Steigenberger. Doctor Horst Steigenberger. Not a medical doctor, a research chemist. He was a patient of mine. Came to me a bit late, though; the tumour was too far advanced. Sugar? There's no milk I'm afraid.'

'Do these things happen to all your patients?'

Edmund offered a wry smile. 'Only to those who don't pay their bills on time. No, he was old. Wanted to return home to Innsbruck to die so that he could see the snow on the Austrian Alps, he always said. He was working away on his own. Had no partners or students and he didn't want to take the stuff next door through customs so he gave it to me.'

'Stuff? Drugs? Heroin?' A growing incredulity spread across Silver's face as he accepted the yellow mug from the doctor's outstretched hand.

'No, more like heroes, as a matter of fact. I'll show you them in a minute.'

Silver was evincing signs of annoyance. 'What's all the mys—' he began, but his words were cut short by a curious rattling noise in the corner of the room.

'What the hell's that?' he cried, his alarmed voice hinting at his increasing unease.

Michaels stepped across towards the window. 'What do you call a girl who has everything?' he enquired, out of the blue.

'I've no idea.'

'Eugenia.' The doctor replied and, in the manner of a magician, removed a pair of tea-towels to reveal a cage positioned at the end of the draining board. The sound of their conversation must have woken up the smooth albino hamster that was now furiously charging round a small vertical wheel.

'I still don't get it.'

'Eugenia. Eugenics. Genie here comes from the best stock man can make.'

'That's Nazi stuff, isn't it?' Silver suggested warily.

'Predated them. It's what I was telling you about the other day. Francis Galton, a nineteenth-century anthropologist – cousin of Charles Darwin, as a matter of fact – worked out that each generation of ancestors makes a proportionate contribution to the total make-up of the individual. He was the first guy to put forward the theory that the human race could be improved by control of breeding – just keep it to the brightest and the best. Now it's done all the time with animals. Veterinary surgeons have shown the way – they isolate the fittest dairy cows, the fastest horses, the sheep with the finest wool. That beef you were eating at lunch was probably man-made or, at least, the cow had been artificially inseminated with sperm from a bull that had been hormone enhanced. The Russians have been doing it since the thirties – a scientist called Ivanov pioneered their plans for breeding millions of horses and cattle and sheep. It goes back further than that. There was a crazy Italian, Spallanzani, who claimed he had inseminated bitches back in 1780. But you know Italian stallions.'

'And bitches,' Dawson observed drily. 'Is this a lecture?'

'You asked who Steigenberger was. He was a guy who experimented with eggs and semen. Genie, there, is a little test-tube baby. Came right out of the cocktail shaker with all her bits intact. A well-bred hamster if ever there was one.'

'Just with animals?' Dawson looked at the creature with evident distaste.

Dr Michaels took a long sip of his coffee, savouring it like a wine in order to allow himself more time to decide how much he should reveal.

'I don't really know. And I don't want to. At one stage he asked me to help him, but he was too old and more than a little eccentric. Besides, he didn't have the back-up to be at the front of the pack. It's already possible to create a child in vitro – in a test-tube, outside of human bodies. But there are problems for anyone who admits to having done it. Legal. Moral. Ethical. When man starts playing God, where does that leave God?'

Dawson sensed he was covering something up but was confused as to exactly what. 'So what did you bring me here to see? Eugenia? Want me to adopt her?'

Michaels looked down at the frenetic animal, still charging round her revolving wheel as if her life depended on it. 'No, I think she'll have to be put down.' He cleaned an imaginary morsel of food from between his teeth with the nail of his thumb. 'I'm relying on your discretion, Dawson, you understand that?'

'You have it.'

'Fine. Forgive me for mentioning it, but I just needed to be clear in my own mind. Dr Steigenberger was something of a collector. Over the years he wrote to a lot of people whose name he saw in the papers. In truth he never really understood America or Americans. He thought the people who appeared on the Johnny Carson Show were our aristocracy. But if they agreed to meet him – men only – he offered to put them in his archive.'

'What – autographs?'

Michaels dropped the tea towel beside the sink and moved across the room to unlock a second door between the kitchen cupboards. 'In a manner of speaking, yes.'

The distinct disinfected aroma of an operating theatre or even a morgue curdled the air as he pushed the door open. He pulled a knotted cord on his right-hand side to switch on the light. An empty enamel table with metal legs stood in the centre of the room surrounded on three sides by what looked like extended super-market deep-freezes.

With delicate caution the doctor gingerly lifted the lid of the one closest to them. Silver stepped forward, fearing what he might find inside. But there was nothing to distress him. Beneath a thick glass canopy was a series of serrated metal baskets crammed full of small brown bottles. They contained varying measures — not very much — of some cloudy substance. Each had the same red label with black writing on it as the kitchen cupboards.

Michaels dropped the lid abruptly as if fearful something might escape. 'They're best if they're kept a hundred and ninety-two degrees below zero. Liquid nitrogen. Don't want them to go off. Some have been there for more than twenty years. Any idea what's in them?'

'Well, from your conversation, sperm,' said Silver. 'Prize-winning bull and pure ethnic hamster.'

'Right fluid, wrong donors,' the doctor congratulated him. 'Steigenberger was, literally, a collector. All this is a strange sort of cryogenics. If people were prepared to give him a sample, he was prepared to preserve it. Not a lot of well-known people did, in fact. Most of those in there are just nobodies. Come back to the kitchen, it's cold in here.'

'Smells of death,' Silver noted as he followed him.

'Life, more like,' suggested the doctor, ushering him past and carefully relocking the door. He went across to a drawer by the sink and extracted an old-fashioned accounts book, bound in dark blue leather. 'Students, mainly, as far as I can see. All their names and addresses are here. Some of them are middle-aged by now — it goes right back to '52. A lot of people did it for the ten dollars he was offering, I think. He's put down some famous names but I think they're probably his fantasies. They're all cross-referenced against the numbers next door. Arranged according to factors like race, blood groups, chromosomes and potential fertility.'

Dawson took the volume from him. It fell open at the section marked 'T'. There was a double page full of names most of whom meant nothing to him. But Steigenberger, clearly a name dropper of the deceased, had underlined some better-known ones: Dylan Thomas, the Welsh poet who had drunk himself to death at the age of thirty-nine; Jim Thorpe, the legendary Indian all-rounder, an Olympic gold medallist and Boston baseball star – another casualty to drink; William Tilden, the tennis champion who died in homosexual disgrace just three months after Thorpe in 1953; Mike Todd, the former husband of Elizabeth Taylor, who was killed in a plane crash; and Spencer Tracy, the Hollywood star who was still alive.

'These names – Spencer Tracy, Jim Thorpe – did Steigenwhatsit really persuade them to give him samples?'

The doctor shrugged his shoulders. 'He said so. He certainly wrote to people like them. But I suspect there's more than a bit of bullshit there – an attempt to make his collection more valuable.'

'And all this sperm,' Dawson continued, 'should it in theory still be effective – even the old stuff?'

'Should be – if it hasn't been warmed up.'

Silver studiously scrutinised the page in front of him. 'Are you suggesting that I contribute?'

'No,' Michaels laughed. 'I just thought you might be interested. It comes down to . . . probabilities. The more we know about the family and the ancestors of a donor, the more we can discount various hereditary defects. We can begin to calculate the odds.'

The actuary appeared not to be listening to him. 'Supposing I were interested?'

The doctor looked closely at Silver whose eyes were still fixed on the page in front of him. 'I've done it before. There's a place in Chevy Chase, just outside Washington DC. Surrogate mother. You could see a photograph of her if you want. Nothing abnormal about it – it's the way forward. There's a book just been published by a writer called Robert Francoeur, *Utopian Motherhood*. I can lend you a copy if you like. He even fears that these mercenary mothers will jeopardise the traditional family structures. Not so; we only use these means when the structure has problems – as in your case.'

'Mercenary,' Dawson repeated. 'How much do they charge?'

'Depends on the woman. Twenty grand, maybe more. You never have to meet them. All you need to do is jerk off into a bottle. Some people say they find that preferable to the real thing.'

Dawson was smiling as he looked up at him. 'And your fees?'

Dr Michaels twitched at the directness of the enquiry and laughingly opened the palms of his hands. 'I'll give you my children's rates.'

· Four ·

'Come on, Winnie.'

Individual shouts from the crowd were usually counter-productive. Ignore them, Moses advised. Don't acknowledge them, don't let them think you even heard. It will only encourage more. You're playing your own game. You control it, not your supporters. If you take heart from them you run the risk of being vulnerable when you're in a hostile environment. Accept the applause after you've won – not till then. Your supremacy's inside you, remember that, it flows from an unlimited spring.

'Fifteen–forty.'

The umpire uttered the score like an admonishing magistrate. No wonder Shimizu had let him serve. He seemed to have direct radio contact with a sensor inside Winston's brain. The Japanese player had moved forward the customary couple of feet to receive, that was a standard tactic in the first few games when the server would be tight and unlikely to attain full pace. But Shimizu was reading him like a daily paper. After putting his practice serves down the middle, Winston had instinctively gone wide with the first ball of the match but his opponent barely had to move his feet to return it, so certain did he seem of its targeting.

His second serve had come back with accumulated interest, stranding Winston helplessly on the way to the net. He had scrambled the third point with an unsatisfactory lob but, again, on the last one Shimizu had punished the ball back into an unreachable corner.

'Fifteen–forty, you've been naughty. Make it whine down the centre line.'

'If you don't kill him, he'll kill you,' Winston repeated to himself as he stared deliberately into Shimizu's unblinking gaze. He lowered his body and released the ball, rifling himself at it with every limb and muscle on maximum thrust. It left him at a hundred and twenty miles an hour. But it hit the net. And so did the next one. 'What does an idiot order in a bar?' he could hear Mo say. 'A double.'

A low groan spread through the Centre Court like a contagious virus. 'Game Shimizu. First game. First set.'

It always seemed stupid to Winston to sit down at the initial changeover. Your body was just warming up and there was no need to rest. One either wanted to capitalise on an advantage or redress a setback, as he did now. But the air temperature at Wimbledon that July afternoon in the year 2000 fell just short of a sauna and there was no danger of losing any body heat during the sixty-second respite.

He automatically picked up his towel to wipe his racquet handle. As he slipped his hand in the pocket of his shorts to check he had sufficient grip he felt the note from Phoebe. Ospreys and storks – he was fighting for more than he had bargained for at the beginning of this venture.

Any further rumination was banished by a hissed voice behind him. 'Jimmy, just a moment, Jimmy.'

Winston turned quickly in his seat and caught the familiar face of Brandi de Soto, leaning over the low wooden barrier that restrained the photographers. She aimed a long lens at him and fired off a dozen automatic shots.

He deliberately failed to acknowledge her. 'Did anyone else hear?' he worried. And, despite the humidity, an arctic shiver slid down his spine.

· *Five* ·

Patriots' Day is unusual among American holidays in that it is only celebrated in the states of Maine and Massachusetts. The inhabitants there have a more lingering sense of duty towards history than the rest of the USA and reward themselves for this virtue with an extra day off on the nearest Monday to 19 April every year. It celebrates the Battle of Lexington, 1775, generally regarded as the opening gambit in the plan to replace the mad George (the Third) with the sacred one, whose name still adorns one hundred and twenty-one towns and villages throughout America, thirty-three counties, ten lakes, seven mountains, and every dollar bill. It might have been simpler to name the country after him.

One hundred and twelve years later the Boston Athletic Association decided that a public holiday without work or pain was debilitating for the soul and, in the wake of the first modern Olympic Games in 1896, decreed that there should be a marathon in the New World. Of course, the idea was immediately stolen by upstart New Yorkers who managed to stage the first one in America the previous fall. But Bostonians are made of sterner stuff and while the Gotham event was not to reappear for another seventy-four years, the Massachusetts race started in the spring of 1897 and has been running, in a manner of speaking, ever since. Even the Great Wars could not put a stop to it, although in 1910 the event was reduced to a ten-man military competition.

In the early races, a nation that had a more valid claim to the continent than George Washington was frequently to the fore: the Hopi and the Narragansett, the Mohawk and the Missassaja, the Penobscot and the Onondaga. It was an Indian from this last tribe,

Tom Longboat, who won the 1907 race in record time through driving sleet. Proof that civilisation had come to Boston earlier than the rest of America was apparent in the willingness of this respectable club to consort with the natives. But not with women. It was to take sixty-five more years after Longboat's victory before Nina Kuscsik became the first recognised female winner of the world's oldest marathon.

Two hundred years, almost to the day, after the historic victory at the Battle of Lexington, the United States was in the throes of its most ignominious retreat. On 17 April 1975 the Communists took control of Cambodia and before the month was out Saigon would finally surrender to the North Vietnamese. So there wasn't very much to feel patriotic about on a grey Monday morning in the trim Massachusetts town of Hopkinton as nearly two thousand competitors – men and women – warmed up for the twenty-six-mile battle to Boston.

'Ice cubes?'

'Yes.'

'Wrist watch?'

'Yes.'

'Legs?'

'One on each side.'

Lenny laughed. 'I don't know why you girls bother with make-up. It's only going to run – faster than you probably.'

'It makes us feel good at the start,' Alice Walker insisted. 'Why did you shave this morning?'

Lenny conceded the point. There were five of them from Battersea, the black-and-white badgers on their vests proudly identifying their provenance. Grace Winston felt unaccountably nervous. She was fairly confident she could go the distance – the fact she had made the qualifying time at Bergerac was testimony to that – but she was aware that she was carrying an additional burden: the need to prove herself to Lenny. It was stupid but it was true. After she had slept with him in France, he had dominated her thoughts like a new-found religion.

He was aware of this, and it made him more confident and slightly cruel. Six of them had trained together as a group since Christmas – one girl dropped out after discovering, unexpectedly, that she was pregant – and had become as close as astronauts with a mutual mission. On four occasions, when Grace had managed to keep up with the men for about the first five miles, Lenny had later come back to her flat in Askew Road on the pretext of giving her a steroid injection but also to make love to her, joking that it was some kind of reward. She was content to participate in the fiction – she was happy just to have him to herself – but she sensed that in his strange way he meant it. Their relationship was predicated on her performance not in the bed but on the track. Maybe it turned him on, maybe she only really became an object of desire in his eyes when she demonstrated her athletic prowess. Maybe, she thought more darkly, he took a perverse pleasure in making her suffer for her sex. But she wanted him, whatever the terms. He wasn't just the man in her life; he was her life.

'We'll stay together till Framingham, it's about a quarter of the way. Then goodbye.' Lenny was addressing his two male colleagues. He turned to Grace and Alice. 'I'm not sure about the starting system here, but if they let the sheep go with the goats, you can come too.'

Alice offered him a dismissive glance and turned her back to loosen up. As Grace's obsession had grown during the winter months, her friend had been a warning siren, anxious to protect her from the inevitable end of the affair.

Grace stood rooted to the road as he came across and put an avuncular arm around her. 'You stick with us, baby. I know you can keep up.'

She wished she could assert herself but the touch of his arm across her shoulders was enough to make her crave for the moment when he would come to her bed in the Holiday Inn.

'You're a patronising shit,' she said, as suggestively as she could.

'I know,' he replied, jogging away.

Dawson Silver sunk his palm into the horn aggressively. He hated to drive himself but even Doherty was entitled to his Patriots' Day off.

'What's the fucking problem?' he yelled at the man with the arm band who was holding the traffic back, feeling confident that he was not a cop.

'It's not a problem,' the steward replied. 'It's the marathon.'

'I know that. I read my papers. And I also know that they don't get here for another hour. Not unless Superman's running.'

'The spectators are here already,' the man replied in a courtly fashion that might have made a more sensitive soul feel apologetic. 'But you can go now.'

As Dawson rounded the Prudential Center he could see that the bleachers were nearly full already. The building was the focal point of the hub, the weather beacon at its tip glowing a reassuring red whenever the Red Sox won a game. Across the other side of Copley Square, the John Hancock Tower had recently obtained a less than sporting reputation as some of the large mirror windows – there to reflect the charms of the neighbouring buildings – had buckled under the high winds and turned into whirling guillotines.

'Sorry, the garage is full, sir.' The black man at the booth was new to him. 'It's the marathon.'

'I know,' Dawson conceded irritably. 'But I have a contract, here.' He jabbed his finger at the sticker on his windscreen.

'It's still full,' the man insisted.

'I'll take my chances,' the owner of the walnut Lincoln snapped back and throttled up the ramp coming to rest, illegally, in a disabled bay.

The elevators from the garage had been shut off, probably to prevent intruders, and for a moment Dawson was worried that the whole building had been closed. He took the emergency staircase to the lobby where, to his relief, he encountered a familiar security guard.

'Good day, Mr Silver. Not running?'

'I'm always running, er . . .' – he had no idea of the man's name – 'just never seem to catch up.'

'I'm afraid the elevator on the right's the only one operational today, Mr Silver. Make sure you're back in time to see Jesus do it.'

Dawson stared at the man incredulously. Was he some kind of Latin American fundamentalist?

'José de Jesus in the race,' the guard explained. 'He's from Puerto Rico, like me.'

'Oh.'

The ping of the arriving elevator thankfully exempted Dawson from any further conversation. It seemed to him curiously presumptuous that anyone should be named Jesus – were there people; he wondered, who went about calling themselves God or Buddha? But there again, the bleak reminder struck him, people did name their children after the disciples.

The engraved sign beside the door on the impressively carpeted eighteenth floor proudly proclaimed the partnership – Silver, Silk and Levinson – but as Dawson, not for the first time, spat with accuracy on the name of Silk and polished the plate with his sleeve it was not with any degree of pride. Rather the reverse: he was anxious to eliminate Sebastian Silk and all he stood for. Two months before Simon's death, Silk had removed the contents of the partnership account – more than a million dollars – and disappeared somewhere south of Mexico to a new life. He had often expressed a desire to get out of the rat race and now, like a rodent, he had achieved it. To raise a hue and cry would have been commercially fatal, so Silver and Levinson had continued to practise as if they had not become virtually bankrupt and the few resources that remained to them had been futilely dissipated on an unsuccessful private investigation.

Dawson felt like a criminal himself as he slipped his key into the first Chubb lock. He certainly had no desire to bump into Hugh Levinson nor any of the slimmed-down junior staff this particular Monday. But it was all right; nobody was there. Like any office after a long weekend, the place had the uneasy atmosphere of an abandoned ship.

The digital clock on his desk clicked forward to one thirty-five. He had a few minutes in hand. Kneeling uncomfortably in front of his private metal safe, he twisted the dial clockwise and anticlockwise through the pre-programmed code. Nobody else knew it. If he were hit by a bus they would have to blow the damn thing up, he thought with some satisfaction. The numbers he had entrusted to Bunny were long since out of date. Besides, she was the last person he wanted to have access to the contents.

He pulled out two unlabelled fawn folders and rapidly closed the door. Just as he was settling at his desk, the sound of the doorbell drilled into the silence of the room.

That would be Quinn, 'Loophole' Quinn as he was known in legal and criminal circles throughout Boston and beyond. Eamonn Quinn to his face.

'I'm sorry I'm late. I had to park miles away. The fellow said the garage was full up because of . . .'

'The marathon, I know.' Silver took his Burberry and ushered him in. 'In fact you're early. We said any time between half past one and two.'

'By my standards, Mr Silver, that means half past one,'

'Dawson,' smiled the actuary, indicating a chair.

Despite the holiday, Eamonn Quinn was wearing the costume of his calling: a thick chalk-striped three-piece suit, which would not have been harmed by a trip to the dry cleaner, a flamboyant green tie – which was his trade mark – and a cream shirt the collar of which refused to settle comfortably around his size eighteen neck. He was a big man and a heavy one, his complexion ruddy with the good life. A mane of red hair flopped untidily across his freckled brow.

Dawson silently disapproved of anyone permitting themselves to become so negligently out of shape, yet it was the lawyer's mind and not his body that he was hiring.

'I apologise for arranging our meeting for today,' he began, 'but if we cannot attain any form of agreement, I think it would be better if nobody else was aware of it.'

'Every day's a working day for me, Mr Silver . . . Dawson,' Quinn assured him. 'Always on call for my clients. That's what they pay for.'

The second remark was not lost on Silver. Quinn had warned him over the telephone that his fees were 'exorbitant times two.'

'Let me come straight to the point,' said Silver, pulling a parchment document out of the top folder on his desk and passing it over to the lawyer. 'I wonder if this is familiar to you.'

Quinn raised the half-moon spectacles that were suspended by a leather cord round his neck and glanced through the three closely typed pages.

'I think I have one of these back in the office,' he noted drily.

'Exactly,' said Silver. 'It was drawn up by your partner. I never met Mr Mitchell but my wife told me they gave him an extravagant send-off.'

'Sometimes it's worth being Irish just for the wakes alone,' Quinn muttered still perusing the document. 'Not that you can enjoy your own. Or, at least, not as far as we know.'

'Coffee?' enquired Dawson, then added, thinking he had just heard a hint, 'or something stronger?'

Quinn shook his head emphatically. 'You know, this was one of the first pre-nuptial things that Bill did. You'd have thought with all that money kicking around this town more people would have bothered. But most look on the bright side. Human nature.'

'Is it legal?' Dawson asked abruptly.

The lawyer glanced over his spectacles as if he hadn't quite heard right.

'Legal,' Dawson repeated. 'Watertight?'

'Anything Mitch drafted would be watertight. Sometimes I think I miss his drafting more than I miss him, if that's not a sacrilegious sentiment. I never bothered to look for another partner because I knew no one could match up to him. I was his clerk to begin with, you know.'

The actuary knew only too well. He knew everything about Eamonn Quinn: his below-the-belt reputation in court, his penchant for publicity and his willingness to bend the rules as far as the fee would go.

'I was just glancing over it' – he tried to sound as casual as he could – 'and I saw that at the top of the second page, certain assets and monies fall under my trusteeship when the issue of the marriage reaches the age of eighteen. We had a son, Mr Quinn . . .'

'No need to go on,' the lawyer held up a slab of a hand. 'I should have written to Mrs Silver and yourself. I'm very sorry. That was a terrible thing. So young.'

Dawson swivelled his chair to look out of the window. The large artificial pond of the Christian Science church far beneath him looked as dark and uninviting as a Scottish loch. Someone had told him once that Loch Ness never yielded up its dead and the notion had lingered in his mind like an unclearable cobweb.

'The fact that the minor never attained maturity effectively invalidates that clause,' Quinn's legalese reawakened his attention. 'Unless, of course, there was further offspring.'

'My wife is fifty-two, Mr Quinn.'

The lawyer glanced at the relevant paragraph again. 'Adopted would probably be okay. Unless either of you objected.'

'Mrs Silver,' Dawson began hesitantly, 'is not really in a position to . . . her condition since Simon . . .'

Quinn came to his rescue once more. 'I had heard. Sad. But understandable.'

'I just wondered,' Silver had rehearsed this moment many times but could find no remotely elegant means of expression. 'Look, if I were to adopt a child, by whatever means, could a court hold that she was not of sound enough mind to participate in the . . . well, what I'm getting at is: could it be done without her being aware?'

'I think you might have difficulty adopting on your own, especially at your age if I may say so. The law requires two parents although there are ways and means . . .' The loophole was never very far from Eamonn Quinn's legal disquisitions.

Dawson decided to come clean. 'I'm thinking in terms of a surrogate mother. There is a system in Chevy Chase.'

'Understood.' The hand went up once more. 'And you would like the child to benefit from this agreement?'

Silver's eyes brightened sharply at the lawyer's intuitive reading of the situation.

'Not a chance, I'm afraid.' Quinn shook his head. 'Mitch has looked after your wife's interests, if I may say, immaculately.'

Silver felt as if he had been stung. A pervasive numbness spread through his system. He had known that this was the situation all along; he had merely hoped that Quinn might have offered him a green light somehow to reinterpret the rules.

The actuary rose from his chair and offered a defeated hand. 'Well, sorry for spoiling your holiday. I know I can rely on your confidence and I look forward to settling your fee.'

Quinn ignored the hand and reached for his Burberry. 'It'll cost you twenty thousand,' he said.

'For what?' The peremptory response fell involuntarily from the dumbstruck Dawson.

'To tear up both agreements and have them redrafted and retyped. I presume you'll want a discretionary advance against maintenance for any child you may have. We can do that, but don't get too greedy.'

'It can be done?' Silver experienced the illicit thrill of overt criminality for possibly the first time in his life.

'Twenty-two thousand,' Loophole Quinn amended his quotation. 'A couple of grand for the fellow who provides the paper. They can test the age of these things so accurately nowadays, you know. Remarkable thing science.'

'You don't have to understand what I'm doing – you just have to assist.'

Leone de Soto was used to the curt manner of Edmund Michaels when he was absorbed in an experiment and continued to ask questions.

'So this is male sperm – right? I thought it lost its . . . you know what . . . when it was exposed to the daylight.'

'You're thinking of Dracula, darling,' the doctor replied sarcastically peering through the microscope with fervid concentration. 'On the contrary this stuff is in tip-top condition. Potentially fertile, free of pathogenic bacteria and T-strain mycoplasma. High sperm count, forty per cent motile after fifteen minutes and only fifteen per cent abnormal.'

'What's motile?' she asked, pushing back her shoulder-length hair still shining from its recent copper-coloured rinse.

'Means it makes you pregnant. Or not you' – he took his eye away from the microscope and transferred his attention to a glass dish that was warming over a paraffin flame – 'the owner of these little oocytes.'

'Eggs, right?' Leone had picked up more than her white coat in the sessions she had spent helping the doctor. She had no medical training but the pay was good, better anyway than what she earned in her regular job in Filene's basement and better still on Patriots' Day. Michaels had emphasised that this Monday was the perfect time for this particular experiment since any unexpected disturbance could violate the sterility of the room.

'Correct. Nice clean pre-ovulatory eggs. Thanks to the laparoscopy we were able to aspirate them from the ovary just after the mid-cycle surge of luteinising hormone.'

Leone was lost again but she obediently steadied the dish with her rubber-gloved hand. Dr Michaels reached for a suction syringe and carefully transferred a few droplets of semen to the solution.

'Now we have to wait for cleavage to occur in vitro,' he explained.

'The embryo should be two-celled at thirty-two hours, four-celled at forty-six, six-celled at fifty-eight and, if it works – eight-celled at about sixty-one.'

'And what then?' Leone hoped he wasn't going to suggest she stay for all that time, she had a date later.

'Then we pop it into Eugenia there and see if her uterus can continue the good work.'

'But you can't grow a human foetus in an animal.' She couldn't disguise the disgust in her voice. 'Not one that size.'

'Of course not,' Michaels replied. 'There'll eventually be a spontaneous abortion. I just need to find out what happens between now and then.'

Grace Winston's legs seemed to stiffen with every stride, as if some atrophying disease were wasting them away. In her mind she ticked off the varying elements of her warm-up routine: none had been left out. Her diet over the past weeks had been as rigorous as the others. Lenny had increased the numbers of injections of late but she was fairly sure that they wouldn't affect her muscles in this way; they never had before. The day was mild although vestiges of cleared snow still bordered the route as she reached the outskirts of Ashland. She needed to speak to Alice but she was some way behind her. Grace didn't want to risk dropping her pace and not being able to catch up with Lenny whom she kept assiduously in her sights. What if it was some form of creeping cramp? What if she had to drop out of the race altogether? What would his reaction be? The prospect was too painful to contemplate – but she found herself contemplating it.

'Mind if I join you?'

The voice was so deeply American that she was surprised, when she looked up, that its owner was black. At home such men would usually still retain the hint of a Jamaican or African accent.

'Please do.' She attempted a smile but feared the pain made her wince.

'You from round here?'

'No,' she replied, 'We're from England. Badgers – you may have seen some of the others.'

'*Wind in the Willows*,' the man replied ruminatively. 'Badger,

Ratty, Toad and Mole. I always looked up to Badger. He seemed so wise.'

'I preferred Ratty,' she ventured.

'Really? Why?'

'I just liked the way he . . . well, his modesty.'

'I agree,' he nodded. 'I don't talk about my river, Toad, you know I don't. But I think about it. I think about it all the time.'

Grace's surprise must have shown in her expression.

'I was reading it to my son last night,' he explained. 'Good pre-race therapy.'

They lapsed into silence and continued to run together stride for stride. It was part of the pleasure for Grace: where else would you get kinship and competition at the same time?

'That's easier, isn't it,' he remarked after a while.

Grace glanced at him again. 'How did you know?'

'I was watching you from behind. You were so tight and tensed up I was amazed you could run at all. Better now. Don't let your mind overrule your limbs. The attainable Zen is for the body to control the brain.'

'Are you a Buddhist?' she asked.

'No, a physiotherapist,' he laughed. 'Take it easy now, Badger.'

He offered a gentle departing wave as he accelerated away. The ache had cleared from Grace's legs and she felt correspondingly stronger in spirit. Lenny was at the back of a group of runners that the physiotherapist was about to overtake and she felt inspired enough to put on a spurt and catch up with him.

'Stopping for me or chasing after Sambo?' Lenny's tone was icy and unpleasant.

'What do you mean?' She felt wounded by the remark. He must have been keeping an eye on her, although he knew the way she felt about him only too well. 'He was a friendly guy. He told me about his son.'

'Darling, you're a free woman to pick up anyone you like. You can even choose the colour.'

Lenny had been offhand before but never so pointedly unpleasant. Nothing he did was other than artful and she feared the motive in his spurious jealousy.

'I wasn't picking him up. Nor was he picking me up. That's unfair. Runners talk, you know that.'

'You, too, from what I've been hearing. It's time you understood that our training methods are not for common consumption.'

Grace was incredulous. 'What do you mean?'

'I'd prefer you didn't discuss the matter of steroids with any outsiders. They're private.'

'I didn't.'

'Oh, no. Not even in the common room at school. I don't think Alice would back you up there.'

'Once,' Grace conceded. 'One day. And only then because the biology teacher expressed an interest.'

'One day too many. Look, Framingham.' He glanced at his watch. 'I'm behind schedule. I've got to get on.'

'Go,' she agreed. 'I'll see you . . . back at the hotel . . . won't I?'

'Not so easy,' Lenny refused to meet her eye. 'My wife's over to watch the race. My son, too. School holidays.'

She had almost known before he had told her. The manner in which he had manufactured an argument was indication enough. Grace cursed herself for her own vulnerability, for putting any sort of trust in him.

'I'm sorry,' he said.

'Fuck off,' she screamed. 'Fuck right out of my life.'

'Stay cool,' he warned, 'you've got a long way to go.'

He tried to pat her reasssuringly on the backside but she brushed his arm away with such venom that he stumbled into the sidewalk, before collecting his balance and accelerating away.

Paradoxically this infusion of anger endowed her with renewed energy and, although she didn't want to catch up with Lenny or indeed ever see him again, she felt a strength within her that she knew would carry her forward more powerfully than ever before.

The bastard, the slimy toad-like bastard. Mr Toad, all pomp and no circumstance. How could she ever have fallen for such a piece of utter excrement? The road began to drop from Natick through Wellesley – wasn't that where that woman in *Love Story* came from? – to Newton Lower Falls. Her legs were moving freely now, running just to get him the hell out of her system. Not that she easily could. She remembered his lecture from the map in the club room. This was the killer: the five-mile climb to the top of Heartbreak Hill. If you make it there, you can make it anywhere. The skyscrapers of Boston beckoned in the slim sunlight of the April afternoon.

There was an increasing number of spectators by the roadside now and they were making more noise, cheering her on, cheering everyone on. Or so it seemed. What Grace saw before her was half hallucination, half real. She sensed there was a television truck alongside, keeping pace with her bunch of runners. She instinctively swept away the lock of hair that habitually fell in front of her eyes in a valedictory act of vanity.

But, in doing so, she staggered, completely lost her balance and plunged forward. And that was the last thing she remembered.

· Six ·

The knock on the door had rarely been more welcome; it roused Dawson out of a confused and fearful dream. Loophole Quinn had been itemising the ways in which Bunny – and all attendant problems – might be eliminated and Silver had been pleading with him not to hurt her. 'Kill her and not hurt her?' the attorney had scoffed. 'I don't run a euthanasia society, you know.'

But Mary Doherty's timid tones brought him back to reality. 'Seven o'clock, Mr Silver. Can I come in now?'

He was relieved to hear her voice. 'Yes, Mary, come in.'

She put her tray by the bed and crossed the room to open the curtains. The sun seemed to have attained its summer strength, although it was merely rehearsing in the April dawn.

'I must water this window box,' she murmured, half to herself. 'Mrs Silver will never forgive me if I let these peonies die.'

Mary's conversation always managed to include a reference to her absent mistress despite the fact that it had been a full eight months since Bunny had last slept in that room.

Dawson pulled himself up in bed and stretched out automatically for the morning paper. He turned immediately to the financial pages. It may have been a holiday in Massachusetts the previous day but not on Wall Street.

'What time do you need the car?' Mary was back by the door.

'Oh, I don't know.' The discomfort of the dream had faded and he was alert enough to resume his usual irritated manner. 'Tell Joe to wait. I'll ring down.'

'Will you be in for dinner?'

Dawson's day ran rapidly through his head. He had made no

arrangements for that evening but he had little desire to spend it in his own company.

'No. I don't think so.'

'Very well, sir.'

'Leave something cold in the refrigerator,' he called after her, half changing his mind as she closed the door.

He flicked the switch by the bed to turn on the large television on the wall in front of him and sank bank into the pillows with a glass of freshly squeezed Florida orange juice. Fuck Vietnam, he thought as he snapped through the channels with the remote-control button. He stopped at a local station which had a blonde ice maiden as its morning presenter. Dawson was intrigued by the way she read the news with the overstated precision of a teacher addressing a kindergarten class.

'Yesterday's Boston Marathon, the seventy-eighth time this famous race has been run, produced both a record field of nearly two thousand competitors and a new American record for Bill Rogers who became the first person to cover the 26 miles 385 yards in less than two hours ten minutes. His time was two hours nine minutes and fifty-five seconds. Well done, Bill, you had five minutes to spare . . . sorry, I mean five seconds. Not so lucky was this English runner who had the Prudential Tower in sight when she slipped and, whoops – there you see it – collided with our travelling camera truck. Overcome with emotion at the sight of the crew, I guess. She spent the night at Karger Orthopaedic but doctors say she'll be just fine. And our own Dr Jack says it looks like being another fine day . . .'

Dawson pressed the mute button to switch off the sound. The joviality of weather forecasters was a continuing anathema to him; he was offended by the way they always seemed to be trying to sell him the weather as if it were a commodity that belonged to them. As he shifted to get out of bed, his eye alighted on a photograph on the front page of the *Globe*. A heavily blanketed individual on a stretcher was being lifted into an ambulance. He picked up the paper. 'Grace Winston, aged thirty, from London, England, is taken to hospital with a suspected ruptured pelvis and broken leg.'

He paused by the window to observe the morning traffic building up in Marlborough Street below, all shiningly eager to be somewhere and attack the day. There was a time when he felt that way himself. But, since Simon, there seemed to be little to hurry for. His eye was drawn, once again, to the photograph of the accident in the paper he was holding. At least she got away with her life, he thought.

'Blue Cross?'

'What . . . what did you say?' Grace's mind was still three-quarters sedated from the anaesthetic. The question came from someone who looked like a doctor. He sported a neat beard and was wearing a white hospital coat but she was unable to focus on his badge.

'Are you Blue Cross?' he demanded.

'We call it Red Cross in England. Are you collecting?'

'You misunderstand me. We call it Red Cross here, too. That's a charity. This hospital, unfortunately, is not. Do you have any health insurance? We need proof before we can proceed with other than emergency treatment.'

'I don't think I do.'

'Any major credit cards?'

Grace had no credit cards, major or otherwise; she kept what there was of her salary in a building society in Shepherd's Bush.

Her focus was becoming a little clearer now. She was wearing a paper night-gown and found herself wedged in a bed with raised metal sides like a child's cot. The plaster on her right arm was not to cover any injury but to hold in place a needle attached to the drip feed which hung ominously from a stand by her head. The room was clean and clinical but someone had thoughtfully provided a vase of red tulips which radiated some welcome warmth. Do they have flowers in prison? she wondered.

'No credit cards,' the man repeated, not unsympathetically.

'Not much of anything, I'm afraid.' She attempted a smile. 'What's going to happen to me?'

'There are ways round this. Charitable foundations, state aid if you make a full disclosure of income. Although you may not be eligible for that, being a foreigner.'

He closed his book and turned to go but the word 'foreigner' triggered something in her subconscious. 'Wait a minute. Travel insurance. We all took out travel insurance. In case of things like . . . well, this.'

'Can I see it?'

She tried to raise herself on the nest of pillows behind her but the lower half of her body was entirely numb. 'It's back at the hotel, at the Holiday Inn. They brought me here in my running things. I'm sure my friends will come.'

'They've been already,' the man said, indicating the flowers. 'If you call them and ask them to bring the policy I'd be most grateful. These things have financial limits, you know. I hope you're feeling better.'

He turned again to go.

'Where am I?' she called after him.

He stopped by the door. 'Karger Orthopaedic Hospital. Boston's finest. You couldn't be in a better place.'

'And what's wrong with me?'

The directness of her question clearly discomforted him. 'Well . . . the race . . . the accident. Not really my department. But they've patched you up just fine. Could take a little time before you're on the road again, though.'

She lay back in the cot and attempted to piece together what had happened. Her legs had begun to buckle under her, long before she fell, and her body had no longer seemed to be under the control of her mind. The image of the world record holder Jim Peters – the first man to break two hours twenty – stumbling and scrambling on all fours with thousands watching but no one to help him, had begun to haunt her. The Commonwealth Games, Vancouver, 1954. He was three hundred yards from home and twenty minutes ahead of his nearest rival. But there comes a point when you can no longer run on determination alone. Just as she started to remember what she had been determined to run away from, sleep descended to offer temporary salvation from her problems.

The next time it was the sound of a familiar and friendly voice that aroused her.

'You need to wash your hair. I'm going to speak to the nurse.' Alice was standing beside her with two large brown paper bags. She saw that Grace was staring at them. 'Your worldly goods. I'll put the clothes in the cupboard but you may need your make-up and your money.'

There were two other people standing beside her. Lenny, looking decidedly uneasy in his Badger track suit, and a short woman, more than a little overweight with matronly grey hair.

'Well done, Grace,' he said, as casually as he could. 'You nearly made it – and you're going to make it now.'

She stared at him enquiringly.

'This is Linda, my wife. She wanted to make sure you were being cared for.'

Lenny and Linda, was all she could think. She had never known her name before. Were the children called Leslie and Larry? Did they all wear identical sweaters with a large L on them when they were on holiday?

'Len broke two-forty,' Linda announced proudly.

Grace stared at the three of them. 'What did I break?' she asked.

'Haven't they told you?' Lenny eagerly seized the opening to become outraged. 'Americans. The tibia and fibula of your left leg are both badly cracked. That's not important; they'll heal. What they're worried about is the pelvis. The collision with that television van pretty well shattered it.'

'Will I walk again?' She felt like a downed pilot in a Second World War movie.

'Of course,' he assured her. 'We'll get you back home, and then they'll fix you up, no problem.'

There was no real need for Dawson to be driven from Marlborough Street to his office in the Prudential Center. If the traffic was snarled, as it was this morning, it was quicker to walk. But less stylish. In fact today he was travelling in the opposite direction. A call to his secretary had erased his appointments for the next two hours – there were no clients sufficiently important that they could not be rescheduled – and a further call to the surgery of Dr Edmund Michaels had elicited the information that the doctor had a thirty-minute gap in his diary between the meetings of various hospital committees. He told her that he had an urgent requirement to see the doctor and the girl had agreed to page her boss.

'What's wrong?' Michaels, professionally clad in an expensive consultant's suit, was already waiting for him at the hospital reception.

'I need to talk, get something off my mind.' As a professional man himself, Dawson had no hesitation about commanding the time of someone who charged it out by the hour, however slight the pretext. 'Got any privacy – and coffee?'

Michaels led him along a brightly lit corridor, pungent with the penetrating aroma of fresh disinfectant.

'We can use the registrar's office,' he remarked. 'I don't think it's bugged. And if it is, I promise not to release the tapes.'

Dawson offered no smile as he accepted the cup of filter coffee; he was bored with Watergate. 'What do I have to do for this donor business?' he demanded peremptorily.

'Perfectly simple. Provide me with some sperm.'

'Well, how?'

'We could try electro-ejaculation,' the doctor replied with a straight face. 'That's the way they do it with bulls. A rectal probe fitted with a ring which gives an electric shock is the standard method.'

'Very funny.' Dawson took a disdainful sip of his coffee.

'Or if that doesn't turn you on, you can do it yourself. Jerk off into a bottle. We even provide the dirty magazines for those with insufficient imagination. What was it that Englishman said: masturbation is the thinking man's television.'

'And then you freeze it, right?'

'Right.'

'So at that stage it's no different from all those other bottles in your friend's ice box?'

'It may look the same but there's all the difference in the world. It's you. All your little nooks and crannies. All your crimes and misdemeanours, although we may be able to clean a few of those up.'

'What do you mean?' Dawson was earnest and in no mood for joking.

Michaels slipped a cigarette out of his breast pocket and leaned back in his chair. 'It takes forty-six chromosomes to develop a human being. An X chromosome indicates a female, a Y a male. That's how we can make pretty sure that you can have a son. But, for instance, it's been discovered that the genetic condition XYY may be linked with criminal behaviour so we'd tend to terminate any little fellow who came along with those initials.'

'Abort?' asked Dawson.

'We call it terminate in here,' the doctor corrected him.

Silver, nervously excited and impatient at the same time, rose from his chair and crossed to the percolator to pour himself another cup of coffee. 'Let's assume it's healthy. To what extent can you play around with genes to make it, say, stronger or brighter?'

'Well, with cattle they do it all the time – although I don't think they spend a lot of effort trying to make cows more intelligent.' Michaels could see that his little jokes, so well received by his students, did not find a receptive audience here. He pulled on his cigarette and batted his eyelids as if to fan away the smoke. 'If you take the growth gene from a rat and inject it into a mouse egg you'd end up with rat-sized mice. But you're not meant to play around with human beings, you know. There are certain exceptions on medical grounds. For instance, Huntington's chorea. It's a fatal disorder of the nervous system which only manifests itself in adulthood. But it's hereditary and it's carried in a single gene. So they've managed to exchange the malign gene for a normal one at the time of procreation and ward off the disease. Pretty clever, huh?'

'So what about my sight – the retina thing?'

'Retinitis pigmentosa. Eventually they may be able to isolate it. Not at the moment. It's true you run the risk of passing that on to any child. I'd chance it, though. None of us is perfect.'

'But aren't there positive things you can do?'

Micheals shook his head sympathetically. 'If you want designer genes you'd better go to a boutique in Bay Street. It's your baby. Well, half of it is. We might be able to improve things with the other half.'

Dawson eyed him inquisitorially; he wasn't quite sure what he was getting at.

'The surrogate mother. We can pick and choose there. Have a look at the medical record, that sort of thing. They say – I haven't seen it myself – they have a directory with photographs at Chevy Chase so it's a bit like a producer checking out actresses. No casting couch, though.'

Dawson stole a glance at his watch; he knew the doctor's time was running short. 'Just take me through it simply, step by step. Prices attached. How much for the girl?'

'That's negotiable,' Michaels shrugged. 'What's more important is to get her to sign a watertight contract so there's no going back on her part. Most of these women who agree to be surrogate mothers do it through reasons of conscience. They've had an abortion when they were younger, something like that. The agency has all their details.'

'Can I go down there and pick and choose? I don't want some screwed-up type.'

Michaels shook his head. 'No, the deal is strict anonymity. The surrogate and the purchaser, as you're known, never meet. Could lead to all sorts of problems. You pay the surrogate company twenty-five thousand dollars. They look after the girl, pay her medical and life insurance premiums, provide her with maternity clothes. It's a fair service. They've made sure there are no hereditary illnesses or birth defects. They place ten thousand dollars in an escrow account and when she delivers, they deliver.'

'What does she have to do?'

'Not have sex, to begin with. At least not within two weeks of the first insemination until conception is confirmed. And stay off cigarettes and alcohol, the usual thing. We insert your sperm twice a month for six months and if the surrogate hasn't conceived by then we say thank-you and try somebody else. No play, no pay. We know from Simon that you're in working order.'

The mention of his son's name took Dawson by surprise. Few people had dared to use it in his presence since the funeral. He looked thoughtfully at the doctor's white coat, a stethoscope trailing from the pocket, that was hanging on the back of the office door. This new child would have a different life. No mother, real or artificial, or none that it would know about anyway. He had deliberately set aside the usual preciseness of his actuarial calculations; this was an emotional decision. Bunny would have no part in its upbringing – save for unwittingly providing the finance – and the child would know nothing of her. He had an aunt, Violet, who lived in Florida on a minimal civil service pension. Dawson sent her an allowance every year cloaked in the form of an excessive Christmas cheque. At the back of his mind was the thought that she could be prevailed upon to take care of the child in its early years – given more money and a permanent nanny. Beyond that he was uncertain of any details save one: he was sure that he needed a son – a companion for his declining years, someone whom he could love and be proud of and who might even love and be proud of him in return; above all, a life that might rekindle the light in his own life.

'Let's go ahead.' Dawson clicked his fingers impetuously. 'When can we start? Now?'

'Hold on,' Michaels stubbed out his cigarette on the ashtray in front of him with a defensive laugh. 'I don't want to be caught with you jerking off in this room. People will talk.'

Grace stared despondently at the figures in front of her. She had already run up a bill of more than five thousand dollars, and that was just for her leg. The corrective surgery to the pelvis was estimated at ten to fifteen thousand and even then there were disclaimers, underlined in red, that the fees were still payable in full in the event of the operations proving unsuccessful. With the hospital charges she was facing costs amounting to more than thirty thousand dollars.

Alice had come back the previous evening with the details of their travel insurance. It only covered each of them up to five thousand dollars. Lenny had cut costs by assuming that anybody seriously ill could fly back to England for treatment. But Grace was still paralysed and would have needed an ambulance plane.

'It would have been cheaper to die,' she thought, not for the first time.

The others would be at Logan Airport by now, ready for the night flight home. Lenny had telephoned and made all sorts of promises to organise charity events to raise cash. He had also made it un-necessarily clear that their relationship had expired with the accident.

Alice had offered to stay on but Grace insisted that she return. In many ways she preferred to be alone in her misery. She needed to sort out the rest of her life. The drugs they gave her provided an artificial high and she took grateful advantage of this temporary balm. She was content just to stare out of the window. From her bed she could just see the top floors of the taller buildings in downtown Boston – the combat zone, she had heard one of the orderlies call it.

The staff sister put her head round the door. 'You got a visitor. All right if I show him in?'

Grace had no time to say yes or no before a substantial figure in a full black overcoat stepped into the room.

'I've come to help,' he announced.

She straightened herself up as best she could. 'Are you social security – or whatever it is here?'

He settled himself in a friendly fashion at the end of the bed. 'Better than that, I'm a lawyer. I've seen what happened. You've got a pretty watertight case.'

'Against whom?' she asked.

'WNTV – the television company. Open and shut negligence. Worth a hundred thousand dollars minimum or me old grandma wasn't born in County Clare.'

The news came like a stay of execution. She was unsure whether it was real or whether she was still immersed in some drugged-out dream. To test the vision she deliberately held out her left hand – the one unencumbered by the drip. 'I'm Grace Winston,' she said.

'I know,' the portly figure smiled, as he leant forward to take it. 'Eamonn Quinn.'

· Seven ·

The following morning Grace actually had an appetite for breakfast, an all-American breakfast like the Badgers had relished at the Holiday Inn: eggs sunny side up, hash brown potatoes flecked with onion and skinny bacon grilled so dry that no evidence that it was ever part of a pig remained. The previous night's visitor remained in her thoughts, however, to the exclusion of virtually everything else. The lumbering apparition certainly cut an exaggerated figure – his Boston-Irish accent had made him sound at times as if he were part of a touring company of *The Playboy of the Western World* – but Loophole Quinn (he had even vouchsafed his nickname as if it were part of his credentials which, indeed, it was) had provided her with much-needed humour and more desperately needed hope.

Only forty-eight hours previously the bottom had fallen out of Grace's world; now there seemed a chance of averting at least one half of her double disaster. Quinn had even convinced her of the probity of making a profit out of her misfortune.

'You look a lot happier. Nothing like a good English breakfast to start the day, is there?'

It was the bearded man with the officious book and white coat who had visited her the previous afternoon.

'Who exactly are you?' she asked.

'Adam Parker, hospital administration,' he announced.

'Are you a doctor?'

Parker became somewhat penitent. 'Yes. At least I was. Still am, come to that. But I tend to specialise in helping our patients, dealing in the concomitant sphere of finance-orientated medically related problems.'

And, most of all, helping the hospital, she thought. Sometimes the American appetite for circumlocution had the merit of beneficially hiding the true meaning of things. Now that he was more clearly in focus, she could see that Parker's beard was an important part of his persona. Not one of the friendly, scraggly beards that young men at university or some of her fellow runners sported, but a precisely brushed and sculpted one – the manicured basement to his roof of immaculately positioned short grey hair with a parting as straight as a missile. The beard was undoubtedly groomed several times a day and she permitted herself the thought that, in the absence of a Mrs Parker – something about him, well everything about him, told her there was no Mrs Parker – the beard was Adam's pet companion. Did he, perhaps, take it for a walk in the park before coming to work in the morning?

'. . . and so there is a very real prospect of a one hundred per cent indemnity situation.'

'I'm so sorry.' She had failed to take in anything he was saying. 'My mind was elsewhere. I was thinking about your beard. It's very nice.'

'Thank you.' He accepted the compliment uncertainly, glancing down at his book. 'Let me recap, Miss . . . er Winston. I am in receipt of your medical insurance details and, as you will have realised, the sums covered fall very far short of the cost of your treatment here at the Karger. Although the world historically looks to Lloyd's of London for leadership in this field it seems that, at a personal level, the British insurance industry is hardly cognisant of the current fee structures in United States hospitals.'

'Couldn't I just fly home?' – like a bird, she thought.

'Unfortunately I am advised by the surgeon with responsibility for your recovery that this is not a viable option. Your pelvis is in a seriously dangerous condition. If it were disturbed while you were in motion in the air and, say, the unthinkable were to happen and you were unable to walk again, the Karger would find the exposure to this liability unacceptable.'

What about me, she reflected, what about my exposure to the liability of a life in a wheelchair? The idea had never impinged on her before and she regretted the full breakfast that now lay reproachfully in her stomach.

Parker was sensitive enough to catch the scent of her emotion. 'That's a worst case scenario,' he assured her. 'There's every chance you'll walk out of here by Memorial Day.'

'When's that?' she enquired ominously.

'End of May – could be earlier?'

'Don't you know?'

'Let me explain,' he stammered. 'Memorial Day is always the last Monday in May, that's fixed. But with a personal injury nobody can calculate the rate of recovery with absolute accuracy.'

'Nor the cost,' she countered pointedly.

'That's what I was coming to.' Parker recovered himself. 'There's a man I want you to see. He's outside now and . . .'

'I think I've already seen him,' Grace interrupted.

'Really? Bill Trentham, vice-president of corporate affairs for WNTV?'

'Oh, no.' She realised her mistake.

'Who have you already seen?' Parker's suspicions seemed aroused.

'Nobody,' she insisted hastily. 'Not him, anyway. It was an almoner, I think, maybe someone from the hospital library. It was when the medication was making me woozy.'

Parker was unfamiliar with the word but appeared to accept the explanation. 'I'll go and get Bill. You'll like him. He's a real straight guy.'

As opposed to a real gay guy, she wondered. Straight guys were people Grace intended to give a wide berth to for the rest of her life, crippled or uncrippled. Only now did she fully realise how possessively she had been in love with Lenny. And how crushingly she had been hurt by his rejection. Always, at the back of her mind, there had been the simmering notion that their relationship would somehow solidify in Boston. Both of them had trained up to their peak and, as they ascended this Parnassus together, there had seemed the real possibility that their affair would flourish on a new, elevated plain. Or so she thought. Evidently he didn't. The fact that he had said nothing about his wife joining him in America smacked of calculated treachery, as if he had wanted to terminate things in the most cruel manner possible.

From the moment he told her during the race, she had become an accident waiting to happen. Without Lenny, what was there to exist for? She had tried to outpace her heart, to run so fast that it would physically collapse just as it emotionally had. There was no known instance of suicide by running, but she had read of soldiers who had died being forced round obstacle courses in full battle gear by some brutal sergeant and she hoped now that some fell sergeant death would respond to her plea and rescue her from the agony of her despair. Instead it had been a television truck. And even that had failed to do the job properly.

'Bill Trentham, WNTV.' The man offered her a card as if to prove that he was who he said and not some intrepid impostor. 'I would have visited with you earlier but the hospital informed me your condition was not receptive at that time.'

Grace smiled wanly. At least Adam and Bill could converse in a common language, she thought.

'It was a most unfortunate accident,' he went on, 'and I bring with me heartfelt wishes for a full recovery from the camera crew involved. They stopped shooting immediately, I hope you realise, and attended to you until the paramedics took over.'

'I'm truly grateful to them,' she murmured.

'The incident is fully recorded on videotape – although I think it would be somewhat distressing for you to view it, especially at this moment in time.' Trentham paused, as if in anticipation of her reaction and seemed thankful when there was none. 'It does clearly record, however, that you – presumably in an exhausted state – lost control of your balance and fell into the path of the accompanying vehicle. There was no negligence on the part of the driver. In fact the speed of his reaction was remarkable. It could have been much worse – much, much worse.'

Grace carefully scanned the sincere expression behind Bill Trentham's equally sincere spectacles.

'He must have saved my life,' she observed with an internal irony of which neither of the two men was aware.

'You said it,' Trentham nodded in relief. 'So let me repeat, as is documented by this tape, there is no evidence of negligence on the part of our company – quite the reverse, in fact. Nevertheless we are appalled that such an accident should happen to a guest in our city and be seen to happen by our viewers. So I have drafted this press release that will be issued this afternoon to the local papers, expressing our heartfelt hopes for your full recovery and offering, without obligation, to cover the expenses of your hospitalisation in full as well as a first class airfare Boston to London when you are fit to travel.'

He smiled, with satisfaction, as he handed her the piece of paper. 'Adam, here, told me about the grievous nature of your under-insurance . . . very wrong.'

Grace felt offended by the man's insincerity. He had no concern with her health or recovery at all, merely with the public image of his television station. To talk in terms of press releases before he had even solicited her opinion was to assume her mind had become as enfeebled as her body – if he had ever credited her with a mind. She glanced at the document without really taking it in. 'It's a generous offer,' she affected to assure him, 'but I think you may be a little premature.'

'In what way?' Trentham was taken aback.

'I'm advised there might be more detailed ramifications from the accident than just these costs.'

'Ah, well' – it was Adam Parker who stepped in – 'this is something we were coming to. What you need here is legal advice, independent legal advice. I'm happy to relate that on your behalf, and free of charge, the hospital lawyers have held an initial meeting with WNTV and, after due deliberation, have ratified this agree-ment.'

'You're very kind,' she replied, 'but I've already engaged my own lawyer.'

'Who?' Parker's voice went up an octave as he asked.

'Eamonn Quinn,' said Grace.

'Jesus Christ,' said Trentham.

With a daunting pall of guilt hanging over him, Dawson Silver locked his bedroom door. Twice. When they had taken over the house from her mother, Bunny had engaged a Parisian designer who had installed French fittings. The phrase *'fermer à double tour'* had become a *double entendre* in the early years of their marriage: it was a shared secret that either could mischievously utter in public to tell the other that they felt like making love. When Bunny came up to bed – in those days the better for a few drinks rather than the worse – and made the deliberate gesture of double-locking the door, it was a signal to Dawson that his services would be required.

'I hold the cash and I hold the cock,' she would whisper tipsily as she moved her naked body beside him. With an expertise that came from her upper-class education, she would loosen his pyjama cord with one hand and coax him into erection with the other. He loved it – but not her. It was this very tartiness that drew him to her in the first instance and then drew them apart. Long after her body had ceased to cause him a flicker of excitement, when her breath was seldom free of the odour of alcohol and even her perfume seemed overspiced, it was a peremptory *'double-tour'* night that conceived Simon.

At first Dawson felt trapped by the pregnancy. He had been drafting schemes to walk away from the match with as much money intact as the law would allow. But when Simon was born he fell in love for the first time in his life. This was a treasure from which he could not bear to be parted.

But now he was. The wrong one had died. In his prayers he would send silent signals to the Almighty that a fortuitous solution to Bunny's mounting alcohol problem might be her early demise. But he must have mocked his Maker and the terrible retribution was the loss of his son. Bunny remained out at the Cape in a daily coma of her own creation. She had lost the desire to fight her disease and Dawson had long since lost any desire to help her. What he was about to produce now would be his and his alone. She would never be allowed to interfere, or even know.

He entered the bathroom with stealth, as if he were somehow breaking into his own home. He was alone in the house, having made sure to select the Dohertys' day off. Slowly and with deliberation he removed his clothes, postponing the moment for as long as possible. On an instinct he seized Bunny's yellow silk dressing gown, which Mary still hung on the back of the bathroom door, and put it on.

Placing Edmund's frozen vacuum flask which he had earlier removed from the ice box, on top of the bidet, Dawson Silver settled solemnly on the closed lavatory seat and attempted to masturbate. At school the problem had been stopping; at forty-seven the problem was starting. He now wished he hadn't so dismissively rejected the doctor's offer of pornographic magazines. True, he had woken with an erect penis after drinking too much on New Year's Eve and had begun the year with an act of onanism, but this was decidedly different. There was something unnervingly sacred about deliberately creating your own son and the religiosity of the occasion left him with a limp dick. He cast his mind back to the good times with Bunny but such recollections were irretrievably polluted by the intervening years of pain.

Sex required relationships and relationships were not things that you could rely on. Not only his own; he could see it in the lives of his clients. The most simple equation would reveal a scale of negative benefits if you were to compute matters over, say, a ten-year period. Dawson had only once experienced bought sex – in a New York club where they kindly took American Express and gave you a hotel receipt beforehand – but the girl they had provided him with had had a waif-like body and hungry eyes and he had felt more used than she.

His member stirred at the memory, but not enough to spark into life. The more he fiddled with it the less it responded, a diminishing return lying short and fat in his reddened right hand. Dawson closed the dressing gown over his knees in disgust and got up to go downstairs. But just as he reached the darkened landing the screech of a bell pinned him fearfully to the spot. Surely Mary hadn't been so stupid as to turn on the alarm system? No, it was the front door. He remained static, shivering uneasily as the silk turned chill against his cooling flesh.

Whoever it was had no intention of going away. Perhaps they had seen his car in its allotted space in the garage. The bell rang again, persistent and unyielding. There was nothing to do but answer the door. Dawson kept the chain on as he edged it nervously open but the substantial figure outside seemed oblivious of his caution.

Loophole Quinn had clearly enjoyed his first cocktail of the evening. 'That bar at the end of your road,' he remarked as Dawson removed the chain and the lawyer stepped uninvited over the threshold, 'they bring the Bushmills over themselves. I know it's an Ulster drink, but if you dilute it with a little Vermouth I think there's no need to mention it at confession.'

The words meant little to Dawson as he ushered the lumbering figure towards the small study that was situated to the right of the front hall.

'Would you like a drink?' he enquired as he snapped on a reading light by the desk. 'I don't think I have any of that Bushman stuff but there's sure to be a Chivas Regal in the cabinet.'

'Mills,' corrected Quinn, still in his heavy overcoat as he lowered himself into a studded chair. 'Dark satanic Bushmills. It's a town in the North of Ireland, don't you see, a Protestant potion. But Chivas Regal would be fine . . . fit for a king, eh?'

Dawson, still discomforted by the surprise arrival, nodded unsurely and opened the glass cabinet beside the unlit fire. He was still shivering as he stooped to search for a match to light the gas jet.

'*Rex, regis*, a king,' the Irishman continued, half in explanation, half to himself and half-pissed. 'It's a great thing the Latin language. When they conducted the Mass in Latin they could be sure that in every country throughout the world the same words would be used and hardly anybody would understand any of them. That's what kept the church strong. Now that they follow what the priest is saying they begin to have doubts. When I was a student we studied the *Institutes of Justinian* in Latin. Did you know that the Romans had a legal system more sophisticated – that's a Greek word – than that of any country in the modern world?'

'On the rocks?' asked Dawson.

'Just water,' Quinn replied, holding a thick finger laterally in front of him. 'A finger of water for every two fingers of whisky – that's the way to achieve the perfect alchemy.'

The actuary carefully used his body as a shield while he made a much weaker drink for himself. He could see from the corner of his eye that his guest had picked up a newspaper from beside his chair.

'What a prat that Bobby Fischer is – ' Quinn seemed to be hopping from subject to subject in a kind of verbal Irish jig ' – he can't even be bothered to turn up in Manila and defend his own title. Karpov's a child – what is he, twenty-two? twenty-three? – but the greatest genius living in America today makes a bloody Russian world champion by default. The trouble is you need more than a mind to win at chess – you need nerve. It's the wrong signal to be sending the Reds at a time when we're crawling home from Saigon.'

Dawson placed the two cut-glass tumblers, one containing liquid of a much deeper shade, on the low table between them. He remained unsure of the reason for the visit but he was beginning to warm to the idea of some company. It had been a long time since anyone had sat with him in this room.

'Books,' continued Quinn savouring the first taste of his drink, 'I like a study lined with books. A little literary womb you can snuggle into . . . my God, I didn't interrupt anything did I?'

'Interrupt what?' Dawson went on the defensive, fearing for a moment that the man had extra-sensory powers.

'Upstairs,' Quinn indicated with his glass, 'no lights. And you, no clothes. You weren't with a . . .'

Dawson drew the dressing gown more tightly around him. 'Good Lord no. I'm still a married man, Mr Quinn, you above all people should know that. I was just . . . em . . . just about to take a shower.'

'I like your robe,' smiled the lawyer. 'Saffron yellow. You're not a Buddhist, by any chance?'

Silver felt caught out and embarrassed. 'Not an anything,' he found himself confessing. 'We live, we die. Actuaries know more about the pattern of men's lives than any priest or pope. Religion trades in the incalculable, I have very little time for that. Why worry about the unknown when the known is worrying enough?'

'Sometimes it's easier to worry about the unknown,' Quinn drained his Chivas and set it down on the table with the strong signal that he expected another. 'If we were having this conversation in the sixteenth century we'd both believe that this life was just a preparation for the next, where the true rewards and punishments lie in store. You've got a document up on your shelves there that testifies to that.'

Dawson followed his gaze inquisitively.

'Hamlet,' the Irishman indicated the leather-bound row of Shakespeare's works. 'That's all it's about, really: the nature of death. We're all going to die, sure, but we're all going to different deaths. It all depends on whether you've made your peace first with your Maker, your shriving time. Won't affect you, though, since you're a self-made man.'

The Irishman chuckled at his pun. Without asking him, Dawson picked up his glass and crossed the room to replenish it. He felt uncomfortable at the turn of the conversation.

'Anyway, it's a different document I've brought for you tonight,' came the voice behind him. 'Not about death, but about birth. This one.'

Silver swivelled on his bare foot to see the lawyer pull a jaundiced parchment document out of the side pocket of his coat. It was a courtroom climax that he had doubtless been working up to.

'The pre-nuptial . . .' He found himself unable to finish the sentence as he stood immobile with a glass in one hand and the bottle of Chivas Regal in the other.

'The post pre-nuptial, to give it its correct Latin name,' the lawyer chuckled as he unfolded the paper. 'You were a little heavy on the water last time, Mr Silver. Just hold the jug close to the glass – for appearances' sake.'

'You did it.' Dawson searched for words but the sheer excitement of the moment seemed to banish them from his brain. He poured himself an equally neat Scotch hoping to reacquire his vocabulary. 'It's legal.'

'Legal all right. Not even the Supreme Court could set aside a clause of it. And maybe not as immoral as you think it is, taking into consideration your honest intent.' It was a phrase that did not fall from the lawyer's lips for the first time; he knew that those who were novices at bending the law were usually in need of reassurance.

'What?' Even if Dawson's mind had been functioning clearly, he would have had difficulty comprehending.

'The child,' Dawson tapped the document with the back of his fingers. 'The whole purpose of this is to give a young child a good life. Now, who could take issue with that?' He raised his half-moon spectacles to his blood-shot eyes. 'Issue being the operative word. If either party – you or your wife – should by birth or adoption have subsequent family, then there is a maintenance provision here of up to fifty thousand dollars a year from the Mahoney trust, exercisable by either of you subject to the approval of the legal partnership of Mitchell and Quinn. Just one word of advice: let the child retain the name of its mother, otherwise some shyster lawyer might persuade Bunny that she has a legal guardianship.'

He threw the document casually on the desk and folded his spectacles. 'Now wasn't that generous of the old man?'

'What about my copy?' Dawson stammered nervously. 'What should I do with the one in the office safe?'

'I think the phrase they used in Watergate circles is to "deep-six" it,' Quinn suggested with evident satisfaction. 'The shredding machine wasn't invented to provide breakfast cereals, you know.'

'Yes, of course. You have my word.'

'Your word is my word,' Quinn fixed him in the eye with the air of a co-conspirator. 'Now, I know I asked for the Scotch with no ice, but if it stays in your hand much longer it will be at blood heat.'

'Sorry.' Dawson could barely prevent himself from shaking as he put the drink on the table. He took a substantial slug of his own and lowered himself into the swivel chair by the desk, not daring to pick up the forged document that lay before him. Instead he pulled open the drawer. 'I can write you a cheque now. The first half of the money. I'm afraid I'm not liquid enough to give you the rest until I've sold some securities.'

'No cheques,' Quinn pronounced definitively. 'You and I have yet to meet. That will happen when you call me to implement the trust. I telephoned your housekeeper to find out her night off. I presume she's not in the habit of returning home unexpectedly early.'

'No . . . no,' Dawson realised how little he himself had thought the matter through. 'Cash, I suppose. I should be able to withdraw ten thousand tomorrow.'

The lawyer shook his head with a smile. 'I can see you've got little experience of arrangements of this sort. Anything that cannot be explained must not become vulnerable to explanation. Do you follow me?'

Dawson responded with a nod.

'You've no off-shore funds, I presume?'

This time it was the actuary who shook his head. He had never even underdeclared his tax return, let alone operated outside the eye of the law before.

'There's the Marlborough Fine Art Gallery just down the street,' Quinn continued as casually as if he were giving traffic directions. 'If you were to purchase a Lichtenstein signed edition for approximately the sum you mention, that would be due consideration. I believe there's one entitled: *'This must be the place.'* It will appreciate nicely on my bedroom wall and I'll appreciate it.'

He swallowed a measure of his drink as if to congratulate himself on the neatness of his scheme and his wordplay. 'As for the rest, I think you'll find provision in clause twenty-two there for pertinent legal fees to be paid out of the trust. We can wait a week or two for those – until after the adoption.'

'Adoption?' The word took Dawson wholly unexpectedly.

'I thought the purpose of this entire exercise was to provide you with a child of your own?'

'Oh yes,' – he recovered his composure – 'yes, it is. There'll be a surrogate mother. I daresay I'll need your services again to draw up the contract there.'

'Be careful,' Quinn warned. 'Are they letting you meet her first?'

'No. Against the rules, I guess, to the extent that there are rules.' He reached across the desk and lifted a loose-leafed folder that looked like a car maintenance manual from the top of a pile of *Actuaries Monthly*. 'My doctor has put me in touch with this surrogate mother agency. They all come highly recommended. But there's something tribal about it – a bit like choosing a wife, only you never meet her in the flesh, or touch her.'

'Let me see.'

Dawson could discern the disapproval in the voice as the massive hand stretched out towards him. He handed over the dossier with a certain reluctance.

The pince-nez were raised in silent inquisition. 'Number twenty-seven,' Quinn called out, as if an usher summoning a witness. 'Aged twenty-four, white caucasian, no hereditary illnesses – both parents still alive. Single parent with daughter aged seven. Must have forgotten to take precautions at the high school prom. Excellent health, above-average IQ, currently receiving social security. Extremely fertile.'

He leafed through the cellophaned pages with evident disdain. 'Here's a nice Irish girl, just right for me – a broad forehead and a mass of freckles. Not that Mrs Quinn would appreciate an addition to the family. Six is quite enough, don't you think?'

'One would be enough for me.' Unused to such doses of strong drink, Silver felt both slightly intoxicated and somewhat morose.

'If you get the son you desire, Mr Silver,' the lawyer demanded in his inquisitorial fashion, 'what exactly is it that you want from him?'

He had touched on a delicate point. The bald man in the saffron dressing gown thought for some time as he gazed pensively into his glass.

'I want him to love me, of course. Even to like me. But not to be like me. What does anybody want from their son? To be healthy and happy. To learn from my mistakes.' He finished his drink with a gulp and the neat whisky burned into his stomach. 'I grew up at a time of caution and austerity. My family were poor. Violet, my mother's sister, lives in a trailer home in Florida right now. I want him to be rich in opportunities. We've produced a generation of men in this country that have led to the mean-minded mess that is Watergate. I want my boy to have some spunk and nobility; to find frontiers and climb mountains, to stroke the Harvard Eight, maybe win an Olympic Gold. I want him to be the best.'

He surprised himself with his own eloquence, like an inauguration speech. Quinn listened attentively and, when he had finished, snapped the book closed with a definitive flourish.

'Well, you won't find him in here. These women are a bunch of misfits. Why else would they be offering their services? You need a mother with some style and intellect – an athlete, too, if you're really serious about your aspirations.'

The implied rejection angered Silver. 'Then what do you suggest I do?' he retorted bitterly, 'go to Bloomingdales and buy a fucking child?'

'Too pricey,' the lawyer's outsize, ruddy face was already ablaze with the solution. 'But I think I may have found the very woman you're looking for.'

· *Eight* ·

Grace Winston felt rather like a tribal chieftain being carried to her coronation. Four heavily built men – all in dark suits with neat white shirts and loudly striped ties, two in sunglasses and two with ostentatious earpieces – lifted her wheelchair up the crowded courthouse steps. The gesture was for the benefit of the media; there was a perfectly workable elevator for the disabled at the side entrance to the building. And the media were not slow to benefit from it.

'How much will you be expecting in damages, Miss Winston?' The young man with the bulbous microphone scrambled crablike in front of her up the steps, nearly knocking over his own cameraman.

'I have no idea.' The Englishwoman gave the pained smile that Quinn had so carefully rehearsed. 'That's for the judge to decide – or is it the jury?'

'They're saying that WNTV offered you a hundred thousand in an out of court settlement. Wouldn't that have been enough?'

Trust a woman to come up with an unsympathetic suggestion like that, Grace thought, as she returned the unflickering gaze of this aspirant Barbara Walters. 'I couldn't possibly comment on that,' she solemnly replied. 'I've merely come here for justice – truth, justice and the American way.'

'Miss Winston, Miss Winston, do you think you will ever walk again?' The person bellowing the question from the bottom of the steps had no microphone but his remark was picked up by every recording machine between him and the top. With his deep trenchcoat and eager notebook the man looked, if anything, too like a newspaper reporter – someone, indeed, he wasn't. Quinn had engaged an out-of-work actor who had been more than happy to accept a fifty-dollar bill from his clerk to make sure this final interrogative would fill both the open air and open microphones.

Grace was disturbed by the fact that the venerable Bostonian had decided not to appear in court himself. He had assured her that such was his fame – or notoriety – that his presence could have an adverse effect on the size of her damages. 'Look at it this way,' he had pointed out. 'You're a poor English girl, thousands of miles from home. If you come barging into an American court with a three-hundred-dollar-an-hour lawyer, the judge and even the jury are going to start getting suspicious. Low key, Grace – low key, large damages.'

As a front, he had engaged Tom Brolly, a young lawyer from Framingham – appropriately a town on the route of the marathon – to present her case. Grace had only met the man for a few minutes the day before and had found him somewhat shifty. He refused to meet her eye or her questions, replying repeatedly, 'Mr Quinn has got it all stitched up.' When she was wheeled into position beside him in the front row of the court, he barely glanced in her direction as he mumbled 'Good morning', almost as if he were the defence lawyer and not her own. Two of the older members of the jury smiled at her as she glanced across at them and this offered her fleeting cause for satisfaction.

Tom Brolly was adroit enough on his feet, however. He looked more like a student than a fully-fledged lawyer, his lank hair flopping over his brow and his brown suit a full two sizes too small for his six-foot frame. But Grace could hear the phraseology of Loophole Quinn flow through him as he recited the facts of the case for the benefit of the jury.

The climax was to be the videotape of the accident. Grace had never seen the footage and Quinn had insisted that it would have infinitely greater dramatic impact if this fact were made known and those assembled in court could see her watching it for the very first time.

The blinds of the courtroom windows were drawn so that the bench, the jurors, plaintiff and defendants could clearly see their separate monitors. But Brolly had tilted his desk light to spill into Grace's eyes and make the contours of her face a focal point for all to behold. She felt tight and apprehensive. They say the camera cannot lie, she thought, well they'd better be wrong.

She was amazed how thin she looked on the television replay. There seemed to be long hollows in her thighs where her muscles should be and her face had the pinched expression of one suffering from oxygen deprivation. She couldn't recognise anyone in her group of runners, nor could she remember the way she had detached herself from them, increasing her pace in some manic gesture as if she were trying to compete with the television truck itself. Grace stared at the screen with mounting anguish. The backs of her hands turned a bloodless white, so tightly did she grip the arms of the wheelchair as the moment of truth approached. Would everybody realise what really happened? The temperature in the courtroom seemed to rise feverishly – or was that just her imagination? Her features froze as she observed the girl on the screen push a lock of hair out of her eyes, as if to see her target better. And then it was over almost before it began: she merely seemed to stumble forward – falling out of the range of the camera with a final cry of desperation.

There remained a nervous silence as the monitors flickered into blackness and the courtroom blinds were raised. Grace looked anxiously at the jury and they, for the most part, looked sympathetically back at her. Was it possible that they didn't realise what they had just witnessed?

'The court will rise for lunch.' The judge's matter-of-fact injunction came as a welcome expression of relief.

Dawson Silver was also watching a television screen at that precise moment – but not the same picture. He bit messily into the tuna submarine sandwich which his secretary had brought into the office. She had strict orders that he was under no circumstances to be disturbed. The only call that she should put through was one from Mr George Bernard Shaw – Quinn relished a dramatic flourish in his pseudonyms. The lawyer had assured him that they might well have a decision by early afternoon. As soon as the defence came to the crux of their case, anyway.

The guest on Chelsea Lambert's lunch-time chat show was Arthur Ashe. He had just returned home after becoming the first black player to win the men's singles at Wimbledon. Chelsea, who had been less than meticulous in her research, asked him if it was his first big tournament win and he modestly pointed out, without any hint or irritation, that he had won the US Open seven years previously. He talked about his early life – growing up as the son of a policeman in Richmond, Virginia – and the struggle he had gone through to gain entry to the South African Open from which he had been barred on the grounds of colour.

'Well, you certainly slammed Jimmy Connors into the ground,' Chelsea purred admiringly. Ashe gently corrected her, pointing out that on the contrary he had taken the pace off the ball so that the championship holder had been unable to send it back with his accustomed pace. Also, he had fed his shots consistently to Connors' weaker forehand.

Silver had watched the match at the weekend. It had been a triumph of strategy over strength. Ashe was undoubtedly the most intelligent player to have won the tournament since the war. The same had been true in the women's final where the cunning of Billie Jean King had allowed the intuitive Evonne Goolagong only a single game.

'Do you think a coloured woman will ever win Wimbledon?' Chelsea enquired unthinkingly.

'Depends what you mean by coloured,' her guest replied patiently. 'Evonne's an Australian aboriginal. Is that colour okay for you? Or how about Althea Gibson who won in 1957 – the first girl from Harlem, incidentally, they ever let into Forest Hills.'

Chelsea flushed: 'I didn't mean to get involved in matters of race but' – she glanced at her clip-board – 'Goolagong only won one game – you think she will ever make a champion?'

'She already is,' Ashe pointed out, 'Wimbledon Champion in 1971, beat Margaret Court 6–4, 6–1.'

Dawson felt like applauding with pleasure. Ashe had all the style and nobility of a true champion.

Grace had been unable to eat anything at lunch-time. A room had been set aside at the back of the court and her minders had brought a selection of soft drinks and sandwiches but she had merely toyed with a Diet Pepsi through a straw. Now the defence counsel, Paul

Prince, with Bill Trentham sitting earnestly by his side, summoned her to the witness stand. Tom Brolly made an elaborate performance of taking the brakes off her wheelchair and deliberately pushing her past the jury to a position just beside the box. Her short hair was brushed severely back and she wore no make-up. Quinn had suggested a simple white blouse and a hospital blanket over her knees.

'Miss Winston, before I begin, may I just confirm that you are apprised of the offer by WNTV to pay a hundred thousand dollars in compensation and damages into open court.'

She nodded.

'Could you reply, either in the affirmative or negative,' the grey-haired lawyer gently insisted. He had a kindly face.

'I was aware of that,' she agreed.

'This morning you heard Miss Winston recite the facts of her case,' her interlocutor now addressed the jury, 'and they are not greatly in dispute. And you saw what happened. This was an accident. Miss Winston fell into the path of the television truck. Thank God her life was spared. What is in dispute – and this may prove an uncomfortable subject but legally it is the essence of the case – is the current nature of the plaintiff's injuries.'

Prince turned back to the table where he had been sitting and picked up a large buff envelope. Fishing inside with his hand, he pulled out some X-rays which he casually glanced at and then put down on the table. Still holding the envelope he returned his attention to the jury.

'Miss Winston suffered fractures of the tibia and fibula – the main bones of the lower leg. Happily both have now successfully mended. Her more serious injury is to the pelvis and this is where a matter of medical ambiguity arises as to the extent of her recovery. Miss Winston, do you expect you will ever walk again?'

Grace felt a spreading sense of unease. 'I . . . I really don't know,' she spluttered.

'Have you been able to walk since the accident?' His enquiry was mild and considerate.

'No . . . not that I can remember.'

Prince delved into the buff envelope once more and produced not a negative but a large positive photograph of approximately the same size. He showed it first to the bench, then Grace, then to Tom Brolly and finally the jury.

'This was taken in the grounds of the Brookline Masonic Nursing Home last Sunday afternoon. You will see Miss Winston standing, unaided . . .'

'I object' – Brolly was on his feet. 'Your honour, we received no prior knowledge of this photograph. There is no proof of when it was taken and it is quite possible that my client could be resting on a crutch on the side furthest from the camera. It is, if I may say, a preposterous and unfairly damaging gesture.'

The judge looked at the defence counsel. 'Do you propose to call witnesses to substantiate this?'

'Just one, your honour.'

Glancing through the documents in front of him, the judge seemed somewhat surprised. 'I don't see any listed.'

'The only witness who can provide wholly reliable evidence is Miss Winston herself.' The lawyer moved away from his table and took up a new position at the end of the jury box.

'Grace,' Prince said, slowly swivelling towards her. 'Would you be gracious enough to get up and walk across to me?'

Her first thought was that she was going to be physically sick. Never in his meticulous preparations for the trial had Quinn even hinted this might happen. He had played defence counsel, hectored her, subjected her to verbal abuse, called her a liar – but apparently overlooked the possibility of this perilous request. She felt more paralysed now than she had at any time in the two months since the accident. Even in the rudest of health, she doubted if she could have risen from her chair without considerable difficulty. At the same time it became absolutely apparent to her that this was the most significant moment of her life. Every day after this, every minute of every day, would be coloured by her reaction now. Most people were lucky enough to travel from the cradle to the crypt without ever having to face such a personal epiphany. But luck had long since proved a false companion to Grace.

The silence of the room screamed at her. This was not an ordeal that she wished to undergo for a second longer. It came almost as a relief as she unfolded her hospital blanket and took her first uncertain steps towards the jury – and towards the rest of her life.

'The judge threw the book at her.' George Bernard Shaw was on the line to Dawson even before Grace Winston had begun to face the ordeal by television that was lying in wait for her outside. 'Said she was in contempt of court. Told her she was lucky not to face criminal charges of false pretences. Hit her with half the defendants' costs – although we'll get them to waive those when they realise they won't get anything anyway. Brolly's feeling a bit stunned but I wasn't to know, was I?'

'You're a shit, Quinn,' said Silver. 'How did you know she'd walk? All the actuarial odds were against it, I told you.'

'Fortunately you formulated an inaccurate equation,' the lawyer gloatingly pointed out. 'You forgot to include the British sense of fair play. I doubt if we even needed to send Prince the photograph. Grace was always going to stand up – even if she didn't realise it herself.'

'How long should we wait now?' The anxiety was apparent in Dawson's voice. 'She's going to go through a pretty tough time.'

'Didn't you ever read fairy tales when you were a child?' countered the lawyer. 'The heroine has to pass through a period of darkness before she gets to the happy ending. Life's like that, you know.'

'Come home now. Just get on the plane and get out of there.' Alice was in tears on the other end of the transatlantic line.

'I can't.' Grace surprised herself at her own composure. 'There's too much to be sorted out. I can't just run away from it,' adding with an ironic laugh, 'even if I could run at all.'

'Then let me come and get you,' Alice implored. 'There must be a British consul there who can help. What's the fucking Foreign Office for if it's not to sort out citizens in distress?'

Grace looked around the spartan trappings of her nursing-home room. She would dearly love to be in England but there was a penance to be paid here first.

'I'm all right, Alice, really I am. There's a lawyer who's been helping me. He was only going to take a percentage of the damages if I had won. I'm sure he'll think of something.'

'Well the last thing he thought of wasn't too brilliant. You need some independent help. You should never even have found yourself in court. It was all so straightforward.'

'I know' – Grace realised that if this conversation continued for much longer she would find herself in an unwanted argument. 'I've got to go, Alice. This is expensive. Money's tight. How's Lenny, by the way?'

'I saw him down at Battersea at the weekend,' her friend sounded slightly relieved at the change of subject. 'He was sort of . . . er' – her voice tailed off as though there were a fault on the line.

'Sort of what?' repeated Grace.

'Oh, just out there training. Back on the track.'

'Training a new recruit, is that what you were going to say? Has she got long blonde hair?'

'Don't distress yourself, Grace. I'd forget him if I were you. You've got bigger problems than a little twerp like him.'

'You can say that again,' she smiled to herself just as the familiar rap, less confident than usual, came at the door. 'I'll ring you, Alice. Don't worry, I'll survive.'

Putting the phone back in the cradle, she paused to compose herself before she let Quinn in.

'What can I say?' – a broad comforting arm snaked immediately round her shoulder – 'you were put in an unforgivable position. No injured woman should ever have to face an ordeal like that, nor a healthy one either.'

'I couldn't do anything else,' she apologised. 'I realised there was no way I could continue to live with myself if I had just sat there.'

'I understand,' he said sympathetically. 'I should have anticipated it. Unfortunately British decency has no place in a Boston courtroom.'

Grace hobbled over to the window with the aid of a stick. There was an artificial pond at the end of the lawn and the usual timorous seagulls had already taken up their safe harbour for the night. They were unlike European birds, with a grey mantle round their black heads and dark pink legs.

'What are they called?' she asked the lawyer.

'Bonaparte gulls,' he replied knowingly, 'they come from Philadelphia originally.'

They watched them settle in silence. 'What am I going to do?' she said eventually.

'There'll be no fee for me,' he assured her. 'You have nothing to worry about on that account. And I've had a word with Parker at the Karger – I don't think they'll be pressing for costs, either.'

'What, no bills?' she turned to him in delight.

'No legal ones.'

'When I was a child,' she said, looking back at the gulls, 'there used to be a notice on a wall we would pass on the way to school. It said "Post No Bills" and I always thought that it was a message to the postman from the people in the house for him not to put any bills through the letter-box.'

Eamonn Quinn laughed – a heaving, hearty artificial laugh. 'That would be a fine thing.'

'There's still the cost of the hospital, isn't there? And here.'

'I'm afraid so.'

'Where am I going to find what, thirty-five thousand dollars?'

The lawyer lowered himself onto the bed. 'There you put your finger on it. Not an easy one. You're going to have to take out a loan, I'm afraid. But I got you into this mess and I'm prepared to stand surety for it.'

She swivelled round to face him. 'But how will I pay it off? I'm not at all certain that I'll even have a job when I get back home.'

He took a considered breath and stared at the counterpane. 'Indeed, you have a problem,' he admitted.

'Don't think I'm not grateful to you for trying to get me some extra money. I should just never have agreed to it. I'm not a lucky person, Mr Quinn, I ought to have told you that at the outset.'

'If you rely on luck finding you, you'll never have any,' counselled the lawyer. 'On the other hand, if you're prepared to go looking for your luck, you'll discover it's nearly always there to be found.'

Grace returned her mournful gaze to the Bonaparte gulls. 'I don't really know where to begin to look.'

'Trust me,' the voice behind her whispered softly.

'Have you ever tasted scrod before?'

'I've never even heard of it before. What is it?'

'Hard to define,' Dawson pursed his lips. 'Snobbish Boston form of cod, I guess.'

'Shouldn't they have called it snod in that case? Too like snot I suppose — forgive me,' Grace apologised. 'That's a word I ought to have left in the playground.'

He looked up from the menu and smiled. Quinn had been right about her: she was forthright and quite witty. He enjoyed this kind of down-to-earth Englishwoman. People like Bunny spent their lives in a vague imitation of the British upper classes but because they lacked the true blood of some mistress of Charles II running through their veins they never really felt at home with themselves and replaced it with alcohol instead. Grace, with her prim dark hair and neatly articulated vowels, seemed like someone out of a Jane Austen novel. He was amazed that she could ever have been taken in by Quinn's obvious blarney.

But Quinn, Grace believed, was the only way out of her present plight. 'Silver's a financial wizard,' he had reassured her, 'as sterling as his name. Let him listen to your problem. There's no one better in the world to analyse it and come up with some solution — maybe a bond against a life insurance policy, that sort of thing. Just have an informal dinner with him. Don't worry — it's not a date. He's still in mourning for his wife and child, both killed in a boating accident last year — although, for Christ's sake, don't make mention of it.'

If she had been intimidated by the prospect of the evening, Locke-Obers did little to alleviate her concern. This was Boston's most hallowed and expensive restaurant, precisely a hundred years old according to the menu. Women had only been admitted to the Men's Café three years ago and it was still the sort of place where no male diner felt quite comfortable unless he was already known to the waiters by name. This presented little problem to Silver who had been greeted like the regular he was and shown to a table quiet enough for a confidential conversation yet well enough placed to observe the arrivals and departures of the other opulent occupants.

'Would madame like a drink?' The waiter in his black tie and long white apron did his best to make her feel welcome.

'What are you having?' she asked Dawson.

'A Manhattan. In fact — I might even have another Manhattan.'

She smiled appreciatively. 'Me, too. Not another one, just . . . well, you know.'

Even the waiter seemed to unbend somewhat as he bowed in

acknowledgement. Dawson had been nervous at the prospect of his intended offer but, fortified by the initial drink, he felt a lot more relaxed.

'What is it?' she enquired. 'A sort of liquid scrod?'

'Wrong city,' he smiled. 'A perfect Manhattan is made with rye whiskey and dry Vermouth. Or you could have it with sweet.'

'Why would one want anything less than perfect?'

'My feelings exactly,' Silver agreed. 'Now tell me a bit about yourself. Do you have any children? Are you married?'

'I thought Eamonn Quinn told you everything about me,' Grace retorted defensively.

'He did, indeed he did.' Silver was contrite. 'But unfortunately I have a memory like a scrod net. At forty-seven the brain cells atrophy at a terrifying rate. It's hard to know exactly when you cross the Rubicon into Alzheimer's Disease. Better not to know, maybe. I can't remember whether he said you were religious. Did that help you through your ordeal?'

She shook her head. 'I'm still searching. I'd be happy to believe like Kierkegaard that religion is born of the unknown. You know, without risk there is no faith and the greater the risk the greater the faith. But I can't. So I'm stuck on Pascal's Wager.'

Dawson was intrigued: these were not things that he had been taught at temple. 'What's that?'

'That the odds suggest it's better to believe. If you do and there is a God and eternal life, you become entitled to it. Whereas if you decide not to believe, you don't actually gain anything and you may lose out on eternal life if you're wrong.'

'That's a very calculating view of religion,' he observed.

She took a wary sip of the drink which the waiter had placed in front of her. 'I thought you were a wizard with calculations. Mr Quinn told me everything about you.'

'Figures occupy a different area of the brain from the imagination. They just roll up like the dials on gas pumps, there's no real need for any creative input.'

'Well what is an actually, actuary?' she blurted out and they both began to laugh.

'That's what your first Manhattan does to you,' warned Dawson. 'Imagine what happens after the first ten thousand. That's an actuarial calculation, as a matter of fact. They say people become actuaries because they find accountancy too exciting.'

Grace smiled. 'No, it's a science,' Dawson continued. 'It began long ago – in your home town in the middle of the eighteenth century. There was a Fellow of the Royal Society called James Dodson who was turned down for an insurance policy because they said he was too old. But he wouldn't accept the rejections so he came up with the very first table of annual premiums based on life expectancy. And that's what I deal in. Probability – or the lack of it – for the benefit of pension schemes, any form of insurance, you know. It's quite possible to estimate the occurrence of various contingencies in human life: marriage, sickness, unemployment, accidents, morbidity, death, birth. And the size of any given policy is shaped accordingly.'

'Morbidity?' she enquired.

He welcomed her interest. 'It's a word we use when dealing with the role of sickness in a specified group or community. For instance, death from tuberculosis has declined in the years since the war – the arrival of antibiotics has changed all that.'

'But death from cancer is on the increase,' Grace suggested.

'Precisely.'

'Could you have anticipated my accident?'

Dawson thought about it for a moment. 'I've never been asked to advise on a policy for the marathon – I'm not sure that they have one. I did read a survey recently which found that eighty-four per cent of all marathon runners were nursing an injury of some sort or other. It's a good question. Let me see, out of two thousand runners running twenty-five miles for approximately four hours that's two hundred thousand hours with athletes on the open road. Yes, it was statistically probable than an accident of that sort might happen – but nobody could have known that it would be you.'

Except me, Grace thought.

Dawson was warming to his subject. 'I have a colleague who adores soccer and he told me that in your country, at the football cup final where there's a crowd of a hundred thousand people, one and a half persons will die from some cause or other during the ninety-minute match. There's a morgue in Wembley Stadium, apparently, and the head of the soccer association is in the habit of going down there at half-time to see if a body has arrived yet.'

'Or half a body.' Grace drained her drink, anxious to move on from the anecdotes to her immediate plight. 'Quinn said you could help me. I'm more than thirty thousand dollars in debt. Can an actuary work that one out?'

He was discomforted by her directness. 'I was hoping to come to that later.'

'Oh, let's get it over and done with. Don't want to spoil the scrod.'

Dawson pensively stirred the maraschino cherry in his Manhattan with his ivory cocktail stick. 'All right. Do you know what a surrogate mother is?'

'Oh God,' Grace exclaimed. 'I've come to dinner under false pretences.'

'No,' he insisted authoritatively, 'you've come for a solution to your financial problems. It can be achieved through your talents. You're a fine-looking woman, Grace, a university graduate and an athlete. A friend of mine would be prepared to pay you money to have a baby – his donor sperm, done by injection.'

'How much?' she asked abruptly.

'There is no rate. But I daresay he'd cover your debt.'

Tears welled up in her eyes. Somehow she had assumed that the man in front of her was capable of waving a wand and taking away her woes. Instead he seemed to be suggesting something that was in essence an assault on her body.

Dawson leant across the table and took a firm hold on her arm. 'Would it make any difference if you knew the person involved? The child would still carry your name – Winston – and, if you wished, access could be arranged for you to keep in touch.' He drew a calculated breath. 'What about if it was from me – for me?'

Grace looked at his pleading eyes and domed head, a man who could doubtless dominate a board meeting with his financial erudition and experience, but who was as vulnerable as any other mortal in the areas of life where intellect and wealth and power were subservient to what nature decided. And what about herself? She could see her own shapeless future spreading out in front of her.

'I'll have to think about it,' she said.

· Nine ·

The murmur of thunder rumbling somewhere the other side of Heathrow caused many of the crowd in the open seats to start searching for raincoats and umbrellas. Even though this Sunday afternoon seemed almost too hot for any imminent downpour. The moisture was already in the air, as if this were not England at all but some God-forsaken colony such as Malaya or the West Indies or Hong Kong, and these invisible molecules themselves presented a shield against the onset of any storm.

'What's he wearing?' Dawson Silver didn't bother to turn his head towards Moses Hoffman who was eternally alert to field his every enquiry.

'Just a shirt and shorts now,' the coach informed him. 'He dumped his vest at the last changeover.'

'The new Goffi stuff, right? With the navy trim.'

'You got it. And the sweatlets, kinda look as if they're black from here. He's made plenty of use of those.'

'Is he sweating all over?' Dawson sounded worried. 'Marks of perspiration?'

'Sure, the kid's had some running to do. You would, too, if you'd covered as much court in this heat. An English summer's afternoon,' Mo reflected ironically. 'You'd think we were back in fucking Florida.'

'Is that going to cause us problems?' The man in dark glasses appeared to ignore the last remark, his whispered tones rising apprehensively.

Problems were exactly what Winston was facing on the grass

beneath them. One problem, in particular, in the shape of Shimizu. The Japanese player had barely made a mistake so far and, as a result, the first four games now belonged to him. Winston knew that unless he held his next service he might as well sacrifice the set.

'Why isn't the bastard even sweating?' he wondered as he towelled the handle of his racquet.

Shimizu stood calmly staring at him, as if he could read his thoughts – something he had done with intuitive aplomb in the match so far, manifesting himself like a genie to crack back every angle his opponent had attempted.

'Take your time, act out a mime, go slow until the going's fine.' Mo had demonstrated to him again and again how losing players tend to rush things, willing co-conspirators in their own downfall. The secret was first to try to control the pace between points and then wrest control during them.

Winston casually threw his towel against the green canvas at the back of the court and summoned two balls from the girl in the left-hand corner. He moved to the centre of the baseline and stared deliberately at his opponent. His clothing appeared to be still crisp and white, an effect heightened by the caramel brown of his skin. Do the Japanese go sunbathing? Winston wondered. And, if they do, does it make them darker? The whole island race seemed to have been born with the same flawless skin.

Shimizu gave him a brief grin and then offered a curt nod of the head, urging him to get on and serve.

Winston deliberately ignored the injunction and instead held out the two yellow balls in his left hand for examination. He paused for three beats, then turned to the ball-boy in the right-hand corner, gesturing with the forefinger and stumped middle finger of his racquet hand that he wanted three more.

Surprised, the boy bounced them across to him. Winston caught them with his racquet and transferred them expertly to join the other two in his left hand. A frisson ran through the more knowledgeable in the crowd who sensed what he was about to attempt. He lowered his body deep towards the grass, drew back his Excalibur Plus racquet and then pistoned it towards the yellow ball which had just reached the apex of its arc with all the might he could muster.

· Ten ·

'You want me to turn the telly on? Our Virginia.'

Grace eyed the substantial black nurse shuffling across the room. The contractions seemed to be coming closer together now, although she couldn't be sure. Certainly they were tugging more remorselessly at her stomach. She had learnt through her abbreviated experience as a long distance runner that she had the capacity to go through the pain barrier but this was something unforgivingly different. How long could she hold out, she wondered, before asking for an epidural injection that would take away her suffering and return her lower body to the numb state it had been reduced to after the accident.

'No, thank you. No television.'

'The Queen's there today,' the nurse remarked, largely to herself, as she stubbornly continued towards the clinical white set suspended from the ceiling. 'Wonder what she's wearing.'

'No,' Grace screamed, partly in pain but mainly in annoyance. 'I don't want it.'

Her outburst brought the nurse to a halt. 'Maybe later,' she reassured her, turning back towards the door. 'Deep breaths now. Fill that brain with oxygen.'

Grace's brain had been filled with nothing other than deep doubts since her waters had broken in the early hours of the morning. This had happened in the middle of a harrowingly troubled dream. Lenny and Alice were apparently living together and had asked her round for dinner because there was somebody they wanted to meet. It was a stranger, a rangy American who chain-smoked his way through the meal. She felt extremely ill-at-ease in his presence, even more so as he repeatedly asked her if she were pregnant and she had kept denying it. Not only did he persist, but Lenny and Alice joined in, demanding to know who the father was. Grace had left the table in tears and made for the bathroom, but there was somebody else already in there – although the four of them were the only people in the flat. As she waited despairingly outside, she wet herself. When she woke she realised she had, in fact, wet the bed. She rapidly realised what had happened from the agonising twinges in her abdomen. She rang the hospital immediately. The duty midwife reassured her there was no need to panic – just to pack her belongings. An ambulance would be along in less than an hour.

Grace had left Locke-Obers agreeing to nothing save that she would discuss Dawson's offer again the following year when she was fully fit. She wished she could have washed her hands of Boston, but the sale of her flat in Askew Road had raised only enough money to pay off two-thirds of her debt to the Karger Orthopaedic. She had been obliged to let Eamonn Quinn stand surety for her so that she could settle the rest by instalments and this made her feel more than a little compromised.

Her life back in Britain had not been a success, although her temporary disability had enabled her to vault the waiting list and obtain a one-bedroom council flat on the fifteenth floor of Stafford Cripps Court in west London. She gave up her job at the school. Word had spread of the attempt to get extra damages in America and she sensed the staff were talking about her behind her back. She needed a new start at a new place where her past would be truly behind her but she had not succeeded in obtaining either of the teaching posts for which she applied. Lack of success bred lack of confidence. No longer able nor wishing to join the Badgers on the track, Grace retreated into her lonely nest with the television, once more, her most trusted companion.

Her outings consisted of a daily trip to P.J. Patel, newsagent, confectioner and grocer, on Rylston Road to collect a copy of *The Times* and whatever provisions she needed. Very often her only conversation of the day would be with twelve-year-old Ranesh. It usually followed the same pattern with Grace trying to convert him to the virtues of running and Ranesh, who had a large poster of Mark Spitz on the wall, insisting he wanted to swim for Britain like

David Wilkie. Once a week she would walk to the post office in Fulham Broadway for her social security, making her way home through the North End Road street market to stock up on vegetables. 'Cheer up, love,' a trader had shouted after her one day, 'it could be worse.' But it couldn't really, she reflected.

In 1976 America celebrated its bicentennial and Britain its hottest summer of the century. Hoses were banned, a Minister for Drought was appointed and the crowd at Lord's actually applauded when rain stopped play for the first time in months. Life in her high-rise flat in the brick-hot heart of Fulham became close to intolerable. Grace had grown to hate each sun-filled dawn. Her salvation lay in the evenings when she watched the Olympics from Montreal. The fourteen-year-old Romanian, Nadia Comaneci, became the first gymnast to attain perfection in the Games when she was awarded maximum marks in the asymmetric bars. Grace obtained trans-ferred pleasure, thinking how thrilled Ranesh must be, when Wilkie broke the American stranglehold on the swimming by winning the breaststroke. Her own hero, however, was Lasse Viren, the Flying Finn, who not only won gold medals in the five thousand and ten thousand metres but then went on to compete in the first marathon of his life and managed to finish fifth. He almost – but not quite – replaced Jim Peters in her affections.

And there was no doubt when Quinn's draft contract arrived that Grace had little option other than to accept. She was deeply in debt and deeper in despair. As she held the initial cheque for fifteen thousand dollars in her hand and gazed out over the stifling city, she acknowledged to herself with sad irony that she had become a womb with a view. Quinn had wanted her to return to America for the baby but Grace wrote back insisting that she would have it in Britain or not at all. Slightly to her surprise, he accepted her terms.

As soon as they had received her signature, a man introducing himself as Dr Edmund Michaels telephoned from Boston and began to give Grace a stream of instructions as if she were some sort of hired help. He cross-questioned her in detail about her menstrual cycle and reminded her emphatically of her agreement to refrain from alcohol, cigarettes and, above all, sex. She hoped he couldn't sense her smile over the phone as she promised she would abstain from the last; there hadn't been a man in her life since Lenny. She was to present herself at 31 Harley Street the following Monday morning with her full medical record. Were her parents still alive? When Grace had told him that they were both dead, the doctor had evinced not a shred of sympathy but merely insisted that she should obtain as much information as possible about their medical records also and, more particularly, details of the cause of their deaths. A London colleague of his, Dr Nicholas McBride, would carry out a detailed health check on her.

Six weeks later Grace had come face to face with Dr Michaels himself. Evidently her tests had proved satisfactory so he had flown over to London in order, as he jokingly put it, to administer the foetal dose.

'Karger Orthopaedic did a real neat job on your pelvis,' had been his words of greeting as he waved an X-ray at her. 'Main cause of infertility in a woman, some sort of pelvic inflammatory disease or, worse still, failed surgery that blocks up the tubes. But yours are ready, willing and able.'

Michaels had taken over McBride's surgery and the fact that he was wearing the doctor's white coat indicated that he, himself, was ready for action.

'I've brought your friend and benefactor, Mr Silver, with me,' he grinned, as he removed a specimen jar from the refrigerator. 'Saves the cost of an air fare if you travel like this.'

Grace found herself constantly on guard in the man's presence. It was a tense enough ordeal for her without his attempted wisecracks. There was something offensively artificial about Michaels; his whole ensemble – club bow-tie, over-coiffed hair and grey-filtered glasses – bespoke a man who had taken his personality off a peg that morning. When he hung it up again at night, she wondered if there would be anybody left.

He looked up from her medical notes. 'As you know, there are two occasions in the month when a woman is likely to be at her most fertile so why don't we give it a hit straight away?'

Grace's spirits sank; this was a moment she would do almost anything to postpone. 'How long have people been able to do this . . . er . . . sort of thing?' she began.

'Centuries,' came the curt reply. 'The Arabs used artificial insemination for horse-breeding back in 1350, although the first properly documented report wasn't until 1784 when a man called Spallanzani successfully inseminated his dog. It's a veterinary science. If you look at a field of cows or sheep today, the odds are their mothers and fathers never met each other – they're all the products of AI. Human beings are infinitely inferior. We have to wait for natural selection and hope that someone as perfect as a Comaneci can come along by sheer chance.'

'But how long has it been done with humans?' she continued nervously.

'Pretty well since the war. There used to be an absurd theory that the sexual act itself was part of the process of insemination, that muscular contractions produced by the general excitement of copulation somehow sucked the semen into the uterus. Absolute rubbish, of course. What I'm about to do has an infintely greater chance of success than some random fuck. With this syringe' – he flourished it with pride – 'I can pinpoint your waiting eggs with Silver's spermatozoa like a low-flying B52.'

Grace looked at the instrument in horror. She felt like a laboratory animal, trapped by her own greed and unable to escape.

'Don't worry,' the doctor reassured her, 'you won't feel a thing. The nurse is waiting for you next door.'

Luckily or unluckily, it worked first time. Michaels returned to London that Christmas and pronounced her healthily pregnant, presenting her with an envelope from Dawson Silver which contained a cheque for a further fifteen thousand dollars. Grace found his inspection of her, without a nurse this time, unsettlingly cold and clinical. Once he had established that she was carrying a child, he seemed to have no further interest in her health or well-being. He wrote an appointment in McBride's diary when she should come for an amniocentesis – 'to make sure we haven't got a little mongol in there,' he explained crudely – without bothering to enquire whether it suited her or not.

This had proved the final straw. Grace could not bear to be touched by the man again; she didn't even want to see him again. Nor did she have to. A detailed perusal of Quinn's contract revealed that, although she was obliged to be impregnated by the doctor and attend consultations with him until conception was confirmed, the only other thing she was legally bound to do was to hand the child over to Dawson Silver within seven days of its birth.

So she telephoned Eamonn Quinn and told him that there would be no amniocentesis. From now on she would be seeing her own doctor on the British National Health Service and she would contact him again when the baby was born. Although he tried hard to make her change her mind – even promising more money – the lawyer was forced to agree she was within her rights. Edmund Michaels was on the phone immediately, asking what was wrong and offering to fly across straight away. But Grace had been adamant. 'I may not be able to enjoy my child once it is born,' she calmly informed him, 'but I intend to enjoy it for the six months before that.'

And she did. The depressions became a thing of the past. Her local GP put her in touch with the pre-natal classes at St Sophie's Hospital and Grace even began to make new friends there. For the time being, at least, she had a renewed purpose in life: the safe delivery of her child. She was no longer some anonymous surrogate that Michaels was free to prod and experiment with; instead she was treated with the respect and care that the community bestowed on a mother-to-be. The first six months of 1977 were a time of treasured tranquillity which Grace had rarely experienced in her adult life before. She even organised a tea party for her thirty-second birthday which three of the other pre-natal mothers attended.

One Tuesday in April, while shopping in the North End Road market, she met Lenny. He must have seen her first and tried to avoid her but once their eyes met – across a stall laden with cabbages and Brussels sprouts – there was no way out.

'I'd heard you were having a baby,' he mumbled. 'Is it in order to ask who the father is?'

'An American,' she replied.

'Oh. And are you going to go and live there?'

'We haven't decided,' she replied confidently. 'Perhaps I'll commute – like David Frost.'

From her bed in the pre-delivery ward of St Sophie's she could observe the hospital's tall smoking chimney which pointed up to the invisible path where the planes settled for their final approach to Heathrow Airport. They appeared to be arriving at closer intervals now and so did her contractions. To Grace they seemed like the striking of a bell, tolling away the final moments of her transitory bliss. In a week or so her child would be taken away by one of those Jumbo storks and she would be back on her own again.

'How are you doing?' The young registrar, whom she had seen on her first visit to the hospital, was on duty this Friday afternoon. He had told her he would be looking after the delivery. Without waiting for her answer, he took her wrist and checked her blood pressure, while glancing at the graph paper print-out from the machine which was delivering occasional bleeps by her side.

'I think we're in business,' he said knowingly. 'Let me have a feel.'

He lifted the bedclothes and pressed his warm hands against the lower part of her abdomen. Did she catch a flicker of concern in his otherwise benign expression? If so, it passed quickly.

He thought for a moment. 'I'd like to give you a general.'

'A colonel would do,' Grace responded, trying to make light of it.

Dr Busfield appeared not to hear; his mind was elsewhere. 'There are minor complications,' he explained. 'The baby's ready to come out all right but just isn't in the correct position.'

'Can't you do it with an epidural? I'd rather be awake.'

'It's looking more and more like a Caesarean,' he warned.

'I still want to be there,' she pleaded.

'Okay,' he agreed. 'I'll get Sister to give you a pre-med and then we'll pop a little needle in your back. You'll be fine.'

'Thank you.'

He gave her shoulder a gentle squeeze. 'See you in theatre. I'll be the one in the fetching green pyjamas.'

Just as he was about to leave the room, he turned back to her, as if he had forgotten something. 'By the way, do you want the telly on? Ginny's evened it at one set all and she's steaming ahead in the third.'

'No, thanks,' she smiled. 'Tennis isn't really my thing.'

Although Grace had never witnessed the birth of a baby before, she sensed there was a contagiously nervy atmosphere in the operating theatre that seemed somewhat out of the ordinary. The talkative Polish anaesthetist was curiously agitated, continually adjusting the flow of fluid into her epidural and anxiously testing her legs with a pin to make sure there was no feeling in them.

She didn't dare ask the junior staff if anything was wrong, as they silently sterilised the instruments for the operation. But her increasing doubts received confirmation when the swing doors of the theatre opened and Dr Busfield came in, followed by an older man also dressed in a surgeon's gown. Oh God, thought Grace, this is someone sent by Michaels. He's done a deal with St Sophie's.

'May I introduce Mr Burton,' said the registrar. 'I'll be assisting him, in fact.'

'What's wrong?' asked Grace.

'Nothing,' the senior consultant replied, 'nothing to worry about.' He placed his expert hands on her stomach. 'You know it's a Caesarean section, don't you?'

They ingeniously erected a small tent over the lower half of her body so that she couldn't see what was happening. Grace felt like part of a magician's act: she was about to be sawn in half and, hopefully, put together again. She observed Burton accept a scalpel from the sister and decided to close her eyes.

Five minutes passed, or maybe three, or maybe ten. There was no real way of telling the time. She could hear the gowned figures in the hermetically sealed surgery murmur to each other in lowered tones. Her ears were anxious for some note of optimism or approval from the consultant but he maintained a professional terseness. From time to time there was a slurping noise, the sound of suction or a sink being drained. One of the nurses dabbed her brow with a damp cloth and asked how she was. And then, without any warning whatever, there came the cry of a child, sudden and strident and transcendent.

'What is it?' asked Grace, opening her eyes to release her tears.

'It's a boy,' said Dr Busfield cheerfully. 'They both are.'

· *Eleven* ·

Because she had undergone what was termed an abnormal delivery Grace was accorded an amenity room, a spare and compact chamber not unlike a small cabin on a ship. In many ways she would have preferred to be in the open ward with the other mothers – she had been isolated enough in the past year – but it did offer her some peace and privacy.

She had slept for nearly fourteen hours following the delivery: exhaustion and a substantial dose of morphine had seen to that. The babies, securely tagged 'Winston 1' and 'Winston 2', had been taken away to the hospital nursery to be cared for until she was fit enough to feed them.

The following afternoon she asked the nurse where the public phones were, only to be rebuked for thinking that her stomach was sufficiently healed for her to walk down the corridor. But the raven-haired Irishwoman – like most nurses, steel on the outside and soft at the centre – promised that a phone on wheels would be brought round in due course.

As Grace sat on the edge of her bed, she realised the nurse was right: she was still extremely weak and enfeebled from the operation. Nevertheless she intended to honour her contract to the letter, and this entailed informing Eamonn Quinn of the arrival of the child within twenty-four hours of its birth.

The twins had been premature – the natural term of her pregnancy had another ten days to run – so she was aware that the news would come as something of a surprise to Quinn whom she had last spoken to the day before she went into labour. As she asked the international operator for a reverse charge call to his Boston office, she reflected that the lawyer would be considerably more surprised were she to reveal the full extent of her news. But she had no intention of doing so just yet.

'Mitchell and Quinn, how may we help you?' The voice of the secretary – breezily cheerful despite the fact that she was working on a Saturday morning – offered little clue to the truth that there was no 'we', just old Loophole operating on his own.

'Will you accept transfer charges from a Miss Winston in London, England?' The English operator sounded priggishly disapproving, rather as if he hoped that the request would be turned down.

'Oh sure, put her right on the line.'

Americans are so much more positive, Grace thought. Their lives seemed to be devoted to making things happen while we take pleasure in preventing them from happening. Perhaps that was why winning matters so much over there.

'Is Mr Quinn in the office this morning?' She could hear the crackling apprehension in her own voice but there was nothing she could do about it.

'Grace,' – the lawyer must have been hovering behind the secretary; he was in the office every morning, Sundays included – 'what's wrong, is anything wrong?'

'No, nothing.' she reassured him. 'I'm calling from the hospital. I've had the baby.'

'How is he? Is he all right? Is everything all right?' Quinn sounded excited and agitated in equal measure.

'How did you know it was a he?' she enquired spontaneously.

'I didn't. It's just . . . It's just a way of . . . you know. So it is a boy?'

'Six pounds and seven ounces,' she told him with pride.

'Small,' he noted, 'a small miracle. And you're okay are you? No problems?'

'I couldn't be more happy,' she replied truthfully.

'You know you could be in a private hospital, all expenses paid. Still could, instead of that St Swithin's place. Are they treating you okay?'

'Like royalty. It's fine, really it is.'

'Good. Well, you did it your way. Let's hope some of that strong female strength of character is passed on to the boy.'

'My son,' she said protectively.

This provoked an audible intake of breath at the other end which was followed by a considered pause. 'Yes . . . er, listen, Grace, I'm going to contact Dawson, tell him the baby's arrived. He'll be specially delighted it's a boy. And he should get over to England early next week. Could he come and collect him, say, Wednesday?'

'I think he and I should talk first. Let him come on Wednesday, by all means, but' – without any warning she was assailed by a barely controllable desire to break into tears – 'there are just things to discuss.'

'Is he sick? Is he going to survive? What's wrong?'

'There's not anything wrong. We just need to talk.'

'There's nothing more to discuss, Grace' – relieved at the news that the child was healthy, Quinn felt emboldened to remind the mother of her legal duty – 'it's all there in the contract. There's no going back on that. From the moment you accepted the advance, you were aware that the agreement became irrevocably binding. Dawson will be bringing the final balance of the money with him and for that you'll be expected to abide by every detail in that document. Is that clearly understood?'

'Yes, I will do everything the contract obliges me to do,' she promised him. 'You have my word on that.'

As she put the phone down, the Irish nurse returned wheeling an incubator. Grace looked down at the two tiny bodies, pink and creased and fragile, lying asleep side by side. She could hold back her tears no longer and they streamed unrestrained down her face. This had been her precious cargo for the past thirty-eight weeks; now it had reached its destination.

'They are all right?' Her concern echoed that of Eamonn Quinn.

'Sure, they're fine. A pair of brave little boyos – screaming all night and sleeping all day. Typical men.'

'Can I feed them?' Her breasts felt uncomfortable and ponderous with milk. Did some celestial dairy send you a double supply if you gave birth to twins, she wondered.

'I'm not too sure about that. You'll have to ask Mr Burton – he's on his rounds now, that's why I've brought them in. You get back in your bed – plenty of rest till those stitches heal.'

The bolt of pain from her stomach as she lifted her legs off the floor underlined the nurse's advice. Grace kept her eyes fixed on the twins, trying to memorise their features in case there was a mix-up and their tabs were lost. Neither of them had a strand of hair – they were similar to Dawson in that respect – but at first sight it seemed from their proportionately long limbs that they were unlikely to inherit his square physique. Their mouths were wide and straight, and their faces narrow with little lantern jaws. Both boys had tiny birth marks on their foreheads, presumably where they had been pressing against each other in the womb.

'You don't object to students, do you?' Burton breezed into the room followed by half a dozen of them before Grace had time to answer. The consultant picked up her chart from the end of the bed. 'You had quite a sleep. Good thing, too. These chaps would have kept you awake, I gather.'

He turned to an Indian girl in a white coat who was standing by the incubator. 'Well, what are they, Shireen? Monozygotic or dizygotic?'

The girl peered diligently at them. 'Almost certainly monozygotic.'

'Which means. . . ?' Burton addressed the question to a young man with close-cropped hair and the build of a rugby player.

'I . . . they're . . . well, twins,' he stumbled.

'Brilliant, Brian,' his professor offered sarcastic congratulations. 'Shireen, explain.'

'They've been created by the early division of a single fertilised ovum.'

'Which means,' Burton repeated, now addressing himself to Grace, 'that they're identical – as you've probably guessed. Did you notice they both have just a little bit of the middle finger missing on their right hands? Every cell the same.'

The class gathered round to inspect this but Grace was surprised and distressed. 'I thought the nurse said there was nothing wrong with them.'

'Nothing to worry about,' Burton responded airily, 'minor imperfection. Five per cent of the population lose a bit of a finger at some stage so they may as well get used to it. No, Winston Two is a touch jaundiced but apart from that they're robust little chaps. Gave us a run for our money.'

'In what way?' Shireen had donned a studious pair of glasses to inspect an enlarged negative against the light from the window.

'They were locked together in the uterus like wrestlers.' Burton clenched his hands to demonstrate. 'It's lucky we got them out when we did. Twin foetuses should interact with each other but here they seem to have been competing for nutrition. It has been known for one twin to kill the other in the quest for food. Murder before they've even been born – interesting legal case.'

'Could that happen with Siamese twins?'

The professor glanced approvingly at his inquisitive Indian student.

'No,' he replied. 'Quite the reverse. They tend to grow in harmony – something that continues after they're born. The original Siamese twins, Chang and Eng, married two sisters and one had ten children and the other eleven. And they passed away in harmony, too. After Chang died, Eng refused to accept a surgical separation and voluntarily died himself a few hours later. A thromboplastin from his dead brother crossed into his circulation and caused disseminated intravascular coagulation – try to remember that, Brian.'

Still befuddled by the remnants of the anaesthetic, Grace felt ignored and alarmed. 'That's not going to happen to my boys is it? You said there was nothing wrong.'

'They're just fine,' Burton assured her. 'Not Siamese. Just the same – but different. What have you called them?'

He had caught Grace unawares; this was something she had yet to resolve. 'If it was a girl I was going to call her Nina,' she said, 'after Nina Kuscsik who was the first woman allowed to win the Boston Marathon. And if it was a boy I was going to call him Jim or James, after Jim Peters. But now it seems unfair to favour one rather than the other.'

'Split the difference,' Burton suggested, 'that's what your egg did. Call Winston One, Jim – he beat his brother into the world by two and a half minutes – and Winston Two, Peter. How about that?'

'I'll have to think about it,' Grace replied.

'Who is Jim Peters?' The professor spun round towards his students; he seemed to treat education as an ongoing quiz, 'Shireen?'

The Indian girl was embarrassed. 'I'm sorry . . . did he discover the monovular . . .'

'I know,' Brian proudly interrupted her. 'Vancouver Games. The guy who collapsed. Lost the marathon.'

'He didn't lose,' Mr Burton told him. 'He won the hearts of everyone who ever saw him. That's why he'll be remembered when all the other winners are forgotten.'

Alice came to visit her the following Tuesday afternoon. 'Why on earth didn't you tell anybody?' she demanded. 'I wouldn't have known if Lenny hadn't met you at the market.'

'I know. It was wrong of me,' Grace conceded. 'You must understand, since Boston I haven't really been myself. It's just been this awful combination of self-pity and anger and envy – until these little people came into my life.'

'Which one is he?' Alice nodded towards the eager head that was clinging limpet-like to Grace's left breast.

'This one's James, the first-born. Peter will hardly take any of my milk, he prefers the mixture they serve in the nursery.'

'How do you know which is which?'

'By the little bands on their wrists.'

'Really?'

'No,' Grace grinned. 'I'm joking. It's strange. I could tell from the first moment I held them. James is more assertive, with my breast, with his grip, already he responds to things. Whereas Peter seems to be in another world, he's more uncertain and vulnerable.'

Alice went across to the cot where Peter lay silently with his eyes open in a state of waking watchfulness. 'They don't look like anybody I know,' she observed pointedly.

'The father, you mean. You don't know him, I promise you that, Alice.' Still holding James to her breast, she reached across with her right hand and searched in the drawer of the bedside cabinet. 'These are copies of their birth certificates. They're official; someone from the registrar's office comes to the hospital on Mondays. Can you keep them for me?'

Alice glanced at the pieces of paper she had been handed – James Winston and Peter Winston. Born: 1st July 1977. Sons of Grace Sarah Winston. Occupation: teacher. Father: unknown.

Grace held up a sealed envelope. 'And there's this. I'm trusting this to you as, well, somebody I can trust. It has the whole story, the truth, everything. But nobody must know. You mustn't open it, Alice. Put it in the bank and keep it – somewhere safe.'

'And then what?' Her friend's tone suggested that she thought Grace was being somewhat melodramatic.

'If anything should happen to me, the boys will know who their mother was – and perhaps you can tell them what she was like. Just the good things.'

'Bloody mysterious, if you ask me.' Alice came across to the bed and took the envelope from her. 'Your luck's turned, Grace. You've got two great guys to look after you the moment you've finished looking after them. I envy you that, you've no idea how much.'

'How's Lenny?' Grace tried to make the enquiry seem as casual as she could.

'The usual,' Alice gave her a parting kiss on the cheek, 'an absolute turd.'

Grace was finishing her breakfast coffee the next morning when Dawson arrived. She had almost forgotten what he looked like. In her memory he had less hair and more girth, but in the flesh he proved to be somewhat squat and better built with a strong surround of neatly groomed grey locks on his domed head. To judge from his clothes, he had clearly not come directly from the airport – his correctly creased suit and freshly laundered shirt were those of a man who had just stepped out of a limousine. Under his arm he was carrying an outsize teddy bear.

'I hope you remember me,' he said unnecessarily. 'I'm Dawson Silver.'

'I'm surprised they let you in so early. Did you say you were the father?'

He shook his head emphatically. 'No, just a friend of the family. Where's the baby?'

Grace had lived in dread of this encounter for nearly nine months now. Like someone frozen in the throes of an accident, she could barely believe it was happening. She had always known that the handover would be as distressing as surrendering a son to the scaffold; worse, in many ways since she, Judas-like, was actually accepting money to give away her infant. In the back of her mind there had lingered a scintilla of hope that Dawson might suffer a heart attack or, at least, a change of heart and allow her to rear the child until it was a teenager. Something would turn up. And, of course, it had – in the shape of her second son.

'They're over there, by the window. They've just had their morning feed.'

In his eagerness for the first sight of his child, Dawson ignored the plural and stepped excitedly towards the light. This was the moment that he had thought about constantly since the news of her pregnancy. This was the culmination of all his hopes. But his immediate joy was abruptly forestalled by his surprise.

'There are two kids here. Where's the other mother? Are you sharing this room? Which one is mine?'

'There is no other mother,' Grace replied with equanimity. 'Just me.'

'Christ. Twins. That's wonderful, simply wonderful.' He looked down at them in astounded delight, afraid to touch their tiny bodies. 'Twins. Both boys?'

'Yes,' she nodded. 'Identical.'

'I'll double your money,' he offered impetuously. 'I knew you were the right woman. I knew from that night at Locke-Obers. Pascal's Wager – you've done me proud, Grace.'

'It's not as easy as that,' she pointed out.

His attention temporarily left the cribs and focused on her. 'What do you mean? Why not?'

'Our contract – the one that Mr Quinn drafted – was for me to provide you with a healthy child for fifty thousand dollars. There's no need to double the money. It was for only one child. The other one is mine.'

'But it's my seed,' Dawson insisted. 'They're both my sons.'

'And mine,' she pointed out.

At first he hadn't been able to believe his eyes; now he couldn't believe his ears. Resisting the temptation to bully her into submission he decided the immediate course was to try to reason with her. 'Don't you see, Grace, this is some kind of miracle. Only 10.1 in a thousand births are twins – 13.4 statistically in the case of blacks, come to think of it. I had a son and he died and now God has replaced him twofold. I can give these boys a way of life and financial support that nobody here in England can enjoy. I'll even grant you an agreed amount of access – although there may be a problem with my wife.'

'I thought she was dead.' Grace was mystified.

'That's Quinn.' Embarrassed, the actuary hurried to cover his tracks. 'He tends to exaggerate things.'

'He tends to omit things, as well,' she responded, gesturing to the document she was holding in her hand. 'We have an agreement for one child, Mr Silver. You could say that the arrival of the second has creaped a loophole in the contract.'

He smarted at her deliberate use of the term. 'Well, what do you suggest we do? Drown one of them?'

Grace was beginning to form an entrenched dislike of the small, puce-faced man in front of her.

'Why don't I bring them up – I'll need some financial support, it's true – until they're old enough to go to university. You can see them all the time till then, holidays and things.' She knew she was pleading but she had no other option. 'And then they'll be free to choose.'

'No way,' Dawson's voice heightened in anger. 'No fucking way. We have a contract which any rational being would interpret as covering a twin birth should that eventuality arise and I'm going to enforce it even if we have to go to the Supreme Court of Massachusetts.'

'We haven't had much luck there in the past,' Grace noted.

'You haven't,' he retorted. 'But I will, and I want my sons.'

She was stirred and provoked by his onslaught. 'You know that's not so. And Quinn knows it, too. I've already registered the boys in my name. We're in English jurisdiction here. If I choose to repay you your money, this contract isn't worth the paper it's printed on.'

Dawson sank down onto the bedside chair. 'So give me back the money,' he suggested sarcastically.

'I can't,' she conceded.

'Then give me the kids.'

'I can't do that either.'

'Whatever else happens you're going to have to give me one.

Think of the boys, Grace. Think of their future. It'd be a crime to separate them.'

'One of them is mine,' the emotion of the moment was proving too much for her. 'I'm never going to let him go. You can never make me. I'd rather die, I promise you.'

Over in the cot one of the boys began to cry. The noise woke up the other, so now they both were screaming.

'Which one will it be, Grace?' he demanded in a final act of provocation, realising that she meant business.

Feeling like a child herself, isolated and vulnerable and alone in her narrow bed, she turned away from him and buried her head deep into the pillows. 'You decide,' she said.

There had never been any doubt in Dawson's mind since the moment he read their names on the top of their cots. Peter. It was all there in the Bible which Bunny used read to their son: Simon, also known as Peter. 'Come with me and I will make you fishers of men.' It was uncanny; Grace had no idea that his dead boy had been called Simon yet she had named one of the children Peter. It didn't have the alliterative ring of Simon Silver, but that no longer mattered. Quinn had warned him that in order to forestall any possibility of Bunny asserting her rights, he should retain the surname Winston. And it was Quinn who was currently on the receiving end of his venom.

'How the fuck could you let that happen? Silver's barrack-room language was at odds with the expensively appointed suite at the Savoy Hotel.

Eamonn Quinn was admitting nothing. 'You wanted a son, I got you a son,' his voice came stubbornly over the transatlantic line. 'If you'd gone to one of those agencies they'd never have told you about a twin brother. They'd had sold him to someone else for double the price. At least this way you'll know where he is. She'll come round. You'll have him back, wait and see.'

'I'm not fucking interested in waiting' – out of the window a glorious evening sun burnished the somnolent Thames but it did little to ameliorate Dawson's mood – 'I want them both. What are you going to do about it?'

'Well, I'm here and you're there, so it's you who's going to have to do the doing.'

'Do what? That's what I want to know,' Dawson bellowed.

'It's quite simple, it's what we call in legal terms the pragmatic approach.' Quinn was relieved that his client had passed on from the matter of the contract; he knew it had been a considerable oversight. Mitch would never have made that mistake.

'What is the pragmatic approach?'

'Easy,' came the voice from Boston. 'Leave it to me to prepare all the necessary documentation and a woman I know will fly with it overnight. She'll be your assistant, call her your nanny. Remember one of the reasons we chose Grace Winston was because, whatever her academic or athletic prowess, she's a loner – no friends or family to get in the way. It should be a cinch. Just do what nanny tells you.'

A pleasure craft, alive with lights and young people dancing on the deck, slid across the window of Silver's suite. 'What are you getting at, Quinn?' he shouted. 'What's the big plan? You want me to snatch the child?'

'You got it in one,' said the lawyer.

Grace offered Peter her full right breast but he refused even to allow her nipple in his mouth and began to cry. She picked up the prepared bottle of milk from the side of his crib and tried that. He took it instantly.

'Here, you let me do that.' The Irish nurse, Sinead, who had brought the boys to her the first time, was helping her prepare to leave. 'You get on with master James, he appreciates his mother.'

The two women exchanged babies and James clung to his mother's breast with possessive ferocity. She glanced at her watch; Dawson would be here at any minute. And then she looked down at little Peter who was timidly taking his feed from the nurse's bottle. He was still somewhat jaundiced and seemed so frail.

'This is a hypothetical question, Sinead,' she said, 'but if both of these boys fell ill, which would have the better chance of surviving? I mean, which one's the stronger?'

'Sure they'd never let you out of here if they weren't satisfied with them both,' the nurse reassured her. 'You must put away such notions – mothers always get a little melancholic at this stage.'

'I know,' she said. 'But which?'

'Well, the one taking the milk is inheriting all your antibodies. But wee Peter here will come round to it once he's feeling up to it, won't you son?' She jiggled the child in her arm.

It was just as Grace had thought. 'You've been very good to me, Sinead,' she said. 'Not too many questions.'

'Sure, who's worried about fathers and the like nowadays,' the nurse responded reassuringly. 'It's we women who finally run the world, isn't it? Men never really grow up, have you noticed that? Whoever they are – I don't care, priest or politician – there's always a bit of them that's trying to get away with something, cheat a little just for the sake of cheating. Always trying to outdo each other for no particular reason.' She smiled at the child in her arms. 'You'll never be as honest as the day you were born, will you, James?'

'Peter,' Grace corrected her.

'Two peas in a pod,' the nurse continued. 'I've never seen a pair so like. Right down to the fingertips.' She immediately realised her faux-pas. 'I'm sorry – you know what I mean.'

Grace wiggled James's foreshortened middle finger. 'I rather like this. It's a sort of identity badge.'

'The Lord thought they were so perfect that He held a little bit back,' Sinead commented comfortingly as she glanced out of the window. 'Is that your friend down there? He's got a very smart car. And a smarter nanny – Norlander by the look of her.'

'He's American.' Grace felt a flush coming over her. 'I met him in Boston. A distant cousin – very generous.'

James had stopped feeding now and she placed him in the Moses basket that sat among her belongings on the bed. It was a warm morning and there was no need to wrap him up. Sinead carefully lowered Peter into the basket beside him. 'Romulus and Remus,' she observed.

'Oh dear,' Grace exclaimed, glancing in her case. 'I think I may have left my dressing gown on the chair in the bathroom.

'Stay where you are,' the nurse made immediately for the door. 'Which one – the one at the far end of the corridor?'

'Mmm,' Grace nodded.

Alone at last she looked down at two little boys innocently lying side by side in their baskets. She knew what she had to do although it broke her heart. Terrified of somebody coming in, her fingers shaking ungovernably, she removed the name-tag from James's wrist and put it on Peter, and then exchanged Peter's for his. Sinead had methodically tucked the boys' birth certificates in the top of each basket and Grace rapidly switched those as well. Now Dawson would still have the name he had chosen – but not the son. It was her duty as a mother to nurture the weaker child, even though he had rejected her milk.

'No dressing gown, I'm afraid. To tell you the truth I don't remember you having one.' Sinead was back sooner than she anticipated.

'You're right,' Grace acknowledged. 'I didn't.'

'Ah well,' smiled the nurse, responding to the rap on the door, 'here's your rich American come to help you home.'

Dawson placed a polite kiss on her cheek as he entered the room. He had suggested on the telephone that they leave the hospital together to allay any suspicion amongst the staff. Grace affected to know Marion, the nanny whom he had brought to help. She gave Sinead a final friendly hug and winced inwardly as she watched Dawson press two twenty-pound notes into her palm. The nurse, however, seemed delighted: this was worth more than her take-home pay.

Marion led the group down the hospital steps, professionally carrying the child now tagged Peter in his basket in front of her. Grace tried to do the same with James but found that she was still weak and could only lug her baby along like a load of shopping. Dawson followed with her battered overnight case.

It was strange stepping into the swirl of a London Saturday morning after the seclusion of the hospital. She sensed how a prisoner might feel when repatriated into the real world. It was all noise and confusion. Dawson, friendly but firm, ushered her into the back seat of the waiting Austin Princess. Grace sat nervously with the newly-named James in his basket on her lap, while the nanny took Peter with her into the front seat. Dawson placed Grace's bag on his knee as he slid in beside her.

'You know where we're going,' he reminded the driver – a young man clad, incongruously, Grace thought, in a T-shirt and jeans. 'First Harold Wilson House to drop off Mrs Watson and then on to the airport.'

'Why the change of names?' Grace whispered as the driver's glass partition closed and the car moved off.

'Best that as few people know as possible,' Dawson replied. 'Harold Wilson is next to Stafford Cripps, right?'

'Yes, there's a vintage Labour Cabinet of tower blocks.'

The remark was lost on the American who was more intent on outlining the immediate course of events. 'Here's a cheque for the rest of your money,' he said, handing her an envelope. 'I've also added a little cash for the inconvenience. May I have Peter's birth certificate.'

'It's in his basket.' She indicated towards the front seat. 'Thank you for the money but it's less important than the other details. You said on the phone I could visit Peter whenever I liked. I don't even know your address. Where will he be? How can I see him?'

He patted her arm to calm her. 'Everything has been worked out, but we need to discuss the matter privately. We can bring both the children up to your apartment, if you like. I know a farewell like this isn't going to be easy. But let's do the best we can.'

He seemed so generous and thoughtful that Grace felt marginally remorseful about her switch. But she resolved to say nothing.

The dark limousine drew up just beyond the newsagency on the far side of Rylston Road from her block of flats. Dawson got out first and came round to Grace's side of the car with her bag. He opened the door for her and lifted the Moses basket containing the baby from her lap. Grace, still feeling an invalid, slid both feet onto the kerb and straightened up shakily.

No sooner was she was up than she was down. At first she thought it was a gust of wind, unexpected on such a warm, calm day. Only when she recovered her senses and could see the car taking off, did she understand what had happened. Dawson must deliberately have placed her case behind her and then pushed her backwards over it. She looked around her to see if James was safe. But he was nowhere to be seen.

She staggered to her feet. 'My baby,' she screamed futilely, beginning to run, 'they've taken my baby. Stop that car. They've got my baby.'

The Austin Princess had by now reached the top of the road and was signalling a left turn that would take it west to Heathrow. But it had been delayed by someone on the zebra crossing just in front of the Fulham Pools.

'My baby' – Grace continued up the road after the car – 'they've got my baby, in the basket.'

The boy on the crossing seemed to have taken the information in. He flung a damp towel and pair of trunks across the driver's window so that the man couldn't see to proceed. Then, slipping across the front of the car to the passenger side, he pulled open the unlocked door and grabbed the basket from the bewildered nanny.

'Drive on,' Dawson screamed from the back and the shocked chauffeur pulled rapidly away, with the wet towel sliding down the window to clear his view.

The boy fell backwards onto the pavement, clutching the basket in his arms as Grace caught up with him, just in time to see the limousine disappearing round the curve of Lillie Road.

'Oh, Ranesh,' she said, sinking to her knees. 'You saved my child.'

The newsagent's son looked into the Moses basket and Peter stared calmly out; he didn't even begin to cry.

'I'll go down to the shop and call the police, Miss Winston,' he said. 'What were those people trying to do?'

Grace put a hand on his shoulder to restrain him. 'No, you mustn't do that. It was a mix-up. My fault. The doctor and nurse were taking the child to another hospital and I wanted him to come home first.'

'Are you sure?' Ranesh seemed unconvinced.

She looked him in the eyes. 'You must believe me, Ranesh. It's all going to be all right now. Well, it will be all right if you never tell another soul what has happened. Not even your parents.'

He nodded sombrely, proud of this sacred secret. 'My mother was wondering when your baby was coming. What's its name?'

'It was going to be James,' said Grace, lifting the baby from the basket and clasping him to her body. 'But now he's Peter – he didn't want to leave me.'

· *Twelve* ·

To anybody who had just arrived it might have seemed as if the final were over. The roar that shook the stadium was akin to that of a giant aircraft taking off. Many people then rose to their feet, clapping like ostentatious opera-goers; others sat back and merely relished the moment with laughter and relief. Up in the seats allocated to the guests of the competitors, Dawson Silver was anxious for enlightenment.

'The fifth ball, Mo, did he throw away the fifth ball at the end?'

'Sure,' the track-suited coach replied. 'Into the corner, though, not into the crowd.'

'And the last ace – down the middle.'

'All four. The whole performance. The whole unnecessary performance.'

'What do you mean – unnecessary?' Dawson demanded. 'He was four games down.'

'The wrong tactics at the wrong time. Two aces, maybe – the first and the last. But the rest was showing off. He should have engineered some longer points to start feeling Shimizu's game – he's not going to be able to spin it out to four sets unless he finds a rhythm. You don't acquire that by using up your big serves.'

'Come off it, Moses,' Dawson was plainly irritated. 'If he can crush the Jap with aces, he's got to go for it. What's the kid supposed to do – serve underarm so that they can have some nice rallies?'

'It's too soon.' The coach was adamant. 'A few more games and Shimizu'll start reading those serves and then what's left in the cupboard? He must get back to the original plan. Try and extend it to something like an hour a set in this heat and we'll have him wobbling at the knees by the time we go into the fifth.'

'You're too unbending, Mo' – this time it was Phoebe, shifting uncertainly in her seat, who corrected the coach. 'Psychologically he had to do it. Just once. You know the reason. And I know him.'

Renewed applause greeted the players as they took up their ends for the sixth game of the first set. Phoebe gazed nervously down at Winston; she could imagine his internal agony at this moment. But his broad, steady shoulders gave nothing away and he held his slim, six-foot-one-and-a-half-inch frame confidently erect as he walked to the baseline. Shimizu still led, by four games to one, but his morale had been diminished and his ego bruised by conceding four aces in a row. He knew his opponent had such artillery within his capability but he had not expected an onslaught like that at so early a stage in the match.

Winston was only too aware that he had disobeyed his coach's game plan, but a desperate situation needed desperate measures, he reasoned. Mo himself had drummed it into him again and again: the primary object in match tennis is to break up the other man's game. Well, he had demonstrated he could do that – maybe not in the first four games but certainly during the last four points. At the back of his mind was the feeling that he could destroy the Japanese player here and now by switching to a power game. But that was not the strategy. The idea was to tire him out: dispatch him to both corners, lure him up to the net, send him back to the baseline, extend every possible rally so that they sapped his strength.

The air was heavy and stifling, as if compacted into the stadium by some invisible roof that turned the place into a greenhouse. Winston wiped away a film of sweat from beneath his eyes with his arm band as he prepared to receive. This was going to be a crucial point. He put his body into a form of static motion, dancing gracefully on the spot so that he was poised to move to the left or the right. He felt the reassurance of his Excalibur Plus in his hand, twenty-nine square inches strung to the tension of sixty pounds to compensate for the heat.

'When the chances look small, read the name on the ball' – Mo's crass doggerel had the merit of lodging in the mind at times like this. Shimizu made contact with the yellow sphere and Winston's eyes narrowed in concentration as he focused on the panther-like logo spinning towards him.

· *Thirteen* ·

'You are all part of the future; it lies right here. Nearly sixty thousand square miles of paradise with ten thousand miles of shoreline. But none of them more beautiful than Longboat Key. Does anyone know who the original inhabitants of this island were?'

A shoal of hands reached eagerly upwards into the tepid afternoon air of the Longboat Learning Center.

'Yes, Kimberley?'

'Please, Miss Lambert,' the small girl sprang up confidently from her seat, 'it was the Spanish, Miss Lambert.'

'Not entirely wrong, Kimberley, but not entirely right either.' The teacher motioned to the girl to sit down. 'I said original – in other words, the first. Now let's have someone who didn't put their hand up' – her gaze travelled across the class, an unerring radar scanner –'yes, James Winston. Stand up, please.'

A tall skinny boy with a strong jaw rose reluctantly to his feet. He pushed back a shock of dark brown hair to clear his small, sharp eyes and shrugged his shoulders. 'The Indians, I suppose.'

'Quite right,' the teacher congratulated him. 'Why didn't you put your hand up?'

'I thought everybody knew that,' he replied, casually dropping back into his place.

'Evidently not,' Miss Lambert replied drily. 'We know they were here from the burial mounds or kitchen middens' – she wrote the word on the blackboard as she spoke – 'which have been discovered on Longboat and elsewhere in Florida. They must have been an extraordinarily well-built tribe – even taller than you're likely to be,

James. One skeleton was seven feet long and another nearly eight. And to judge from the shells of clams and oysters and conches that were buried with them they had a very healthy seafood diet. They might also have hunted some deer, as we can deduce from the weapons, skilfully made from shells, that were found in these graves or middens' – she pointed at the word on the blackboard. 'Now why would they bury food and weapons and tools with a dead person – Myron?'

The overweight child with a severe, straw-coloured fringe of blond hair stopped sucking his pencil. 'Well, in case they weren't really dead, Miss Lambert, and they needed to dig their way out of the grave.'

The rest of the class sniggered cheerfully – Myron was usually good for a laugh – but the teacher cut them off with an admonitory hand. 'Not as wrong as the rest of you think. The Indians certainly didn't believe that death was the end, so their friends and family buried these supplies and artefacts with them to support them in the afterlife. And this is where your Spanish come in, Kimberley. In 1539 Hernando de Soto' – the name and date went up on the board – 'landed here in his long boat, hence our name. He treated the Indians like animals, cruelly exterminating them. And those that didn't fall to the Spanish sword fell victim to the white man's illnesses. Just imagine, Myron, you might have to take a week off school if you caught chicken-pox but what would happen to an Indian?'

The pencil was once more withdrawn from the chubby face. 'Two weeks, ma'am?'

This time the teacher laughed. 'Worse than two weeks, I'm afraid. They had no resistance at all and died. A plague of chicken-pox killed most of the Indian population. So the land was free for settlers from the Civil War to come here by wagon and then by boat and start to farm. Some of them were your ancestors.'

Not mine, thought James as his eyes focused on the fern-like palms pressing listlessly against the outside of the classroom window. Aunt Violet had driven down to Sarasota from New York in her ancient Oldsmobile in the winter of 1951. She had told him the story more than a dozen times. They were making a movie, *The Greatest Show on Earth*, and Aunt V. was paid seventy-five cents an hour to sit in the Big Top. Imagine actually being paid to watch the circus. The Ringling Brothers and Barnum and Bailey Circus, the greatest show on earth – they wouldn't have said so if it wasn't true. The name Ringling chimed like magic in his ears. They used to own the whole area and built castles and causeways and bridges and hotels. When Aunt Violet took him to the John and Mable Ringling Museum of Art and pointed out all the ancient statues they had brought back from Europe, he would tug her hand and urge her to come with him to the Circus Galleries where you could see the wagons and whips and trapezes and even the costumes worn by the original Tom Thumb. Could he really have been a fully grown man and as tiny as that? – he was much smaller than James was now at the age of seven.

Sometimes on Sundays his aunt would drive him over to the trailer park where she first 'hitched her wagon' as she used to say. She had lived there until he had come along and her old neighbours, one-eyed Mike and Mary-Louise, would welcome her back with a can of Miller's beer and a Dr Pepper's for Jim and reminisce about the old days. Sarasota had been known as Circus City when they arrived. Every November endless silver trains would bring the performers and paraphernalia and animals back to their winter quarters.

'Ninety railroad cars, there were,' Mike recalled, 'to take the circus all over America. And you should have seen the parade when they got home. First the elephants, dozens of them got up like maharajahs, and then the tigers and leopards and black panthers in their cages and the zebras led by the clowns, followed by the long-legged showgirls and the acrobats – doing cartwheels down Beneva Road – and, last of all, the high-wire walkers and the midgets.

'Some of them would come and live in this park, right here,' Mary-Louise told him, 'and some of their children would go to your school. My goodness, the stories they would come back with. There's a whole nation out there, Jim, from Connecticut to California, holding up their dollars waiting to be entertained.'

He loved the trailer park; it was a great place to run around and hide, although there weren't many children there. But it was much more fun than their apartment in Pollux Palisades on Siesta Key where Violet moved when he had come as a baby. That was too quiet and tidy. Aunt V. said the view of the Gulf of Mexico was worth a million dollars but Jim would have much preferred to live in a trailer and act out his fantasies as a performing clown or high-wire artist on Mike and Mary-Louise's temporary dividing wall.

'. . . the bomber pilots had to learn somewhere and since the US Army was stationed here, one of the offshore islands was used as a practice bombing range.'

'Were the people on it killed, Miss Lambert?'

'No Errol,' the teacher gave him a withering look. 'There were no people on it. That's why it was used for bombing. It was an uninhabited island. But for safety's sake they cordoned off the south of Longboat close to the county line. They would close the gates at eight in the morning and they wouldn't open them again till five in the afternoon. At that time there were no real grocery stores on the island so most people went to Sarasota to do their shopping. But they had to get up early to beat the barrier and then they would have to stay there all day. This happened throughout the war. Now in the early fifties the new Ringling Bridge broke down and people were stranded . . .'

But the ringing of the school bell put a temporary halt to another Ringling story and the teacher acknowledged with the slackening of her shoulders that it would have to keep for another day.

Aunt Violet was waiting for James as he leapt agilely down the last three wooden steps from the Longboat Learning Center. He could have gone home by the school bus – it dropped Myron in Siesta Key – but he knew she enjoyed the afternoon drive to come and pick him up. Sometimes she would take him down to Eckerd Drugs on the Avenue of the Flowers if there was no need to hurry home; on other occasions they would visit the Mote Marine Science Center and look at the turtles and manta rays and tarpons in the tanks there.

She always stood beside the car – like an attentive chauffeur – a slightly stooped woman with thick-lensed spectacles who looked her seventy years despite her cheerful summer dress and the appropriate violet tint in her grey hair. James, who was already nearing five feet, would soon be taller than her. He was growing as fast as she was shrinking, she would observe with just a hint of remorse. Her car had shrunk as well: a compact Japanese Toyota had taken the place of the trusty Oldsmobile.

'Aunt V. were you here when they bombed Longboat?' James searched in the pocket of the passenger door for the familiar tube of peppermints.

'Who bombed it?' She peered intensely through her glasses at the road ahead, the top of the steering wheel cutting off the bottom of her field of vision. 'Not in my time.'

'The American Army or maybe the Air Force. During the war. Miss Lambert said they did.'

'Well I never heard such a thing . . .' she began, before cutting herself off in mid-sentence. 'Wait a minute, yes, yes I did. Tomasz told me about it – the island would be cut off all day.'

'Who was Tomasz?' James innocently enquired, knowing already but knowing also that this was the one man his aunt loved to talk about.

'I must have told you. He was a member of the Czechoslovak National Band. He wore boots and a scarf and a finely buttoned waistcoat and a white silk shirt decorated with hand-stitched patterns. I'm sure I told you. They were famous in Europe and they all arrived, twenty-five of them, at Ellis Island in 1926.'

'Wasn't it twenty-six of them in 1925?'

'You may well be right,' she continued, too caught up in her memories to care. 'That's where all the immigrants landed. But they wouldn't let them in because they had no means of support – just their talents. However Otokar Bartik, the ballet master of the New York Metropolitan Opera, heard about their plight and went to Ellis Island to see them perform. He thought they were wonderful and paid for them himself to tour America. One night John Ringling went to see them in New York and he was spellbound and brought them down here for the grand opening of St Armand's Key. Christmas Day 1925. They gave a concert that no one there will ever forget with songs from their native land and jazz and American music – even the Star Spangled Banner. And many of them thought they had found the promised land here and so they stayed.'

'When did Tomasz die?'

His aunt pushed her spectacles more firmly back on her nose. 'It must have been twenty years ago, maybe twenty-one . . . oh James,' she looked reproachfully across at him, 'stop leading me on. You've heard all this before.'

'And you never wanted to marry anyone else,' the boy asserted seriously.

Violet glanced at the Gulf, vast and placid beyond the passing palm trees. 'One day I'll visit Czechoslovakia,' she said, 'and I'll take you with me.'

'You see they want to introduce daylight saving time,' Dawson Silver pointed to the article in his magazine, 'because they think it will be better for the community. But what they haven't calculated are the costs incurred with curtains and other fabrics fading more quickly.'

'Take a look at this.' Edmund Michaels was bored with his companion's analysis and shoved a newspaper in front of him. It contained a photograph of a young man's corpse, his features caught in an artificial rictus. The doctor covered the caption underneath the picture with his hand. 'When did this kid die? Note his fingers – near perfect, teeth too.'

'It's no good, I've got to change my glasses.' Dawson Silver struggled to pull another pair out of his shirt pocket. He peered at the picture of the body. 'I've no idea. Two days, maybe three. Why do you want to know?'

'One hundred and thirty-six years. That sailor died a hundred and thirty-six years ago. Two of them in fact have been found in the Arctic, frozen to death and perfectly preserved. Incredible.' He removed a thin diary from the inside pocket of his jacket and began writing with a pencil. 'Owen Beattie, Professor of Anthropology, University of Alberta. I'll give him a call when I get back and see if I can get a sample.'

'Of what,' Dawson enquired distractedly.

'Oh . . . skin tissue . . . you know, see what the system was like before the invention of any modern medicines. No antibiotics then, nothing like that. This is a primitive man, died 1848.'

Silver was more absorbed in his own problems. 'Can't modern medicine do something for my eyes? I can see less and less out of the sides.'

'That's the nature of your condition, I'm afraid. Retinitis pigmentosa – I told you. It's like the picture on a television set getting narrower and narrower until it disappears altogether.'

'Thanks a lot,' said Silver bitterly.

'You're not so bad,' the doctor reassured him, folding the newspaper back to the front page. 'Take off your glasses and read the headline.'

'FERRARO HUSBAND FAILS TO COME CLEAN OVER FINANCES.' To his delight Dawson could see it reasonably clearly.

'As long as it's in front of you and you can focus, your eyes are as good as mine,' his companion continued. 'No point in pretending they aren't atrophying around the edges, but then we're all getting older. What are you now, Fifty-seven? – you'd be dead if you were that sailor's age.'

Dawson tried to work out the convoluted sentiment. 'Yes, assuming he died at – what? – twenty-four, that plus a hundred and thirty-six would make him a hundred and sixty. Not too many people that age running around.'

'Except those Russians in the yoghurt ads on TV.'

'I'd take those with a pinch of salt. I don't see them waving their birth certificates at the camera. It's true, though, statistically Russians do survive longer than us,' the actuary noted, 'largely because they don't live on a diet of McDonalds.'

'The evil empire,' Michaels murmured, glancing at the front page. 'Fucking Ferraro – landed us with four more years of that Hollywood ham.'

Silver took immediate issue with this. 'If Fritz Mondale had got into the White House, we'd be back to the spineless days of Jimmy Carter and the Iranians shitting all over us.'

'You misunderstood me,' the doctor was anxious to correct him. 'I wouldn't want Fritz Mondale collecting my garbage. What I want is a proper leader, an Eisenhower, someone who'll tell the Hispanics that if they come here they abide by our laws and constitution, and remind some of the Blacks about that, too.'

'Can I offer you some more champagne, sir?' The Delta Airlines stewardess appeared not to have heard his final remark or, at least, affected not to. Her flashing white smile emerged from a face that had its ancestry in Africa.

Michaels covered his glass, embarrassed. 'No, thank you. How long have we got?'

'We shall be landing at the Sarasota-Bradenton Airport in

approximately forty-five minutes. Going to your family for Thanks-giving?'

'Sort of,' Michaels answered awkwardly.

'Enjoy the rest of your flight.' She took away his glass and switched her attention to the passengers on the other side of the aisle.

Michaels turned to Silver. 'Is Violet bringing the kid to the airport?'

'Depends whether there's school today. James stays on in the afternoons now. He's a big guy, you know, and going to be bigger. Luckily didn't inherit my shape. How long is it since you've seen him?'

'Nearly two years,' the doctor's memory was precise. 'Christmas '82 – Violet brought him up to Boston. You built that snowman on the Common, remember?'

As Dawson gazed out of the cabin window at the endless carpet of luxuriant, white cloud beneath them, the memory came back to him with pure pleasure. In truth it had never left him. In his mind he blended the childhood experiences of Simon and James in such a way that they often became one, so that Simon had never died but – like that sailor in the Arctic – had merely been frozen at a certain age until James could come along and liberate him. It wouldn't be long now.

'When are you going to bring him back to Boston permanently?'

'What?' Dawson had heard the doctor's question quite clearly but the remark had punctured the comfort of his thoughts.

'When are you going to bring James home?' Michaels repeated.

'In a way he is home,' Dawson answered ruminatively. 'He's with his own blood. Violet's his great-aunt and they love each other. He's happy enough down here. Bunny has no connection with him. Quinn says to take him permanently to Boston at this stage would risk her trying to interfere.'

'I heard she went into that new clinic out on the Cape, is that so?'

'You know as much as I do,' Dawson replied. 'Some weeks I hear she's going to dry out completely and then the next she's as bad as ever – worse even. I can't let the kid near her.'

'Does she know about him?'

Silver shook his head. 'Nor will she. She killed one son of mine – that's enough for one lifetime.'

He knew the accusation was unfair – grossly so – and Dr Michaels did as well, but Dawson had persuaded himself that his wife was wholly responsible for Simon's death the better to justify both his subsequent actions and his secrecy about James.

'How about Violet, though?' Michaels enquired. 'She must be getting on – over seventy. Are you sure that's the right environment for a young boy to grow up in?'

'She's happy about it. Even got rid of the nanny after a year.'

'But are you happy with it?' the doctor persisted. 'I know James goes to school with other kids and spends time with you in the holidays, but his overall environment is that of an ageing woman. This isn't necessarily the ideal way to attain a fully formed character.'

Dawson rounded on him accusingly. 'Are you suggesting it's going to turn him into some sort of faggot?'

'I didn't tell him you were arriving today. I thought it would be nice if it were a surprise.' Violet had permitted Dawson to drive and accordingly the Toyota was speeding down Washington Boulevard at more than its accustomed trundle.

'But you told him we were coming?' Dr Michaels sounded slightly concerned in the back seat.

'I told him his father was coming. I didn't think I'd tell him it was time for his check-up. He tends to worry about that sort of thing, you know.'

'Why so?' asked Dawson.

'I don't know. I'm looking forward to a free medical myself. I suppose James feels fit and healthy and he's a little afraid that the results of all those tests that you do will mean that he's not – if you see what I mean.'

'The kid's in great shape,' Michaels assured her. 'And the way to keep him like that is to keep monitoring his growth and progress. I know you're doing an excellent job, Violet, we just need to check a few things the eye can't always see.'

'But the other parents at his school seem happy enough with the local doctor and I . . .' the old lady interrupted herself, '. . . right Dawson, turn right here, along the 758.'

'Where is he?' Silver asked her. 'Who did you say was looking after him?'

'He's with the caretaker's wife. She has a boy the same age. They're probably out on the beach.'

The car lurched abruptly forward as he jabbed violently on the accelerator. 'Violet, you shouldn't do that. You should've brought him with you.'

'It's all right,' his aunt insisted, aware of his agitation. 'Take it easy, Dawson. There's no surfing on Siesta.'

Nevertheless Silver propelled the Toyota with determined haste into its parking place in front of Pollux Palisades.

'Edmund, can you take up the bags?' he shouted, jumping immediately out of the car. 'Where do you think they are, Violet?'

'Just the other side of the condo, probably.' The old lady frowned at his unnecessary panic.

Disregarding this, Dawson dashed round the side of the block and anxiously scanned the public beach. It was relatively quiet; the Thanksgiving throng would not be out in force until the end of the week. There were a few figures by the water's edge but the strength of the silhouetting sun made them impossible to identify. He loosened his tie and threw it and his jacket onto a low wooden bench. Sitting down he kicked off his shoes and removed his socks, leaving them haphazardly where they fell.

Running as fast as his unfit frame would permit, he set out across the clean quartz sand of Siesta Key Public Beach – judged by experts to be the whitest and the finest in America – towards the sound of shrieks and laughter on the sea shore. If only he had been on the Cape that day, he would have heard Simon, he knew he would have heard him. He glanced ahead at the ocean: it looked tranquil enough but you never knew. Violet was an idiot to let the boy out with strangers. It was against his express instructions. If James were still alive he would have to find someone to help her. Please God, he prayed, make him safe, don't do this to me . . .

'Daddy, daddy, daddy!'

James, angular and stringy in his striped Bermuda shorts, tossed the white plastic football to the chubby Mexican child he was playing with and charged, exhilarated, towards his father.

'Daddy, daddy, I thought it was tomorrow.'

Silver felt weak-kneed with relief and could barely retain his balance as he spun his son round and round, high and low. 'We thought we'd surprise you.'

'We?' enquired the boy.

'Dr Michaels came down as well – for a bit of a rest, and to make sure you're as good as you look.' Deliberately to dispel the look of disquiet on the boy's face, he added: 'And guess where we're going Friday. Aunt V. has the tickets already.'

'Venice?' James was almost afraid to suggest it in case he might be wrong.

'You bet,' shouted his father. 'Clown school to begin with and then the first circus of the season.'

'Fantastic,' cried the child, cartwheeling away, his long limbs casting spidery shadows on the crimson afternoon sand.

'I'm just going to put this newspaper up here on the mantelpiece and I want you to try and read it from where you're standing.'

James felt awkward when he was left alone with Dr Michaels. He was wary of his bright bow-tie, he found the grey spectacles sinister and he hated the way Michaels blinked continually as if he were receiving a succession of small electric shocks. He wished his father would sit in on these tests but he didn't like to ask him.

Michaels propped the paper up, holding it with one hand against the wall. 'Begin with the headline. That should be easy enough.'

The boy stared at it uncomprehendingly and said nothing.

'Come on, James, for Christ's sake you must be able to read the top line.'

Still nothing. The words wouldn't come.

The doctor was getting irate. 'How many fingers am I holding out?'

'Three.'

'Fine. So what's the first word?'

'Fer . . . ferrer . . . Ferrari? I just don't know it, Dr Michaels – I'm only seven.'

'I'm sorry, I forgot,' the doctor laughed, realising his mistake. 'You're so goddam tall you could be eleven. Ferraro, Geraldine Ferraro. Didn't you hear about her on the news?'

'I don't think so.'

'Well, you're not likely to hear about her again so it doesn't matter. Just give me the next line – the one in small print.'

James narrowed his already narrow eyes. ' "President Reagan, after his sweeping victory in" ' . . . the dot on the "I" is smudged but it must be . . .'

'You can see the smudge, James?' the doctor interrupted him. 'From there you can see the smudge on the dot?'

'Just about,' the child replied with pride.

'You're fine,' the doctor lowered the paper and put it away. 'You haven't just got good sight, you've got supernatural sight. Come over to the window, now, and let me have a look at you.'

He slipped an unwelcome arm around James's shoulders and guided him to the light.

'Dad says he has a problem with his eyes,' the boy confided. 'Sometimes he'll just hold me and look at me and when I ask him what he's doing he says he's taking it all in, just in case one day he won't be able to any more.'

Michaels was surprised that Dawson should have been so candid with the child. 'He's okay at the moment and with a bit of luck he'll stay okay for a long, long time.'

'But' – the boy seemed unconvinced – 'he also told me there was a chance I might get his bad eyes.'

'You mustn't worry, James.' Michaels put both hands on his shoulders to reassure him; he seemed absolutely positive. 'There's no chance of that, no chance whatever.'

'Why – have I got my mother's eyes?'

'That's it, that's precisely the reason.' The doctor seemed, if anything, over-anxious to agree with him.

'What was she like?' The boy stared questioningly into his eyes.

'Who?' Michaels prevaricated, playing for time.

'You know, my mother.'

'Hasn't your father told you?'

James looked uneasily at the syringe that the doctor had taken out of his black bag. 'He said she was a runner. She could run for ever. And in a race she was killed by this truck. In England, I think. That's all I know.'

'That's right. She was a fine athlete, James. Maybe one day you'll follow in her footsteps.'

'But what did she look like? Dad says he's got some photographs in his office but he keeps forgetting to bring them.'

'I'll remind him next time. Now roll up your sleeve, we just need to take a little blood.'

The boy backed away, distressed. 'I won't. There's no need. None of the kids at school has to do this. Why do you keep hurting me? I won't let you.'

'It's only a little prick,' Michaels pleaded. 'The thought is worse than the real thing. Just don't look. Watch that yacht out there and think of happy things.'

'I won't make a fuss if you tell me what my mom was like.'

'Very well,' conceded the doctor, 'but you mustn't tell your father I told you. Close your eyes now and try to visualise her. She looked just like you, James. A tall woman with long thin limbs, broad in the shoulders with light brown hair. She had tiny blue eyes that were always twinkling, a nose that was thin and straight, a perfect smile and an honest jaw, strong and determined. There, I've popped in the needle and you never even noticed.'

'I did but I just didn't say anything.' James, his eyes still tightly closed, set his own strong jaw in a resolute fashion.

'Good boy,' Michaels dabbed his arm with some cotton wool and put a small adhesive plaster over the point of entry. 'Now, keep your eyes closed. I've brought you a present. See if you can tell what it is.'

'I don't need to feel,' the boy replied. 'It's a tennis racquet.'

'How on earth did you know?' This was uncanny. For a split-second Michaels was assailed by the most disconcerting sensation.

'I saw it in the back of the car.'

· *Fourteen* ·

The snapping metal tongue of the letter-box aroused Grace for the second time that morning. She had got up at seven thirty to make Peter a chicken sandwich for school but had then returned to the warmth of her bed. Nevis was still abroad, not due back until later that afternoon, so she had plenty of time to tidy up before his return. The basement flat lacked central heating and was inadequately insulated against the damp November chill. Her body badly needed heat or her lower back and hip joints became stiff and arthritic. So bed was the most satisfactory place to be.

But the sound of the mail hitting the mat was terribly tempting. She leant across and felt for her watch behind the assorted bottles of pills beside her bed. It was nearly ten o'clock. More important, it was that day again – the first Thursday of the month.

She could contain her curiosity no more and swung shivering out of bed into the tired tartan slippers that had served her since her university days. Christ, it was cold. Although she was already wearing her quilted dressing gown, she pulled the lilac eiderdown from the top of the covers and turned it into a shawl of sorts. Opening the door, she discovered that the hall was several degrees cooler with eddies of icy air biting at her uncovered ankles like uncontrolled corgis.

There it was on the edge of the mat, distinguished from Nevis's mail by its light blue texture, the colour of the shallows round a coral reef. She was fearful of touching it in case it wasn't what she expected but, gingerly turning the envelope over as if it were a burning coal, the familiar Marblehead postmark confirmed that it was. She hastily gathered up the rest of the letters, all for Nevis – she would take them up to the studio later, and sought the refuge of the bathroom with her precious possession.

Peter had thoughtfully left the wall heater on and as soon as she ran the bath the place rapidly filled up with welcome warming steam. Grace wiped the mist off the mirror with her dressing-gown sleeve and gazed remorsefully at her dominant gallic nose and uneven front teeth. Even if she wanted a man – which she didn't – she doubted if any man would want her. She ran a comb through her hair. Nature had acted with autumnal preciseness: she could have sworn she had begun to go grey on her thirty-fifth birthday. Or maybe she just noticed it on that day. Still, the petrol-black thatch that had stayed with both her parents until their deaths was not going to go the distance with her and the short, steel helmet made her wide emerald eyes seem pallid and less luminescent.

Since the birth of the twins and the subsequent trauma, she had used the alibi of being a single parent to avoid any thoughts of returning to teaching. In truth, she no longer had any stomach for the job nor interest in other children now that she had a son of her own. An almost mystical bond had been forged with Peter by the perverse circumstances in which he had fallen into her care. She had rejected him in favour of his weaker brother and yet it seemed to be his very tenacity that had caused him to be returned to her.

Still in a state of shock, she had taken no steps that fateful Saturday to interrupt Dawson's departure from the country. And on the Sunday it had all seemed part of a pattern. Grace, knowing she had only an uncorroborated witness in young Ranesh, had feared that if the question of parentage and guardianship were to reach the Supreme Court of Massachusetts she, once again, would not have had a leg to stand on. So she did nothing. And waited. And, on the other side of the Atlantic, Dawson Silver must have done the same. He honoured his cheque and she used some of the money to move to a guest house in Southampton for the first months of Peter's life, telling St Sophie's Hospital and the Hammersmith and Fulham Social Services that she had gone to stay with a cousin. Somewhat to her surprise they were not concerned about the adoption of his twin, having received the correct documentation and – as the health visitor remarked – 'a very generous letter from your lawyer in Boston.'

In her isolation on the south coast, looking out across the Solent at the dreary outline of the Isle of Wight, she had anticipated a renewed tryst with depression but the reverse had been the case. A door opened in Grace's life which she simply didn't know existed and she experienced a daily feeling of contentment and joy and pure love of a kind she had never before given or received. With the American's money she was able to afford private medicine and additional help when she needed it. But most of the time all she needed was Peter.

In the autumn of 1978, when he was just over a year old and her funds were beginning to look less than infinite, a small ad in *Harpers and Queen* caught her eye. 'Housekeeper required for household name photographer,' it began, 'Fulham area, own flat, suit single parent. 'And it did. She had never heard of Bert Nevis – Ben Nevis to his detractors and just Nevis to the artist himself – but then she had never bothered to read the captions under photographs in magazines. He lived in St Paul's Studios, a time-warp row of eight houses on the edge of the Talgarth Road in West London, rarely noticed by the passing motorists urging their cars along the six lanes of highway, anxious to reach the freedom trail of the M4 or eager to get back into the city again.

'They were specially designed by Frederick Wheeler in 1891 to suit the requirements of bachelor artists,' Nevis proudly pronounced as he showed her round after the interview. 'Dame Margot Fonteyn used to live a couple of doors along to the left, just next to the Royal Ballet School. You could sometimes see Rudy panting past after a night out with the boys.'

Grace warmed to Nevis, with his tasselled smoking jacket and silver hair and camp references to his 'snaps', although she warmed less to his basement which was a darkly cheerless place, assaulted from the front by the furious roar of the road and from the rear by the ceaseless chatter of trains entering Baron's Court tube station. But she began to harbour a growing affection for this reassuring noise. On summer Sundays and bank holidays when Grace sometimes experienced the disconcerting sensation that she and Peter were the only people still in London, even the sound of the empty carriages offered a form of companionship. She could hear a train coming in now as she lowered her body into the bath.

There was no need to open the air-mail envelope; the steam had done that already. As always it was without an accompanying letter inside, merely a cheque for a thousand dollars drawn on the Narragansett Bank of Boston, with its cigar-store Indian insignia. The signature was indecipherable but the account was in the name of the WTT Trust Fund. She had written to the bank when the money had first started to arrive five years ago in order to enquire who was sending it, but the manager had replied that it was simply a charity of which the trustees wished to remain anonymous. Eamonn Quinn, who had been so solicitous during her pregnancy, would no longer accept her phone calls personally but had communicated through his secretary that as far as he was aware Dawson was not sending her any more money. That debt, she was authoritatively informed, had been paid in full.

The cheque was both welcome and unwelcome. Nevis pretended not to notice that the year was now 1984 and expected her to survive on a stipend more suitable for the sixties: there was no spare cash after she had bought food and clothes for Peter and herself. But the sight of the word Boston by the Indian's head at the top of the cheque served as a regular monthly reminder of the existence of her other son. It wasn't so much that she missed him; it was just that she didn't know him. Grace would sometimes speculate, as she did now in the bath, on how he had turned out. Did he wear his hair long or short? Was he as prematurely tall as Peter and did he have those narrow athletic shoulders presiding over his attenuated body? Did he have an American accent? Of course, he must. She could never bring herself to try and find out about him – that would only cause greater agony – but she could never erase from her memory the fact that James was the one she had chosen, the one that got away.

'I am old, Peter. I'm ever so much more than twenty. I grew up long ago.'

'You promised not to.'

I couldn't help it. I'm a married woman, Peter.'

'No, you're not.'

'Yes, and the little girl in the bed is my daughter.'

'No, she's not.'

Peter, his dagger clasped in his right hand, strode across to the cot and glanced in. With a heart-rending groan of despair, he cast the knife away and threw himself on the floor in floods of tears.

'Very good, very good' – a man with a pronounced Adam's apple, tucking his clip-board under his arm in order to applaud, came across and helped him up. 'I don't think you should flourish the dagger quite so threateningly. You're not Lady Macbeth, you know. It's only an instrument of self-defence, from Captain Hook and the like.'

'Who's Lady Macbeth?' Peter could taste the salt on his cheeks; to his amazement he had been able to cry for real this time.

'The very personification of femininity,' their teacher, Tom Hall, stifled an inward chuckle at his own observation. 'No, she was a woman in a play by Shakespeare – we mustn't mention the name in here – who would stop at nothing to help her husband's ambitions.'

'What's ambition?' the girl playing Wendy asked innocently.

'It's a thing that Americans have a lot of but that we tend to . . .' Hall decided not to pursue this line of thought and instead offered a more simple explanation. 'It means wanting things we can't get.'

'Like Wendy wanting to stay young,' suggested Peter.

'Well, if she did want to stay young that indeed might be considered her ambition,' Hall admitted. 'But my interpretation of the play is that she is not interested in arrested growth. That is the province of Peter Pan. Wendy is quite content to mature normally – as I hope you all are.'

'But she can't fly any more,' Peter pointed out hesitantly. 'It must make you feel very sad to be able to do something wonderful like that and then . . . well . . . not to be able to do it any more.'

'It's called growing old,' said his teacher.

'You only got the part 'cos you're called Peter.' Matthew Kuttner was secretly envious and hoping to provoke a fight.

'That's not true.' Peter Winston felt furiously aggrieved.

''Tis.'

'Well, why wasn't Wendy Tanfield made Wendy then instead of Tessa?'

''Cos she's ugly and she's got a snotty nose.'

Both facts were undeniable. Peter decided to go on the offensive. 'I suppose you were made a Lost Boy because you've lost your marbles.'

At the age of seven verbal arguments tend to be of limited length and rapidly replaced by physical ones. Peter knew he had gone a remark too far and tensed his body as his burly classmate swung out at him.

'Stop it. At once.' The angular figure of Tom Hall made a timely appearance at the changing-room door. 'Any more fighting from you, Kuttner, and there'll be no football. Save your energies for the soccer field. Winston, you take care of yourself now. We can't have a Peter Pan with a black eye or a broken leg. Got to keep yourself fit to fly.'

Hall must have told Mr Verity, the sports master, to put him in goal, Peter realised later, when found himself trying to keep warm on the edge of the sodden soccer pitch in Bishop's Park. The chances of a broken leg might be reduced by being made goalie but in the bitter November drizzle, with no opportunity to run around, his mother always said it was the surest way to get a chill. He hoped she wouldn't arrive to collect him until after the game was over. If she saw him in goal today she would insist that he had caught a chill, whether he had or not.

The whistle sounded in the murky distance. Rather a quick game today, Peter thought, must be the weather. In fact it was a free kick. The struck ball rose high over the halfway line and landed at the feet of the dread Kuttner who was stationed, unmarked, close to the left-hand touchline. He controlled it expertly, gathering momentum as he came powering towards the lone goalkeeper. Peter stationed himself in the centre of the goal crouching like a predatory panther, ready to dive to either side. If only Charlot were here to help him, he thought, they could cover one side each. Kuttner loomed closer and closer and then slammed a mighty kick with his left foot. Peter lunged acrobatically to his right just as the ball cannoned into the opposite side of the goal.

'Peach,' he remarked to himself as he turned to collect it from the netting.

'What you should have done,' Mr Verity had by now caught up with the play, 'was come right out and dive at his feet. It's the only real option in those circumstances.'

'He wanted to practise his flying, sir,' Kuttner gloated, flapping his arms to emphasise the point.

'That's enough from you, Kuttner,' reprimanded the master. 'You were probably offside anyway. And I think that's enough for all of us. Time.' He planted the silver whistle in his mouth and let loose a prolonged blast.

Grace had been watching the end of the game from behind a cluster of trees around the rubber-tyre swings that lay at the entrance to the playing field. Once she had spotted her son in goal she thought it prudent to stay out of sight until the game was over. She knew he got teased by the other boys if she was seen to be overprotective. But now she joined the trickle of parents who were making their way to the changing hut to pick up their offspring.

'Did you see my final save?' Peter demanded as soon as he emerged.

'No,' she lied.

'Just as well.'

'Not a good one?' she enquired.

'It looked good,' replied her son, 'providing you were on the other side.'

She smiled at the serious-faced seven-year-old who was trotting along beside her, his strong chin plunged into the collar of his anorak and his tiny blue eyes tightened against the sweeping drizzle. He's soon going to be as tall as me, she thought, casting a glance at his willowy body. He had a natural form of wit, whether or not he was aware of it, and the flow of his gestures made it more probable that he might do something artistic rather than athletic.

'Couldn't Charlie have helped you?' she suggested with a grin.

'Charlot, mum,' he corrected her. 'He doesn't answer to Charlie any more, and also he doesn't like football.'

Charlie had been his invisible friend almost from the moment when they had settled in Talgarth Road. At first Peter had kept his existence from his mother but, in a moment of intimacy, he had decided to make him a shared secret. Ever since he had begun French lessons, however, his chum had demanded to be known as Charlot.

A tenacious jogger in singlet and shorts overtook them as they reached the puddled towpath beside the Thames.

'What's he training for?' asked Peter. 'Doesn't he know the Olympics are over?'

'They're never over,' said his mother. 'There's always another lot in four more years.'

'Yea, but there'll never be another Sebastian Coe. He's the greatest, isn't he?'

Grace chose her answer carefully. 'One of them – certainly.'

'Who else then?' Peter paused to pick up a swollen horse chestnut that lay among the soaking leaves on the path in front of him.

'I named you after a great runner,' his mother bent down to gather some chestnuts herself but also to avoid looking him in the eye. 'A man who ran marathons.'

'Did he win a gold at the Olympics?'

'As a matter of fact he didn't.' She straightened up, heartened by his interest. 'He was the favourite for the Helsinki Olympics in 1952. He even set a new world record to qualify. But he was hit by cramp and had to abandon the race. Poor Jim never had much luck on the big occasions. But the following year he set world record after world record in nearly every marathon he ran – just to show that he could do it.'

'I thought you said you named me after him?' The boy had split open the spiky green shell of the chestnut to discover a pair of conkers, glistening like mahogany, their touching edges un-naturally flat as they nestled symmetrically beside each other.

'I did.'

'Jim?'

Grace became flustered. A sonorous blast on the foghorn of a police launch chugging its way through the gloom distracted her son's attention for a moment and gave her time to compose her thoughts. 'No, not Jim. His full name was Jim Peters – so I thought I'd call you Peter. You see.'

Peter saw but somehow wasn't entirely convinced. She was keeping something from him. As he turned away and tossed one of the conkers far out into the river, not even the gathering dusk could wholly disguise his mother's discomfort. They walked on, side by side in silence, to where the sodium lights of Putney Bridge curved mistily over the river.

'Do you see this arch? She indicated with her hand, attempting to take his mind off the subject that she feared was preoccupying his thoughts. 'It was specially constructed so that the Prince and

Princess of Wales could drive under it in a horse-drawn carriage to a great banquet. That was in 1902. They held it to celebrate the Coronation of King Edward VII. Only the poor were invited, fourteen thousand of them. They sat in marquees and ate roast beef and plum pudding, washed down with pints of beer.'

Peter was always intrigued by historical details, especially when he could associate a place with its past. 'Did you have to drink the beer?' he asked. 'Suppose you didn't like it?'

'There were temperance tables for those people,' said his mother.

The boy was unsure of the word. 'Does that mean they had to keep their temper?'

Grace's laugh softened the chill of the evening. She hugged him tightly to her and warmed his freezing cheek against hers.

'Get me another pair of lamps. The tungsten ones in the corner.'

Nevis had shown him on previous occasions which the tungsten ones were, but Peter had completely forgotten. He decided not to risk the photographer's ire by asking again and crossed the studio floor to those that were nearest.

'No, no, silly boy. I said tungsten. Over there, by the window.'

The seven-year-old had been summoned upstairs to help in the studio. Nevis usually had a professional assistant if it was a shoot for *Vogue* or an advertising agency. But when it was merely a private client who was prepared to pay a thousand pounds for the privilege of a portrait, he would prudently economise on the two hundred pounds he would have to pay out of his own pocket and use child labour from downstairs to prepare the shot.

Peter loved it. As soon as the call had come, he rushed through his homework and dashed upstairs. The depressing darkness of the day was dispelled by the excitement of the studio. It was fragrant with the Eastern incense which Nevis burned whenever clients were coming and the white cyclorama which blended the wall and the floor into one shone shimmeringly bright under the powerful lights.

'Take two cushions and go and sit on the chair.' Nevis would sometimes use Peter as a stand-in to prepare the lighting. 'No, one cushion. I think it is just a little girl.'

The boy did as he was bid, holding himself silent and erect while the white-haired master – in the full artistic drag of silk scarf, wine smoking-jacket and monogrammed slippers – busied himself behind the camera.

'Why do you need so many lights?' Peter asked attentively.

Nevis moved a stand closer to him and began adjusting the flaps. 'With these lights,' he announced, 'I am God. I can recreate anyone in my own image, or – at least – the image in my eye. I can make ugly women beautiful and plain men mysterious. I can make people twenty years younger or twenty years older. I can see right through to a person's soul and X-ray their emotions. When you sit there, Peter, you are created by me. I paint you with light.'

The boy didn't fully understand everything that Nevis was saying but he was mightily impressed by it none the less.

'Now I take a Polaroid,' the photographer announced, bending over the camera. 'Wait. We need something. Something to link you to those pillars in the background. Take your shirt off.'

Peter did so, reluctantly.

'Ah, now I see you,' Nevis smiled. 'Nearly there.' He skipped across to the plaster bust that stood impressively at the top of the stairs and lifted the artificial laurel wreath from its head.

'Do you know who this is?' he asked, patting the touselled hair. 'Pan, a Greek shepherd-God. He danced and sang and played pipes. Beautiful music. Look, he even has his own pipes which a friend of mine found in the Portobello Road.'

He came back over to Peter, placed the little fan of pipes in his hand and lowered the wreath onto his brow. 'I want you to think that you are Peter Pan, just like your play, and you are about to soar into the sky. Look up, up to the window and believe that you have no weight at all. That a hot draft could suck you up like a feather. Empty your eyes.'

The unexpected flash caught Peter unawares; he was sure he had blinked. Nevis pulled the paper out of the camera with a flourish and stepped into the light.

'Mr Pan,' he observed looking at the boy. 'Eternal youth. I can offer you that as well. You will grow old but the image in my hand will stay the same for ever.'

He tore the back off the Polaroid and examined it. 'Not enough light in the eyes and too much on the chin. We can rearrange your features if ever we do a portrait of you but this evening . . .'

He stopped at the sound of the infirm bell in the hall. 'Go and give them a warm welcome, Peter. They are Americans. And they are paying cash.'

The boy pulled on his shirt and sprinted down the stairs, hauling open the front door with both hands. A lady and a little girl, of about his own age, were shaking the rain off their umbrellas.

'Have we come to the right place?' The woman had a deep-throated American accent, almost like a man.

'Yes,' said Peter, anxious to agree.

'How do you know? I didn't say which place we were looking for,' she smiled, nevertheless stepping into the hall. She undid her transparent plastic hat and shook down to her shoulders thick tresses of damp copper-coloured hair. 'England!' she said.

He felt embarrassed. 'Oh, I just assumed . . . you wanted your photographs taken.'

'Stop teasing him, auntie.' The girl turned to him reassuringly. 'She always teases. She's a teacher, can't you tell.'

'A teacher and a teaser,' pronounced her aunt closing the door. She handed the boy her umbrella which he grasped by its carved pelican handle and placed in the stand in the hall. 'Now where do we find Mr Nevis?'

'Upstairs,' Peter indicated, pressing his back against the Welsh dresser in the hall. The woman looked slightly familiar; he was sure he had seen her near the school playground earlier in the week. But there was no chance to examine her further. Nevis wouldn't let him remain in the studio when the clients actually arrived, so he made his way reluctantly downstairs.

'This is my niece, Cherry,' the American woman informed Nevis as he helped her off with her raincoat. 'Some day she intends to become a photographer but, for the moment, what we need today is a wedding anniversary present for her parents. Make her look like a princess.'

'She already does.' Compliments were included in the price of Nevis's package.

'Where's the little boy? Is he your son?' The woman had settled herself at the photographer's work-desk and was sifting through the pictures on the surface.

'No,' said Nevis. 'He's the housekeeper's boy. He occasionally gives me a hand up here.'

'Doesn't look like you,' acknowledged the American, holding up the recent Polaroid which she had found on the desk. 'Strong features – mind if I keep this?'

Whether Nevis minded or not was academic. She dropped the picture into her handbag and clicked it shut. When she was paying a thousand pounds the client knew she could behave exactly as she liked.

'Can I get out?'

'No, stay for a little bit longer. You're bound to have caught a chill on that soccer pitch.'

Peter ran some more water from the hot tap. 'I didn't catch one, promise. I didn't catch a chill or the ball.'

'How did rehearsals go?' Grace shouted from the kitchen.

'All right.'

'Very informative. Did you remember your lines?'

Peter spread his face-cloth out on the surface of his bath and bombed it with some small perfumed balls that he had found in a bottle on the ledge. He spread his thumb and little finger as wide as they would go to form wings and made aeroplane noises in the back of his throat.

'Your lines, did you remember them?' His mother's voice contained more than a hint of exasperation.

'Yes,' murmured her son, coming in for the attack again. 'Mr Hall said I had to be careful with the dagger in the nursery at the end.'

'I didn't know Peter Pan had a dagger,' Grace replied, half to herself as she tested the baked potatoes to see if they were ready.

'Mum,' Peter remembered the question that had been nagging him on and off all afternoon. 'You know when Wendy is making up all those games so that Michael and John and all the Lost Boys won't forget what their mothers and fathers look like. You know, they have to write down on their slates the colour of their parents' eyes or the sound of their laughs.'

'Yes.' Grace had recently read him the book in preparation for the play.

'Well, why doesn't Peter join in?'

'He can't read or write, that's why.'

'But if he could, would he be able, say, to describe what his own mother and father looked like?'

She knew what he was getting at but she wasn't prepared to play along with him. 'He didn't have a mother or a father. He's like Tinker Bell, a fairy. That's why he can fly.'

'What about Tiger Lily, then?'

'She's an Indian. They just lived in tribes, not families. You can get out of the bath now, supper's ready.'

Grace strained the water from the cauliflower and set it in a bowl. The sausages were overcooked so she scraped away some of the worst burnt patches with a sharp knife.

'This Indian isn't my daddy, is he?'

She turned round abruptly to see him standing in the kitchen doorway, the outline of his childhood birthmark on his forehead, probably noticeable only to her, more pronounced after the heat of the bath. He was wearing her quilted dressing gown and his wet hair dripped steadily onto the shoulders. In his right hand he held up the cheque which she must have left in front of the bathroom mirror.

· *Fifteen* ·

It's true what they say, thought Winston, utterly inscrutable.

He had not taken his eyes off Shimizu for a single second after the Oriental player had won the first set and had just stood, without emotion, waiting for the applause to die down. The crowd, for the most part, had been disappointed by this early setback but traditionally sporting in their appreciation of a favoured foreigner. If psychiatrists' waiting rooms were frequently painted pink in order to calm the patients, then the predominant green of the All England Club – from the grass to the stadium to the shops to the canvas backings to the ivy to everything, in fact, except the balls – seemed to instil a code of behaviour on those assembled there. It was as if everyone had been vaccinated on entry with some time-warp drug and an Edwardian sense of etiquette and decorum was preserved in this sacred place.

'If you lose the opening set, it sometimes is the better bet.' Well, it was better than losing the third or the fourth or, certainly, the fifth, Winston thought, but no better than winning it. Mo's consoling couplet only illustrated his contention that the player in the lead was at his most tense at this stage. There was a nervousness that came with taking the initial advantage – as if somebody had given you a precious glass bowl and you were terrified of dropping it, was the coach's example – and now was the time to exploit this vulnerability.

But as Winston monitored the physiognomy of his opponent for any signal of nerves he could see nothing. It was like opening a book and discovering the pages were blank. Shimizu's eyes, almond and unblinking, stared without focus into the middle distance as if he had entered a trance. He didn't even throw a glance up to his own coach seated in front of Mo and Dawson.

Instead it was Winston, himself, who was feeling unsettled. What does he wear that headband for, he wondered, his hair's too short to need to be contained. What do those slashed stripes on his shirt mean? Is it some form of martial arts emblem? The Japanese player seemed impervious to the increasing humidity in the Centre Court, cooling himself with his own confidence as if he were about to perform a ritual execution.

Winston looked at the confirmation of his status in the gold electronic letters of the scoreboard – 4–6 – and then let his gaze slip across to Phoebe in the players' box. She was waiting to catch his eye but, knowing that a television camera was pointing in her direction, deftly brushed her lips with her forefinger and indicated with an imperceptible jerk of her head, that Mo was anxious to make contact with him. Coaching, during any match and especially during a Wimbledon final, was strictly prohibited but most players and their trainers had evolved a system of signals that would at least let them communicate certain basic information.

Mo was zipping the top of his tracksuit casually up and down in an almost abstracted manner, as if it were a mere fidget. But Winston knew what he was telling him to do. Slowly, slowly, was the repeated message. Take your time, spin it out; lengthen the rallies and protect the points. Play a Pasarell. He had no need to be reminded: the seeds of their entire strategy had grown out of the opening Men's Singles in 1969 when the American Davis Cup player, Charlie Pasarell, wore down forty-one-year-old Pancho Gonzales in one hundred and twelve games, including a 24–22 first set, the longest ever Wimbledon singles match.

But at this very moment he was, unfortunately, feeling more like Gonzales.

'Stay in your seats, please,' the umpire counselled the crowd. 'Second set. Mr Shimizu to serve. Play.'

· Sixteen ·

James sensed something was wrong even before he left the classroom. Mr Hanson had spotted that his thoughts were elsewhere and had thrown him a curved ball, asking him to name exactly where in the States Christopher Columbus had landed. The boy could remember from his lessons with Miss Lambert, who had dwelt luridly on Columbus's slaughter of the Indians, that the explorer had never set foot in North America at all – the nearest he got was Haiti. So he came back with the correct answer: 'Nowhere.'

'Quite right,' conceded the teacher, 'however, your attention would be very welcome here, especially at the Longboat Learning Center.'

Still the worry would not go away. After the bell rang he couldn't bring himself to look out of the classroom window and deliberately dallied in the locker room, hoping that his fears would prove unfounded.

But unfortunately he was right. When he sprinted down the school steps Aunt Violet wasn't there. She always parked the Toyota in the same spot under a pair of pineapple trees to make sure of some shade if the afternoon sun was too strong. But today they had no one to protect.

He didn't know what to do. Maybe she had gotten a puncture or been delayed at the market. Only once before had she failed to turn up but that was during the flu epidemic and she had telephoned the school secretary to tell him to come home with Myron on the bus. James ran back to the secretary's office to see if there was a message today. It didn't surprise him to learn that there was none. Not wishing to panic the woman, he said that his aunt had been unsure that morning whether she could make it or not but, if she did eventually turn up, could she be told that he had gone ahead on the bus.

He nearly missed it as he careered down the wooden steps once more and hammered on the driver's door to get him to stop.

'Where to, my man?' demanded the elderly Jamaican at the wheel.

'Same as Myron,' gasped James, throwing his books on the seat beside his classmate and settling himself across the aisle.

'Your auntie ill?' Myron was somewhat jealous of James's chauffered trips to and from school and also more than a little upset with his own parents that they wouldn't permit him to accept a ride because they didn't trust Violet's driving.

'Just a cold,' James replied, as casually as he could.

When they reached Pollux Palisades he followed Myron, who had a key, into the entrance lobby and then charged up the stairs, promising he would try to meet up for softball on the beach at the regular time.

She didn't answer the door. He stabbed desperately at the bell, hoping that a succession of rings might wake her up from her afternoon nap more effectively than a single prolonged one. But neither method was any good. So he dashed down to the apartment of the caretaker, Mrs Lopez, in the basement to get a pass key and in order not to arouse any suspicions, told her that his aunt had accidentally locked her own keys inside.

He knew there was no need to knock on the bedroom door. She was there, still in bed, with her spectacles carefully placed on top of the neatly folded copy of the *Sarasota Herald* on the bedside table. It was her habit to read the paper after lunch and then close her eyes for half an hour before coming to pick up James. But as the sad October sun filtered through the lace curtains highlighting the violet tint in her hair, it was clear to the ten-year-old that she had begun her final rest.

He tiptoed over to the side of the bed and whispered her name, softly at first. 'Aunt Violet, Aunt Violet.' There was no response. He put his hand on her frail grey arm that lay outside the covers. It was cold and clammy and touching it made him shiver.

'Aunt Violet,' he shouted, angry that she should have left him this way, 'wake up.'

And then he climbed onto the bottom of the bed, curled up as tightly as he could and let the tears bleed from his eyes.

Monday, 19 October 1987 had dawned dark and drizzly but by mid-morning the Florida sky was rain-washed and its usual cloudless self. There were only six people at the Sarasota crematorium: James and Dawson; one-eyed Mike and Mary-Louise from the trailer park; Myron's mother, Mrs Connell; and Mrs Lopez, with whom James had stayed until Dawson had managed to get down from Boston the previous Friday.

There were no hymns or anything like that: just some prayers spoken by a solemn man in a collar and tie who didn't look like a priest or a rabbi. James could barely concentrate since he spent his time biting his lip, determined to show his father that he was not a cry-baby. As they walked together back down the narrow aisle, he could hear the electronic whirr of the coffin being guided into the trap door that lay ominously in the wall behind. In his imagination the boy had seen hungry flames licking the other side.

'Does it go straight into the fiery furnace?' he asked with concern.

'No,' Dawson reassured him. 'They do all that when nobody's here.'

The undertakers had left the four wreaths that had accompanied the coffin on a freshly-watered patch of grass just outside the door. Dawson bent down to inspect the labels. 'With deepest sympathy, from Karen the daughter of Tomasz,' he read. 'Do you know who that is, James?'

'I don't know Karen,' the boy replied. 'I didn't know that Tomasz had a daughter.'

'Tomasz?'

'He was Aunt V.'s friend. But he died. She always said she was going to visit the country he came from – Czechoslovakia, I think, he used to be in the Czechoslovakian National Band – but now she won't be able . . .'

The boy could contain his emotions no longer; he turned away, embarrassed at himself and devastated at her death, and buried his face deep into his hands.

'Don't worry, Jim,' came a familiar voice. 'It was the happiest passing I ever heard of. No pain, no problems, just a deep sleep. We all should be so lucky.'

It was one-eyed Mike who had walked across to put a consoling hand on his shoulder. Dawson regarded the man resentfully, as if this were an illegal intrusion into his parental territory.

'Can you introduce me, James?' he demanded.

'This is Mike,' the boy sobbed, 'and that's Mary-Louise. And they were all part of *The Greatest Show on Earth* with Aunt V.'

Mike held out his hand to the uncomprehending Dawson. 'Mr Silver, Jim has often spoken about you. I'm very sorry. Violet was a good woman. Lived here all alone until this little lad came along and then she discovered how much richer life can be when you have someone to care for.'

Dawson murmured a muffled assent, unsure whether the remark was meant to be a criticism of him. But it appeared not to be.

'We were wondering,' one-eyed Mike went on, 'Mary-Louise and me, whether Jim might come and stay with us for a year or two. It's only a trailer – well, you know it, it's where Vi used to be – but it's a safe home.'

'And a loving one,' Mary-Louise added, slipping her arm through that of her husband as if to confirm their bona fides as a couple.

'No,' Dawson forced a smile and backed away. 'That won't be necessary. I mean, thank you. I appreciate it. Very kind. So does my son. But we've already made other arrangements. You understand.'

'Dad, watch out!'

'What?' Dawson seemed not to have noticed the articulated truck overtaking them until the last minute. When it grazed the wing-mirror of his rented Thunderbird, he stepped on the brakes in panic and veered off to the right. Fortunately there was a slip road into a small shopping mall just ahead and he managed to steer into it, pulling up by the Custom Pie Café.

James could see that he was sweating profusely as he switched off the ignition; his driving seemed even worse than that of Aunt V. The boy had been feeling apprehensive ever since Dawson had used the expression 'other arrangements' to one-eyed Mike. Throughout the past weekend he had given every indication – without putting it in so many words – that James would return to live with him in Boston.

As he scrutinised his brooding father, who was leaning forward on the steering wheel and looking in a glazed fashion at the old folk slowly making their way into the Custom Pie for an early dinner, he wondered what these 'other arrangements' were going to be. The one person in his life whom he truly loved, who had been mother and friend and family to him, was dead and now there was no one left to protect him. Of course he loved his father, too, but more in the respectful way reserved for a favourite uncle than with the undiluted emotion he felt for Violet. He always looked foward to Dawson's visits – inevitably they were accompanied by presents and nice surprises, especially trips to see the clown school down in Venice. At one stage Dawson had even joined in the softball games on Crescent Beach, but lately he had begged off, claiming that his eyesight wasn't good enough.

They had never really been chums, not in the way James had observed the relationship some of the boys at school had with their fathers. For one thing, Dawson rarely dressed in a particularly relaxed manner: even his sports clothes had a formal air about them. James could never imagine him in sneakers and jeans. He could see him out of the corner of his eye now, regaining his composure as he tightened his black tie into his starched white collar. His chunky body seemed heavier than ever – certainly there was an increasing expanse of shirt at the waist – and the sparse perimeter of hair circling his head was turning snow white. Dawson Silver was beginning to look like an old man.

At last his father spoke. 'I'm sorry.'

'That's all right, dad.'

'It's my eyes,' – Dawson had taken out a blue linen handkerchief and was reflectively polishing his glasses – 'damn doctor's given me the wrong prescription, I'm sure. I can't see a thing at the sides any more.'

'It's that pig thing, isn't it?' said James.

His father laughed ruefully. 'You're right, it's a pig of a thing. I can live with it, providing it doesn't get much worse. I just don't want you having to live with it.'

'Oh, that's all right,' James countered innocently. 'Dr Michaels told me there was no danger of that. He said I had uncanny sight.'

Dawson stopped polishing and looked sceptically at him. 'Did he now? He never mentioned that to me.'

'Perhaps he was just trying to make me feel good about it,' the boy suggested, backing off a little.

'Perhaps.' Dawson seemed unconvinced. 'Listen, I want to talk about the future. Your future, my future – our future.'

James knew this moment was coming and could feel the ice cold pebbles piling up in his stomach. He tightened his lips and said nothing.

'You know what I do for a living, don't you?'

The child managed a smile. 'You're an actually.' It was their joint joke; he had never been able to get his lips round the correct word when he was younger. In truth, he had no real idea what his father did, save that he worked in Boston and it was to do with figures and money.

'I sort of calculate the future,' his father went on. 'I don't know what's going to happen tomorrow any more than anybody else but I do know what's *likely* to happen tomorrow – because of what's happened in the past. Do you follow?'

'Yes, I think so.' James didn't really follow at all but was anxious to appear willing at such a crucial crossroads in his young life. 'Surely nobody knows about the future – except, perhaps, God. I mean, it's ahead of us. And the past is behind.'

'That's true,' his father nodded in assent, 'but we're all the product of our past. You see, from knowing the details of people's personal history and, more particularly, from studying the behaviour patterns of thousands of other individuals I can advise insurance companies on the likelihood of accidents or illness or death. I can tell pension funds how much money they are likely to have to pay out. See those old folk in the restaurant there – it's possible to compute, on average, how long they're likely to survive. There was a survey done in Salt Lake City a few years ago and they found that out of seven hundred and forty-seven deaths, forty-six per cent occurred in the three months following the deceased's birthday. Dying's a psychological thing and at that age the only milestone you have to stay alive for may be your birthday. A major cause of death is lack of the will to live.'

James tried to seem interested but he remained confused and still somewhat uncomfortable.

'You're ten years old and I'm sixty,' Dawson continued. 'I'm nearly ready to retire. I've made some prudent investments on Wall Street – against the natural caution of my calling, I might say, but you can't go very far wrong with blue chip stocks today. You'll learn about them soon enough. So I'm going to come down here to Florida to live with you.'

The boy reached out, relieved, and took hold of the safe anchor of his father's arm.

'Oh, dad, that would be great. We could go to Venice all the time.'

'Sure, and the original Venice, too. Do they tell you about that at school?'

'Aunt V. did, I think. The one where the streets are flooded with water?'

'We'll ride in a gondola' – Dawson found himself warming to the notion – 'and the boatman will serenade us with arias from the finest operas and then we'll go and eat the best pizza in all Italy.'

'Yea,' shouted James. 'Can we go tomorrow?'

His father laughed. 'You're going to have to wait a little while longer,' he cautioned. 'It'll take some time to put my affairs in order, tidy things up in Boston and find a place down here.'

'How long's a while?' The boy searched his eyes for a clue, like a prisoner scanning the face of a sentencing judge.

'Let's say a year. Maybe less. None of us was to know that Aunt Violet was going to die. I can't upsticks straight away, there are things to be settled.'

'And till then,' James pleaded anxiously, 'can I go and live with Mike and Mary-Louise?'

His father's expression was resolute. 'No. They may be nice folk but they're not quite suitable.'

'Can I come back to Boston, then?' The child tightened his grip on his father's arm.

'It's not appropriate at this time,' Dawson stated decisively without any further explanation. 'No, you're going to be okay. There's a good place near by that will take care of you. I've talked to the guy who runs it and it's a lot of fun. Have you heard of the Osprey Academy?'

James shook his head. He had visions of some terrible school like the ones he saw in old English films on TV where the masters wore funny flat hats and beat the pupils with canes. Even if it wasn't as disciplined as that, he still had little desire to go there and he also had a strange hunch who was at the back of all this.

'It was Dr Michaels' idea, wasn't it?' he demanded.

His father looked at him in amazement. 'As a matter of fact it was.'

'I've got a present for you.' When they arrived at Pollux Palisades, Dawson decided to break the uneasy silence that had lain between them during the drive home.

James said nothing but climbed mutely out of the car and set off in a subdued fashion for the front door.

'Don't you want to know what it is?' his father called after him.

The boy turned wearily back to him. 'What is it?'

'A surprise.'

'Why are you giving me a present?' James didn't mean to sound rude but at the same time didn't want his father to think that his compliance could be bought with a gift.

Dawson stepped out of the Thunderbird and carefully closed the door. 'I had meant to let you have it on your tenth birthday if that conference in Seattle hadn't stopped me from coming down. I wanted to be here to show you how it works. They should've delivered it this morning. Take a look in the garage.'

James paused for a moment, uncertainly, and then his curiosity got the better of him and he ran ahead to see what it could be. The garage door was unlocked. He pushed it open and there it lay in front of him – low slung and gleaming midnight blue, with a highbacked seat and a scaled-down leather steering wheel.

'Is this for me?'

His father had reached the door and beamed his assent.

'But I'm too young to drive. I don't have a licence.'

Dawson laughed. 'You can't take it on the highway but it's okay around the block here and we might get away with it on the beach if no one's around in the evening.'

'What is it?'

'It's a go-kart. Haven't you ever seen one before?'

James thought he had but he had never actually known anybody who owned one. 'Maybe at a fair,' he said. 'I think I've seen them on a sort of a track.'

Dawson helped him to wheel it out of the garage and onto the concrete path that skirted the shore.

'Want to have a go?' he asked.

'Sure,' said the boy.

'Well, jump in. I asked them to make sure the tank's full. Always check that it's in neutral. You just turn that key and it should start.'

James did so, jerking back in shock at the unexpected roar of the engine.

'You strap yourself in like this.' His father snapped the buckles closed on either side of the narrow seat. 'Only two gears, in or out of neutral, and two pedals – one for stop and the other for go. Take it away.'

He stood back and watched as his son cautiously clicked the kart into gear and then set off at a sedate pace along the path. It seemed to have done the trick, temporarily distracting him from his apprehension about the uncertain time that lay ahead.

James gained in confidence and in speed, turning around a wooden bench two hundred yards away and then navigating in and out of the street lamps on his way back.

'It's great,' he yelled. 'Can I try the beach?'

'Why not?' Dawson had no doubt they would be informed soon enough if it was against local regulations.

The boy guided it cautiously down the slip road and then opened up the engine when he reached the safety of the shore. The tyres carved curling signatures on the sand as he circled round and round etching figures of eight. Without realising it he was getting closer and closer to the sea and the softer sand slowed his progress until finally the kart stuttered to a halt.

Dawson, panting as he ran, caught up with him and slumped down on the beach beside the vehicle attempting to get his breath back. The sun had dipped beneath the Gulf of Mexico, but its legacy tinged the twilight blood-red. He gazed at his son, resolute as a young fighter pilot sitting at the controls.

'It's fantastic,' James enthused. 'Didn't these used to be popular? I mean, before I was born.'

His father had been playing with the sand in front of him, heaping it up and patting it down. Deliberately he concentrated on the task, not looking up at his son as he spoke. 'You're right. That's about when they were popular. In fact this one was meant for someone else, but he never saw it.'

The boy said nothing but held firmly onto the steering wheel. Dawson picked up some shells and began to decorate the top of the compressed heap of sand in front of him as if it were an Indian burial mound.

'You see,' he began, 'I had a son before – when I was a younger man. Not with your mother but an American woman. And he lived in Boston and he liked doing many of the things you like doing. Didn't look a lot like you – his hair was blond and curly, just as mine was once – but he would have adored you. You would have been buddies. He loved the sea, loved to surf. Too much, perhaps. And then he had an accident, out on Cape Cod, near Boston. It was a freak – not the sort of thing that anybody could have expected. His surf board hit him and he died. Just ten, just your age. Only he'll always be ten.'

'He was called Simon, wasn't he?' James had climbed out of the kart and now sat beside his father on the sand, helping him to make the mound.

'How did you know that?'

'Aunt V. She told me about him one day. And then she said I wasn't to tell anyone, especially you. I couldn't quite follow her but she said – I think she said – that the clock in your life had stopped and it would only start again when I could' – the child felt embarrassed and played more furiously with the sand – 'when I could sort of stand in Simon's shoes.'

Dawson awoke early the next morning; he slept badly when he was at home and worse when he was in a strange bed. He got up and gingerly opened James's door but the boy was still firmly asleep, clutching the driver's gloves which – along with a helmet – had come with the go-kart. A barrier between them seemed to have fallen away last night although he acknowledged that there were several more to go. They had pushed the kart back to the garage and then gone upstairs to cook spaghetti. James grilled some bacon and chopped it up to make Violet's favourite sauce. And afterwards they had sat in front of the artificial log fire and played game after game of chess. At first Dawson let his son win but later he found he had no need as the boy took the initiative.

He felt more than a little guilty about sending James so peremptorily to Osprey Academy but this had always been the plan in the event of Violet's premature demise. Edmund Michaels had indeed suggested the place since he knew the man who ran it. Better that James stay there until the pension plan was sorted out and Dawson could restructure his business to make himself a consultant rather than a partner. He went into the kitchen to prepare breakfast but there was no milk or bread in the refrigerator so he returned to his room to get dressed and then quietly slipped out of the apartment. Although it was barely seven o'clock, he suspected the store further down the road might be open.

It was. But before Dawson could make his way to the back of the shop where the provisions were kept his gaze was caught and then fixed by the newspaper headlines arrayed along the counter in front of the till. Crash, crash, crash: the word screamed out from every one of them with terrifying unanimity. Was this some kind of practical joke? He sought out the *New York Times* and extricated it from the pile. All the News That's Fit to Print. Tuesday October 20, 1987. 'STOCKS PLUNGE 508 POINTS, A DROP OF 22.6%; 604 MILLION VOLUME NEARLY DOUBLES RECORD.'

He hastily pulled his spectacles out of the breast pocket of his shirt; his eyesight must be much worse than he thought. But in fact it was the news that was worse. 'Stock market prices plunged in a tumultuous wave of selling yesterday,' the *Times* reported, 'giving Wall Street its worst day in history and raising fears of a recession.'

'I think it's gonna get worse than they said on TV last night.'

Dawson realised that he and the elderly shopkeeper, who was opening bundles of magazines behind the counter, were the only people in the store so the remark must be addressed to him.

'I didn't see any television last night,' he replied, still transfixed by the story in front of him. 'I haven't really seen anything or spoken to anyone for the past three days. What's been happening?'

'Worse than '29, they say, and I can remember that only too well. All those – what do you call 'em, puppies? – are going to be jumping out of Wall Street windows thicker than a ticker-tape parade.' The jeremiah of the counter didn't seem too distressed himself; on the contrary he exuded the underlying satisfaction old people often obtain from imparting bad news. 'Where've you been – out on a boat?'

'No, I came for my aunt's funeral.'

'Violet Silver,' the shopkeeper nodded without even seeking confirmation that this was who it must have been. 'Sad. Sadder still about the little boy. She was his aunt, too – but you must know that.'

Dawson decided to avoid further explanations and handed the man a quarter for the paper.

'Fifty cents down here, mister,' the tone was reprimanding, 'it's come a long way – like you.'

Dawson eagerly offered the extra quarter, a small price to buy his exit and an even smaller one compared to the hundreds of thousands of dollars he calculated he must have lost in the past twenty-four hours. Outside, the morning sky was grey and forlorn; it must have heard the news itself, he reflected. In the bull market of the eighties all that glistered had not been gold but stocks and bonds had regularly ascended by leaps and bounds with such predictability that nobody thought it possible that they would ever go down again. Dawson settled himself on a bus-stop bench to read the rest of the story. The old timer was right: it was more catastrophic than the Crash of 1929. According to the *Times* the worst day of that was a 12.8 per cent drop; yesterday shares had fallen 22.6 per cent – the most disastrous day in the history of Wall Street.

These must be mainly junk bonds, he thought, surely his blue chip stocks would resist this yuppie panic. But no – IBM, which had been $176 in August, was down to $104. General Motors and Exxon had both fallen in value by twenty-five per cent. The rout had obliterated more than $500 billion in equity value from the nation's stock portfolios and at least a quarter of the value of his own with, he suspected, worse to come. He was not alone but there was little comfort in being in good company.

He wasn't ruined – but his pension plan had suffered a crippling blow. It could take years to reflate it again. Why, he cursed himself, had he been so stupid as to listen to Quinn and enter the equity market?

A bus drew up in front of him, making him take his eyes off the paper. The door crumpled open automatically, revealing it to be empty except for its driver, a young man with hippy-length blond hair. Dawson motioned to him apologetically, indicating that he didn't wish to board it.

'Just you keeping reading the paper, my friend,' the driver tittered, as he re-engaged the forward gear. 'Reckon all those smart folk in New York got what was coming to them. Maybe they wasn't as smart as they thought they was.'

Dawson felt tempted to screw up the *Times* and throw it at the now receding vehicle. But as he watched it disappear up the highway he could see a telephone booth further along the road and decided it would be better to vent his anger on a more appropriate target.

'Did I wake you?' he demanded hopefully, as the transfer charge call to Boston went through.

'That's not possible at present,' Loophole Quinn was quick to counter. 'I haven't slept in three days. Where the devil have you been? Where are you now?'

'I'm in a phone booth in Florida and I'm feeling pretty pissed.'

'You're not alone in that,' the lawyer was on the defensive. 'Why don't you tell your office where you're going? If I could have contacted you yesterday we might have been able to get out early enough to avoid the worst.'

'Well, get me out now,' Silver yelled.

'Too late,' the lawyer countered. 'Nobody's buying — I've been talking to the money men all night. No sense in joining in the panic and breaking up your portfolio now — it'll come back, eventually.'

'Eventually isn't soon enough for me. Violet's dead, didn't Michaels tell you? I need to be here to look after the boy. And I need my capital.'

'Listen,' Quinn's voice dropped to a conspiratorial whisper. 'There's a guy in Framingham who's very close to some major fund managers. I haven't spoken to him yet but if we square a few people, we may be able to backdate some deals to before the weekend.'

'Forget it, Quinn.' Dawson's disgust was enunciated in no certain terms. 'I've got to take my son to school.'

· Seventeen ·

It was as if a giant plane had crashed, ripping its way through the foliage until it had reached some final resting place beyond the horizon. The trees closest to the riverbank had sustained least damage with only broken branches and crooked backs as a reminder of the torrential winds. But those that had stood individually in the centre of the park, with no neighbours to offer some protection, were the worst hit. Several had been physically uprooted from the ground. The oldest had suffered most cruelly: trees that had been there for centuries, forty or fifty feet tall, lay forlornly by the cavities that once contained their foundations. Some divine dentist seemed simply to have plucked them out with a pair of mighty pliers. Others – the sycamores and horse chestnuts mainly – had put up a more valiant fight, holding the line and not budging an inch in their position. But many of them had finally succumbed in the face of the 110-mile-an-hour hurricane, their proud trunks snapped in two. If anything, their caracasses looked more sorry than those of their fallen fellows, with the jaundiced wood of their wounds lying jaggedly open and exposed.

'If there were a God he would never have let this happen.' Tom Hall swerved his bicycle to avoid a fallen branch. 'He even prepared the way, you know. If it hadn't been such a fine summer this year the trees wouldn't have still been in such full foliage in mid-October and the damage would have been a tenth of this.'

'How can he not exist and still prepare the way?' Peter, following behind, was more than a little nervous of arguing with his teacher but Hall had seemed to contradict himself.

'You know what I mean,' sighed the older man in the way that adults always do, Peter reflected, when you don't.

'Didn't he make the trees in the first place?' His pupil didn't want to get into an argument, but that was what he had always been taught.

'So the Church would have us believe,' his teacher shot back tartly. 'But I didn't read about any vicars explaining from the pulpit last Sunday what motivated the Almighty to inflict this particular act of destruction. I can understand him punishing the ill-gotten greed of the money-worshippers with the Stock Exchange crash but I don't see why he had to take it out on nature as well.'

'Didn't someone know about the crash before it happened?' On his smaller bike, the boy had to cycle twice as hard in order to keep up. 'Mummy said they rang the BBC to say it was coming but the BBC told everyone it wasn't.'

'You're nearly right,' Hall laughed. 'Only it wasn't the Stock Exchange crash, it was the hurricane. They assured us it wasn't going to happen. Trust the Beeb – if anyone has a hot line to God it's surely that place but on this occasion they must have got their wires crossed.'

They made an odd couple as they traversed Bishop's Park in the late October sun. Despite the benign weather Hall was clad in a long blue raincoat from which his thin white legs emerged in a cartoon-like fashion as he pedalled along. His old-fashioned spectacles and pronounced Adam's apple did nothing to detract from the bizarre image. Behind him, Peter Winston – tall for a ten-year-old but looking no older in his white shorts and school sports shirt – was riding his compact thick-tyred BMX bike which caused his knees to come up to meet his arms as he sat in the saddle. A youthful Sancho Panza to Hall's Don Quixote, he faithfully followed the winding trail his master navigated through the wreckage.

'We'd better step on it,' Tom called back to him. 'If we don't get there by five, we'll never get a court.'

They veered to the right at the northern gate of the park by the small aviary of white doves and multi-coloured canaries and dismounted as they arrived at the gravelled entrance to the grounds of the Bishop's Palace. This proudly built red-brick edifice, its unattended façade indicating a shortage of funds for any running repairs, harboured one of the nastier secrets cloistered in the annals of the Church of England. Since the ninth century it had been the official home of the Bishop of London. But towards the end of 1867, during the bishopric of Dr Esau Penderick, a palace coup secretly took place, most probably perpetrated by Penderick's twin brother who was about to be appointed Bishop of Fulham and Gibraltar (quite what religiously connected two such disparate places was a mystery that the Church of England hugged secretively to its bosom, but the link remains to this day).

Jacob Penderick claimed that since the palace fell within his see it should be his official residence. His brother resisted the idea but – like the one-month Pope, John Paul I, a century later – met with a timely death. His drowned body was washed up on the other side of the Thames, just where today the Oxford and Cambridge crews lower their craft into the water for their annual boat race. Nobody ever proved that he was murdered but the speed with which the church covered up the story prevented anyone from even trying to prove it. Nevertheless Jacob managed to acquire both jobs and his desired control over the Palace from 1869 until he died peacefully – although possibly not at peace with himself – on the eve of the Coronation dinner for the poor in June 1902.

Some bishops, as a reminder of their earthly powers, leave behind churches or even cathedrals, but Jacob's legacy was to sow the seeds in the Palace gardens of the future Fulham and Gibraltar Lawn Tennis Club. In 1872, on a trip to his Mediterranean diocese, he had observed the Spanish game of pelota being played by some of his rock island flock and decided to import the sport to the stately grounds of his London home. For many years lawn rackets, as it was known, was the sole preserve of chosen clerics but officers recuperating in the Palace after the First World War were intrigued by the game and those who were fit enough were permitted to join in. The surge of democracy heralded by the Labour Government after the Second World War extended this privilege to local civilians and on 15 July 1952, five months exactly after Elizabeth II became Queen of England and ten days after Maureen Connolly – Little Mo, as she was known since she was short and only seventeen – became Queen of Wimbledon, the FAGLTC was founded.

A temporary wooden pavilion had been constructed on the boundary with the local allotments and, indeed, looked like a larger version of the makeshift huts dotted among the cucumber and cabbage patches. Up until 1958 play on Sunday was prohibited but a shortfall in members had caused the Church to rethink the rule. The only concession to the Sabbath now was a note pinned by the bar asking members not to use profane language nor to shout too loudly on that day, in case the Bishop were to come by. That apart, the club no longer had much connection with the Church save for the tradition that the Bishop's archdeacon was its honorary president – although he rarely attended any committee meetings, his presence there usually indicating that the biannual ground rent was overdue.

Four gently undulating and generally unkempt grass courts that stretched between the clubhouse and what was once the bursar's office in the main building comprised the entire facilities on offer. An overweight Irish caretaker from a local school, Dermot Gould, arrived on Monday and Friday mornings to mow the lawns but not if it was raining. He claimed to be unavailable at any other times so during particularly inclement summers the grass would grow to the height of a low savannah. Some members claimed actually to have lost a ball on the court – although this was open to question. Suffice to say that only Dermot possessed the key to the hut where the lawn-mower was kept, so no enthusiastic amateur could cut the courts if he didn't.

And nobody at all could roll them. Dermot debarred himself from this activity because he claimed he had a bad heart. People newly elected to the committee would often question his qualifications for the job, but since he was officially the Palace part-time gardener – a role that for the most part entailed keeping the paths clear of leaves in winter – they discovered the club had no control over his appointment. Some would even suggest that it was strange that an Anglican bishop should employ an anarchic Irish Catholic for this sinecure, debating whether it was the Bishop's desire to put Catholics in their place or to put tennis players in their place which had motivated the decision.

Besides, one of the secrets of the Fulham and Gibraltar Lawn Tennis Club was its remarkable home record in the fourth division of the Middlesex League. Teams that would annihilate them in away games, would frequently come to grief on Dermot's lawns where the practised members knew every kink and slope and valley in the courts. These matches were but one of many contentious issues that divided the club. It seemed insane to many members that three of the four courts should be reserved exclusively for this purpose from 6.30 p.m. on at least one night a week and sometimes two. People would point out that the fourth division of the Middlesex League was of such an inauspicious standard that many of London's better clubs would just field anybody who volunteered to play and often not even enough of them. It was not unknown for visiting teams to turn up with only five or sometimes four out of the requisite six players, but the FAGLTC could usually make up this shortfall having a coterie of members, aged nearer seventy than sixty, who were always looking for a game but whom nobody much wanted to play with, standing by to help the opposition.

If a poll had been taken, a majority of the club would have been found in favour of abolishing these court-consuming matches, but the chairman – a pet insurance salesman called Ken Worple – warned that they might not get their treasured annual allocation of Wimbledon tickets from the Lawn Tennis Association if they were not seen to enter into the amateur spirit of league competition. The other pest that many members would have liked to see exterminated were the 'juniors'. However persuasively Worple might argue that the future of the club and, indeed, of the very nation's tennis was dependent on encouraging the young, most Fulham and Gibraltar stalwarts would be happy to encourage them to be somewhere else when they arrived for a game and found the courts full in the evenings or at the weekends.

A good old British compromise had been reached in this matter which, in its good old British fashion, was satisfactory to neither party. Juniors were obliged to forfeit the courts to senior members at certain times, unless they had attained the status of 'privileged juniors' which allowed a maximum of two of them to remain on court for a doubles with two senior members providing not more than six senior members were waiting to play. The rule was almost impossible to interpret and harder still to apply, as there were endless debates about which juniors were in fact privileged. The club coach used to decide but since he had been pensioned off to a nursing home near Bournemouth, the juniors themselves had demanded the right to nominate from their number. As a result the matter seemed always to be in a state of permanent and probably deliberate altercation. Even more perplexing problems were caused by the second half of the rule regarding the mental state of senior members on the verandah of the clubhouse. A man might be deemed to be 'waiting to play' when he was, in fact, just waiting for someone to buy the next round.

No such complications arose in the case of the bridge players who solidly occupied the only three tables in the club house on Tuesday, Thursday and Saturday evenings and Sunday afternoons. Age and infirmity usually safeguarded anyone from mistaking them as being likely to be waiting to play anything except the next hand. Quite why they needed the premises of a sports club to carry out their sedentary pleasure was unclear – save for the further pleasure they undoubtedly obtained from telling younger members to keep quiet or loudly shouting 'three no trumps' just when the club radio broadcast the latest cricket score. This may not have been a wholly intended act of malevolence since many of the elderly bridge circle hailed from Hungary, Poland, Czechoslovakia and Austria – territories where the latest news from Edgbaston and Lord's did not carry the same imperative as it did in the home country. Various attempts were made over the years to shift these social members to a more secluded location such as a church hall or the back room of a pub but they invitably ended in failure.

'Bridge and tennis, zey have always go together,' insisted their spokesman, Adolf Hann, 'like love and marriage, rain and dogs and cats.' His similes may have been mixed but his message wasn't: they weren't budging. And he was not without historical justification; before the advent of television bridge was the traditional pastime of tennis players, even those competing at international level, when rain stopped play. In addition, as Worple annually pointed out, older members liked to enjoy themselves in the company of young things in short skirts and breathe in the intoxicating bouquet of new-mown grass – when Dermot had got around to doing it.

The presence, or rather absence, of young things in short skirts was another cause for concern at the Fulham and Gibraltar. In order to join the club a new member not only had to stump up a combined entrance fee and subscription of £314 but also pass a playing-in test. This used to be administered by the coach, indeed it was during one such test with a twelve-year-old girl that old Desmond finally had his stroke and was taken away in an ambulance. When he was admitted to Charing Cross Hospital the driver gave his address as the Bishop's Palace and this subsequently enabled Desmond to obtain a preferential rate at a south coast home for retired vergers when, after his recuperation, Worple finally informed him that his days of staggering round the court were over. Now the play-ins were administered by Vivien Bradley, the ladies' team captain, an unmarried woman in her late thirties who was quite determined that, until she acquired a husband of her own, no younger or prettier female player would be admitted to impede her progress. The latter qualification put a radically low premium on prettiness and it was said by some that a young woman would have to have an astigmatic squint or a hare lip before she could be invited to join.

Tom Hall was an honorary member by virtue of his voluntary position as tennis master at Parsons Primary School which, having no grounds of its own, rented two courts from the club on Tuesday and Wednesday mornings. Cricket was the official school sport for boys but after an initial assessment, promising pupils could choose to play tennis instead and catch up on their art and woodwork classes in the afternoon. Four places in the junior section of the Fulham and Gibraltar were traditionally kept open for Parsons pupils and it was Tom's prerogative to make the selection.

Peter Winston had not expressed any particular enthusiasm for the game; he was only ten and seemed happy to try his hand at all sports. But he was an only child from a single-parent family and Hall, whether he admitted it to himself or not, gravitated towards pupils without fathers. He had no children of his own, nor wife, nor likelihood of wife. Most women, he discovered, reminded him of his own mother and irritated him just as much. If one was able to exist without the permanent partnership of a nagging and capricious woman so much the better. He had lived like this for the first quarter of his life and it amazed him that so many men rushed into similar bondage for the remaining three-quarters.

In another age he would have been regarded as an old-fashioned bachelor but in the late eighties he had to suffer the insinuation of being a confirmed one, the gossip column argot for homosexual. Occasionally, through mischievous or honest intent, people would send him invitations to Gay Rights Marches. The thought filled Hall with horror: he was as allergic to overt queers, as he called them, as he was to overweening mothers. Like a latterday Jean Brodie, the cream in his coffee was provided by the satisfaction of shaping and maturing young minds.

'It's all too jerky,' he reprimanded Peter as his pupil slithered to return the ball. 'The backhand is the most artistic shot in the game. It's like the cover drive at cricket or a perfectly swung wood at golf. Grace, timing and the follow-through. Cross with your right foot and lower your centre of gravity. It's essentially a balletic movement.'

The analogies left his pupil confused. Peter was experiencing enough difficulty connecting with the ball, let alone doing so with grace. Having hit nothing but backhands for the past forty minutes he was beginning to become bored and tired but help was at hand in the sun-blotting shape of Ernie Ebam, followed faithfully by his Filipina wife, Tang.

'You nearly finished then?' In terms of territorial acquisition tact was not the foremost element in Ernie's vocabulary. He had spent too many years at the helm of a black London taxi, a position that licensed the driver to scream abuse at those ahead and half-inaudible opinions at those behind, to have acquired any veneer of sensitivity. Despite having hung up his medallion many years previously, the thought of manoeuvering into an already occupied parking space greatly appealed to him.

'No we're not, Ernie,' Tom Hall retorted, pointing to his watch. 'This court comes free at six o'clock – seventeen minutes by my reckoning.'

'But the other courts are full.'

Tom stopped feeding balls to Peter who was beginning to feel uncomfortable and looked around him. 'You're right, Ernie, they are. They have that in common with this one.'

'But you're playing with a junior. Tang and I have priority.'

'Not until after six o'clock.' Tom's lips started to tighten. 'Then you may have the court. In sixteen minutes.'

'Is he a member?' Ernie indicated Peter with his venerable wooden Maxply, clearly intent on pursuing the argument for the next quarter of an hour.

'He is a fully paid-up junior member and, if I may continue with this coaching session, likely to become a privileged one.'

'Erlie say too many of those arleady,' Tang chimed in. 'Too much pliverege, too few room.'

Tang was a consistent echo of her husband's thoughts. Although younger than him by more than thirty years, she remained for ever – or for as long as he was likely to remain – in his debt for buying her a marguerita at the Matsuoka Club in Soho (a place known mainly to Filipinas and taxi drivers) and rescuing her from a life of penurious au pairdom. Their marriage worked as well as most: during the day she was his energetic doubles partner, scampering to areas of the court prohibited to him by his belly, and at night they sat in front of the television, each with an A–Z in hand as he guided her in 'the knowledge' – the minute details of London streets that aspiring cabbies must commit to memory. It was unlikely to be of much practical benefit to Tang as she was unable to drive. But it proved an unusual game and a poignant pointer for many of her husband's reminiscences.

'Whatever Ernie may say' – Tom was determined not to lose this battle, especially in front of his pupil – 'the rules say that juniors may not only play but be treated as normal human beings up until six o'clock. Then, like cattle, you may shoo them off the pasture.'

'I couldn't agree more.' Ernie Ebam's tone altered from belligerent to condescending. 'Your recollection of the rule is absolutely word-perfect. Unfortunately it also confirms that you are currently breaking it.'

Tom was astounded. 'In what way?'

'The salient word is "play", junior members may "play". But this young lad wasn't playing. He was being coached. And a game takes precedence over that.'

Hall opened his mouth to answer back but was given no time.

'I'll tell you what, we'll compromise,' Ernie conceded as he wobbled over to Peter's side of the court.

It was game, set and match to the former cabbie before a ball had been struck.

'You serve, Tang,' he called to his wife and then turned his attention to Peter. 'Now listen son, no fancy footwork and big swings. Just put the ball in the court – if we don't have a rally we won't get pally, all right?'

• *Eighteen* •

'You can do anything you like to me. Anything you want. That's how I feel today.'

Dawson paused, his trousers in his hand, as the information wafted out of the lighted bathroom. He placed the turn-ups under his chin and folded them in his usual deliberate fashion. With an invitation like that, he wondered if he should have flung them across the room in reckless abandon. Instead he carefully unknotted his tie and rolled it up, placing it by his cuff-links on the bedside table.

'I guess you've never had an offer like that before, Dawson. I'm like a very expensive restaurant with no menu. You can eat anything you like.' The woman giggled at her own remark.

He slowly unbuttoned the front of his shirt, experiencing a pleasure from it akin to undressing her. Not only had he never had such a suggestion, he hadn't had sex at all since his ill-fated experience with a New York call-girl twelve years, ten months and twenty-seven days ago. Helena Bell had come out of the blue. She had telephoned his office, informing him she had been impressed by a short piece he had contributed to the *American Actuary* – 'The Benefits of Early Death on the Corporate Pension Fund'. She, herself, was a freelance financial journalist and was doing an article on what prominent Boston people thought about Dukakis's state fiscal plans – whether they would translate into a national success if he were elected President next month. Dawson had thought the prospects of the Governor of Massachusetts beating George Bush were an actuarial impossibility, let alone bothering about his financial plans in the unlikely event that he formed a first administration.

But he didn't say so. He said yes. The woman on the phone sounded bright and friendly and was prepared to stand him lunch at the Ritz-Carlton where she was staying. Although she had run a small tape recorder during the meal, the conversation on any potential Dukakis budget had been extremely limited. He worried that he was not giving her enough information but she assured him that he would, unfortunately, only be forming a brief part of a long article. Instead she did most of the talking, telling him about her marriage and her little girl and what a worthless shit her husband had turned out to be. He had gone back to Barcelona – where he came from – to resume his practice as an architect. She suspected he had only married her for a Green Card and because she spoke Spanish. Marta, their daughter, was spending the rest of the year with him but she was going to collect her at Christmas.

He had started the meal with a pair of Manhattans and had managed to consume most of the Californian Sauvignon before they got to the main course. Intoxicated with Helena's attentive company and his intake of wine so far, he ordered an expensive bottle of Mondavi Opus Dei, insisting he would pay. Dawson had found himself empathising with her predicament. He told her about his own son, glossing over the exact details of the child's birth but merely indicating that he and the boy's mother had also split up. Enthusiastically he outlined his plans to go and live with James in Florida when the financial tide turned.

'In some ways it's sad,' she said, 'to have only one child. Not sad, more unfair to them, bringing them up on their own with no brothers or sisters.'

Unprompted but curiously proud, Dawson announced: 'In fact we had two.'

'Really?'

'Twins, funnily enough. The other boy lives with his mother but at some stage we'll sort things out.'

He realised he had revealed more than he intended and asked her never to tell anyone about this, explaining he was still not free from the tangles of his marriage. Helena put her hand on his – both a gesture of reassurance and a strong sexual signal – and requested him to keep a similar silence regarding her misfortune. If any over-eager immigration official were to get wind of the possibility that she had been involved in a Green Card marriage, then all sorts of trouble might ensue.

Their shared secrets created an intimacy between them and, from the moment the blackcurrant sherbet was served there was little doubt that the meal would end in bed. So he found himself now, palpitating with excitement, barely daring to slide off his boxer shorts because he was in such an agitated state of arousal that he feared he might ejaculate all over them.

Helena appeared from the bathroom. She had fluffed out her shoulder-length hair, her breasts were full and motherly and her skin looked dark and delicious.

'Do you want these panties on or off?' she demanded, slipping her thumbs into the elastic.

'You decide' – his voice came dry and faint – 'off eventually.'

'You may have to earn that,' she warned, advancing towards him. 'Now lie on your front and close your eyes. We need to make you a little less tense.'

He happily did as he was bid. He would have done anything for her at that moment. The total sexual freedom that she had apparently put on offer had the paradoxical effect of making him the servant.

'Just relax,' she said softly, as she lifted a small jar from the side of the bed and rubbed a warm sticky substance into the back of his neck and the top of his shoulders. It loosened him slightly but, further down his body, he could feel the silken grip of her thighs on either side of his buttocks and the occasional caress of her pubic hair as she moved gently to and fro.

'That's better,' she whispered on his behalf as she worked her way down to the small of his back. She was no longer astride him but was now kneeling on the bed to his left with her hands resting on the other side of him. He could feel the touch of her aroused nipples traced lightly across his back. Without warning his body contracted in shock as he felt her tongue dart deep into his rectum. It was not a thing he had ever experienced before, the equivalent of a starving man being offered a scoop of caviar.

'You like that, don't you?' she murmured as she turned him over and attacked him again with her tongue, licking round his scrotum like a cat confronted with cream and then slowly working her way up his penis as if it were a stick of seaside rock.

'Come,' Helena commanded as she dropped her mouth over it and he instantly obeyed, the years of abstinence flowing out of his body in juddering waves of ecstasy.

She gulped it down with evident pleasure and, for the first time since she had come to the bed, brought her lips up to meet his.

'There,' she smiled. 'Feel good?'

'Wonderful,' he gasped.

'With all that inside you I think you could have fathered a regiment of sons. I'm not surprised you had twins. It's a wonder you managed to avoid quintuplets.'

'I don't think the two factors are mathematically . . .' he began. 'Well, who knows? What the hell.'

'How did you decide?' Helena had begun to caress him again and to his amazement there was still life, or renewed life, in his empty member.

'Decide what?'

'Which twin to choose. It must have been difficult. Or did your wife do it?'

He found it hard to believe but he was actually beginning to harden again. 'No, I chose. I chose the first-born. I suppose that's the natural heir.'

'How romantic. You are a romantic, aren't you – once you set aside your calculator?'

'I suppose we all are.'

'Are you sure he was born first? I mean, did you witness the birth? Your wife could have said anything.'

'I wasn't there but of course I'm sure. Why do you want to know?' Dawson was suspicious of the turn in the conversation but at the same time greedy to have her.

'I just want to know a little bit more about you,' she said, tickling his chest with her copper-coloured locks.

'Do you know enough?' he asked.

'Almost,' she smiled, 'we've found out what you can manage with my panties on. Now let's see what you can do when you take them off – no hands allowed.'

The following day Dawson had his doubts and the day after that he was certain. His worst fears had been realised. He examined his penis in the bathroom mirror and though there was no sign of any blotches or suppuration or anything like that, he was convinced he felt pain when he urinated and a general itchy discomfort that had never been there before. He had undoubtedly contracted some sexually transmitted disease.

When he was a student others in the fraternity would joke about such things and shrug it off after they had been to the clinic for a penicillin injection. But sex was more serious now. You died of it. He leafed through the medical dictionary to find out the early symptons of AIDS but the book was five years old, too ancient even to mention the disease.

What a gullible idiot he had been. He should have seen it coming. There was no such thing as free sex any more. He, above all people, should have been able to assess the risk in having intercourse with someone who offered her favours so eagerly.

It was well after hours at Dr Michaels' consulting room on Beacon Hill and all he got was a recording machine referring him to another doctor at Karger Orthopaedic. Dawson was damned if he was going to publicise his problems by taking them to someone else. They might become all too public in the end, anyway, if he were to be condemned to some hospice, wasting away.

Yet he needed help. There was no chance of him falling asleep that night with his mind in the state it was. Should he contact Helena Bell and confront her with the problem? He would have done so unhesitatingly, only she had left Boston the following day and he had no number for her in New York.

'Shit,' he snarled for the hundredth time as he did up his belt. 'Shit, shit, shit.'

There was nothing else for it: he would go and search for Edmund Michaels. The doctor might be at a private dinner party but he was more likely to be eating at some restaurant. Dawson grabbed a local guide from the bedroom shelf. The chances were that someone earning a hundred and fifty to two hundred thousand dollars a year would expect to spend more than a hundred dollars on dinner for two – that should narrow the field. He circled the most fashionable restaurants in this category, noting ironically that Locke-Obers, where he had initiated his sex-free mating with Grace Winston, was at the top of the list. God, how on earth was he going to explain it to James if the worst came to the worst?

The moment he hit the remote-control button to raise the electronic garage door, inspiration struck. Maybe it was the presence of the scientific gadget in his hand. There was just a chance – but a better than even one – that Michaels was sequestered in a laboratory rather than sitting in a restaurant. On the last occasion they had met, the doctor had mentioned he had bought the lease to the little lab he had taken Dawson to after their lunch at the Orson Welles cinema and said he was embarking on some exciting research work. Dawson racked his brains to try to remember where it was; it had been a walk away, just around the corner. He pulled a map out of the glove compartment and tried to look for it. But, in the dim light of the car, his sight wasn't strong enough. He would drive towards Cambridge and see if he could remember.

His eyes may have been weak but his memory was acute and he found the place without difficulty, as if he had been there the previous day: Castor Street, just off Massachusetts Avenue. The small backwater was packed with cars on both sides but there was a space by a fire hydrant. Dawson decided to risk it. They said the firemen would ram their hose through your windows if they needed to get to the hydrant, but Dawson had always calculated that in an emergency they could hardly spare the time to administer the punishment.

There was a light on in number eighty-eight. His luck was holding. Dawson scanned the door for a bell or even a knocker but could find neither. Perhaps Michaels preferred not to be disturbed. Well, tonight would have to be an exception: he was the only person he could trust. The actuary hammered unrepentantly on the solid wooden door.

The surprised and defensive expression on the doctor's face as he edged it open immediately confirmed that his privacy had been violated.

'Thank God you're here. You must help me.' Dawson began directly.

Michaels was mystified. 'What's wrong? Are you injured?'

'Worse than that. Can I come in?'

'Couldn't you come to my surgery tomorrow? We're at a vital

stage in an experiment.' But as he looked at Silver he could see the man was clearly in a state of acute distress. 'You'd better come in,' he conceded.

Dawson thankfully followed him up the ill-lit stairs. Not much had changed in the dozen years since he had last been there, certainly not much in the way of paint.

'We're going to have to share the room with my lab assistant,' Michaels called back over his shoulder. 'It's okay, he's a very bright boy.'

'No.' Dawson halted on the stair. 'This is highly confidential. Can't you send him home? It's late.'

'I told you, we're in the middle of something. If we stopped now we'd have a lot of dead cells on our hands. He can take ten minutes – any more and we're in schtuck.'

'That'll do,' Dawson breathed gratefully.

A youthful-looking black man in a long laboratory coat which almost reached down to his boot-like sneakers, his hair militarily short but oiled like a pop star, was labelling a bottle as they came in. Dr Michaels, sensitive to Dawson's state, didn't introduce him by name. 'Kelvin, this a patient of mine – having a bit of difficulty sleeping. I need to check out a couple of things before we pop some pills in him. Could you give us ten?'

'Sure thing, no problem.' The assistant carefully placed the small bottle with some others in the metal sink. 'Three mils of rohypnol does the trick for my mamma,' he added with a grin as he passed Dawson. 'Makes her feel pretty good the next day, too.'

'I dread to think what else he prescribes her,' Michaels whispered under his breath after the door was closed. 'She probably runs a tab at Superdrug.'

Silver was not interested in anybody else's problems. He grabbed Edmund by the elbow. 'Listen, I'm in big trouble. I went to bed with this woman and she gave me a dose. Worse maybe. What does AIDS feel like?'

'Nothing on earth,' the doctor replied drily. 'When did this happen?'

'Two days ago – Thursday.'

Michaels adjusted his bow-tie condescendingly. 'Determined to be the first heterosexual male over the age of sixty to contract AIDS in the State of Massachusetts. You actuaries are all the same.'

His patient was not amused.

Edmund gave him a reassuring pat on the shoulder. 'Bit premature for your diagnosis of AIDS – it usually takes a year or two to germinate. Early even for herpes simplex.'

'It hurts when I pee,' exclaimed Silver.

The doctor lifted a pair of thin white rubber gloves from the side of an instrument tray and began to powder them, preparatory to slipping them on. 'Let's have a look at you. Take down your trousers – over there by the light.'

Dawson felt like a truant schoolboy as he meekly obeyed, a tremble shooting up his spine when Michaels gently lifted his scrotum.

'It's okay. I'm not going to hurt you.' He knelt down and explored the area with a slim pencil of light. 'Neither did she, by the look of things. No purulent urethral discharge. No sign of pediculosis pubis.'

'What's that?' Dawson asked anxiously.

'Crabs,' Michaels straightened himself up. 'Good old Boston crabs. I don't think you have much to worry about.'

'But the pain . . .' Dawson began.

'Pain takes place in here.' Michaels tapped the side of his head. 'You think you have pain when you urinate because you think you have a sexually transmitted disease. Maybe you think you deserve one. But you have no symptoms – not at the moment, anyway.'

'They could come later.' Dawson was not persuaded.

'Oh for God's sake.' The doctor was beginning to get annoyed. 'I'll give you a shot of penicillin – just to set your mind at rest – and I'll put you on some pills for the next five days. Don't pull up your trousers just yet.'

'Thank you.' For the first time since he had left Helena's bed Dawson began to relax a little.

Searching the shelves, Michaels found the ampule he was looking for and drained it with a hypodermic syringe.

'Turn around,' he ordered, 'it works better in the butt.'

'What do you do about these diseases when you're dealing with pregnancies?' Dawson put the question as much to prevent an uncomfortable silence as to satisfy any real spirit of enquiry. 'With your donors and surrogates and people . . . isn't there a danger?'

'None whatsoever.' The doctor targeted the needle into the soft flesh of his rump. 'We have the only flawless way – we can check out everything in lab conditions. Just like this, I can microinject a pure sperm into an egg after superovulation. One day human sex will become just an irrelevant sport – and maybe a rather dangerous one. I don't know why you bother.'

'Me neither,' agreed his patient penitently.

Michaels withdrew the hypodermic and patted the point of entry with some cotton-wool. 'Don't have to trouble so much with surrogates these days. We can mix it all up in vitro, as you know. I've been working on a preimplantation diagnosis to make sure the child is pretty well flawless. We take a single cell from an early embryo – the rest of the embryo is frozen and stored – and we grow the removed cell in the lab and screen it for chromosomal damage. Any problems and we eliminate the defective gene and pop in a new one. There, you can do up your trousers, but I wouldn't sit down for a moment.'

With his state of acute panic somewhat assuaged, Dawson was better able to absorb his surroundings. Beneath the window-sill, well away from the work surfaces, there were two large cages: one with sleeping rats, the other with tiny mice moving silently around.

'What happened to Eugenia?' he enquired.

'Oh, she died,' Michaels noted with mock-sadness while slowly drying his hands. 'But in a good cause.'

'And Dr Steigenberger, is he still alive?'

'Dr . . . who?' The twitch that, until now, had been absent from the doctor's eyes made a rapid return.

'The old guy you told me about – who rented this place. Horst.'

'Oh, Horst.' The name seemed to prompt his memory. 'Him, too. Dead. Back home in Vienna. Got a better funeral than Mozart, though.'

Dawson was almost certain it had been Innsbruck: his recollection of facts and figures was rarely wrong. He was about to point this out but the clattering return of Kelvin, angrily brandishing a copy of the following day's *Boston Globe*, put paid to that.

'What a dumb-headed dude. They breed 'em up there in Canada.

To get caught like that. They've taken away his gold medal. Quite right, too. Take it away for stupidity.'

Michaels removed the paper from him and Dawson glanced at the front page over his shoulder.

'Ben Johnson – the Seoul brother,' Kelvin went on. 'The Olympics have certainly become amateur again – a load of amateur pharmacists. What a fuck-up, they're all so little league.'

'What do you mean?' Dawson felt unsettled, intimidated even, by the young man's onslaught.

'A few anabolic steroids don't make no difference. Not compared with what we got.' Kelvin made a dramatic gesture towards the cages by the window. 'See those rodents there. Those big boys took the right stuff. They all brothers.'

'Not exactly brothers,' Michaels intervened. 'We isolated a gene for growth hormone from rats. And then we removed the eggs from female mice and fertilised them here, in a test tube. And when fertilisation occurred, we injected the rat's gene, the one for growth hormone, into the eggs and put them back inside the mice. As you can see for yourself,' he indicated the cage on the right with the sleeping animals, 'the result was rat-sized mice. Nearly twice the size of their litter mates.'

'But you're not suggesting that this can be applied to humans?' Dawson addressed his enquiry to Kelvin.

'They do it all the time, man. How do you think we deal with dwarfism? Pat the little kid on the head and tell him to grow up? No, the guys extract human growth hormone from the pituitary gland in the brain of some dead dude and pop it into a tiny child who grows up nice and tall. If old Ben Johnson's doc had given him a couple of shots of that, he wouldn't need to be fooling around with no kiddies' candies.'

'It's only used in the most extreme cases.' Michaels was keen to play down his assistant's notion of laboratory-created athletes. 'Besides, it's not our field. But we are coming close to isolating the single gene that makes the difference between men and women. It may soon be possible to change the sex of the embryos of those mice over there by injecting the newly fertilised eggs with just a fragment of DNA. So far we've failed but they've been encouraging failures. We could be on the verge . . .'

'When was that taken?' Silver was no longer listening to him. Kelvin had opened a cupboard door to put away the remainder of the syringes and his attention had been caught by a photograph stuck on the inside. 'I've never seen that picture of James before. I didn't know you had it.'

'Oh that, Edmund Michaels was looking discernibly flustered. 'Let me see. I think Violet sent it the Christmas before she died. Said he was in a school play or something.'

Dawson could remember no such play. He leant over, his buttock still smarting from the injection, for a better look at the fading Polaroid. His son appeared to be dressed as a Greek god – Pan, to judge by the pipes – and his head was garlanded with a laurel wreath.

· Nineteen ·

The return of serve surprised Winston. It came blistering back towards him, homing in on his heels. He knew he should have followed his second service into the net but the ball had left his racquet so uncertainly that he feared a forward run would have left him vulnerable on either flank. Instead he was vulnerable at his feet. He hopped deftly to his right and lowered his racquet head to the ball's probable point of arrival, praying that it might land out.

But it didn't. It rifled into the ground just short of the line as if it were intent on damaging the court. Mo always insisted it was impossible to keep visual track of a fast ball in the last five feet of its approach so Winston attempted this blind block shot, trying to anticipate the point of impact. To his amazement he connected. The half-volley ballooned back over the net but straight into the waiting racquet of his opponent who ruthlessly punched it into the opposite corner and the point into oblivion.

Worse, much worse, than losing the point was the noise. The crowd loved it. They rose to their feet and crashed their palms together and howled their delight while at the same time managing to signal their derision.

He was close to tears but close was as far as he intended to get. After retrieving the offending ball from the corner he prepared to serve again, ostentatiously not bothering with another for a second serve. There was no wind as he threw it precisely into the air, lowering his centre of gravity as if he were sitting down on some invisible rocket which would propel him upwards. He blasted off accordingly, making contact with both feet flying from the ground.

The screeching ball satisfyingly nuzzled the outside of the centre line, leaving his opponent flat-footed and outmanoeuvred.

'Out,' called the umpire without hesitation, and the crowd cheered in agreement.

'What?' Winston had turned to pick up the balls for his next serve. He should now be only 30–40 down. This was outrageous. 'Could you repeat that call?'

The lean man in the white tracksuit, the sparse strands of his remaining hair educated across his balding dome, looked impassively ahead. 'Out,' he repeated.

'What do you mean?' Winston strode towards the chair. 'It came off the line. You saw it yourself. It was an ace, a pure ace.'

Any further remonstration was impossible amid the uproar from the crowd. They howled and hissed and cheered and booed. The umpire held up his watch and indicated that he was allowing Winston only twenty more seconds to get back for his second serve.

The player shook his head in anger and amazement and returned deliberately slowly to the baseline to see if the guy would have the nerve to penalise him. But that would have been too much.

He removed the ball from his pocket and began to bounce it methodically, one, two, three, four . . . still no penalty. So he arched his back and released it in the air, bringing his racquet down with less impact than before but equal accuracy to see if he could find exactly the same spot on the line. He did, to within a millimetre. But this time the ball came back, with interest, pummelled straight at his stomach as he moved in towards the net. His feet feinted to the left but he angled the head of his racquet to the right and the ball crashed with brutal accuracy into the opposing service court and spun out across the tramlines well beyond any hope of return.

The crowd reacted with unbroken silence. Not a murmur, not a sound save the umpire's 'deuce.'

His next service was fast and deep but the return came back faster. It caught Winston before he had found his balance, and when his uncontrolled volley flew past the baseline without touching the ground the place once again burst into joyous life with prolonged whoops and cheers.

This time he could do nothing to stop himself. As he took his position on the baseline for what could be the final point he looked across the net but he could barely discern his opponent. His eyes were moist with involuntary tears and there was little he could do to hide them. He tried to brush them away with the alternate sweatlets of either wrist but he was fooling nobody as the cruel catcalling and slow hand-clapping duly informed him.

He served two double-faults and that was that. Walking reluctantly to the umpire's chair, his head lowered in ignominy, he tried to console himself with the thought that when this round of cheers came to an end it would at least be the last one.

'You did okay, Jim,' acknowledged Dr Bob, stepping down from the chair. 'You held out longer than most. I've seen some kids crack in the first game. Never managed to win another.'

Jenny, the blonde teenage girl in shiny green satin shorts who had just taken the set 6–4, offered him a hand and a smile. 'Wow!' she said to the umpire. 'What a high. I felt like Mick Jagger out there.'

James had grabbed his striped brown-and-white Osprey towel from his stool by the net and, after responding to Jenny with a reluctant handshake, threw it over his head.

'None of you leave' – Dr Bob had brought the portable microphone down from the umpire's chair – 'we've got some lessons to learn. I know a lot of you will have attended one of these "foreign field" sessions before but you may as well get the message again so that it stays with you for the rest of your lives.'

He adjusted a strand of hair on his brow and cleared his mouth behind his hand as if he were about to commence an electoral address. 'There are some countries in this world that are not as fairminded as the United States of America. I'm not going to name any names – we've got some students from abroad among us – but if you were to find yourself playing the final vital rubber of a Davis Cup tie in, say, Argentina or Italy or France you could well be facing the biased mob you provided for Jim Winston today. Not just the crowd – there are some videos in the library of the final of the 1976 Italian Open at the Foro Italico won, as you can see for yourselves, not just by Adriano Panatta but also by ten thousand fellow Romans, most notably the line judges. In these circumstances it's human nature for the foreign competitor to find himself playing two opponents: the other guy and the home crowd – which, incidentally, was pretty good this morning. A lot of you seem to have Sicilian blood in your veins.'

The students struck up again in mock applause. There were less than three hundred of them but they had managed to achieve a decibel level of several thousand.

'However, here at Osprey,' Dr Bob quietened them down with an admonitory wave, 'we're not interested in human nature. We're on a journey beyond that venturing into the realms of the super-human. Now Jenny, here, according to our computer records would only take three games off Jim in a conventional set, all other things being equal.'

'Four, last time.' The blonde girl was still ecstatic but anxious to set the statistics straight.

'Thing's weren't equal on that occasion,' Dr Bob shot back – he didn't take kindly to being corrected. 'Jim was nursing a shoulder strain and serving at seventy per cent. Anyway, that's not the point. We only permit a student to play a foreign field match here when we think he or she is on the top of their form mentally and physically. Now, normally you practise with no crowd reaction and all your motivation and emotion comes from within. And that's how it always should be, whether you're on the center court at Flushing Meadow or playing in the park: you have to have as much control over your mind as you do over your shots.'

'But what if the crowd gets behind you, like we did with Jenny?' The questioner was a heavily muscled senior student seated at the top of the bleachers.

'It's a variable,' Dr Bob was adamant, 'and we don't deal in variables. What you have to have, Bruno – and here's the crux of this experiment – is the ability to create the noise of the crowd in your head as if you were wearing a Sony Walkman. I've always thought the ideal tournament player should be deaf, if he didn't have to listen for the sound of the other guy's stroke. So when you're out there we teach you to become selectively deaf.'

'But I felt so fantastically pumped up,' Jenny was still in a state of physical exhilaration. 'Like, if my friends and family came to every game nobody could beat me.'

'It wouldn't last. It's an artificial stimulant, a dangerous drug even, because you'd find yourself unable to win without it. In here'

– Dr Bob pointed to a spot between his eyes – 'are all your supporters. Those fuckers out there' – his arm waved round the rising rows of benches that surrounded the court – 'don't know what you know. They don't know when a winner was a mis-hit from the top of the strings; they don't know when your zipper down the line was intended to head cross-court; they don't know when you hit an accidental ace because you mistimed the kick and your opponent read it wrong. But you know. Only you know where perfection lies. And, in your head, you isolate your errors and cheer yourself on towards perfection. Now, Jim,' he poked the microphone under the towel that was still covering James's head, 'you still alive in there? How did it feel?'

Winston emerged from under his Osprey towel, his eyes still rheumy and red.

'That call,' he looked bitterly at Dr Bob's thin lips, 'the first serve at 15–40. It was good.'

'Yep,' the teacher agreed impassively.

'So why did you give it out?'

'A major part of the foreign field experience. All the A-grade seniors and juniors have suffered the same. Larry, up there, got an identical call when he was serving to save and his ball was inside the line. However, he stood his ground and argued the point. The crowd threw shit at him but he didn't allow it to get to him. And after a couple of minutes I agreed a let. You gave up too easily, Jim.'

'But . . . like in the Italian Open . . . there's no way some Roman umpire is going to change his call.'

'You never can tell.' Dr Bob now addressed his remarks to the students at large. 'If you really believe the call was unfair you have to let the linesmen, and the umpire, and the crowd, and even the people watching on TV know. You probably won't get that point but the next close call won't be given against you that easily. Your ma ain't going to come and change your diapers any more, Jim. You've got to deal with your own shit.'

The remark stung the twelve-year-old child with particular venom; he wondered if the instructor had made it because he was aware that James had never known a mother. He had treated Dr Bob with circumspection since the day he had been dumped in Osprey. The only Dr Bob he had come across at that point in his life was the chuckling one in the loud sports coat who delivered the weather forecast on television. For a while, James thought he was a real doctor who cured people in his spare time. But Aunt Vi had ended this illusion. She said he just called himself that to make him sound more authoritative; he probably didn't have any qualifications at all – save the ability to get the weather wrong.

Now James harboured similar suspicions about Dr Bob Borogon. The day after he had arrived at the academy, a boy in his class had slipped and cut his knee badly on the concrete entrance steps. James remembered seeing the word 'doctor' on a door just off the hall and knocked on it to summon help. However Dr Bob seemed annoyed at being interrupted and took time to indicate to James the term 'Sports Psychologist' on his name-plate before he came to look. After examining the injury with professional concern, he pronounced that it called for stitches – and confessed that this was not something he was able to perform. He helped the child along to the school surgery where Sister cleaned the wound and said a strong bandage would be quite enough.

Dr Bob had little to do with the younger students and initially James wondered whether a sports psychologist was someone like a television weatherman, only he guessed the results of tennis matches as opposed to warm fronts. Sometimes when children cried at night because they were homesick they were sent along for a chat with Dr Bob, but the result was usually that they cried even more since his traditional advice – even to ten-year-olds – was to 'toughen up'.

There was a distinctly military air about Osprey Academy, not least because the place occupied the former camp of the Third Florida Infantry Division who had abandoned it shortly after the cessation of hostilities in Vietnam. An astute Brooklyn property developer, Melvin Lacey, had bought it cheap from the Department of Defense, even down to the sheets and bedding. With minimal refurbishment, Lacey rapidly turned it into the Osprey Children's Camp.

He found, however, that while it was busy in the school holidays his capital investment was earning nothing during the rest of the year. The solution had come from his part-time tennis coach, Moses Hoffman, a wiry, wizened Californian who claimed once to have played on the West Coast circuit. The children loved the little man – he taught them rhymes to remind them of techniques and told them stories of the great players of the past. Much of the repeat business at the Camp was attributable to him.

At the end of the summer of 1977 Moses tossed a new tennis magazine across the proprietor's desk. 'Page five – beaten in the Davis Cup by Argentina, would you believe? This is the country that produced Johnston and Tilden and Patty and Kramer and Ashe and now we get pushed around by the Third World.'

'So?' Lacey seemed unimpressed by the lament.

'So the government's going to do something about it.' Moses took the magazine back from him and flicked through the pages, stopping at a small article near the back. 'See, the National Council for the Promotion of Physical Fitness is prepared to offer interest-free loans of up to two million dollars for any approved plan to benefit the tuition of tennis in this country.'

At the words 'interest-free' Lacey's attention was immediately galvanised. His eyes eagerly scanned the conditions to see where the catch was; there always was one. But on this occasion the offer seemed straightforward.

'What are you suggesting, Moses?' he enquired guardedly. 'That I build a couple of courts here with a government loan? Why not?'

'No,' the coach kept a poker face. 'What I'm suggesting is that you build twenty-four courts here and a further six inside those hangars over by the helipad. Turn it into a tennis camp. Help me to make a new American champion and help yourself to a great deal of money.'

At first James Winston hated the place. The gloom of that October morning in 1987 when Wall Street crashed and the world went with it permeated the unwelcome wooden building that was to be his dormitory for the forseeable future. He was right about Edmund Michaels: the doctor seemed to have made all the contingency plans. As Moses Hoffman sat on the upright chair in his sparse room he glanced through hand-written medical notes on James that had been faxed down from Boston. Even his father had been surprised by this. He was less surprised not to meet Melvin Lacey who had left town over the weekend on urgent business matters – doubtless to try and stem his own stock market losses. As Dawson sat beside James on the ungiving army bed, he feared that it might now be many years before his retirement plan could take shape. Always remember, had been his professor's parting words at college, always remember to watch out for the incalculable.

Moses sensed the child's nervousness and the parent's concern – he was used to this experience – and tried to set both their minds at rest. He acknowledged that the surroundings were still primitive but assured Dawson that when they entered the next phase of the five-year plan, children would have new quarters with thick carpets and individual bathrooms. The place looked spartan with nobody in it, he explained, but when the rest of the kids returned from their obligatory morning classes at the local high school it took on the life of an extended happy family. James would be able to join them for lunch and then would go into the Little Hawks tennis class that afternoon.

Dawson apologised for the fact that his son did not come with a record of any prowess at the game but Hoffman cut him off with the avowal that they preferred it that way, otherwise the first term was wasted undoing other people's inept coaching. There was an Osprey Method, he said, to which all the teachers adhered.

After the coach had left them, promising to send Sister along to help the boy stow his kit and asking Dawson to drop by the office on the way out to sign a few forms, father and son sat side by side on the narrow bed, subdued into silence by the shock of the past few days and the unspoken uncertainty about the future. There was a continuing fear at the back of Silver's mind that one day James might learn everything: the nature of his conception; who his mother was; the fact that he had a twin brother; even the manner in which his upbringing had been fraudulently financed. But he would not hear about any of these things from his father's lips. And if he learned about them after he died, well, too bad. It wouldn't harm Dawson. Death was final: nobody had ever asked for a pension from beyond the grave.

He was still trying to work out in his mind how much money he had lost in the crash. It was a futile exercise; the news on the car radio on their way to Osprey had said that prices were continuing to plunge. He needed to get back to Boston as soon as possible and see what he could retrieve from his portfolio.

'Well,' he shrugged, getting up from the bed. 'At least you've got a racquet.'

'Have I?' enquired James sourly.

'Sure, the one Dr Michaels gave you.'

'Oh that, I threw that away.'

Dawson knew better than to ask why. Instead he searched in his inside pocket and removed his wallet. 'Here,' he insisted, handing James two fifty-dollar bills, 'I should imagine you can get the sports stuff on credit at the school shop but you may need some liquid cash. Go easy though. Listen, I have to get back – you heard the chaos in the car.'

As he patted his son on the head he failed to read the look of resentment and betrayal on the ten-year-old's face.

'Put your racquets down on the ground, everybody, and all hold hands.'

It was the familiar start of Dr Bob's shoot-to-kill lesson. The students jockeyed for position to avoid being next to the sports psychologist himself: his grip was bone-crushing, and his breath smelt. Today, however, James couldn't avoid it and only the security of his room mate, Andy, at the end of his other arm made his situation minimally more bearable.

'Dear Godabove' – Dr Bob yelled the phrase into the sky as if it were all one word – 'guide us this day with thy heavenly instinct to fight the good fight. May we cast aside worldly problems, doubts, insecurities and injuries, and in thy abiding light find a heavenly pathway to victory, through Jesus Christ's name. Amen.'

It was more than a mere grace; Dr Bob incanted the prayer with the zeal of a Crusader, as if there were some infidel foe that needed to be taught a lesson and then destroyed. Get into the mind of the enemy, he always insisted, think the way he thinks, know what he is going to do before he knows it himself – and then outwit him. Every match was a battle to the death with only one survivor. There are no second acts in American life, he would warn, quoting Scott Fitzgerald. Not all his sources were so literary: he loved to adapt the words of the former Liverpool soccer manager, Bill Shankly – 'Tennis isn't a matter of life and death – it's much more important than that.'

The class – there were twelve of them – released hands and waited for the day's parable.

'Jenny, over here.' He beckoned James's recent conqueror to come towards him. She approached with some trepidation, fearing he had seen the smile on her face during prayers.

Abruptly pointing towards her Osprey Academy T-shirt with his racquet, he demanded. 'What does that symbolise?'

She looked down at her maturing breasts in some surprise. 'Well, the college, I guess. Numquam non paratus. Never unprepared. Always ready.'

'That's true,' Borogon agreed, warming to his theme. 'But it means much more than a motto. An osprey is a hawk, the shrewdest and the wisest of the hunting birds. Its prey is a mindless fish. It doesn't even get its head wet to catch it. It waits and hovers, observing its victim's progress through the water. And when the time is right it plunges, feet first, to catch the fish with its long curved talons. The grip is as tight as your hand on your racquet, secured by sharp spicules on the underside of its toes. And then it takes the fish onto its own territory, to some favourite perch, to make a meal of it. And when it's all over the osprey flies low over the sea in triumph, washing its feet in the water.'

He regarded the class with his own hawk-like eyes. 'Do I need to make my message any clearer?'

'No, Dr Bob,' they chorused.

· Twenty ·

'Yours, Clarissa.'

The tooth-clenched military command echoed across the damp and undulating courts of the Fulham and Gibraltar Lawn Tennis Club and on to the smoother and unruffled waters of the River Thames beyond.

Alas, it was no use. Clarissa Crichton-Greene was a woman of a certain age, certainly the age when barked messages to her brain took more time to reach her trusty plimsolls than they might have done ten years ago. But she had evolved a style of tennis that ensured she had remained woman's singles champion at the FAGLTC for all of those ten years: she changed the racquet from her right to her left hand at will, thereby removing the vulnerability of a backhand; she refused to acknowledge the existence of the volley, playing nearly all of her game from the baseline; and, when in doubt, she lobbed – high, slow, painful and accurate. The fact that Vivien Bradley, who had cruelly dispatched this short ball to Clarissa's side of the net, had admitted no women under the age of thirty-five to the club during that period had assisted Clarissa's domination of the singles tournament. In fact, for the past seven years, she had beaten Vivien in the final.

But this was doubles and Clarissa was not prepared to embark on the journey from the baseline to the spot where Vivien's drop volley was about to commence its second bounce. Instead she rounded on her partner, Major Miller, and snapped back: 'No, yours.'

He knew better than to complain. Several years ago when he had wrongly interpreted a signal she had given off at the Christmas cocktail party and had attempted to give her a more than seasonal kiss Clarissa had made it clear to him that his tongue was not welcome in her mouth. When, emboldened by Dermot's Killarney punch, he had attempted to justify his presumption by expressing an emotional alibi for this lingual assault, she was quick to tell him that she had once been engaged to a Sandhurst man. A can of Mace could not have been more effective in rejecting his advances. Major Miller knew that she knew he had risen from the ranks and had left the army with the substantive rank of captain. The catering corps had once allowed him the temporary status of major which he now accorded to himself permanently. Besides, he was married with three children.

So while any intimate physical partnership was completely out of the question, Clarissa was quite happy to have him as a partner on court where they were anxious to win the Jacob Penderick Mixed Doubles Cup for the third year in succession and thereby make the replica of the trophy theirs to keep. But she was not prepared to have him shout at her, a fact her glare made abundantly clear as the yellow ball trickled past her gym shoes.

'Come on, Clarissa, hit a few winners and get it over with. We was due on this court twelve minutes ago. Bloody tournament.'

Ernie Ebam and his wife, Tang – their racquets at the ready – formed part of the sparse crowd watching the final on this damp September Sunday in 1990, but were not its most enthusiastic supporters. The heightened howl of the evening Concorde turned the heads of all towards the sky as the supersonic pilot throttled down route Ace 20 on his way home to Heathrow. Just over three hours ago he and his passengers had been in New York where a few days previously nineteen-year-old Pete Sampras had beaten both Ivan Lendl and John McEnroe to reach the final of the US Open and, at this very moment, was about to enter the Stadium Court at Flushing Meadow and do the same to André Agassi, thereby becoming the youngest-ever American champion.

Although six years younger than Sampras, another Pete – or rather Peter – was in his first major final as well. Vivien Bradley had kept a watchful eye on Peter Winston's progress over the past three years as he practised with Tom Hall when they could get a free court after school. She had noted how he would also turn up towards dusk on weekends, when most members had repaired to the bar, knowing there would be a free court and hoping there might be an available opponent. Ernie Ebam had always partnered Vivien in the mixed doubles tournament until that fateful night at the Matsuoka Club when he met Tang. Since then, nobody had asked her. So when Peter's game matured sufficiently she not so much requested as commanded him to be her partner. Coming from the ladies' captain, this was – as Tom Hall had pointed out – an offer he couldn't refuse.

Clarissa Crichton-Greene, sensing the danger to her doubles title from this pairing, had brought the matter up at a committee meeting, arguing that the juniors had a tournament of their own and were therefore disqualified from the senior one. Ken Worple, the chairman, had promised to read the rule book carefully and report back. Alas, the prelate who had drawn up the rules of competition in 1877 had failed to foresee such an eventuality: no mention of any minimum or maximum age requirements was anywhere to be found. So there was nothing to prevent Peter Winston playing and, at nearly six feet, he certainly fitted the bill physically.

'Keep it on Clarissa's side of the court,' Vivien whispered to him as she resumed her position after the winning volley. 'And if she summons up the energy to run, aim for her ankles.'

'No coaching, Vivien, you know the rules.' Clarissa, unable to eavesdrop on what was being discussed, had a more than fair idea that it was probably about her and was determined to interrupt it.

'It is quite permissible for doubles players to discuss tactics.' Vivien Bradley stared coldly at her opponent. 'If you had followed the careers of Nicola Pietrangeli and Orlando Sirola' – she gave the names the culinary flavour of an Italian waiter itemising a menu – 'you would know that they spent more time discussing the game than actually playing it.'

'The behaviour of a couple of wops is hardly the yardstick by which to re-interpret the rules of lawn tennis . . .'

'If you ladies are just going to carry on a conversation,' Ernie Ebam was looking pointedly at his watch, 'perhaps you could do it in the clubhouse.'

'We could not.' The ladies' captain switched her attention to her erstwhile partner. 'If you and Tang' – the name fell from her lips with a form of onomatopoeic disgust – 'had not been beaten by Clarissa and the major in the semi-finals, you would have the right to be on this court, Ernie. Having forfeited it, I would ask you to remain silent.'

'Erle onry wannagettagame beefor too dalk to pray.' Tang's interjections on her husband's behalf were rarely well-timed or beneficial.

'You too, Tang. Silent.' It was Clarissa Crichton-Greene, temporarily united with her opponent, who turned on the Filipina member.

'Come now,' Major Miller was anxious to stop this spat from escalating out of control, 'or it will be too dark for us to finish. Four–two to you, I think, and young Peter to serve.'

Peter Winston had become accustomed to the petty squabbles that attended nearly every match at the Fulham and Gibraltar Lawn Tennis Club. So much so that it seemed to him a normal aspect of the grown-up game that people should argue interminably about whether a given garment was white – and therefore permissible clothing under club rules – or the courts were dry enough to play on, or the ball was in or out or on the line or had bounced once or twice. He took it to be part and parcel of the entertainment members obtained from their tennis although he was prudent enough never to voice an opinion of his own. Another privileged junior had once tried that and a letter had immediately been posted to his parents informing them that he was no longer welcome at the club. Juvenile behaviour, Tom Hall sombrely pointed out, was the sole preserve of adult members.

'Peter, a word.'

The boy stopped his preparations to serve as Vivien came back to him from the net.

'Yes?' He wondered what he had done wrong.

'No need to soften your serve for Clarissa any longer,' Vivien was almost menacingly conspiratorial in her instruction. 'She's had a set and six games to get her eye in. Turn it up to full volume.'

'Play.' The intrusive shout, not without a hint of belligerence, came from the lady in question, stamping impatiently in the advantage court.

He cracked his first serve to the major who stabbed it tentatively back at Vivien, the ball hitting the top of the net and falling stonelike in front of her.

'Terribly sorry,' he said, with a gesture of regret. 'I really am sorry.'

'Yes, I'm sure you are,' replied Vivien, turning to Peter with rancour in her eyes.

'He did apologise,' the boy pointed out, *sotto voce*.

'It is one thing to say you're sorry,' rasped the ladies' captain, 'it is another to mean you're sorry. Now stick it to the bitch.'

Taking his captain at her word, Peter let loose a thunderbolt to Clarissa's backhand, or rather where her backhand would have been had she moved four paces to her left. Her only riposte was a look of lingering contempt. The major fluffed his next return into the net. 30–15. Was it Peter's imagination or was Miss Crichton-Greene mouthing the words 'don't you dare' at him as he threw up the ball again? Nothing daunted, he whacked it with his full force down the centre line, and this time his opponent spreadeagled herself like a fallen ballerina as she tried to alter direction. Peter immediately averted his eye to avoid her expression. The major looped his next return to Vivien at the net who snapped it away with tigerish satisfaction shouting simultaneously: 'Game, five–two to us,' loud enough for those on the clubhouse verandah to hear.

'I would have expected you to have been brought up with rather better manners,' Clarissa hissed in Peter's ear as they passed at the net to change ends.

'What did she say?' Vivien waited until their opponents were out of earshot before she made the enquiry.

'I think she was upset about the speed of my serves.' Peter was duly penitent. 'She does have a point. Mr Hall always says it's bad form to ace ladies.'

'As a general rule, yes.' Vivien attempted to put his conscience at rest. 'But there are always exceptions. Like this evening – failing light, people waiting to play. Besides, the result's a foregone conclusion. Sometimes it's fairer to shoot a wounded animal between the eyes to put it out of its misery.'

The result *was* a foregone conclusion. Clarissa, no longer retaining any stomach for the encounter after her inelegant sprawl – an incident made all the more humiliating by Tang's stifled snigger – served two double-faults in the final game and hardly bothered to run to return Vivien's winning volley.

'Jolly good. Four and two. Well done. Too fast for us, I'm afraid.' The major seemed oblivious to his partner's distress as he held out his hand across the net.

Peter was concerned that Miss Crichton-Greene might strike him over the head with her racquet as she made her reluctant way towards them but the deeply imbued requirement to be a good loser, a seminal element in English sporting education, took precedence over any immediate emotions. So even Clarissa proffered her congratulations, with the caveat 'quite a little cannonball you've found there, Vivien.'

'Hurry up will you, it's beginning to drizzle.' Ernie and Tang were beside them, eagerly unsheathing their racquets ready for play.

'The weather is hardly under our control, Ernie' – Clarissa was pleased to have found a target for her pent-up anger – 'although if your wife is under yours, you might inform her that it is not the tradition in this club – or country – to take delight in the misfortune of others.'

The drizzle had turned to a more sustained shower as the four finalists reached the clubhouse and the small chalice known as the Penderick Cup, which had been awaiting the winners on a table outside, was filling up with raindrops. Ken Worple shook out the water and attempted to dry off the trophy on his russet cardigan as he carried it in.

One or two faces looked up from the three Sunday afternoon bridge fours in progress there, half-annoyed at the unexpected invasion by the dozen or so people from outside. They became more wholly annoyed when Worple embarked on his speech.

'I would like to pay tribute to this year's finalists for a fine, sporting game and their excellent timing in getting it completed before the weather broke.'

'Four no trumps,' came a voice from the table nearest the bar.

'An upset is always an agreeable result,' the chairman continued, 'except, of course, for those who have been upset. But congratulations to Clarissa and the Major for making it to the final once more, while at the same time saving the club the expense of having to purchase any more replicas of the trophy.'

A ripple of uncertain clapping blended with a heightened cry of 'Five diamonds'.

'And it gives me great pleasure to announce that the 1990 winners of the Jacob Penderick Cup are Vivien Bradley, our esteemed lady captain herself demonstrating the high standards she sets for entry to this club, and young Peter Winston who at thirteen must rank as the youngest champion Fulham and Gibraltar has ever known.'

'Five spades,' croaked a guttural Hungarian voice by the fireplace.

'I think Vivien might like to have the trophy for the first six months – it needs a bit of a polish,' smiled Worple, 'and for Master Winston we have something special: this book, *Lawn Tennis* by Lt.-Col. R.D. Osborn, which was written in 1881. It should offer him some tips for his future progress in the game.'

Peter stepped forward beside Vivien to accept the battered green volume with its cover half hanging off. But the benign applause was interrupted by a barked reprimand from Adolf Hann: 'Can't ve haf no peace in here, bloody tennis.'

'Bloody weather,' came the echo from the door which swung violently open to reveal Ernie and Tang Ebam, sodden and windswept like survivors from a shipwreck.

'Can't we stop, please?' Peter screamed at the umpire. The storm around them had reached preposterous proportions. In fact it was almost impossible to see the umpire as the rain drove across the court with the force of a waterfall. 'Charlie, you can't go on, can you?'

His partner pushed the hank of dripping hair out of his eyes and merely shrugged his shoulders.

The umpire, however, was adamant. 'Play on,' he insisted.

It's all right for you, Peter thought, you're dry. With his spreading layers of dark green oilskins and his yellow sou'wester the official looked like the bosun of an old-fashioned lifeboat.

He tried one more appeal to the man, the logic of which seemed unimpeachable. 'Look, this is entirely pointless. Even our opponents have gone. There's no point in serving to no one.'

'Play on.' The umpire looked straight ahead, oblivious to the howling weather, as he repeated his stentorian verdict.

A dagger of lightning temporarily illuminated the gloom, as if someone had snapped on some floodlights for a fraction of a second, and then found its target like a laser in the forest, causing a protruding pine tree to erupt into flames. The uppermost branches of a horse chestnut on the edge of the court started to snap, as if in sympathy, under the swirling force of the hurricane.

'Play on. Play on, or you default.' The umpire's injunction seemed to be a direct challenge to the elements as if, in some supernatural way, he was in control of them as well as the game.

'Are you ready, Charlie?'

Peter's partner had assumed his crouched position at the net. He raised his racquet to indicate that he had heard. The question had been unnecessary: Charlie was always ready. He had been – constantly and unwaveringly – for as long as Peter could remember.

There seemed no other option but to serve. Peter threw the ball up against the force of the rain but a punishing gust of wind curved it over his head and, as he himself arched back to try and make contact, he lost his balance and let loose a silent scream that he knew nobody could hear as he fell deep into nothingness.

'You won, then?'

His mother's presence at the half-open door was outlined by the thin light from the bathroom.

'Yes,' he replied, stretching his arm back to switch on the lamp above his bed. 'How did you know?'

She came in and sat on the edge of the bed. 'Your prize. This book. I read the inscription.'

He sat up, re-arranging a pillow against the head-rest. 'I didn't know it was inscribed. I hadn't even looked at it.'

Grace opened the broken cover. 'It says: "A worthy tomb for a worthy winner. K.R. Worple." I hope he means worthy tome – do you think you should tell him it's spelt with an "e"?'

'I wouldn't dare tell him anything. He'd probably have me kicked out of the club. Not much of a prize, is it? Must have cost him at least forty pence in some second-hand bookshop.'

'I wouldn't be sniffy about it, if I were you,' countered his mother. 'Most people go through life winning nothing.'

'Including you?' As soon as he let slip the remark he wished he hadn't said it.

She appeared unperturbed. 'I won you,' she smiled. 'It was more of a struggle than most parents have to go through. One day . . .'

'One day, one day, always one day,' Peter's frustration was still inside him from the dream. 'If it's such a great bloody story why do you keep refusing to tell it to me.'

'Don't swear. You know why – the pieces aren't all in place. There's no point embarking on a tale until you know the ending.'

'But what about the beginning – at least you could let me in on that.'

She shook her head with a curious certainty. 'Sometimes the ending is part of the beginning. Life isn't as simple as a race with a starting gun and a finishing tape, you know.'

Peter knew that if he continued the line of questioning about his father it would only distress her. She had told him that he was an American who was married to someone else and who occasionally sent cheques. Furthermore she had promised that once he turned eighteen she would provide him with the information on how to find him, if he wished. So instead he changed the subject.

'You must have won prizes, with the running and that.'

'It was a very short career. No sooner had I learnt how to run than I had the accident. After that I was lucky to learn how to walk. Once you lose the ability to do something you've always taken for granted, you tend to stop taking anything for granted. Life seemed that much more precious.'

Peter noticed how his mother had begun to move less easily as if some creeping arthritis was taking hold of her joints. But he had said nothing. He knew her and he knew he would be told what was wrong when she deemed the time right.

'Where were you tonight?' he asked. 'Upstairs?'

'Sunday night,' she reminded him. 'Nevis and the whirling dervishes.'

'I thought I heard the sound of chanting. What do you hope to gain by it all? Life everlasting?'

'I told you, you should come up one Sunday and find out for yourself. You never know, it could help. It certainly can't harm. Might even improve your backhand. People tend to get out of Bali Yoga whatever they're prepared to put in. A bit of meditation might put a stop to those nightmares.'

'What nightmares?' Peter stared at his mother, more uncomfortable than upset at this intrusion into his privacy.

'I'm sorry, I didn't mean to mention that.' She moved up towards him and put her hand on his brow. 'Bali Bhava teaches that it can be beneficial to release your demons in your sleep. That way they're no longer inside you. Sometimes I look in on you at night and I can tell your consciousness is asleep but your brain is alive. Your face is still damp.'

'Charlie,' Peter confessed. 'It's always Charlie. Always there beside me. Sometimes I think he leads me into these terrible situations. He certainly never wants to leave.'

'I thought he'd gone,' said his mother.

'He has during the day. You know that. Years ago. But he's there in my dreams. Not every night. Just the bad ones.'

'When you were little,' his mother recalled, 'he was there all the time. Your invisible friend. We couldn't close the door till he came through, you used to keep a seat for him on the bus and even put a pillow out so that he could sleep beside you.'

'Oh, shut up.' Peter squeezed her hand in mock anger. 'If you ever breathe a word about him to anyone I'll deny it all.'

'I'll tell your bride the night before your wedding. After all, she needs to know the partner she's replacing. Now go back to sleep.'

Peter obediently pulled the pillow down onto the bed. 'Mum?' he asked.

'Yes.'

'Can I have a story? Just a short one.'

It had been more than two years since he had made such a request and she was unable to disguise her delight at the warm feeling of satisfaction that it generated.

'Of course. How about your winnings?' She picked up the book from the bed. 'Lawn Tennis by Lt.-Col. R.D. Osborn.'

'That'll do,' he grinned as he closed his eyes.

Grace reached in the pocket of her dressing gown and unfolded a pair of glasses. She opened the green volume on her lap, pressed down the yellowing page so that the spine creaked, and began to read:

'The scene should be laid on a well-kept garden lawn. There should be a bright warm sun overhead and just sufficient breeze whispering through the trees and stirring the petals to prevent the day being sultry. Near at hand, under the cool shade of a tree, there should be strawberries and cream, iced claret mug and a few spectators who do not want to play but are lovers of the game, intelligent and appreciative. If all these conditions are present, an afternoon spent at lawn tennis is a highly Christian and beneficient pastime.'

Glancing down at her son to gauge his reaction, she could tell from his breathing that he had now found an untroubled sleep.

'I've always thought paradise might be something like that,' she murmured to herself, as she closed the tome.

The twin Victorian towers of London's Natural History Museum – sharp as a spire and intricately castellated as if they were a model for Cinderella's castle in Disney's Magic Kingdom – seemed to curve through a magic of their own in the unnatural September heat wave. Peter felt sorry for the crocodile of young boys in thick knee-length woollen shorts and long fawn socks who were crossing the Cromwell Road ahead of them. At least his new school allowed you to wear any clothes you liked. The boys tended to stick to blue jeans but many of the girls – save the overweight like Wendy Tanfield – had adopted the fashionable athletic fad of skin-tight shiny cycling shorts.

David Rooney, the science teacher – a man known in the staff common room as the proselytising prophet – summoned his class around him. 'Right, today you're going to find out where you came from. Any questions?'

Samantha Bergen stuck up her hand with a saucy giggle. 'Is that like the facts of life, Mr Rooney? Some of us know those already.'

'It's more important than the facts of life,' – the teacher ignored the smut in her question – 'it's about life itself. When you leave this great temple of knowledge this afternoon, Samantha, you will realise your utter insignificance in the universe.'

Peter had no idea what the facts of life were although he had felt an unspoken attraction for Samantha from the first day at school. She had such confidence, and her blue-eyed open face and ash-blonde hair and skin like silk made her stand out from the rest of the girls in the class.

The museum was actually on the same road as Nevis's house, only a mile closer to the centre of London. Peter had often passed the daunting edifice before on the top of a bus, marvelling at the stone sculptures of jaguars and jackals and fish and wolves that perched like hungry gargoyles on the roof. Nothing had prepared him, however, for the colossal bronze-coloured animal that seemed to fill the entire building.

'This is Dippy,' smiled Rooney proprietorially, pleased that some of his pupils were seeing it for the first time. 'He's American. Or was.'

The children clustered round the small plaque by the creature's mighty front left foot. Or not so mighty, proportionately, it informed them. *Diplodocus carnegii* was indeed an American – from Wyoming – but he hadn't been there for the past sixty-five million years after becoming extinct, and that was two million years before the arrival of mankind. Weighing ten tons and measuring twenty-six metres, his feet would have been too small to support him in swamp ground. Most creatures of his size were amphibious.

'It's a shame they died out.' Wendy Tanfield evidently felt some empathy with the creature.

'I wouldn't worry,' her teacher assured her. 'The species existed for more than eighty million years; the human race will be very lucky to last a tenth of that time.'

He led them up the stately stairs, past the stuffed llamas and pterodactyls and tortoises, to the stern stone bust of Charles Darwin, 1809–1882. He had such a melancholy face, Peter thought, and seemed to have grown as much hair as possible to hide his features – save on the top of his head where he probably wanted it most. For just a second he wondered if this could be anything to do with his Charlie – there was a resemblance – but the thought passed as rapidly as it had arrived.

'Right,' said Rooney. 'You can follow it for yourselves. It's all set out in ten easy sections. But nobody is to enter Seven B – it's not relevant.'

'Why not?' Matthew Kuttner's tone was inevitably combative.

'Because it's about genetics, something that Darwin, like you, Kuttner, knew nothing whatever about.'

'Why not, if he was so clever.' The obdurate pupil was not to be so easily dismissed.

'Because the science wasn't invented until forty years after he died,' Rooney put down his least-favoured pupil with some satisfaction.

Peter's attention had already been caught by some diagrams demonstrating how dachshunds' legs had been progressively shortened by two-thirds over the past century, as if they had been gradually worn away by a grindstone. He had never realised before that when people spoke of dog breeding, they literally meant manufacturing dogs. Models of a bulldog and a terrier showed how the Staffordshire bull terrier had actually been made by man. Sometimes such skills could be put to beneficial use: the St Bernard rescue dog had been deliberately created out of the great dane, the mastiff and the Pyrenean mountain dog.

'They have to hang the brandy cask on him later,' Rooney noted wrily as he joined him. 'Come and take a look at the mule. It's a hybrid, only produced when a horse and a donkey breed. A mule can't reproduce itself, poor old thing. Elephants on the other hand are a pure species and can't stop. See this pair. Theoretically they could produce sixty offspring in their lifetime. Exponentially that would fan out to a dynasty of nearly twenty million in seven hundred years, just from this old couple. Africa should be jammed coast to coast with elephants – like the road to Brighton on Bank Holiday Monday – if it weren't for the ivory trade.'

Peter, baffled but intrigued, made his way through the various exhibits illustrating Darwin's observations on natural selection: even though there was this superabundance of offspring, it was the struggle to survive in their enviroment that ensured the ultimate strengthening of the species. Suddenly his attention was stolen by an unexpected tug at his sleeve.

'Do you want to do something naughty?' Samantha Bergen had a challenging glint in her eyes.

'What?' he enquired nervously.

'Come with me,' she insisted, dragging him round a full-scale model of the extinct Quagga.

'Where are we going?' he asked lamely, somehow constrained to follow but anxiously glancing back over his shoulder.

'Where do you think? Seven B. I've been before.'

'Why do you want to go again?'

'Because I want to share it with you. Don't you see,' she indicated the notice at the entrance to the forbidden section. 'This is about sex. You can learn things that Darwin didn't know.'

Peter wasn't at all sure he was going to learn anything but was flattered into following her.

'We inherit characteristics as instructions called genes,' he read. 'A creature that has a new characteristic is a mutant.'

'Like the Ninja Turtles,' Samantha added knowingly.

The model demonstrating how DNA molecules could make exact copies of themselves was lost on him and, he was relieved to observe, on Samantha.

'It doesn't matter,' she claimed excitedly. 'It's all on this television over here. See, the chap who used to play Dr Who.'

Indeed, the actor Tom Baker was explaining how cells might be altered to create new characteristics. For instance, a bacteria ring could be opened and something like a growth hormone inserted. The television showed pictures of sheep trotting through a meadow apparently on a mercy mission. Newly fertilised cells had been removed from them and DNA added. This put a blood-clotting factor nine in their milk which could then be used to cure haemophiliacs.

'But here comes the exciting bit,' Samantha grabbed his arm. 'Listen to the warning.'

Dr Who was worried about the repercussions of genetic engineering. 'What if someone found it possible to create a super race of extra strong people?' he questioned, but the rest of his message was lost as Mr Rooney emerged behind them.

'That's for another day,' he observed kindly. 'For the moment let's remain on the straight and narrow.'

The rest of the group were gathered back at the entrance to the exhibition, many somewhat bored, most with their pocket money in their palms eager to get to the coffee shop. But Matthew Kuttner was unpopularly impeding their progress.

'What's the point of this lot, sir? I mean, it's all very obvious. Things come from other things, that's what he's saying, innit?'

Rooney had not intended to take the lesson any further than this but he was damned if he was going to let Kuttner upstage his outing. He turned on his heel and let him have it with both barrels.

'The point, Kuttner, is to make you think. And if you were capable of doing this you would wonder why Darwin, having developed his revolutionary theory of evolution, kept it like a guilty secret known only to himself for half his professional lifetime. He only published it because another naturalist was about to scoop him. And why was Darwin terrified of publishing it, Kuttner? Because he was about to suggest that we, *Homo sapiens*, were part of a species called apes. Descended from chimpanzees. They've even taught baby chimps to talk in America.'

A respectful silence overtook the group, broken only by Wendy Tanfield's timid voice.

'What about God? He made me. The Good Lord made us all.'

'Let's go downstairs.' David Rooney, worried what her parents might say, deliberately ducked the question. 'You can buy little rubber dinosaurs in the bookstall.'

On the way out, Matthew Kuttner, aware of Peter's enthusiasm for tennis and envious of his new-formed friendship with Samantha, stopped him at a glass case. 'Look at that swede. It says it's a hybrid originally bred from a cabbage and a turnip. Now we know were Stefan Edberg comes from.'

Peter glared at him; he was a devoted admirer of the Wimbledon champion and accompanied his mother on shopping trips to the nearby Sainsbury's only because they had twice seen Edberg pushing his trolley there.

But their teacher had overheard the remark and answered back for him. 'On the contrary, Edberg is the perfect example of what Darwin could see was happening to the world. Healthy, well-adapted individuals are likely to increase. In other words, the survival of the fittest.'

· Twenty-One ·

Winston was having difficulty seeing the ball. He could not recollect any previous Wimbledon final being stopped because of bad light – how bad could it get on a July Sunday afternoon? But the lowering grey clouds had formed a canopy over the stadium and the air was as humid as it could become without actually breaking up into rain. It was as if they were playing in some jungle clearing, certainly not in London SW19.

Shimizu seemed unperturbed by the conditions; indeed he appeared positively to relish them. The number one seed, who was seeking his third successive title, prowled his patch like a proprietor. Although his unseeded opponent had demonstrated degrees of versatility that had brought the crowd to their feet on his way to the final, today he was playing as if his shoes were laced to one another.

Shimizu had watched Winston closely in his semi-final against Garland and this seemed not to be the same man: all the strokes were there but none of the emotion. What had happened to the white heat of anger that had carried him home? The player was not centred on his game. He seemed preoccupied with a strategy that encompassed more than the point in play and this could prove suicidal.

Winston desperately scrambled to the corner of the court to retrieve the perfectly pitched forehand drive and popped it feebly back towards the Japanese player who had followed it into the net. From there, the reigning champion smacked the return away with effortless command.

The largely British crowd applauded with polite appreciation. But not the nutmeg little man clad in the black tracksuit in the players' box.

'Go for the line,' Moses mouthed to his protégé, not caring who might notice him. 'At least go for the fucking line.'

• Twenty-Two •

'It's Mr Quinn.' Mary Doherty was on the extension in the hall.

'Tell him to come up.' Dawson put down the receiver and rotated his high-backed swivel chair to look out at the gas-lamps of Marlborough Street which burned throughout the day. It was snowing; strong, pure, New England snow, falling in obedient ranks to brighten the sullied streets of Boston.

'My most sincere condolences.' The words emerged from Eamonn Quinn even before his substantial figure had fully emerged through the door. There were still traces of snow on his shoes.

Wondering whether Quinn was capable of being sincere about anything, Silver inclined his head in acknowledgement and indicated a studded leather chair by the fire.

'Of course it was inevitable,' Quinn went on, settling himself down. 'The wonder was that it came later rather than sooner. The heart, I believe. Well, you always said that once you lost the desire to live, it was only a matter of time. Still, sixty-eight. Not old.'

'Did you bring her will?' asked Silver.

'That's why I came.' The veteran attorney shifted uncomfortably in his seat. 'I have the one she drew up on marriage to you, of course . . .' His voice tailed off.

Dawson came round the desk and seated himself on the chair opposite. 'Of course what?'

'No good, I'm afraid.' Quinn winced slightly, as if he feared repercussions like a Roman messenger bearing bad tidings.

'No good? What do you mean?'

'You know, you should have gone to see her. She'd fallen in with a local religious order out on the Cape – the Sisters of Rathlin. They started to visit her in the last years. In fact I believe she was on the road to some sort of rehabilitation.'

'So?' Silver's mystification was rapidly giving way to anger.

'These people are highly sophisticated nowadays. They even instruct their own lawyers. He rang me last night, a Mr Sproule – W.P.R.A. Sproule – regarding the contents of her last will and testament.'

'She left them the lot.' Silver knew immediately.

'Not quite.' Quinn was relieved to be the bearer of at least some good tidings. 'Evidently she agreed that you should live out your life in this house – Mr Sproule must have guided her generously through that clause – but then it reverts to the Sisters. Of course, we'll challenge the whole thing. It was made when she was of unsound mind. I should imagine you can count on half, maybe more.'

'No, Eamonn.' Dawson rose to his feet with as much dignity as he could muster. 'That's not a thing I'm prepared to go through in public. There are occasions when we just have to accept our fate.'

'Did you prefer it the colour it was?'

'I can't remember what colour it was.' Edmund Michaels surveyed the packing cases crammed together in the bay window. The snow had completely coated the beach beyond and it was becoming hard to distinguish the divide between it and the foaming tide.

'Well, copper was the quick description. But Leslie of Boylston Street always described it as a grey reddish orange that is redder and darker than Etruscan red or hyacinth red, and yellower and darker than Persian melon. Made me sound kind of classical.'

'Leslie certainly has a way with words,' Michaels agreed, taking a sip of his coffee. 'And what does he call it now?'

'Black,' said Leone de Soto. 'You sure you don't mind if I take these glasses with the lemons. It's just that Brandi loves them so.'

'Take anything,' the doctor shrugged. 'I'm going to have the place done up, anyway. Probably rent it out.'

'You're crazy. You should use it yourself – at least as a summer home. You didn't even come to see the yachts last July. They were wonderful. Marblehead's quite a historical place you know. The man in the bank said it was founded in 1629 by fishermen from Cornwall in England.'

Michaels appeared uninterested. 'Did you tell them to make sure to keep up the standing order?'

'Everything.' Leone took her own mug of coffee from the window-sill and perched on the edge of one of the boxes. 'There's one thing I've been meaning to ask you. The umbrella. Why did I have to put that plastic bag over the handle?'

'Fingerprints. Simple as that.'

'I thought so. But I still don't follow. I mean you always said they were identical in every way, genes and everything, down to the last detail.'

'Every detail except that,' acknowledged the doctor. 'Even identical twins have different fingerprints. I guess God wanted to keep the cops happy.'

'Is that why you think there was a mix-up?'

'There was always a chance they might have fingerprinted them at birth, just for safety's sake. But I guess British hospitals aren't that sophisticated. However, the records you did get from St Sophie's clearly record that the birth mark on the first baby spread to the left – the opposite of James.'

'I've never seen any birth marks,' she confessed.

'They're not strawberry marks,' Michaels explained. 'They fade in infancy. But they're always there, just beneath the skin.'

'But Dawson Silver had no doubts,' she pointed out.

'Thank you for that,' said Edmund. 'There was no need to go quite so far.'

'I wanted to.' Leone responded with a wicked smile. 'You know every woman would like the excuse to be an absolute whore, just for one night. You have no idea the feeling of power.'

'I'd better go.' Michaels put down his cup. They were getting into territory that made him feel uncomfortable. 'Thank you for looking after the house for all this time. It will miss you – and Brandi.'

She came across to kiss him goodbye. 'Ring me if you need me. Chicago isn't so far and Hernando isn't the jealous sort.'

'I will.'

Leone was reluctant to let him go. 'Do you realise that we've been friends for fifteen years now – I counted them – and never once have you . . .'

Edmund Michaels put a finger against her lips to silence her.

'There are more important things in this life than sex, you know.'

• Twenty-Three •

'And there's your enemy Scud missile up there in the sky, lazily lobbed and hoping to pass over your head and land before you can get back and secure the defences. Some hope. It's a gift. Accept it as such. You're an American marine, you're so brutally trained and fanatically fit that you can retreat towards the baseline before it's even crossed the net. You've had time to assume a secure and steady position, knees slightly bent, left arm outstretched and forefinger pinpointing this useless thing like radar. And then, boom! You bring back your Patriot and annihilate the Scud out of your airspace. You crater it into your opponent's court before he knows what's hit him.'

The Gulf War had come at an opportune moment for Dr Bob Borogon's Tactics, Timing and Tenacity classes at Osprey Academy. It enabled him to add an additional angle to his brain-washing seminars which had otherwise changed little over the past ten years. Tucking his carbon fibre racquet under his arm like a swagger-stick, he turned to address his audience of thirteen- and fourteen-year-olds.

'Right, take up your positions in the front two rows of the bleachers. We have come to a seminal moment in your education. I am about to impart to you the single most important piece of information you will ever learn in this academy — or anywhere else in life, for that matter.'

The air of anticipation could hardly have been keener as the young players settled themselves on the wooden benches beside Osprey's main competition court. The morning was unusually humid for late February and the training session had been especially arduous. James Winston, his hair dripping with sweat, tucked a towel round his neck like a boxer as he leant forward to attend to the words of the sports guru.

'This information is strictly classified.' Dr Bob regarded his troops with a challenging and collusive expression. 'And you have only gained access to it by attaining the required standard of play. You would be ill-advised to pass it on to anyone else. Careless talk costs matches. Do I make myself clear?'

'Yes, Dr Bob,' came back the unanimous chorus.

'What we have in this great country,' he went on, pausing for effect and emphasis, 'unknown to anybody else in the world, is The Magic. No other nation has this – nor do they know how to acquire it. Why do you think the Russians can't make Coca Cola? Because however much they analyse the stuff, they can't quite break down the ingredients. That's because The Magic's in there and they don't realise it. What I'm going to tell you today are the three external elements of The Magic. If you manage to acquire these skills and blend them together, then nothing can stand between you and the ability to become a champion.'

'This is what I've been waiting for.' Jenny Dalton sat staring at her hero with undiluted adoration.

'First,' Dr Bob began, 'total commitment, which means working twenty-five hours a day every day of the year if need be. Second, belief in yourself. You have it within you to achieve anything you want. You make use of a quarter of your brawn and a twentieth of your brain. Just you double that capacity and your horizons are limitless. And third, and most important, undying faith in God Almighty. He's waiting there to help you but he needs to be asked. The Lord wants to do a deal with you, just as surely as a sportswear sponsor or a real-estate agent selling you a condo. But if you don't enter negotiations with God, you don't get nowhere.'

The brevity of the statement took some students by surprise. They sat attentively waiting for more. But it became clear that none was forthcoming.

'Is that all there is?' Tom Semple had been furiously writing down Dr Bob's three-point formula in his bulging filofax. 'I mean, if we can combine these things will we find The Magic?'

'Good point.' Dr Bob looked admiringly at his most assiduous disciple, fixing him with his intense, messianic gaze. 'Let me put it in a reverse fashion, Tom. Without these three things, you have no chance of finding The Magic.'

'You haven't quite answered the question.' James Winston had grown in assurance during his time at Osprey and his acknowledged prowess as one of the top players of his year gave him the courage to speak out. Besides, his initial misgivings about Dr Bob had been replaced by a growing affection. He was the first man to take any real interest in him. By adhering to his advice, James had transmuted much of the isolation and bitterness that had attended his first months into more ruthless determination.

Dr Bob was not offended by James's observation but indicated with his opened hands that no precise response was forthcoming. 'I've answered as far as I can, Jim. The rest of the answers are inside you. The truth is you can only go so far towards finding The Magic. At the end of the day you have to rely on something else happening, the unknown part of the equation. You have to wait for The Magic to find you.'

There was a purposeful silence as the students tried to take on board this new shard of philosophy. People fumbled with their racquets or jiggled the tennis balls in their hands.

'We've gone further than I intended.' The sports psychologist was on his feet and ready for another demonstration. 'Now let's look at another weapon in your amoury: it's like a smart bomb. From the moment you program this shot on your racquet it knows the precise route to its target . . .'

'Do they teach you anything in that academy of yours?'

'What do you mean?' James was immediately defensive. 'We're on court four hours a day, six sometimes. Mr Hoffman says we train harder than the Bolshoi Ballet. Often you hit serves until your arm becomes red hot with pain.'

'No, I'm not concerned about the tennis thing.' One-eyed Mike gave him a reassuring squeeze on the shoulder to calm him down. 'I mean lessons and things. School work.'

'Sure. We spend every morning in class. We've got workbooks just like anyone else. There are homework assignments every evening – geography, math, science, language, arts.'

'So you don't all have to become tennis champions to survive?'
There was a look of parental concern on Mary-Louise's face. In the
four years since Violet had died she had tried to keep a distant eye on
James's progress although she sensed that Dawson disapproved of
the continuing relationship. But every six months or so, on an
agreed Sunday morning, they would drive down to Osprey in the
pick-up truck and take James to the Sarasota crematorium where
they would spend a silent half-hour in memory of his great-aunt.
Then it was back to the trailer park for hamburgers and hot dogs and
pyramids of french fries – foodstuffs as illegal as drugs in the strict
dietary regimen of the academy.

'Only ten per cent ever get as far as playing even the satellite
circuit,' James explained. 'The rest of us are aiming for sports
scholarships. They send out scouts from the best schools in America
to recruit promising players – Stanford, Yale, Princeton.'

'You've got to be careful, though,' warned Mike, indicating the
newspaper on his lap. 'You've still got to pay your passage with your
tennis. Say you got fed up with the game. There's this girl here,
Heather Gottlieb, been playing tennis since she was eleven and she
got a scholarship to the University of Nevada in Vegas with high
school grades certified by her principal in subjects like marketing
and oceanography. Can you imagine that, oceanography? Anyway,
she doesn't want to play tennis any more and' – he ran his finger
down the page – 'yea, it seems the National Collegiate Athletic
Association are now saying she hasn't fulfilled the academic
requirements. I bet if she was out there winning for Nevada they
wouldn't be so concerned.'

'Well, she's crazy,' James retorted dismissively. 'I can never think
of a time when I wouldn't want to play tennis. It's the greatest sport
known to man. You can get rid of all your tension and aggression
and nobody gets hurt.'

'Unlike these games in the Gulf. Mrs Collie over there' – Mary-
Louise indicated the rusting trailer across the track – 'had a boy
wounded and coming home.'

'Hit by a Scud?' James enquired.

'No, by a US army jeep. Driven by somebody who'd been out
celebrating.'

Celebration seemed to be the order of the day in the Longboat trailer park. There were, unfortunately, no old oak trees round which to tie yellow ribbons but nearly every telegraph pole or post or prop holding up a makeshift awning was festooned with them. The Stars and Stripes abounded, little flags poking out of the metal mail boxes in front of the houses, larger ones stuck in windows and not a few front doors entirely enveloped in the national emblem. At the entrance to the park someone had erected a banner with the proud words 'God Bless Our Boys in the Gulf'.

'It's strange,' the fourteen-year-old looked around him. 'All this patriotism. It's almost as if people were enjoying the war.'

'In a way they are.' One-eyed Mike returned from the cramped camper kitchen with a fresh Budweiser for himself and a Dr Pepper's for the boy. 'There's more than a bit of guilt here. They're making up for their failure to support the last one.'

'Vietnam?'

Mike nodded. 'The only flags that time were on the coffins. You gotta understand, James, most of the people who live here in Longboat are old folk. They've worked hard all their lives and they've come down to Florida for a bit of sun to warm their retirement. And they remember the Second World War when it wasn't a crime to be a patriot. In fact it was a crime to be anything else.'

'Made you proud to be an American.' Mary-Louise squeezed the top of the aerosol can in her hand and covered the pecan pie on the table in front of them in an excess of artificial cream.

'Would you like to fight for your country, James?' she asked, handing him a heaped helping of the forbidden pudding.

The boy filled his mouth with a forkful of pie to give himself time to take on board the implications of the question. 'No, I don't think I would,' he replied, 'but I'd like to play for it.'

The joyous outbreak of jingoism was manifest across the whole peninsula of Florida, clearly visible from the windows of the Toyota Space Cruiser as it hit Interstate 4 en route from Tampa to Orlando. Nearly every electronic billboard seemed to alternate its designated message with the universal prayer: 'God Bless Our Boys.' Many of the hotels beckoned custom with the offer: 'Half Price Accommodation for All Service Families.' And, most precisely of all, one bold outpost of the favoured chain of wayside halts proudly announced: 'Starvin' Marvin hails Stormin' Norman.'

James had been pleased, but not altogether surprised, on his return to the academy that Sunday evening to find his name included on Moses Hoffman's Honor List. He had hit a timely winning streak of late, in time anyway for the occasion every semester when five chosen students, one from each academic year, who had made most progress on the tennis court were singled out for a treat − traditionally a trip across the state to visit the theme parks near Orlando and the Kennedy Space Center at Cape Canaveral.

'Welcome to Dr Bob's Magical Mystery Tour,' muttered a darkly tanned girl in a white tracksuit as she stowed her bag under the seat and settled beside James at the back of the vehicle.

He was flattered that she had chosen to sit there. Phoebe Carter was an Australian and something of a star at Osprey. Two years older than James, she had shamelessly outmanoeuvred him on the last occasion they had met in one of the open competitions. Moses always liked to give precedence to Americans over foreigners when he admitted people to the academy but her lawyer father back in Sydney was rich enough to have endowed an additional pair of indoor courts which had secured her entry. However she had proved a prodigious player in her own right. Classmates who had seen her tackle the downhill at Telluride during the winter vacation predicted she might be the first woman to represent her country in both the summer and winter Olympics.

When the gods were handing out their gifts, Phoebe Carter was one of those people fortunate enough to be accorded a wholly disproportionate share: a build that was both athletic and statuesquely feminine, deep bush-baby eyes as wide as the Pacific rim, obedient dark hair that she could curl round her jaw to achieve a Cleopatran allure and an effervescent sexiness that was all the more annoying to other girls because it was so effortless. She could have pretty well any male she wanted eating out of the palm of her hand. Not that she wanted any; her ambition, like that of all the other pupils at the academy, was singlemindedly to become the best tennis player possible. She had been on Hoffman's Honor List twice before.

' "Magical Mystery Tour" – it's a song,' she explained to James, who had been too diffident to reply immediately. 'You know, by the Beatles. Ever heard of John Lennon?'

'Sure,' he found a barely audible voice. 'John Winston Lennon.'

'Ah yes,' Phoebe remembered, 'James Winston. Perhaps you're a distant relative.'

'I doubt it. Although Winston's my mother's name and she was English.'

'Mother's name? Something to hide?'

Her enquiry was only semi-serious but he treated it with candour. 'I guess there was once. Something to do with tax. My dad never really explained it fully. I think it's sorted out now but why bother to change?'

'With parents it's nearly always about money,' Phoebe agreed reassuringly, adding: 'You said "was". Is your mother dead?'

The rain that had been threatening since they left Osprey had now broken. For a moment James took in the passing landscape of gloomy grey rectangular warehouses and cheaply built motels, their illuminated vacancy signs like beggars' outstretched hands.

'She died when I was born,' he lied. 'She died in a London hospital giving birth to me.'

'I sometimes wish mine had gone the same way,' his companion casually remarked without a hint of remorse. 'It might have saved sixteen years of hassle and neurosis. But mothers don't die in childbirth in Australia, they're far too tough. It was more common in the last century, mind you. My grandma told me that people would always reassure themselves with the belief that if a woman died like that, her soul passed directly to the child in some mysterious way and so remained alive. But I think that's a crock of shit. The only things that have soles are sneakers.'

James had never heard this theory before. He had rarely thought about his real mother while Violet was alive. But since his aunt's death, in his four years at Osprey, he had wondered about her more and more. She had been a runner but that was pretty well all he knew. His father had promised that one day they would go to London and visit her grave and then he would tell him the whole story. But there had been disconcerting moments in James's life when he felt curiously feminine, as if he were in a way experiencing the part of him that was her. Of course he had never told anyone about this, not even Dr Michaels – especially not Dr Michaels. He wondered if other boys ever had the same sensation but he was not prepared to risk their derision in order to find out. It had always been his assumption that being brought up alone by Aunt Violet might have caused this occasional split in his personality. Now Phoebe had put forward another possibility.

'She died without seeing Florida, then?' The Australian girl evidently had little respect for mothers or death.

'I think she only once came to America and that was to take part in the Boston marathon.'

'Good on her. I hate the way people come to this place and just wait to die. It's as if they've given up on life before they need to. You see them sitting outside their tacky mobile homes in canvas chairs. Contented couples, their arms folded, doing nothing, just nodding in the sun wondering if this will be the day the big hand comes down to collect them. The whole state's like a waiting room for death, people hiberating in these sort of open-air crematoriums warming themselves up in preparation for the big oven to come.'

'You're sick.' James was just as provoked as she intended. 'There are lots of kids and ordinary folk here. I grew up in Florida.'

'Let me tell you, this place is not real.' A possible reason for Phoebe's presence next to him was explained by the relish with which she unleashed her sermon on a fresh pair of ears. 'Melbourne, Venice, Naples, Panama City, Hollywood,' she itemised the towns on her fingers, 'they even have a Marathon but not the one that gave its name to the race. These are imitation towns. The people who live there know the real ones are somewhere else. Have you been to Nalcrest? It's a place actually named after a union – the National Association of Letter Carriers. It's where the retired postmen go. Did you know that dogs are banned there because of all the aggro they gave them during their working lives?' She pushed her hair back from her brow and laughed at the thought of this. 'And where else in the world could you find a place called Niceville? Niceville, I mean, it's too much.'

'Dr Bob says Orlando's the second biggest tourist centre in America,' James responded defensively.

'Sure, for people whose idea of adventure is a theme park. Has Borogon given you his Magic talk yet?'

'The Magic? Yes.' James nodded. And then he made the connection. 'Oh, I get it, the mystery tour.'

'Well done, pilgrim,' Phoebe patted him on the back. 'Stand by for the plastic pleasures.'

The following day was spent in an inexhaustible exploration of Walt Disney World with nobody more inexhaustible than Dr Bob himself. As on the tennis court, he became the children's guide and mentor.

'You know what they say about this place,' he announced the moment they passed through the gates. 'They say this is the place God would have built for himself if he had had the money.'

As James followed the others up the spotless Main Street, with the hedges trimmed to look like Mickey Mouse ears and other favourite animals, and into the turn-of-the-century Town Square he felt constrained to agree. Sweet music filled the air which seemed to have a special fragrance of its own – did they scent it every morning? In the distance lay the beckoning enchantment of Cinderella's castle and familiar creatures from Disney cartoons mingled with the tourists bidding them welcome with unflagging good humour.

'Hi,' smiled a petite Snow White with immaculate black hair and shining pearl-like teeth, 'you all enjoy yourselves now, do you hear.'

'Doesn't it make you want to vomit.' Phoebe had pushed her own dark locks under a New York Mets baseball cap and still wore the ultra-white Tacchini tracksuit that she had travelled in the previous day. She signalled her aggression towards the place not just with her whispered remark to James but by her cool-to-casual demeanour with her hands deep in her pockets and her mouth mobile from constantly chewing a large wad of gum.

He was reluctant to be intimidated. 'Hey, lay off. I'm having fun. What's bugging you about this place anyway?'

'It's too perfect,' she replied, 'and it just isn't natural.'

Nobody said it was, he thought, as a Mickey Mouse with a small human frame and giant nodding head and outsize hands welcomed them into his Magic Kingdom.

Dr Bob was as relentless as the powerful February sun as he urged them on in the non-stop pursuit of pleasure: the swashbuckling

Pirates of the Caribbean boat trip in Adventureland; the Mad Hatter ride in Fantasyland; the submarine voyage 2000 Leagues Under the Sea; the Big Thunder Mountain roller coaster in Frontierland.

James was intoxicated by the contagious atmosphere of so many people hell-bent on having a good time. At the end of the day as they queued for Space Mountain, the most intimidating ride of all – a roller coaster to 2001 – he was pleased to see even Phoebe had let her hair down a little.

'What do you hope to be doing when you get to 2001, Jim?' she enquired as she pushed in beside him.

'Looking back on my incredible career,' he replied.

'Are you pregnant?' she asked out of the blue.

'What?'

She indicated the sign ahead of them which warned that the ride was unsuitable for pregnant women or people with a heart condition or who were susceptible to motion sickness.

'I have a heart condition,' she moaned pressing her palms to her left breast and assuming an American accent. 'I'm in lerv.'

'You're not allowed to be in love, Phoebe.' Despite his cheerful grin, Dr Bob was as earnest as ever. 'Bad for the concentration. Stow it until you have a couple of big wins behind you.'

'What about Chrissie and Jimmy – Wimbledon '74?' she countered provocatively.

'They may have won then but they both lost their titles the following year,' the coach was quick to point out. 'Never should have if their private lives had been sorted out. The only love you need on a tennis court is your opponent's score.'

They had reached the front of the queue and were whizzed into the world of Tomorrowland. Phoebe held tightly to James's arm while they hurtled into outer space, dodging meteorites as they sped through galaxies millions of light years from the earth.

'Does it still make you want to vomit?' he asked as she emitted a high-pitched shriek when they started to tumble into black nothingness.

'Yes,' she admitted, 'but in a different sort of way.'

It was the last ride of the day. 'Phenomenal,' remarked Dr Bob as he led them out of the park and he then divided the word into two: 'Phe-nomenal.'

They stopped and lingered over one last look at Cinderella's castle, to James more mystical than ever as it was blushed by the dying light of the sun.

Dr Bob inhaled a substantial breath, almost as if he were holding back a tear. 'America,' was all he said, shaking his head in awe.

After breakfast the next morning James found a position on the first floor balcony of the Peabody Hotel to give him a clear view of the famous duck walk. He wanted to avoid going back to the bedroom he had been obliged to share with Dr Bob who he assumed would still be there. Nothing untoward had happened although the coach had strolled around naked after his shower vigorously massaging himself with his towel and indulging in what James assumed to be jock-talk. It made the boy feel uncomfortable and determined to spend as little time in the room as possible.

A loud fanfare caused the other residents of the hotel on the floor beneath him – well-paunched men in chequered shorts and long socks, an obligatory Florida uniform, and women with brightly tinted spectacles and hair – to form an honour guard on either side of the red carpet that ran from the elevators on the edge of the lobby to a small pool with a fountain in the centre. A troop of six ducks followed by three hotel staff in braided white jackets wobbled their way towards the artificial pond serenaded by brash music and applause.

'Magic.'

James turned to find Dr Bob standing behind him.

'It's a great tradition here, Jim. The product of pride and training. In what other hotel in the world would you see that?'

The question appeared to be rhetorical so he did not feel obliged to respond.

'You know what the Orlando basketball team's called?' the coach went on. 'The Magic. Load of no hopers at the beginning of the season but look at them now. What about Scott Skiles, short, fat and white but he'll be voted the most improved player in the NBA.'

'Weren't they beaten by the Lakers last night?' James hoped his point would appear knowledgeable rather than impudent.

Dr Bob shrugged his shoulders as if the information underlined his own contention. 'That's what happens when magic meets magic.

Magic Johnson, the most perfect player in the league. He could score as many baskets as he wanted but, you see, by playing him point guard the Lakers are virtually unassailable.'

'Where are we going today, Dr Bob?' They had been joined by Bruno Hill, eager as ever to get on with things and improve himself.

'The Experimental Prototype Community of Tomorrow.' The coach enunciated the words with considered clarity. 'To you, Epcot. Americans don't need to go abroad, this is where abroad comes to America. You'll see why no other nation can quite match up to the good old USA. First we discover what made this country great with Ben Franklin and Mark Twain and then we travel into the future with Michael Jackson. You know, those guys at Disney don't do anything by chance. It's all carefully thought out. Why do you think they chose Michael Jackson for the future? Because he's a prototype American, that's why. He knows how to get to the top. He doesn't spend his time womanising and doing drugs. He remodelled his act and he remodelled his face. With commitment and dedication, you can be anything you want to be. Just isolate your aim and then go for it.'

'Personally I preferred Michael J. Fox.'

The following day was the last of the Magical Mystery Tour. The Toyota Space Cruiser sped west along Route 528 heading for the John F. Kennedy Space Center at Cape Canaveral.

Phoebe had resumed her position at the back beside James. The morning was hot and she was clad in a white tube top and candy striped satin shorts. If it was her intention to look provocative she had succeeded.

'I don't know why Disney needed to pinch Peter Pan from the Brits,' she continued, 'when you've got your very own Peter Pan here at home.'

'Who?' James asked.

'Michael J. Fox, dummy.' Phoebe pushed him flirtatiously in the ribs. 'What is he, about thirty or something, and he doesn't look any older than you.'

'It was a fantastic ride,' James agreed. As a group they had filled an expanded De Lorean car which twisted and soared and dived in a vacuum filled with Imax and Omni screens recreating the small star's ride in *Back to the Future*.

'Universal Studios are better than Disney. They're more real somehow.' The Australian girl was never slow to advance an opinion. 'All that smiling gets to you after a while. If I see another Snow White I think I'd strangle her.'

'How can they be real?' Bruno Hill's face appeared over the top of the seat in front of them, eager to join in discussion with Phoebe. 'They're both fantasies. It's only the movies, you know.'

'In America,' Phoebe pronounced contrarily, 'few things are more real than the movies. Film stars are treated like royalty, studio chiefs are paid like emperors – what did they say that guy at Disney earned, thirty million a year? – and people talk about movies the whole time. They're real all right, you'd better believe it. More real than most things.'

'I preferred Disney.' James was anxious to be seen to be assertive in front of Bruno who was considerably older than him. 'Can you imagine the thought and the planning that went into that place? It's twice as big as Manhattan, you know.'

'Me, too.' Bruno followed his lead. 'I think you have to be an American to truly appreciate it. I believe in The Magic, too. I can make myself shiver just thinking about it. It's there for sure.'

'Do you know what employees are told to do if they have a problem there?' Phoebe asked them.

'No.' The replies were simultaneous.

'Sprinkle a little magic dust on it.' She put her hand over her mouth to cover her laugh. 'Can you imagine that? Sprinkle a little magic dust.'

'How do you know that?' Bruno demanded.

'Dr Bob told me last time. He used to work there as a guide.'

'Really?' James was surprised.

'Sure. Told people to watch out for sharks on The Pirates of the Caribbean. They even say his doctorate's from Disney, although I can't be sure about that.'

'Okay troops.' The erstwhile guide had resumed his duties in the front seat. 'Time for the final countdown – Spaceport USA. It's no accident that the only country in the world to put men on the moon blasted off from a place less than an hour away from the heart of The Magic.'

Like many before him on the tour, James was duly stunned by the size of the Saturn V rocket, longer than a football field the guide proudly announced as if she had built it with her own hands. In fact everything here seemed and was infinitely larger than life: the massive six-million-pound Crawler Transporters that carried the Space Shuttles to their blast-off positions, the endless acreage of the Vehicle Assembly Building – one of the largest structures in the world, she informed them, and the launch-pads themselves, stretching up to touch the coral ceiling of the sky as if they had no need to send up rockets to do so for them.

While the other students were buying souvenirs back at the Spaceport, James strolled among the small copse of upright rockets that lay to the left of the building. He felt uplifted and inspired by what he had heard and seen. Despite Phoebe's cynicism he had no doubts about the reality of The Magic. He could sense it in the air around him here, in this otherworldly atmosphere with pride and death and glory all intermingled. At the far end of the Spaceport was the new Astronauts' Memorial where those who had given their lives in the conquest of space were accorded, if anything, a more legendary status than those who survived.

But his solitude was short-lived; Dr Bob Borogon was all too soon at his side. 'Only twelve men have ever walked on the surface of the moon – same number as there were disciples, what do you make of that? – and do you realise two of them were called James? James Lovell whose space-suit we saw in the museum in there and Colonel James B. Irwin, the seventh moon walker. Apollo 15, July 1971. Twenty years ago.'

'Is he still alive?' James asked.

'Sure, continuing his mission.'

'What's that?' James was uncertain what Dr Bob meant. 'I mean, he's already been up there.'

'Already walked on the moon, yes,' the coach agreed, 'but he didn't find what he was looking for. Jim Irwin was looking for God. He said he felt the power of God as he never felt it before when he walked on the moon and he resolved to spend the rest of his life spreading the good news of Jesus Christ. He brought back the

Genesis Rock, four thousand million years old. The only pure white rock in the mountains of the moon. That's inspired him to search for more evidence of the proof of the Lord. Why, he's even led expeditions up Mount Ararat in Turkey searching for Noah's Ark. You can't be much more certain than that.'

'He's looking for his Magic, isn't he?'

'You got it, Jim,' the coach put his arm around the boy. 'You and I are going to get along just fine.'

· Twenty-Four ·

'Before we begin our meditation this evening I'd like you all to welcome Dr Abigail Weghofer, our guest speaker. Not only is she a practitioner of Bali Yoga and a doctor of philosophy, but she is gifted with remarkable psychic powers which, as you will learn, she has turned to great good.'

Nevis paused for effect and studied the two dozen people who were sitting cross-legged on the carpet which Peter Winston had earlier helped him pull across the floor of his studio. The camera stands and the lights had been pushed back to the walls, save for one orange-filtered lamp that was angled across the white cyclorama for theatrical effect. The only other source of illumination was provided by four thick cream church candles strategically placed on elegant wooden tripods that marked the borders of the carpet. The strong sweet scent of incense dominated the room, endowing it with a religiosity redolent of a sixties ashram. Outside, the Sunday evening traffic was making its stop-start way along the Talgarth Road back home into London. The arrival of March, coupled with general relief at the cease-fire in the Gulf, had inspired motorists to take to the countryside as if this had been a mid-summer weekend.

'Dr Weghofer is both a psychic and a healer,' Nevis looked across at their small, unsmiling guest with pride. 'Not only has she the power to see into people's previous incarnations, but she can also use past life therapy to deal with illnesses and problems that might beset us in our current lives.'

Peter, who had assumed a position beside Grace nearest the stairs to try to be as inconspicuous as possible, had been to these strange Sunday evening gatherings twice before. On both occasions Nevis had made references to past lives as if this were a commonly held belief that everyone in the room subscribed to. When he had tackled his mother about it later she had been evasive on the subject, saying only that people should be free to believe whatever they chose to believe in. The boy sensed that she might have doubts herself but was unwilling to give voice to anything that could upset their landlord.

'Also before we commence our meditation let us give thanks to Bali Bhava for bringing peace to the Middle East and making the ground war to liberate Kuwait so swift and certain. We apologise to him for any misgivings we might have entertained that his divine powers would not answer our prayers so completely. Hari Bali Bhava.'

'Hari Bali Bhava,' those on the floor reiterated in enthusiastic unison. Peter joined in automatically although he had no clear idea of what it was he was saying; he merely assumed it was some form of worshipful expression. He felt privileged because he was the only child there. Nevis had previously asked Grace if he could help in preparing the room and she in turn had requested that he might stay on for the yoga meetings. The average age of people there seemed to be somewhere between fifty and sixty. Peter thought he recognised two of the women present as members of the Fulham and Gibraltar Lawn Tennis Club, although he knew neither of their names.

'Bali Bhava, Bali Bhava.' Nevis was wearing what looked like a white towelling kimono, a garment he had in fact removed from his hotel room on a trip to Tokyo when he had realised how much he was paying to stay there. It had the effect of making him appear more like a wrestler than any form of religious guru. The rest of the people there – primarily women – were more conventionally clad in loose-fitting slacks and sweaters. Everyone had left their shoes by the darkroom and now sat upright on the carpet, with legs crossed and eyes closed in preparation for their meditation.

'Bhava Bhava, Bali Bali,' Nevis continued in a low liturgical chant. 'You who are the power, the light, the day, the night, move within us now and take away all that is negative from inside us – all bitterness and envy and hatred – and fill our souls with love of life. Bali Bhava, Bali Bhava, Bhava Bali.'

A low hum – like a subdued opera chorus – rose from those seated on the floor. This, combined with the flickering candles and the growing pungency of the incense, blended into a suble intoxicant that pervaded the room. Even a complete sceptic might fall prey to this heady brew. Peter glanced at his mother who seemed carried away by the atmosphere, her eyes lightly closed and an expression of calm serenity on her lips.

'And now let us feel our bodies. We start with our toes. Wiggle them a little, feel that they are there and sense that they are under our control. But slowly we move through the ankle, up through the tibia and the fibula up to the knee. We have reached base camp. And there we rest for a moment. Just take stock, twitch your kneecap if you can. And now on up through the thighs to our sexual organs. Don't be afraid to sense that they are there and sense that they can give pleasure. But know, too, that you must control them and they must never control you. Now up into the stomach, we can feel the space in it, we have fasted a little today and later we shall fill that space with rice and salad and pure vegetables.'

Grace had spent the afternoon preparing precisely these foods in her kitchen which she would bring up at the end of the evening. It had been her usefulness as a cook that had effected her entry to Nevis's yoga evenings.

'And above the stomach the lungs, so strong and powerful. Experience them as you take deeper and slower breaths, as the rhythm of your breathing alters pace into the peace of meditation. Now higher into your shoulders and you feel the tension of the day as it grabs the back of your neck like a pair of angry hands. But you can loosen this grip as you assert mastery over your own system and you relax and let those cares fall away. Now your feeling moves up through your throat and lubricates your mouth and touches your tongue and all is well with you. Bali Bhava, Bali Bhava.'

Peter found that he had, involuntarily, closed his own eyes the better to concentrate on this journey through his body and the words Bali Bhava fell automatically from his lips in chime with everybody else.

'And now' – Nevis's voice took on a dreamy, echoing timbre that further combined with the candles and the incense to infuse the studio with a surreal dream-like quality – 'you have reached your destination. Your mind. The coming together of the conscious and the subconscious. The control room of your body and your being.

And there – feel it – directly behind your eyes you make contact with your spirit. Take tight hold of it for this is where we transcend our mortal frame. Are you holding it firmly? You and the spirit are now one, the spirit and you. This is the moment of release. Bali Bhava, Bhava Bali. Let us go higher, higher, let us leave our mortal frame. The spirit does not need it. The spirit does not need it. Our eyes are firmly closed. And we rise out of our bodies, just for a moment. We can look down and see ourselves. We see the person sitting beside us, we see the candles burning bright. We have reached the highest state. Nothing can harm us here. Bali Bhava, Bhava Bhava, Bali Bali.'

On the previous occasions when Peter had attended Sunday yoga this was the moment when he felt a fraud. Try as he might there was no way his spirit was going to leave his body. He would secretively half-open his eyes to see what was happening to everyone else. Certainly nothing physical: they were just sitting on the carpet, their eyes intently closed, murmuring Bali Bhava to themselves.

But tonight something was happening to him. He had been aware of it from the moment Nevis had led them on the journey through the body. A wholly unexpected sensation had started to grow within him, as if he were no longer completely in control of the exercise. He knew that he could stop it at any moment, that he had only to open his eyes and this alien sensation would evaporate. But he didn't want it to. He wanted to see if he could transcend his mortal frame with his spirit.

Bali Bhava, Bali Bhava, Bhava Bhava, Bali Bali, he chanted inwardly, again and again, letting his subconscious assert its ascendancy. When it happened, it happened almost naturally. It was as if he was now standing looking down from the gallery above the studio. He could see everyone as clearly as the soft light from the flickering candles would permit. There was Nevis, gently rolling his body forward and back. And beside him Dr Abigail Weghofer, a plump figure in her black cotton pyjamas, her raven hair gathered in a single plait that ran down her back to rest on the floor. Peter could make out Grace, her grey head bowed in prayer, and there, beside her, he could see himself as certainly as if he were looking in a mirror. He deliberately stretched out his arms to be sure and the arms of the boy beneath him stretched out simultaneously.

'And gently, gently we come back.' A firmer element of command had entered Nevis's intonation. 'Once more into the body. Once more marrying the spirit with the soul, the unconscious with the conscious. Once more we are one again. Bali Bhava. Bali Bhava. And, in your own time, open your eyes and be present with us.'

Peter did so and looked towards his mother, anxious to see if she had undergone the same mystical experience as him. She smiled back at him, a maternal but enigmatic smile offering no clue as to whether she had.

Nevis unhurriedly rose to his feet. 'Don't worry if you failed to achieve the out-of-body experience. Bali Bhava teaches us that it can be enough to aspire to achieve it. But he also tells us that it is dangerous to remain outside too long. Our spirit might return to the wrong body and then where would we be?'

A ripple of nervous laughter arose from the floor as people relaxed, happy to be in contact with someone other than themselves once more. Peter found himself laughing more forcefully than anyone else, not least to banish the sense of fear from his system, as if he had just come off a ride on a ghost train.

Nevis glanced across at him with just a hint of reprimand in his expression. 'Let us welcome now our speaker, Dr Weghofer. She tells me she will be happy to answer any questions at the end of her short talk and, more important, should any of you wish to consult her privately, all you have to do is make an appointment. She has, thoughtfully, left some of her cards by the darkroom door and you may take one as you leave. Abigail.'

Respectful applause greeted the small figure as she rose from the carpet and repositioned her plump body in a canvas director's chair facing the assembly.

'Thank you.' From her first words, conviction and confidence shone from her firm, unblinking expression. 'Reincarnation. As Henry T. Buckle once said: If immortality be untrue, it matters little whether anything else be true or not.

'I think that most sentient and intelligent people now accept reincarnation as an undeniable fact. Let me quote to you from the words of two great Englishmen.' Dr Weghofer leant forward and extracted a well-worn notebook and a pair of rimless glasses from the carpet bag at her feet. 'David Lloyd George, your legendary

Prime Minister. He said: "The conventional heaven, with its angels perpetually singing et cetera, nearly drove me mad in my youth and made me an atheist for ten years. My opinion is that we shall be reincarnated." '

She looked over the top of her spectacles in evident satisfaction, with Nevis nodding in agreement beside her. Peter had always thought Lloyd George was Welsh; he knew about him from the never-ending ditty 'Lloyd George knew my father, Father knew Lloyd George.'

'And Judge Christmas Humphreys, a man renowned for his sagacity and learning.' The doctor leafed through some pages of her book to track down the quotation. 'Here we are: "When the day's work is ended, night brings the benison of sleep. So death is the ending of a larger day, and in the night that follows, every man finds rest, until of his own volition he returns to fresh endeavour and to labours new. So will it be for all of us, until the illusion of a separated self is finally transcended, and in the death of self we reach enlightenment." '

She whipped her glasses from her face in a swift, challenging gesture. 'Now some of you may be thinking to yourselves: "But Christmas Humphreys was a Buddhist so he would say that, wouldn't he?" '

Peter certainly wasn't. He had never heard of anybody called Christmas before and he felt certain that someone with a name like that was almost bound to be a Christian.

'But I am here to tell you tonight' – Abigail's voice, her slight Austrian accent now more identifiable, had taken on an evangelical tone, more suited perhaps to a larger gathering – 'that reincarnation was one of the tenets of the original Christian church. Why do you think the Second Council of Constantinople in 553 decreed that anyone who believed in it from then on was committing heresy?' She glanced once more at her book. ' "If anyone assert the fabulous pre-existence of souls, and shall assert the monstrous restoration which follows from it: let him be anathema." The answer is simple: because most Christians did believe in it at that time. But the leaders of the Church realised that there was no way they could control their errant flocks with hell fire if they thought they were going to be born again in a healthy body. Who do you think the Inquisition tracked down most zealously and murdered most heinously? Yes, anybody who still believed in reincarnation. In the Pyrenees in the South of France there was a Christian sect, the Cathars, who believed the material world was evil and continued to have faith that the reward for leading a good life was to experience an even better one in a subsequent body. Where are they today? Wiped out – they represented too much of a threat to the Christian church. Most of them burnt at the stake thanks to the holy orders of Saint Louis the Ninth. He let the Inquisition loose on them. The Church knew that there was no hell fire in the hereafter, so they brutally visited it on these innocent souls in the here and now.'

One of the candles guttered with ominous timing, adding poignantly to the sense of unease amongst those seated on the floor. Dr Weghofer seized her moment and rose to her feet.

'Now let us go from the dark foothills of the Pyrenees in the thirteenth century to the somnolent town of Bath in Britain precisely thirty years ago. We have a housewife, Mrs Smith, aged thirty-four. She has two children and a part-time job while they are at school. Perfectly normal. Except that since she was a small child she had been cursed with recurrent nightmares. And she can take them no longer. She goes to her doctor. He cannot help her. So he refers her to a local psychiatrist – Dr Arthur Guirdham. And she tells him her dream, her horrible, horrible dream. I have it here.'

Once again Dr Weghofer slipped on her glasses and searched through her notebook: 'Here it is: "I felt suddenly glad to be dying. I didn't know that when you were burnt to death you'd bleed. But I was bleeding heavily. The blood was dripping and hissing in the flames. I wished I had enough blood to put the flames out. The worst part was my eyes. I hate the thought of going blind." '

She snapped the book closed with an artful shiver. 'I'll spare you the rest but I suspect you've guessed it. This woman was the reincarnation of a Cathar, a man – it's quite possible to change sex when you change life – probably a priest who was burned at the stake. Was she making it up? Not for one moment. She brought Dr Guirdham lurid stories she had written as a child about those nightmare days in France seven hundred years previously – and she had never heard of Cathars till he told her nor studied any history at

· 224 ·

all. But she came up with accurate dates and names of places, such as the destruction of the great fortress of Montségur in 1244. She had no gift for languages but she began to dream in fluent French. Not only that, she identified seven people she knew who also lived in Bath as being fellow Cathars. And when the psychiatrist regressed them, they acknowledged, every single one of them, that they had been Cathars in a previous incarnation. They even fell ill on the anniversary of a notorious mass burning. Nor am I making this up. It's there for anyone to read in the public library – *The Cathars and Reincarnation* by Dr Arthur Guirdham, 1970.'

She let the message sink in as she herself sank back in her canvas chair, deliberately dropping the notebook with finality into her carpet bag.

'Before you come to me with any illness to be cured,' her voice had dropped to a modulated, bedside tone, 'you must believe. Otherwise I am unable to help you. You might as well go to your local GP for a packet of pills as come to my consulting room with doubts. As the profound philosopher, Erich Fromm, so truly wrote: "The majority of a psychoanalyst's clientele these days are sick because they know that life runs out of their hands like sand, and that they will die without having lived." In past-life therapy we can surmount that fear. I will regress you to the moment in your previous existence when the pain occurred – maybe you suffer from irrational claustrophobia and we discover that you were a rear-gunner in a British bomber in the Second World War, unable to escape when your plane caught fire. And when we find the source of your suffering we can begin to cure it.'

So saying, Dr Weghofer pressed her palms together in a symbol of peace and nodded a bow to the audience. People seemed uncertain whether to clap or not, but her smiling response to the first diffident note of applause ensured a stronger, more sustained ovation.

'Abigail,' Nevis came across to her, still clapping himself. 'I have always believed but never so certainly as I do at this shared moment. Now, are there any questions?'

'Dr Weghofer, could you tell me, approximately, what your success ratio is? I mean, what proportion of the people who come to see you are cured?' It was one of the women whom Peter recognised from the Fulham and Gibraltar Lawn Tennis Club.

The question carried with it a suspicion of doubt, something that was inimical to Dr Abigail Weghofer whose therapy was predicated on the absence of such thinking.

'One hundred per cent,' she replied crisply. 'Those who do not enjoy a total cure in this life will find it completed in the next.'

'Okay, let's hit a few to warm up, let you get used to the lights.' Nigel Bergen sported a towel arrayed around his neck like a cravat with the collar of his tracksuit jauntily turned up to graze the back of his neatly cut hair. He allowed the jacket to fall open in order to reveal a freshly laundered college sweater with a pair of crossed racquets on the front. Peter had no precise idea what they stood for but knew that his opponent's ensemble proclaimed the words 'Public School' as loudly as if they had been written on his chest.

The fourteen-year-old felt ungainly and uncomfortable. Moreover the speed with which Mr Bergen was whipping back his forehand returns indicated that Peter was unlikely to provide more than cannon fodder for the older man.

The game had been Samantha's idea to try and soften up her father. After their experience at the Natural History Museum she and Peter had embarked upon a friendship of sorts. They had twice been to the cinema on Saturday afternoons – on both occasions to see an 18-rated film at Samantha's insistence. And Peter had willingly accompanied her after school on Mondays to Queen's Ice Skating Rink in Bayswater where, following her class, he was permitted to join in the final twenty minutes of free-skating. He stumbled along, a natural fall-guy in every sense of the word, but it was a price worth paying to observe her limber legs and the provocative thrust of her posterior as she glided across the ice in her micro-skating-skirt.

Now it was her turn to watch him, as she draped herself over the gallery high above the indoor court. Her parents had apparently heard that their daughter was seeing more than a little of this particular classmate and had suggested that it should stop. At fourteen she should have a wider variety of friends and not just single out one, especially a boy who came from a basement in the Talgarth Road. The Bergens lived in a double-fronted neo-Georgian house on the fringes of Holland Park and had hoped their daughter's friends might equally emerge from such seven-figure mansions. But Samantha's insistence that she should not board but attend the local comprehensive school had inevitably plunged her into the company of the immigrant and the indigent. At least Peter Winston was one of the latter.

Nevertheless her parents had forbidden any more Saturday afternoon matinées until they had met the young man formally. At first Samantha had resisted, pointing out that he was hardly asking for her hand in marriage. But when she saw that her father was unbending in this — he had been unbearably tetchy ever since his Lloyd's syndicate had posted its last results — she had evolved a stratagem which she thought would put Peter in the best light possible. Although he never mentioned it himself, she knew he was a promising tennis player. He had even won a tournament at that strange club of his. So she prevailed upon her father — instead of subjecting her friend to ordeal by tea in the living room — to have a game of tennis with him.

At first Peter was wholly opposed to the idea. He couldn't see any need to meet Samantha's parents, especially since their daughter steadfastly resisted his attempts to kiss her on the lips. But he had reckoned without her trump card — the location of the suggested encounter. As the word fell from her lips his mouth dropped open as if to catch it.

'Wimbledon? Not the. . . ?' he stuttered.

'Yes, The All England Lawn Tennis and Croquet Club to give it its full moniker.'

Nigel Bergen had his father to thank for his admission to this charmed circle comprising only 375 members — as he had for his Holland Park house, his seat on the board of the family financial services company and, to a less grateful extent, for his Lloyd's syndicate. His father had played in the championships before the war and, although he had failed to progress beyond the first round, had succeeded in obtaining membership of the club. Nigel's name had duly been put down at birth, although it was only after he had been awarded his Oxford Blue that he was elevated from the ranks of temporary members.

So it was that on this blustery March afternoon Peter Winston first set foot on the hallowed Wimbledon turf or, to be more accurate, the synthetic surface of the indoor courts belonging to the club on the western side of Somerset Road. He had hoped that they might play on grass but, of course, it would be another two months before the groundsman would permit any player on this pampered surface.

'You serve.' Nigel Bergen threw the balls down to Peter's end, apparently unconcerned whether the boy was ready or not.

Peter took the opportunity to hit some practice services while Bergen removed his tracksuit and went through an exaggerated warm-up routine by the umpire's chair.

'You show him, Peter,' Samantha called mischievously from the balcony but the encouragement, if such it was, only made him more nervous. He double-faulted the first point and also the second. After that, when he reduced his pace to ensure the ball actually went in, Bergen smacked successive returns to either corner which he barely managed to get his racquet to.

Peter walked slowly to the net for the changeover, his head hung low and his spirits lower. But Samantha's father instructed him to stop. 'No need to change. We do it after every set in here – no sun, no wind. The sides are the same.'

Or not the same, Peter thought as Bergen's serve curled into his chest causing him to miss it completely. He had never played on the compressed artificial surface before and while he was trying to accustom himself to it, his opponent seemed intent on humiliating him. No points that game either.

He was down three–love before he began to hit the ball with any bite but even then, when he followed it into the net, Bergen managed to pass him at will. However, he was determined to stay with his serve-and-volley game at all costs. Tom Hall said it was the equivalent of waving a white flag at your opponent if you reverted to a baseline game in the first set.

It proved a short-lived affair, six–love. As he approached the net, Peter reluctantly cast a glance up the balcony where a silent Samantha was still standing. 'I'm going to do some shopping,' she called down, 'I'll see you in the members for tea.'

'Don't be too long,' warned her father as he picked his towel out of his tennis bag and sat down beside the umpire's chair.

Peter assumed it was in order for him to do the same. His only guideline for etiquette had been to follow whatever Bergen did. But the remark needled him. Sure, the man had won the set easily enough but there was no need for him to imply that the next would be just as easy. Especially to his own daughter in front of her friend.

Since Bergen seemed in no hurry to address him, Peter pulled his towel over his lowered head and began to replay the vital points, as Tom Hall had taught him, in order to analyse what had gone wrong. Maybe it was the darkness or maybe the silence – the indoor courts were empty except for them – certainly it was through no act of the boy's own volition, but he found himself inwardly chanting 'Bali Bhava, Bali Bhava, Bhava Bhava, Bali Bali' as if he were back in Nevis's studio. Almost automatically he went through the parts of his body, like a pilot checking his instruments before take-off. And, like a pilot, he took off. Without any warning he found himself standing on the balcony, where Samantha had been, looking down on his own towelled head and Nigel Bergen who was now getting up to resume the contest.

'Come on, then,' the man's voice was peremptory to the point of irritation. 'It's you to serve.'

His words immediately lifted Peter out of the trance, if trance it was. But not too far out. After he assumed his position on the baseline ready to serve, he closed his eyes for a moment and, to his amazement, found he could resume his viewpoint from the balcony instantaneously. Bergen was edging to his right, in preparation for a serve to the forehand corner. So Peter immediately opened his eyes and smacked one down the centre. The older man got a racquet to it but only to push up a powerless return which Peter punched into the corner of the court for a winner.

So it was throughout this strange set. Peter Winston discovered he could call a momentary view of the court at will by merely batting his eyelids. It offered him an immediate advantage over his opponent since he could now read Bergen's shots twice as well, in addition to getting an objective reading of the position of both players. The image descended like a sense of *déjà vu*; it was with him for only a transitory moment but he found it lingered in the mind with clarity.

Against any other opponent he might have felt the employment of such psychic powers was cheating and unfair. But Nigel Bergen had shown him so little consideration or mercy in the first set that the boy wondered if the great Bali Bhava had not loaned him this gift to balance things out. His volleys now connected with uncanny accuracy, his serves forced Bergen into a defensive position and he found himself hitting groundstroke winners down both sides of his opponent's court. On occasion he glanced up to the balcony, half-expecting to see himself. Instead, where Samantha had been standing, there was now an elderly man in long cream tennis trousers and a crumpled mackintosh. There were wisps of white hair on his reddened cheeks and an unkempt mass of it on his head.

The old chap seemed to be following the game intently. It was still a struggle – Bergen was undoubtedly the better player – but Peter persisted and triumphantly took the set seven–five. He was unsure whether his luck would hold for the decider but this was not something he would discover. To his surprise, his opponent came to the net and held out his hand.

'Well played. Let's leave it at that.'

No further explanation was offered. Bergen threw his racquet and towel into his tennis bag and gathered up his tracksuit. 'Need a bath?' he muttered.

'No,' Peter replied. 'I came already changed.'

'Fine. Give me twenty minutes and then meet me in the main hall. I'll give you a shifty of the Centre Court.'

'That man,' the boy felt he had earned the right to speak by his prowess in the second set. 'The one who was watching. Do you know him?'

Nigel Bergen set a sprightly pace across Somerset Road and nodded with such authority at the uniformed guard on the West Gate that even if he had not been a member, Peter reflected, he would probably have been let through.

'Jonathan Birdwood. Curious fellow, hangs round the club like a stray cat. Member, of course. They say he was handy in his day, played Davis Cup for Ireland – before the Boer War I should imagine.'

With that he sprinted up the steps and pushed open the polished teak door to the All England Club. Peter was left alone – in the land of his dreams. He had seen the club before on the television, of course: the banked ivy, dripping from the Centre Court like a waterfall, the grid of grass courts, each with its separate cover like a horse-blanket and, at the end of them, the Water Tower which no longer served any useful purpose save that of a legendary landmark. He breathed it all in. This was real. This was Wimbledon.

Since Mr Bergen had given him no indication as to how to fill the next twenty minutes, he decided to take a further look around. But his tour was cut short for there, admiring the statue of Fred Perry playing a forehand off the wrong foot which graced the East Gate, was old Birdwood sitting on a shooting stick and smoking a cigarette.

'Good game,' he said. 'Young Nigel's a tough nut to crack. Not a patch on his brother, though. That one could've beaten the best of them.'

'Could have?' Peter Winston was unsure what the old chap meant.

'Dead, long before his time. Found in his bath. A brain haemorrhage his parents said but some people say it was suicide. Two brothers chasing the same girl – bad business. Better if they'd wasted their energies on the court.' He inhaled thoughtfully. 'It'll take brothers to get this country back at the top, though.'

'Why?' Peter was not only intrigued by the contention but welcomed some companionship while waiting to be allowed inside.

'Because brothers were how we won in the past.' Birdwood stamped out his cigarette. He, too, welcomed some companionship; not many people gave him the time of day any more. 'Look at the Dohertys, Big Do and Little Do. Both of them born right here in Wimbledon. Big Do won the Championships four times, beat his brother second time around, and then Little Do went on to win it five times, just to show him. Together they won eight doubles titles and together they brought the Davis Cup here from Boston and here it stayed for five years. Never lost a Davis Cup rubber, Laurence Doherty.'

Birdwood searched in the pocket of his raincoat and pulled out a packet of Silk Cut cigarettes. 'Smoke?' he enquired, as he offered Peter one.

'No, no thank you, sir.' The boy felt flattered to be thought old enough.

'And then there were the twins.' Birdwood's shaking hands struck a Swan Vesta match on its sizeable box and lit the small cigarette in his mouth. 'The Renshaws. They came from

Cheltenham. They had to put on special trains to bring the crowds from there. If anyone was the father of tennis it was William Renshaw. Won the title seven times. No man is ever going to do that again. Beat his brother three of those times. Five doubles titles they won. And the year Willie got tennis elbow – he was father of that injury, too – Earnest won the title to keep it in the family.'

He took an appreciative puff of his Silk Cut and emitted a sort of choking chuckle.

'Were they identical?' Peter asked.

'Not as identical as the Baddeleys, the Baddeleys from Bromley. Wilfred was the youngest chap to win Wimbledon until that German fellow. Only nineteen. And he won it twice more. He and Herbert won the doubles four times and no one could tell them apart. So much so that if Wilfred thought Herbert was having a bad day he'd do all the serving himself and not a soul would notice – least of all their opponents.'

'That's amazing.' Peter raised his voice as he observed that his companion was hard of hearing, cupping his left hand to his ear in order to listen. 'You're very fortunate to have seen such great British players.'

Jonathan Birdwood took a final puff from his cigarette and began to shake so much with laughter that Peter feared he would fall from his shooting stick. 'I didn't see any of them. I'm not that old, you know. Wilfred Baddeley won the Championships in 1891, a hundred years ago.'

To cover his embarrassment Peter indicated the statue of Fred Perry in front of them. 'Well, you must have seen him.'

'Saw him indeed, saw him indeed. Three successive finals. Fine player. If you think about it, Bunny Austin was his brother – not his blood brother, though.'

'Tom Hall, the person who coaches me, says Perry is the greatest player of all time. But he never saw him. Do you think. . . ?'

His question went uncompleted. Samantha was waving agitatedly from the balcony of the main building. 'Peter, come on. Dad's been waiting for hours. He's in a hell of a bate.'

'I'm sorry.' The boy made his apology to Birdwood and began to run in her direction. But he could still hear his companion's voice behind him.

'You tell your Town Hall that I've seen every final here since the war – since the first war. There'll only ever be one candidate for the greatest player.'

Peter had now reached the bottom of the steps but he stopped and turned. 'Who's that?' he called.

'Big Bill.' Birdwood held his left hand up in the air. 'He'd pick up five balls, serve four aces and throw away the fifth. There's no one could do that now.'

'Hurry up,' Samantha seemed as short-tempered as her father. 'He was going to take you round but now he says there isn't time.'

'Ah, there you are.' Nigel Bergen was at the top of the steps, shining from the shower. He glanced at his watch. 'Only time to show you the Centre Court, I'm afraid.'

Peter went inside and penitently followed the father and daughter up the stairs.

'Look up.' Mr Bergen's command sounded as if it came from a schoolmaster. 'Kipling.'

The boy gazed at the words embossed above the door. 'If you can meet with triumph and disaster and treat those two impostors just the same.'

'And here's the most famous tennis court in the world.' Bergen seized both handles to open the double doors but they were locked.

'Shit,' he said frustratedly. 'Some other time, then.'

· Twenty-Five ·

"Peach!"

Winston stood at the net, his racquet tucked under his arm, and applauded Shimizu's passing shot along with the rest of the crowd. It had, indeed, been a do-or-die effort with the Japanese player diving deep to his right as he rescued Winston's return from the edge of the sideline and had then curled the ball unreachably past him to the back of the court.

'Are you all right?' Winston placed both hands on the net and looked across to his fallen opponent, still prostrate against the rolled-up canvas in front of the court-side seats. 'We can stop for a bit if you like – let you get your breath back.'

Shimizu eyed him with suspicion. What was his opponent up to? He was already a set down and about to lose the second if he conceded the next point and here he was offering some form of temporary truce. He decided it was a piece of underhand games-manship to which he would not respond. So he ignored the gesture, slowly picked himself up and walked deliberately back to the baseline, employing his racquet to knock the soil out of the treads in his shoes as he went.

'What did he say? What did he say?' Moses had temporarily left the players' box and Dawson Silver addressed the enquiry to Phoebe.

'He offered him a rest. Shimizu took a tumble – not a bad one. He's up again now.'

'But the Jap won the fucking point, didn't he?'

'Yes, it was an incredible shot. You should have . . .' Phoebe stopped and corrected herself. 'Well, nobody could have anticipated that one.'

'So now Shimizu's serving for the second set, right?'

' 'Fraid so. Things don't look too good.'

'Well, where's Hoffman?' Silver clutched frustratedly at her arm. 'What's he doing in the john when we're in this sort of shit? There's no sense in waiting any longer. It's time to do something.'

'I think that's just what he is doing.' She spoke especially softly to calm him down and defray any attention that might have come their way.

· Twenty-Six ·

'Hi.'

James Winston stirred in his bed and fought open his eyes. He had already entered the twilight zone between waking and sleeping. The figure at the door was hard to distinguish, backlit by the hazy hall light. But the voice was familiar.

'Hi, are you asleep?'

'No,' he pulled himself up against the pillow and fumbled for the bedside lamp. 'Come on in.'

It was Phoebe Carter, clad in a long Osprey Academy T-shirt and seemingly little else. She was carrying a card and a small box, no bigger than a pack of cigarettes, both wrapped in the same cheerful Christmas paper. Closing the door carefully behind her, she tiptoed across the room and sat down on the empty bed beside his.

'I saw Andy's mother collect him at lunch-time today. What a woman – all that white pasty make-up and ghastly jewellery. Where were they going?'

James grinned. 'It's the fashion in Palm Beach. They dress like that to go to the shops. If you don't, people will think you've hit hard times.'

'Anyway,' she said. 'I guessed you'd be on your own so I came to say goodbye. And give you this.'

She handed him the card and the package. 'Go on, open them.'

'I'm afraid I haven't bought you anything,' he apologised as he struggled with the wrapping paper. 'Christmas sort of snuck up unexpectedly this year.'

'No worries,' she assured him, pulling her long bronzed legs under her chin and revealing a skimpy pair of white pants.

'Hey, what are these?' He dangled the keys in front of him with delight for he knew already.

'I wanted to leave Madame Butterfly in loving hands and yours were the best I could think of.'

Phoebe Carter owned a scarlet Suzuki motorbike which she nicknamed Madame Butterfly because, she always told the un-initiated, Suzuki was the name of her faithful friend in the Puccini opera.

'Jesus, that's generous.'

James leant across to kiss her cheek but she caught his face in her hands and twisted it round to give him a long, deliberate kiss on the lips.

'Two presents,' he smiled as he shyly withdrew his head back to his pillow.

'More if you want it.'

He affected to overlook the offer and opened the card. There was a leaping tennis player on the cover. 'May 1995 be a smashing year. Thank you for being my friend. See you sometime,' he read. 'So you're really going home?'

'Sure. It's summer in Sydney right now. It's incredibly beautiful there. Where we are in Watson's Bay, right out by the Heads, you can sit on the porch and watch the ocean racers return to the harbour on a Sunday evening. You should come some time. And guess what my Chrissie prezzie is?'

'I don't know. A framed photo of Ron Laver? You talk about him enough.'

'Rod Laver, you arsehole,' she retorted, jumping onto his bed and settling herself astride the covers. 'No, better than that. A wild card to the New South Wales Open in Sydney. Local girl makes good. If I get through a couple of rounds there I could make it down to Melbourne.'

She bounced provocatively on top of him. 'You'll be able to see me on the television all the way from the Australian Open in Flinders Park.'

'Be careful.' James put a finger to his lips. 'If Hoffman finds you in here I could get canned.'

'What the hell, it's nearly Christmas.'

'But you aren't coming back next year and I am.'

'No,' she laughed. 'I've got an absolute discharge. I'm free. That's why I came to say goodbye. Can I get into bed, it's kinda chilly out here?'

'Sure,' he assented cautiously.

Without waiting for any encouragement Phoebe crossed her arms in front of her and pulled off her T-shirt. James stared mutely at her athletic torso, strongly shaped by hours in the gym and tanned by the Florida sun, and her breasts, white and firm and frightening.

'Did you know that whenever you get anxious, you can just see the outline of what must have been a birthmark, here.' She traced it for him on his forehead.

'I'm not anxious,' he lied.

She slipped into bed beside him and lovingly ran her hands through his long, dark, hair, at the same time nibbling provocatively at the earring in his left lobe. James felt under attack. He hadn't bargained on this and he had no idea of how to respond.

'Are you a virgin?' she asked. 'You shouldn't be at seventeen.'

'I'm not, it's just . . .'

'Just what?' She took his right hand and pressed it against her breast. 'Do you have any feeling where the top of your finger is missing?'

'Yes. The nerves are pretty well normal.'

'How about here?' she asked, sliding her hand through his shorts and gently squeezing his testicles.

'Phoebe, don't,' he protested.

'It's all right. Nobody's going to find us. They're all sound asleep after that awful rum punch. Come on, now. Can't you stiffen up a little to say goodbye?'

'You don't understand,' cried James, drawing his body away from her and throwing it round to face the wall. 'I'm sorry, Phoebe. You think you know me, but you don't.'

He needed to talk to someone but there was no one at Osprey he could talk to. Also he felt he owed Phoebe an explanation – if she knew the truth she would be less offended – but when he went to her room the following morning she had already left for the airport. Her Suzuki, however, was still in its usual place at the end of the bicycle sheds.

James thrust the key into the ignition, looking anxiously around him as if he had no right to take the machine. It roared expensively into life. He had no helmet nor any kind of protective clothing but he didn't care. He felt reckless; he felt the need to take risks. If he was going to meet an early death, today would be a very good day for it.

He turned onto Route 41 North and twisted back the throttle. The machine nearly threw him off as it bounded erratically forward, smearing the highway with scorched rubber. There was other traffic about so he reduced his speed and tried to look reasonably responsible. He had no idea where he was going. Just north. Just away. He kept his eyes assiduously on the road ahead. But when finally a red traffic light forced him to come to a halt he leaned back and, looking up, saw a sign. Stickney Point Road. Then he knew where he was going to go. He made a left turn. He was going home.

James brought the bike to a halt beside Pollux Palisades and sat, short of breath, in the strong morning sun. He gazed reflectively at the empty beach where he used to play and the glistening Gulf of Mexico beyond. Although it was not far from Osprey, he had not been back here since the weekend of the Wall Street crash, more than seven years ago. For one thing he had never had any transport before. He had Phoebe to thank for that – but for little else.

He felt unhappy, uncertain and chronically confused. He desperately wanted to turn the clock back to the time when he used to do cartwheels on the sand with Domingo, the son of the Mexican caretaker, and his aunt would call him in at sunset with the promise of home-made pecan pie. If she was in a good mood she would let him snuggle up next to her on the sofa later and together they would watch her favourite television programmes – *All in the Family* and *The Cosby Show* and *The Golden Girls*.

Why did she have to die? Why did she have to leave him alone in the world? Why hadn't she told him what life was going to be like before she departed? It had all seemed so completely uncomplicated then. Like the people on the TV, problems were things you laughed at and then they went away. But James knew that his would haunt him till the day he died.

Leaving the bike against a tree, he walked down the path to the caretaker's entrance and pressed the bell. Perhaps Domingo would be there to cheer him up. A heavily built black woman with a restless baby in her arms answered the door.

'I was looking for Signora Lopez or her son, Domingo,' he asked diffidently.

'They gone away.' The woman seemed irritated by the enquiry.

'Do you know where?'

'I dunno. Just away.'

Returning to the Suzuki, he hit upon the idea of going to see one-eyed Mike and Mary-Louise. It had been more than a year since they had paid a visit to the Sarasota crematorium together. His weekends had become increasingly occupied with junior tournaments and Mary-Louise no longer bothered to ring to suggest they come and take him out. He felt guilty about not keeping in touch, so he stopped at the local store and bought them a fluffy snowman stuffed with candies as a Christmas present.

A scraggly Christmas tree bearing strands of tinsel like a weeping willow had been placed at the entrance to the trailer park with the words 'Have a Cool Yule' chalked on the notice board leaning against it. In fact, it was anything but cool. The temperature had reached the low eighties and was climbing. Many people had attempted to decorate their mobile homes with cotton snow sprinkled over the awnings and artificial holly with wax berries arrayed around the windows and strings of Christmas lights shining redundantly in the baking morning sun.

There seemed to James a sense of desperation about these gestures, as if people were wishing they were somewhere else and hoping to convince themselves by these tokens that they were. Maybe Phoebe was right. Maybe Florida was God's waiting room where you sat passively until you were summoned. He was relieved to observe, as he turned the corner, that such attempts at festivity were nowhere to be seen on Mike and Mary-Louise's trailer.

Neither were Mike and Mary-Louise. The doors were firmly padlocked, the windows shuttered closed and there was no truck in the driveway, only a rusting go-kart – his.

'Looking for Mary-Lou?'

James turned round to see an elderly man in a baseball cap and tartan shorts sunning himself beside the trailer opposite.

'I was looking for both of them. Mike, as well.'

'Aw, he hasn't been here since the summer. Not since the stroke. Didn't you hear?'

'No.' James switched off the engine and pulled the bike back onto its stand. 'What happened?'

'Are you their son?' asked the old man.

'I'm just a friend. A friend of a friend really. We'd kinda lost contact this year through one thing and another.'

'Well, he was hit real hard.' The neighbour shook his head at the memory of it. 'The paramedics were down here, five of them. Didn't think he'd pull through at first. But he's a tough old critter. Paralysed right down one side, though. Don't think he'll be jumping the five-barred gate again.'

James was stunned and filled with unease. 'Did you see him? What did he look like?'

'Nope, never did. They took him away in an ambulance. He'll not be back here again, poor fella.'

'But Mary-Louise?'

'Oh, she came back all right. Very shaken, though. Tried to learn to drive that pick-up they had but it was too late. Some things you have to do while you're young and healthy. Took two buses every day to get to the Citrus Memorial Hospital. Began to take its toll on her, as well.'

'Is he still there? Do you know how you get to it?' The news made James more desperate to see them than ever before. At least Mike was alive and he could make a sort of peace with him.

'No, sir. Not at those prices. They had to sell the truck to pay the bill. Don't think they were well enough covered by their insurance. That's a thing to remember, young fella, while you're still hale and hearty. Make sure your insurance policies are as well. I should know. Used to sell them for near on forty years.'

'But where are they now?'

'I think they moved him to one of those free Medicaid nursing homes over in Orange County. Mary-Lou told me the name when she came to say goodbye but I don't remember too good now.' He pushed his cap further up his forehead as if to clear his brain. 'Sure wish she'd have stayed here for the holiday period. We could've gone to Starvin' Marvin together. Full Christmas dinner for old folks for only three dollars if you get there before noon. Not too much fun going on your own, though, no one to pull your cracker with. But no one's pulled my cracker for a long time.' He dissolved into a thin snigger.

'Is she going to come back?' James asked.

'Said she would. But who knows? Lots of folks say they're coming back and you never see them again.'

For a split second James looked at the frail figure in the chair and could see himself: vulnerable and old and alone. Despite the warmth of the day a shiver went through his system. He reached back into the pannier behind his seat and pulled out the candy snowman.

'Here,' he said, stretching over and handing it to the old man, 'Happy Christmas.'

'That's very kind. Thank you.' He was clearly touched and not a little emotional. 'Didn't think I'd be getting anything this year, so a surprise is all the sweeter. You have a happy Christmas, too, and mind how you go on that hot rod of yours. Old age ain't so bad, you know. It's worth trying once.'

'Okay, let's see how you handle a tie-break.'

Aside from any academic work, Moses Hoffman made a personal annual assessment of each student at Osprey. It was done in alphabetical order so Winston inevitably came close to the end. His opponent that afternoon was Al Williams, a Southerner from a patrician family whose ability to pay the full fees enabled Hoffman to subsidise another scholarship boy more likely to make it in college tennis.

Whether it was due to his exacerbated remorse at not being able to explain things to Phoebe or his lingering melancholy at the thought of one-eyed Mike possibly passing the last Christmas of his life in some soulless nursing home, James played with coiled anger inside him and whipped and drove and snaked the ball mercilessly into the corners of the court. Any fraternal Christmas spirit was conspicuously absent from his game and The Magic informed his every shot. Williams, a weak player at the best of times, was left looking inept and incapable at this, the worst of times.

'Okay, break it up.' Mo deliberately sounded like a boxing referee as he came onto the court after Williams had virtually been knocked out 7–1. 'Albert, take a shower and be back in ten minutes. There are always going to be days like this – you've just got to wash them out of your hair.'

'Yes, sir.' The sporting Southerner congratulated James with a firm hand and sprinted off towards the boys' quarters.

'Jim' – the veteran coach would have put an arm round the seventeen-year-old's shoulders had there not been an eight-inch disparity in height between the two men – 'come and sit down.'

He led him back to the bench beside the centre court where his charts and personal files were laid out on top of his briefcase.

James, his tennis shirt sodden with perspiration, undid the red bandana that held back his matted hair and took a prolonged swig from the water bottle that was a compulsory part of every player's equipment at the academy – the 'dehydration is dangerous' rule was reiterated at the start of every semester. He sunk onto the bench and waited to be congratulated.

Hoffman took his time reading through the boy's report, then removed his trade-mark black peaked hat and wiped the sweat off his forehead with the back of his arm. 'Son,' he said at last, 'you've fucked up.'

The remark hit the boy like a blow from behind. 'In what way?' was his immediate riposte.

'Well, at the Juniors at Kalamazoo for starters,' Mo pointed to the result with his finger, 'but you didn't need me to tell you that.'

'I came up against Sid Wood. He's the best in Saddlebrook. I wasn't in with a chance.'

'But you didn't give yourself a chance. You've got to be out of your mind to tank a match like that. There were scouts there from every decent school in the country. If you'd run him three and three they'd have given you a second glance.

'I was feeling sick,' James lied. 'And I wanted to save myself for the doubles later. We won that.'

'Nobody bothers with first round doubles matches,' the coach patiently explained. 'They take an interest from the quarters on. By then where were you?'

A sullen silence confirmed where Winston then was. Nowhere, as far as the university talent scouts were concerned.

Hoffman stubbed the bottom of his pen into his briefcase. 'You have the potential to take any kid in your age group in a single set. Your problem is that most of them have the potential to take you out in the next two. It's a best of three game, Jim, and if you make it to the big time best of five. You'll never sustain the sort of sprint tennis you just played against Albert in a three-setter.'

'But it wasn't a three-setter. It was a tie-break. That's why I went for them.'

'Okay, point taken. Nice work. Your eye was in.' Mo held up a hand in acknowledgement. 'But what we have to do is groove your game so that you can spread the pressure instead of expending it all in a ten-minute burst.'

'Sure.' James sounded more than ready to listen and learn. 'What schools do you think I could go for? I wouldn't mind Stanford. Or Yale.'

The coach shook his head. 'At the moment, no chance. Your best bet is to start with something in the Boston area. Stay at home, steady up. Some people develop later than others.'

'But there are kids younger than me already turning pro.'

'There are no two players the same, remember that.' Moses put down his notes and looked pensively at him. 'I'm going to tell you something. Do you know what I used to be known as back in California?'

'No.'

'Little Mo. And do you know why?'

'Because you're short, I guess.'

'Nope. I'm not that short. Five foot six on a good day.' Hoffman smiled at his own humour. 'I was called it after a woman who was born the same year as me – 1934 – and won Wimbledon at the same age you are now – seventeen. Stubby little girl, stubby little nose. Won it three years in succession as a matter of fact. But at the age of twenty – two weeks after her third victory – she gave up the game for ever.'

'Why?' James was intrigued.

'Crushed her leg in a riding accident. Never really recovered. Little Mo. Maureen Connolly. She couldn't volley as well as you, in fact she was still learning to in the year she quit. Hit nearly everything off the baseline. But she had concentration you would kill for, never made an unforced error. This is a quotation from her, see, I pasted inside my case to remind me.'

James moved beside him and read the fading piece of card. 'I hated my opponents. This was no passing dislike but a blazing, virulent, powerful and consuming hate. I believed I could not win without hatred. And win I must because I was afraid to lose – Little Mo.'

'Let me tell you what her concentration was like,' Hoffman went on. 'The day before she died of cancer, although she was under heavy medication, she wrote out a list of books that she wanted her two little daughters to read after she was gone.'

'What age was she?' asked James.

'Thirty-four. Pretty well the same age as Martina when she won Wimbledon for the eighth time. You should never second-guess God's timetable, Jim. Arthur Ashe didn't win it till he was thirty-two. And Big Bill managed it at thirty-seven. You don't have to hurry.'

'Sir,' William was back from his shower and running across the court. 'My father's come to take me home. Could he have a quick word with you? He's anxious to know how I'm doing.'

James's sleep that night was made restless by jumbled dreams of death. First Aunt Violet, then Mary-Louise, then Little Mo and the the faceless mother that he never knew all telling him what to do with himself as their coffins creaked along the electric ramp of the crematorium towards the crackling flames. He awoke and sat up, wet with sweat. There was someone at the door.

'Hi, are you asleep?'

Dr Bob carefully closed the door behind him and silently crossed the room.

'What happened last night?' said the boy. 'I was waiting for you but you never came.'

'I looked in,' smiled the coach as he slipped out of his dressing gown, 'but I could see you were otherwise engaged.'

· Twenty-Seven ·

The X-ray hung on the illuminated screen in front of Grace Winston like a death warrant. First it was clear and then it went in and out of focus as if someone were fiddling around with the lens on a camera. Her head seemed to fill with invisible fumes and for a moment she feared she was going to faint.

'Are you all right?'

'Very far from it — if what you've just told me is true.'

The consultant smiled at her spirited irony. 'I mean would you like to lie down, or a glass of water or something?'

'No,' she stopped looking at the negative and returned her attention to him. 'I'll be fine. For the moment, anyway.'

'There's no reason why you shouldn't remain fine for quite a few years to come. The majority of patients don't die from cancer, you know. We can cut it out and control it.'

'You just can't cure it.'

'Not yet. One day. We all carry cancer inside us, it's just our genetic immune system that becomes fallible. Sooner or later they'll find a way of strengthening that up.' Mr Hartley-Smith, smart as a stockbroker in his custom-made suit and his silver silk tie, opened the well-worn file in front of him. 'Quite a history. This accident, back in Boston. What happened exactly?'

Grace shrugged defensively. 'I was hit by a truck. Simple as that. It was near the end of the race, I was tired and they were following the runners for TV. Nobody's fault really.'

'You were lucky to escape with your life.'

'Or unlucky,' she replied enigmatically.

'The Americans did a good job on the pelvis.' Hartley-Smith

turned back to the X-ray. 'Patched you up just fine.'

'So that's not the cause of it.'

'No, not at all. It could possibly have speeded the onset of your arthritis but it wouldn't have had any effect on the bile-duct.'

'What caused it then?' Grace leaned across the desk imploringly. 'You say the biopsy revealed cancerous cells in the cysts. Where did they come from?'

Hartley-Smith eyed her sympathetically. 'If we knew, we could prevent them.'

'Fate,' said Grace, tightly puckering her lips.

'There are grounds for optimism. I think you'll be around to help with your grandchildren.' The consultant turned his attention back to the file. 'Twin sons, I see. Nice. Eighteen this year so you may not have too long to wait. By the way, there seems to be a mistake here, we've only got one listed as next of kin – Peter. Shall I put in James as well?'

'No, don't.' Grace immediately realised how panicky she sounded. 'There's only Peter . . . the other . . . it's complicated.'

Mr Hartley-Smith was experienced enough not to pursue the matter further at that moment. But there was another matter he wanted to pursue. 'When you were in training, preparing for your marathons, did you take any additives to help your performance?'

'No, nothing.' Grace looked across at him with open-eyed sincerity.

'You're quite sure?'

'I'm as certain as . . .' she began, and then it came back to her.

'What?' The consultant jerked his head forward like a beagle that had picked up the scent.

'There was this man,' she recalled reluctantly. 'Our trainer, I suppose. He offered injections. Some took them, others didn't.'

'But you did.'

'Only a couple of times. Maybe three. Four at the most.'

'Steroids?' asked Hartley-Smith, but he already knew the answer.

'I think so. But surely they can't have . . .'

'I'm afraid they can.'

She was just in time to take the short cut home through Margravine Cemetery at the back of the Charing Cross Hospital. It closed early, at four o'clock, in January.

Did they always build graveyards so close to hospitals, Grace wondered as she cautiously made her way along the icy path between the sprouting sepulchres. She used to take Peter for walks through here on summer evenings when he was a child. The headstones seemed to have remained the same. She supposed it must be a full house; you probably had to be cremated if you died in London today.

The very thought of it made her shiver. In many ways she feared the unknown period between now and death more than death itself. Although her expression was as glazed as the ice that clung stubbornly to the tombs, she obtained some comfort from the recognition of old familiar friends, many of them military, who had been there when her son was a toddler and had remained peacefully undisturbed by the passing of the years. 'Waldegrave Rock Thompson' – Grace had always liked the Rock – 'Doctor of Medicine and Surgeon, Late 46th West Indian Regiment.' 'Zenobia, dearly loved wife of Major T.W. Francis of the 9th Lancers.' T.W. was to join her sooner than he expected. And many young men in their teens and twenties who died at Ypres in June 1916. 'Leonard Horstead June 4 – dearly loved'.

Leonard – the name came back to haunt her. Fucking Lennie, she thought, dearly hated. How ironic that the only man she had ever felt any emotion for should also have been her executioner. And then she remembered that, but for him, there probably would have been no Peter. Her executioner and her saviour. She had no idea where he lived now. Perhaps he was in here, pushing up the daisies. He had taken enough of the stuff himself.

And there was Bunnie – the sight of the familiar head-stone unlocked another nostalgic memory – 'Bunnie, dearly loved child of Percy and Blanche Berrif – aged seven.' Peter had been just that age when he was first able to read the simple hymn inscribed on it:

> Jesus loves me. He will stay
> Close beside me all the way.
> If I love him when I die,
> He will take me home on high.

That must have been more than ten years ago, she reflected. Now her son was preparing to leave home whereas little Bunnie would always remain little Bunnie.

The tomb opposite caught her eye – 'Maurice Cockerell who fell asleep 1920'. She had never noticed it before but several of the graves clustered there, all of people buried around the time of the First World War, used the expression 'fell asleep'. Perhaps their children found comfort in intimations of immortality. How did the poem go? She used to teach it to her pupils.

> Our birth is but a sleep and a forgetting;
> The soul that rises with us, our life's star,
> Hath had elsewhere its setting,
> And cometh from afar.

As the rust-coloured cornices of Baron's Court Tube Station beckoned from across the wintry road, her recollection of the words of Wordsworth ignited a burst of inspiration. Grace now knew what she was going to do. She would telephone Dr Weghofer.

Peter was in the kitchen when she let herself in.

'Which hand?' he teased snapping his arms behind his back as if he had been caught looting the refrigerator. In the course of the past few months he had developed an almost flirtatious relationship with his mother.

She deliberately took off her coat and put it on top of his on the rack at the bottom of the stairs. 'I'd like an entirely new hand. A new pack of cards, come to that.'

His face registered her fear. 'The cysts? I thought that once they were out it would all be okay?'

'It would have been' – Grace came into the kitchen and, without thinking, ran the tap for a cup of tea – 'if they'd been okay.'

'And they're not.'

Her back was to him as she reached across for the kettle. ' 'Fraid not.'

'Oh, Mummy.' He came across and held her round the waist. 'What are they going to do now?'

'They want to put a piece of radioactive metal inside me. Apparently there's a chance it will kill off the cancer.'

'I'm so sorry. It's worth a try, I suppose.'

She released herself from his grip and struck a match to light the stove. 'Why aren't you at tennis training? Doesn't the Sutton squad meet on Thursdays?'

'It does. I just thought you might like some company tonight.'

Grace reached for the kettle. 'Tea?'

'Please.'

'Left,' she said.

'What?'

'Left hand.'

'Oh.' Peter had forgotten that he still had letters in both of them. He handed her the airmail envelope. 'Our daily bread.'

His mother took a knife from the draining board and slit it open. It was the usual Narragansett Bank of Boston cheque, now for two thousand dollars. Whoever was sending them had been thoughtful enough to increase the amount in line with inflation.

'WTT Trust Fund.' Peter read the words over her shoulder. 'Why don't we know who they are?'

'I tried once but the bank refused to disclose it. And, in truth, since then I've been afraid that if I did find out maybe the money would stop coming.'

'WTT,' he repeated. 'There used to be a sort of competition in America – I read about it – called World Team Tennis. Cities would play each other, like at baseball, but it never really caught on. Do you suppose they might have decided to distribute what was left among promising . . . you know?'

'Doubt it.' Grace shook her head. 'This started coming long before you picked up a racquet. Now what about the other letter.'

'You open it.' Peter thrust the buff envelope into her hand. 'I couldn't bear to. I'd been waiting for you to come home.'

His mother looked at the postmark. 17 Jan 1995. Cambridge. 'Oh, dear,' was all she said.

'Make it quick. I've failed I know.'

His mother didn't bother with the knife this time but anxiously tore the end off with her hand and extracted the single white piece of paper from inside.

'I'm sorry,' said Peter, attempting to read her expression.

This time it was Grace who put her arms around her tall son and brought his head down to rest on her shoulder. 'Selwyn College,' she said. 'You've got a place. A new home next September.'

In the four years since she had spoken at Nevis's Sunday gathering Dr Abigail Weghofer had moved her consulting room from her flat in Kilburn to Number eighty Harley Street.

'Business must be good,' Peter observed as he pressed the buzzer. He had insisted on accompanying his mother to her appointment.

Abigail, her raven hair still in the same long single plait, had expanded a little with the passing of time and now sported a white consulting coat over her generous frame. Clearly the intention, like the address, was to add a medical veneer to her metaphysical technique. She remembered the evening at Nevis's and could even recall Peter as the boy in the corner. 'Your meditation worked well – I noted the expression on your face.'

Because of this she permitted him to remain in the room while his mother embarked on her past life therapy. To begin with she made copious notes about Grace's medical history and current condition. 'He's very good, Mr Hartley-Smith. As good as surgery can be. But sometimes that's not good enough. Right, now I want you to take off your shoes, loosen any zips or buttons that might be holding your body in. Just lie down on the table and and close your eyes. Try and shut out the world completely. I'll play you a little music to help.'

Dr Weghofer touched a button on the desk and a chorus of otherworldly sounds emanated from hidden speakers in each corner of the room. She pulled down the blind which had a Japanese sunset printed on the back and lit two slender incense candles positioned on a sort of altar in front of a wall-mirror. Picking up a basket from the floor, piled with what looked like quartz crystals, she circled the table placing them randomly around Grace's inert body.

'The hospitals can only cure the illnesses of this lifetime. But here we can go to the heart of the matter, to the cause of the cancer. One patient came to me with a constant nagging pain in his chest. It disappeared when he re-lived the time he was a Roman centurion and we discovered he was pierced in exactly that spot with a spear. Another woman suffered terrible loneliness, utterly unable to make friends. We ascertained, through her regression, she had been a Trappist monk in the Middle Ages. Always, there is a reason.'

She placed both hands on Grace's brow. 'We don't use hypnotism for this, instead a form of theta brain wave relaxation. Together we re-enter that earlier existence and I guide you towards the source of your ills.'

Moving her hands down Grace's body she brought them to rest on her stomach. 'And this is where the pain is, yes?'

'No pain,' Grace replied, 'but yes, the problem.'

'Very good. Now clear your consciousness and tell me a year that comes into your mind.'

'1920.' Grace was unsure why she said it at first but then realised she had been thinking of Maurice Cockerell, in the cemetery, who simply fell asleep.

'And tell me a country.'

'France.' The rows of graves at Ypres filled her imagination in unending ranks.

'Perfect. Just relax completely. We are in France. It is the twenties. The war is over and it is now a time of champagne and laughter. There is music playing. Do you hear it, Grace?'

She nodded dreamily. 'Saxophones. Jazz. The Charleston. Josephine Baker.'

'Very good. And you are there. What are you wearing?'

'I'm wearing silk. A silk pleated dress – calf length. It's the flapper generation. What fun.'

Abigail Weghofer lifted a quartz crystal from the top of the table and held it over Grace's head. 'I can see you now. Just as you said. We are in the South of France. In Cannes. You are a star. You are wearing a salmon pink bandeau and white rabbit fur coat and everybody is applauding you.'

'Is it at the film festival?'

'It could be.'

'Surely that didn't start until much later?'

'Anyway,' Abigail was not put off, 'you are not beautiful like a film star. Your skin is sallow – maybe from childhood jaundice – but you are triumphant and your personality is such as to hold everyone enthralled. But now I see a dark cloud on the horizon. It is taking you north, away from the sun and the fame.'

'To Paris. It must be the Second World War.'

'I hear voices of young people around you.'

'I'm a teacher.'

'A teacher, yes. You are not married. But you have found

contentment. Only the corpuscles in your blood are in rebellion. It is not good.'

'Leukaemia.'

'It's so sad. You are called before your time. Your spirit is needed for another body. But your name does not die. You remain a star.'

'Who is she, who was she?' Peter was unable to contain himself any longer and had joined Dr Weghofer beside his mother.

'I see four men. Four famous Frenchmen following you to the grave. There are flowers, beautiful flowers . . . but no, it is gone.'

'Oh dear,' Grace opened her eyes. 'No good?'

'Very good,' Weghofer reassured her, indicating the crystal which she had been rotating over her stomach. 'Already we are beginning to release the accumulated centuries of pain. We have not yet found the problem but we have found one lifetime. On your next visit we will find another.'

Grace sat up, wondering if she could afford another hundred pounds and how many more hundreds after that. Past-life therapy was not, as yet, available on the National Health Service.

Dr Weghofer registered her concern. 'We have time left. Perhaps your son would like some therapy. No extra charge.'

'But there's nothing wrong with me,' Peter protested.

'There are many things wrong with all of us,' the doctor insisted. 'The more we come to terms with our past lives, the more we understand our present existence.'

'Yes,' Grace sat up. 'Go on, give it a go.'

It took a full twenty minutes for Dr Weghofer to guide him through the relaxation ritual. He had taken off his tennis shoes – he was on his way to an indoor training session at The Queen's Club – and his six-foot two-inch frame was too long for the table with his white-socked feet flopping off the end.

'Now I think we are ready. You are a bright student, no? I can sense learning inside you and I see ancient seats of learning before you.'

'I'm going to Cambridge, yes.' Peter's voice was sleepy and slightly slurred.

'A student and an athlete. A tennis player. A warm summer's afternoon, a freshly mown court, everyone so smart in white and the smell of the grass on the ball, the sweetest scent you ever can remember.'

Peter breathed in heavily. 'Yes,' he agreed.

'Now I am going to take you back, before that time, when you were small, so small. What is the first thing you ever remember, Peter? Take your time.'

Grace gripped tightly onto the arm of her chair. She didn't like the way this was going. Surely he could have no memory of the kidnap, the car, the basket?

'My mother is taking me into the sea. The water is cold. I don't like it. I don't like it because there is green seaweed all around, some of it with slippery pods. I am afraid of standing on it. I want to go back to the sand. Please, Mummy, please.'

'It's all right.' Grace was standing up.

'Sit down,' Weghofer commanded, waving her away. She had found a more than receptive patient. 'We know now why you stay away from the water. But we are going further back. The soul has an existence before it comes into this world. It is already there in the womb. And sometimes the moment of birth is traumatic. So now we are there, in the womb. It is dark, it is safe. Although you are alone you are not afraid . . .'

'No . . .' Peter interrupted her, 'no . . . I am not alone . . . I . . .'

'Stop it.' Grace was on her feet again. 'No more. I forbid it. Stop it at once.'

· Twenty-Eight ·

Eamonn Quinn, solid and florid in his lime green summer suit, had somehow obtained a seat exactly opposite the umpire's chair, beside the gangway that separated G and H Blocks. He was near the back, close to where a female corporal manned her post, pulling a thin chain across the entry while play was in progress. Quinn had been up and down from his seat at every changeover like a cuckoo on a clock. Winston had observed this from the corner of his eye, feeling certain it was sooner or later bound to arouse suspicion.

But no one seemed to have taken much notice except him. Then, when he had lost the second set, Quinn had disappeared totally and his place had been taken by Moses. Winston could see him with utter clarity even though he was in the penumbra of the overhanging roof. And he knew with equal clarity the signal that Mo was sending out to him as he tugged with increasing fervour at the peak of his cap, first with one hand, then with the other, finally with both.

But he chose to ignore him. This was an agreed counsel of despair and he was not despairing yet. The second set had gone to seven–five and they had now been on court, according to the digital time on the Rolex scoreboard, for more than two hours. It was his intention to detain Shimizu there for another two before his task was done.

He felt more confident and in control now, as if his isolation had become his inspiration, and by taking the pace off the ball managed to tease out the rallies for much greater duration, almost as if it were a women's singles. When he served he no longer went for the easy ace – not that any ace was easy against the Japanese champion – but hit for position, neither following the ball into the net nor giving his opponent the opportunity to come in himself.

At three games all it was Shimizu to serve at the start of what was known, even to club players, as the vital seventh. His first ball was a clean ace, catching the edge of the centre line and then curving into an unreachable orbit.

'Out,' called the lineswoman behind Winston, snapping her arm into the air like a fascist salute.

'Come on, what do you mean?' Shimizu cast aside his second ball and strolled querulously towards the net. 'How can it be out when it hits the line? The only person who could call that ball out is his mother. Are you his mother?'

The sections of the crowd that could hear his questioning were suitably amused. But not the umpire. 'Mr Shimizu, please,' he warned. And then, directing his attention to the woman still with her arm in the air, he enquired: 'Are you sure?'

She nodded emphatically, not wavering an inch.

'Second serve,' called the umpire. A succession of catcalls and boos came from various parts of the stadium; obviously there was a feeling that the Japanese player had been the victim of an unfair call.

'If I hit the same spot with my second, will it be out as well?' Shimizu called to the official. With a lead of two sets he could afford to see the funny side.

But he didn't hit the same spot. He put a slow, heavily spun ball securely into the back third of the service court. However it still proved to be an ace, since Winston made no attempt at all to return it. The head of his racquet remained resting in his left hand as he watched the ball bounce by.

'Were you ready, Mr Winston?' The umpire seemed concerned.

'Yea,' he replied, walking towards the other side of the court.

The applause started slowly as some spectators realised he had conceded the point and when people informed their less knowledgeable neighbours it grew in volume, so much so that, despite the umpire's calls for silence, Shimizu had to stand back and wait for it to die down.

'Did he hit a winner?' Dawson asked Phoebe, perplexed.

'In a way,' she replied.

• Twenty-Nine •

Moses Hoffman hated Boston. A city of snobs and students, his father always used to say, and his own infrequent visits to the place had done little to disprove that assessment. Admittedly Jews were tolerated in the better clubs now, but there was still the club within the club from which they would always be excluded. Besides, he had enough students and more than enough snobs among the parents he had to deal with down in Florida.

The flight from Sarasota had been crowded and uncomfortable. He had been put in a bad mood from the moment he boarded when an officious cabin attendant had forced him to leave his tennis bag by the aircraft door for stowing in the hold. 'It won't fit under your seat, sir,' she had insisted with the sort of smile that came with the uniform, 'federal regulations, I'm afraid.' If he had been forty years younger and on his way to a tournament, Moses thought, she would probably have leapt at the chance to look after it for him.

So now he stood with a hundred other passengers vacantly watching a vacant carousel. At least, half-watching it. The other half of his attention was on the look-out for the girl Edmund Michaels had sent to meet him. 'Don't worry about finding her,' Michaels had insisted on the phone, 'she'll find you. Black cap, black tracksuit, right?'

Mo had reluctantly acknowledged that his outfit had not changed over the years but, ever mindful of the negligence of other people's arrangments, had demanded to know what the woman looked like. 'She's a beautiful blonde,' the doctor had laughed. 'Would I send anything else?'

There were no blondes, beautiful or otherwise, that he could see outside the choked luggage collection area, just two uniformed black men in peaked chauffeurs hats. Boston, thought Hoffman.

He had been extremely reluctant to come. June was the peak period at Osprey with students setting off for tournaments all over the place. 1998 had been a vintage year and Bill Clothier had already left for England to play the pre-Wimbledon qualifying event at Roehampton. If he made it, Mo intended to go over for the tournament itself. He hadn't been since 1980 when he witnessed the Borg–McEnroe tie-break, which he always cited as the most spectacular tennis match he had ever seen or was ever likely to see. So he was in no hurry to return. Various Osprey graduates had played there over the years but none had made it as far as the second week. Besides, he was committed to a lucrative adult coaching course during the Championships which traded on people's heightened interest in the game at the time and involved Mo in giving expert analyses of the matches in the evenings. However, Clothier was the brightest prospect he had had in years and well worth the sacrifice of handing over the course to his deputy.

But Edmund Michaels had been unyielding on the phone; it was essential that Hoffman come to Boston. Ninety-nine times out of a hundred the veteran coach would have ignored such an injunction but he felt doubly indebted to the doctor. It was Michaels, more than thirty years ago, who had saved his late wife's life by diagnosing the urgent need for an appendectomy while all the other medics at Leucadia Naval Hospital had insisted she was merely suffering from food poisoning. And Mo also felt a lingering sense of remorse about asking James Winston to leave Osprey – expel was too strong a word – because of his unfortunate liaison with Borogon who, unknown to the students, was living on borrowed time because of a previous similar offence. When he was discovered in the boys' block on this occasion Borogon was asked to have his bags packed and his office cleared by Christmas Eve.

Maybe Hoffman had been too harsh on Winston. He had taken him at Edmund Michaels' behest and the boy had proved both able and enthusiastic. He might even have hacked it on the satellite circuit. The teaching staff had tended to dismiss him as a one-set wonder but Mo was convinced he could train his temperament and concentration to last out longer. However, the same staff had been unanimous that if Borogon went, Winston went, and Hoffman had been obliged to defer to this decision. He softened the blow to the boy's father and his old friend Michaels by saying that James had seduced an under-age Australian girl – a fiction to which Winston himself seemed happy to subscribe.

Somebody had stolen his bag. Moses had seen it at last emerge through the slatted rubber at the far end of the carousel and was waiting for it to pass the anxious crowd and come to him. But it had gone. He decided not to shout – it was against his nature to create a fuss – but moved swiftly towards the sliding doors to block the thief's exit. He caught sight of him almost immediately, a man actually smaller than himself with his back to him nonchalantly retreating towards the glass partition with the brightly coloured Goffi bag in his right hand.

Moses stepped smartly forward and grabbed him by the arm. 'Where the fuck do you think you're going?'

It wasn't a him; it was a her. The Chicago White Sox cap had disguised the blonde tresses but there was no mistaking the hazel eys and open rouged mouth that registered such surprise.

'Mr Hoffman, I'm so sorry. I looked for you everywhere. Ed said you'd be wearing a tracksuit.'

Moses glanced down at his blue blazer and grey flannels. 'I had a Trustees' meeting before I left,' he explained. 'I was going to change on the plane but the stewardess took my bag away.'

The girl offered a beguiling grin, cheerful and cheeky. 'It seems to be living a life of its own today. By the way, I'm Brandi de Soto.'

'Where are we going?' Moses uneasily watched the sign for Downtown Boston disappear to their right as Brandi kept the Camaro on a course north along the John Fitzgerald Expressway.

'Cambridge,' she shouted over the thud of heavy metal that was emanating from the four corners of the vehicle. 'Ed has a place there. Sort of hush-hush. To tell you the truth I've never been in it.'

Hush-hush? Moses began to wonder if the doctor had switched his line of work. First the promise of revelations too important to be uttered over the phone. Now this girl was talking in these clandestine terms. He was badly in need of some explanation but he wanted it from the horse's mouth.

'What exactly do you do for him?' He tried to make the enquiry seem as casual as possible.

'Oh, my mom's one of his oldest friends. She'd sometimes help him out with the aftercare of patients, things like that. She's married again, though, a dentist in Chicago. So I suppose I carry on the family business.' Brandi let free a tinkling laugh as if the expression had just occurred to her.

'Is that a full-time occupation?'

The girl leaned forward and, softening the music, removed a compact camera from the glove compartment. 'No, not at all. It comes in fits and bursts. I majored in photography.' She held the camera up in her left hand and flashed a shot into Hoffman's face. 'Had a cover picture for the *Boston Globe Magazine* at Christmas – children playing in the snow. But most of my stuff's for *Snap!* They pay a good retainer. Have you heard of them?'

'It's a sort of scandal sheet, isn't it?'

'Nah, not scandal really. Just about famous people. Give the public what they want to know.'

'Doesn't it snoop into their private lives?' Moses had seen it and knew it did.

'Nobody asked them to become famous,' Brandi replied with a defensive shrug, turning up the music to curtail their conversation.

'And the work you do for Edmund? Is that similar?'

She pursed her lips and once again offered him a smile of wicked innocence. 'I'm not meant to talk about that.'

Brandi dropped him a third of the way down Castor Street off Massachusetts Avenue with the assurance that the doctor would be waiting for him inside Number eighty-eight. Moses noted the sophisticated video surveillance system by the door; Michaels was evidently not in the habit of opening it to casual callers.

'Mo? That you?' The familiar voice responded instantly when he pressed the bell. 'Where's your tracksuit? Come on up, anyway.'

He hadn't seen Edmund Michaels since James Winston's fourth year at Osprey. The doctor seemed to have aged considerably since then. He had lost a lot of weight and, despite the perkiness of his bow-tie, his skin lay loose and grey at his neck. Moses was sixty-four and he calculated that Michaels must be at least nine years older than him.

He noticed that his friend made no attempt to come down the stairs to greet him but the two men embraced warmly when he reached the top. Michaels, clad in a full-length white medical coat, led him into a small laboratory off the landing, bombarding him with irrelevant questions about the journey and his job as he took his bag and handed him a cup of lukewarm coffee.

'I've booked you in at the Cambridge Intercontinental – Nobel Prizewinners stay there,' the doctor informed him proudly.

'Do they jack up their rates accordingly?' Moses was less than impressed.

'Don't worry, it's on me,' Edmund assured him. 'Brandi will take you there after dinner.'

'What's up doc?' Hoffman was anxious to get to the point. 'What's so special about Jim Winston that it can't be dealt with on the phone?'

'Sit down,' Michaels indicated a high wooden stool beside the cluttered work bench. 'It's good of you to come. It's not without reason. There are two things here that I needed to show you, not things I could put in the mail. And also I wanted you to talk to James.'

'How is he? Still at Boston University?'

'I'll tell you in a moment,' the doctor replied guardedly. 'But take a look at these first.'

He slid a slim folder of photographs across the work surface and then sat back and removed a single cigarette from the packet in his breast pocket. Snapping open the Zippo lighter which he had been fidgeting with in his right hand, he carefully lit up and pulled pensively on the cigarette to allow Hoffman time to take in the pictures.

'It'll kill you,' Moses warned without looking up.

'At seventy-three,' the doctor replied, 'I think the calendar will probably do it first. I'm sure Dawson Silver can verify that with his charts. What do you think of them?'

'The short hair certainly suits him,' the coach was purposely tempering his surprise. 'And I'm glad he's lost the earring. That hippy look was taking him nowhere. But I don't recognise the college. These blue blazers with the crossed racquets seem very Ivy League. Isn't that some sort of cricket game going on in the background?'

'You're absolutely right. Fenners, to be precise. Cambridge University cricket ground – and tennis ground, as you see from the grass courts.'

'Your old college,' Moses remembered.

'University,' the doctor corrected him, straightening his yellow and maroon Hawks Club bow-tie.

'So Jim made the team. Is that the firsts?'

'The Blues. You're awarded one if you're selected to play against Oxford.'

'Well that's great.' Moses looked down again at the photograph of the eight players, proudly erect in their light blue blazers with Winston standing at the back on the right with his usual slightly sheepish smile on his lips. 'Very good. I thought the kid would make it. Just shows what a change of environment can do.' He finished his coffee. 'You could have posted these to me, you know. I promise I would have sent them back.'

'But I needed to explain.' Dr Michaels was being deliberately cryptic.

'I have heard of Cambridge University. It's in England, right?' Moses betrayed a groundswell of irritation. 'You could have written it on the back to make sure I understood.'

'That's not the point,' said Michaels, coming to his. 'The point is that that is not James Winston.'

Moses picked up the team photograph again and held it beneath the angled light in front of him. 'Then it's his double,' he shrugged after studying it for a while.

'His twin, in fact.' The doctor stubbed out his cigarette with dramatic satisfaction.

The coach perused the picture once more. 'Amazing. Identical. And a tennis player, too. Don't ever remember Jim mentioning him, though.'

'He wouldn't have, for one simple reason. He didn't know about him. Still doesn't. The boy – he's called Peter – grew up with his mother in England. Dawson didn't want to know.'

'But you said his mother was dead' – Moses was now more than somewhat mystified – 'died in an accident. He was brought up by his great-aunt over on Longboat.'

'Siesta Key,' Michaels corrected him. 'True, that's the version his father taught him. But this is his mother, Grace, alive and reasonably well and shopping at Sainsbury's in West London.' He pushed another photograph across to him.

'You seem to have quite a family gallery.' The coach was starting to feel just the slightest bit uncomfortable as he perused the photograph of the short, grey-haired woman pushing a supermarket trolley. 'Are you the official biographer or something? Where do all these pictures come from?'

'My amanuensis – you met her – Brandi de Soto. She's my eyes over in England. I'm sort of the family doctor rather than the biographer. More than that actually. When Dawson and Grace – that's the mother – agreed to split the twins, I supported Peter. Financially. Still do to an extent. Monthly cheque, you know.'

'Why are you telling me all this?' Something about Michaels' smug manner was getting to Moses.

'Nobody else knows. Not all the details. I thought it was time to put you in the picture.' He pulled another cigarette from his pocket. 'As you said, I might not be around for ever.'

'But surely Silver must know.'

'Not really. Of course, he knew about Peter. But he's deliberately kept well away from him, and the mother. There's a history of litigation, not good. And he knows nothing of my, er, financial involvement. That's strictly shtoom.'

'But doesn't he want to see the boy? I mean, Cambridge and all that. He was pretty keen for Jim to crack it.'

'He's not going to see anything for very much longer.' The doctor exhaled a thin taper of smoke and watched it disappear towards the ceiling. 'His sight is going fast now. Like a door closing. I'm surprised it lasted so long, as a matter of fact. And the tragedy is that James and he no longer speak or meet. Silver discovered what really happened with that coach of yours and although he was prepared to come to terms with it James wasn't. The boy was living at home but he moved out and now he's rooming with some other students at the Wellesley end of Commonwealth Avenue. Brandi knows where.'

'I'm sure she does,' Moses observed drily.

Dr Michaels appeared oblivious of any irony. 'She also knows what he's been doing ever since the snow melted in the spring. He didn't touch a tennis racquet for two years after he left your place, did you know that?'

'I had heard.'

'But now he seems to be getting his act together. He'll be a junior at BU next semester and his grades are good. And all this summer he's been teaching kids tennis, nearly every afternoon in a park near where he lives. There's a practice wall there and Brandi says he'll sometimes spend hours in the mornings just hitting the ball on his own. It's not far, the other side of Brookline. She'll take you to it tomorrow.'

Both the assumptions and the imposition grated intrusively on Moses Hoffman. He had better things to do with his time.

'Why do you need me?' The surface ice in his tone was scant indication of the spreading anger that was growing beneath.

'There's a tournament at Longwood Cricket Club next month, some good players come from the big tennis schools – Nevada, UCLA and the like.'

'I know it.'

'Well, I have a friend who's a member – a lawyer – and he can probably fix James a place in the draw if you could just assess him, make sure it won't be an embarrassment. The boy needs it. You never know, it could turn his life around, give him confidence in himself. Might even bring him back to his father. Dawson's very lost without him, not in good shape at all.'

Whatever sympathy Moses felt for the father and son was outweighed by his anger at being duped and tricked. If Michaels had levelled with him and told him all this on the phone, he would have expressed sympathy and then passed on it. He wasn't into social work and, besides, there were other kids who needed him more. But the doctor presumably thought by bringing him here he could somehow blackmail him into helping out. Well, he couldn't.

'Why the hell should I?' he exploded, getting up from his stool as a firm indication that he was about to leave.

Dr Edmund Michaels folded his hands and fixed the veteran coach in the eye with an almost penitent expression. 'Because of what I am about to tell you,' he said gently. 'These twins are very special.'

*

'Do you want me to come with you?'

Brandi de Soto pulled the Camaro into a gravelled clearing on the edge of Newton Lower Falls Park. She turned off the ignition, and thus the thumping music, clearly expecting an affirmative answer.

'No, I don't think so.' Moses hoped it sounded as if he were considering the request although he couldn't wait to get out of the company of this amateur Mata Hari. 'Does he know you?'

'Sure. Like, he knows that I hang out round here sometimes and take photographs. I mean he doesn't know I'm connected with Ed or anything. And he sure as hell doesn't know I've taken pictures of his brother.'

'What's he like?' Moses paused for a moment before climbing out of the car.

'Jim?'

'No, the English one.'

'Peter?' She screwed up her face to help herself think. 'Different, I guess. Speaks different for sure. Just very English. I've never actually been introduced. Kinda cute, really. He has this faraway look that comes over him sometimes as if he was, like, daydreaming. It's sorta sexy. Not that I'm allowed to get involved, you know. Besides he has this real stiff British broad that doesn't let him get that far out of her sights.'

'Really?' said Mo. 'Lucky guy. Well, thanks for the ride. I guess those are the tennis courts, where they're playing tennis.'

'That's right.' The remark passed over Brandi's eager head. 'Jim doesn't start coaching the kids till after lunch but if he's got no classes in the morning he'll hit up on the practice wall. All morning if nobody else wants it. There was a guy he'd sometimes play with but I think he's gone now. Are you sure you don't want me to come?'

'Certain.'

'I'll wait, if you'd like.'

'Please, I'll be fine,' Moses assured her as he closed the door. 'Have a nice day.'

It was a nice day, he reflected to himself, as he stumbled across the tall, tufted grass of the football field which had been allowed to grow wild in the off-season. The New England air was much more bracing than Florida, even as the temperature rose, and the sky, decked with the occasional cloud, seemed somehow higher and cleaner.

At dinner the previous evening Michaels had pointed out the irony of the location which James had chosen for his lonely quest to train himself. It was less than fifty yards from the precise point on the highway where his mother's athletic career had been terminated by the television truck. One day no doubt, Mo surmised, he would be apprised of exactly what happened there in 1975. And one day, no doubt, he would even learn that his mother was still alive.

But not today. As the coach, garbed once again in his shiny black tracksuit and peaked cap, ran his eye along the speeding traffic on the highway that formed part of the perimeter of the park, he had no intention of breaking his vow of secrecy regarding the facts he had learnt in the past twenty-four hours. He merely intended to find out if Jim's tennis was up to scratch.

All three courts were occupied by what appeared to be a school lesson and there were a couple of young black players alternately thumping the ball against the practice wall as if they were intent on knocking it down. Initially Moses thought Brandi must have misinformed him about Jim being there that morning. A couple of men were sitting on the bench outside the court, presumably waiting for their turn, and a blond-haired enthusiast was doing press-ups on a patch of worn grass by the water fountain.

But no Jim. Moses decided to remain a little way off. He dropped his tennis bag on the ground and hunkered down beside it. Now that he concentrated, he could see there was something familiar about the guy working out – that greyhound shape with a back like a shield, strong shoulders tapering to what could be the waist of a woman.

He waited for him to finish and his suspicions were confirmed. The streaked blond highlights were new. Moses was content to observe for a few moments as the young man went through his warm-up routine. The graceful pace and languid mannerisms were only too familiar. And when he held up his head so that his golden tresses were licked by the morning sun, that long lean face with its narrow eyes and lantern jaw could belong to nobody else. It was so obvious. Hoffman could have kicked himself for not realising years ago.

'Jim.' He tried to say the name in a controlled whisper so as not to arouse anybody's attention.

The blond head turned immediately towards him. 'Mo,' he immediately responded. The coach had no doubt that he would know who it was. Those gimlet eyes could read the name printed on his cap even at a hundred and fifty yards.

He rose to his feet as James sprinted towards him. He wanted to take the boy in his arms and cradle him and apologise and explain everything. But he knew he couldn't.

'What on earth are you doing here?' James seemed staggered to see him but the broad grin on his face also signalled his delight.

'I came to look for you. They said this was your practice wall. Don't those two know it?' Moses nodded towards the occupants, still sledge-hammering away.

'Aw, that's Ashley and Lucius. They'll let me on whenever I want. Who told you?'

Moses was prepared for this. 'Down at Chestnut High. The school secretary.'

'But why?' – James seemed lost for words – 'You . . . here . . . I don't understand.'

'I was in town on business,' Moses lied. 'And we like to keep up with our former pupils.'

'You must have some intelligence network.'

'Let's just say The Magic led me and leave it at that. Now how've you been?'

'Things are looking up. I had a bit of luck during the winter. There was this guy advertised in the paper for someone to coach his son – two hundred dollars a week. Turned out he had an indoor court with a wooden floor. I never knew such a thing existed.'

'They all used to be wood,' Moses informed him. 'Fantastic surface. Faster than grass.'

'You can say that again,' James enthused. 'It was part of the stable block of this mansion out at Framingham. The boy wasn't very good but he got better. And I found I got better, too. I mean, in a strange way by teaching him I was at the same time teaching myself. The family went to France for the summer but one of my professors at BU has a kid at Chestnut High and he told me they were looking for someone to help coach. So, well, here I am.'

'Got your appetite back for the game,' Moses suggested as they strolled towards the courts.

'I never lost it.' James swung his racquet at an errant dandelion, decapitating it with precision. 'I just lost my appetite for life. Things weren't wonderful when I arrived here as you can imagine. Thanks for . . . well, you know.'

'I spoke to Dr Michaels,' Moses spared him the misery of dredging up the past any further. 'He put me in the picture. I hear your relationship with your father isn't so good.'

'I guess if I'd grown up with him we might have been able to sort things out better. But all I ever seemed to do with him as a child was go to circuses. He'd become a sort of stranger somehow and when he had to face the facts . . . well.'

'Don't worry.' Moses gave his elbow a reassuring squeeze. 'Look, there's a court free. Want to have a knock?'

'Sure.' James turned his head and yelled across to the boys on the practice wall, 'Yo, Lucius. You can stay on there. I don't need it right now. This is my main man here, come up from the Deep South to put me in my place.'

'You sure need putting in your place, asshole.' The cheerful rejoinder bounced back off the wall.

Moses could see immediately a marked improvement in his ground strokes. The young man was now the possessor of a topspin backhand which he had never mastered at Osprey, and he managed to alternate between it and a finely timed slice with equal facility. His eye seemed keener than ever and his pick-up shots on the half-volley exhibited masterly control and accuracy.

'Not bad,' the veteran coach offered his highest verbal accolade as he came to the net after they'd been hitting for twenty minutes or so.

'It's largely theory at the moment,' James explained. 'I'm short of match practice. But the strange thing is, as I said, when you teach those kids you teach yourself. It's as if you learnt more that way than when you're actually being taught. Crazy.'

'You still needed to have the fundamental grounding.' Hoffman was defensive about his *raison d'être*. 'If you hadn't spent seven years at Osprey you wouldn't be anywhere. After that, a little individual application can work wonders. What are you going to do with it all?'

James undid the candy-striped band around his head and his

thick golden hair spread down nearly to his shoulders. 'Carry on coaching, I guess. I like it.'

Moses studied the earring in his left lobe and tried to give the impression of working out a plan. 'Tell you what, we're running a teaching course the last two weeks of this month. I suspect I could squeeze you in if you wanted.'

'That would be great.' James seemed initially appreciative. 'But I don't think I can afford it. I don't take my allowance any more. Got to find a vacation job.'

'Don't worry,' Moses replied. 'We can probably manage a scholarship. I think we owe you that.'

'Hey, you dudes going to stand around gassing all day or you prepared to face some black power?' Ashley and Lucius had arrived on the court and were now positioned ready to do battle.

The name of the Longwood Cricket Club, founded in 1877 – the same year as the first Wimbledon Championship – was not one that was easily forgotten by the pioneers of British tennis; in fact it went with some of them to their graves. In 1900 one of Longwood's younger members, twenty-one-year-old Dwight Filley Davis – a Harvard undergraduate – thought it might be a fine idea to have an international tennis competition for countries. So he went down to the Boston silversmiths, Shreve, Crump and Low, and ordered up a sterling silver punchbowl, thirteen inches high and lined with gold. The thousand dollars which it cost barely dented his family trust.

Dwight duly played in the first Davis Cup match at Longwood in August 1900. America's opponents were Great-Britain who had condescended to send across a B team which was annihilated 3–0. The British, sporting to the last, blamed everything except themselves.

'Picture yourself a court in England where the grass has been the longest you have ever encountered; double the length of that grass and you have the courts as they were at Longwood at that time,' wrote Herbert Roper Barrett, one of the discontented losers. 'The net was a disgrace to civilized lawn tennis, held up by guy ropes which were continually sagging, giving way as much as two or three inches every few games and frequently requiring adjustment. As for the balls, I hardly like to mention them.' But he did. At length.

The British came back wiser and stronger two years later with the Doherty brothers, Big Do and Little Do. Although the latter had won Wimbledon a few weeks previously, the British captain unaccountably failed to select him for the singles, maintaining he didn't want to tire him out for the doubles, so the Americans won again, 3–2.

At this stage Dwight Davis became bored with playing international tennis – he was twenty-three, after all – and decided to get on with the rest of his career which involved becoming Secretary of War and Governor-General of the Philippines. In his absence the Brits twigged how to win his trophy – play your Wimbledon champions – and the Davis Cup left Longwood for a world tour before returning to the United States for an unbroken period of seven years immediately after the first war.

The reason for this American dominance lay in the photograph that James Winston was now examining as he sheltered in the Longwood clubhouse: the unstoppable team of Dick Williams, William Tilden and William Johnston, or Big Bill and Little Bill as the latter two were inevitably termed.

'People were prepared to play for their country in those days,' observed an elderly lady who was finishing her tea at the table beside him – a reference to the fact that the Davis Cup competition had been abandoned three years previously. 'You young men just want to play for money nowadays.'

'I'd play for my country,' James replied defensively, 'if they chose me.'

'See that woman,' his companion indicated an adjoining portrait with her cake fork. 'Hazel Hotchkiss Wightman – she was a member here, too. Went to the same jewellers as Dwight Davis to get her trophy. Those were the days.'

He was about to agree but the amplified voice of the tournament secretary booming in from the verandah announced the resumption of play. James could see through the window that the rain which had interrupted the 1998 New England Open had stopped and the ground staff were already removing the covers from the twenty-four immaculate grass courts. His match had been abandoned at one set all with his opponent taking a three-love lead in the third so he was none too optimistic that he would remain in the tournament for very much longer.

The two weeks back at Osprey had proved a tremendous tonic. It was an adult course, since the students were either away at tournaments or on vacation. So there were no players there who knew him from before. The people that did – several of the coaches and some of the catering staff – greeted him like a prodigal son with no mention made of the indiscretion that had effected his exit.

He realised he had only infrequently trained under Moses Hoffman when he was a student and the rigid religion of Dr Bob was replaced by a much more reasoned and analytical approach. 'The primary object in match tennis is to break up the other man's game,' the coach repeated at the start of every session and then demonstrated the ways and means of accomplishing this. Winston was gratified to find that the lonely hours spent at the practice wall were now paying dividends on court. He grew in confidence and, more than that, managed to exorcise the demon of the place which had hung uneasily around his neck since the day he left.

James wondered how Moses managed to fix him a wild card for the New England tournament – he presumed his Boston base must have helped. Although he recognised several of the names in the draw, especially the main seeds, he had been fortunate enough to avoid them, finding himself matched against Beals Wright, a sturdily built left-hander from New York State.

The court was damp and unsteady underfoot when the two men resumed. James had already lost his first serve in the final set and was determined not to do so again. The break had provided him with renewed energy and he threw himself at the ball as if he were charged up like an Atlas rocket.

The thought of that journey across Florida imbued him with the memory of The Magic. And he knew it was within him at this moment. He didn't know why nor did he know from where. But it was as if Wright were now facing two players; every time he looked up from a stroke there was Winston at the net, precisely placed to put the ball away.

James won the set 6–4 and the match. His opponent took his defeat with good grace, wishing him all the best in the next round. For most of the game they had played wholly unobserved, without even an umpire, but towards the end an isolated figure in a blue raincoat had taken up a position by the copper beeches that bordered Dunster Road on the far side of the courts from the clubhouse.

James had had his back to the spectator for much of the set, and even when he had switched ends had been too absorbed in his mental game to take any notice of him. But he did now as he gathered up his racquets and windcheater and prepared to leave the court.

'Did you win?' the man enquired politely as he approached the court.

'Yes, Dad,' James replied, clearing the catch in his throat. 'I won.'

· *Thirty* ·

'Come with me.'

Samantha was standing at his bedroom door in a striped dressing gown with a towel round her head, a large slab of pink soap in her hand and a mischievous glint in her eye.

'Where to?'

'Come and have a bath. The Watsons say there's only enough hot water for one, so we may as well double up.'

'They'll kill us if they find out,' Peter protested.

'No guts no glory,' she retorted, setting off down the corridor challenging him to follow her.

Two sisters, Maud and Lillian Watson, were the formidable proprietors of Log's Lodging House in Tanner's Close. They were, as Maud was never slow to inform arriving travellers, daughters of the manse and expected their hotel to be treated with appropriate respect. Lilian, the elder, had a basso profundo voice and a glass eye which had the disconcerting effect of making her appear to be ignoring the person she was talking to. Neither had ever married and the narrowness of the beds they offered their guests indicated that they considered them a place for sleep and no other activity. Not that the Watson sisters would have been able to sleep in them themselves since their joint weight must have fallen not far short of forty stone.

Log's was the temporary home of all thirty-four members of the Cambridge Theatre Group for the duration of the 1998 Edinburgh Festival. The students were putting on two productions in the church hall two doors along: William Shakespeare's *Comedy of Errors* at nine o'clock and Peter Winston's musical version of *Dracula* at midnight. Samantha, who had gone up to the university at the same time as Peter, was much in demand as an actress: she played Adriana in the Shakespeare and then opposite him in his musical as Lucy, Dracula's love-interest.

Brackish brown water that looked as if it had only recently left a Highland glen trickled uncertainly from the ancient gas heater at the end of the bath as Peter gingerly lowered himself in behind her.

'Do my back,' she commanded, holding a soaped sponge over her white, marbled shoulder.

'What if they catch us?' he whispered, worried that if the Watsons were to get wind of such perversions the whole of the cast could be kicked out of their lodgings.

'They won't,' she assured him. 'And even if they do, it's too late for them to fill up this dump with anyone else this festival. You realise who they are, don't you?'

He stopped sponging for a moment. 'No.'

'We'll you're the New Age man, I thought you'd have twigged straight away. Reverse reincarnation, Burke and Hare come back to life. This is the very place they operated from.'

'But they're fictional. Like Frankenstein. Or Dracula, come to that.'

'Dracula existed,' said Samantha, 'in Bram Stoker's imagination. He saw him as an undead man, hovering between this world and the next. Bit like you sometimes.'

'Is this an amateur psychology lesson or a bath? Whose imagination did Burke and Hare spring from?'

'No one's, you dodo, go on sponging. They existed in their own right. William Burke and William Hare. Big Bill and Little Bill. Hare honestly was the keeper of Log's Lodging House. They used to smother the guests and sell the corpses to Robert Knox, the surgeon, for seven and six a time. Why do you think Edinburgh became such a good medical school? They had plenty of fresh meat to practise on.'

'I'm sure you're mistaken. You'll be saying next that Shakespeare didn't make up *The Comedy of Errors*,' he teased her, 'that there really was a merchant who named both his twin sons Antipholus and they were actually separated by a storm at sea and then spent their lives running round the place trying to find each other.'

'As a matter of fact,' Samantha took a firm hold of his left toe and twisted it less than playfully, 'Shakespeare didn't make it up.'

'So they existed. And they also had twin servants both called Dromio. Come off it, Sam, pull the other one.'

She shifted her grip to his right toe and did exactly that. 'Shakespeare didn't make any of it up. He pinched the lot from Plautus. If you played less tennis and studied a few more classics you'd have read *The Brothers Menaechmus*, where the wife mistakenly has it away with her husband's twin. Hadow told us in rehearsals.'

'Oh really.' Peter pulled her back so that she was now lying on top of him and began to soap her breasts. 'I just hope you didn't have it away with Hadow, by mistake or on purpose.'

'Don't be stupid, he's far too fat.' Although her words denied it, her body didn't. Peter could feel the truth through his fingers on her stomach which tightened the very moment he made the accusation. From the beginning of the Shakespeare rehearsals with Hadow he had sensed that some part of her was slipping away from him. She used to accompany him on away tennis matches against the county teams so that they could stay in the relative luxury of hotels. But ever since she became caught up in *The Comedy of Errors* Samantha had chosen to remain in Cambridge. Now he had an inkling why.

'Shakespeare had twins, you know,' she went on, seemingly oblivious of his realisation. 'Judith and Hamnet. The boy died when he was only eleven. That's why he kept coming back to the subject, like Viola and Sebastian in *Twelfth Night*. Although he got that wrong.'

'In what way?' Peter's mind was elsewhere but he managed to keep up the conversation.

'I would have thought it was fairly obvious. You can't have identical twins who are a boy and a girl. And she can't have this.'

Her hand dropped onto his penis that lay flaccid in the water. It responded almost immediately and she responded to it, with a forceful massage until it was fully erect. Then she turned her body in the bath to face him.

'You're sleeping with Hadow, aren't you?' he said.

Samantha smiled. 'That's an unfair question to ask a girl with her mouth full.'

She lowered her head into the water and took him between her lips, softly to begin with and then more and more vigorously as the excitement transferred to her own supple body and rippled through the bath.

Peter placed his hands on her shoulders, silk and slippery with soap as they moved rhythmically to and fro, and lay back and willingly surrendered himself.

'Who's that? Who's in there? Open up at once if you please.' The accent was deep and Scottish and the hammering on the door was angry.

Samantha pulled up her head in shock and stared at Peter for guidance.

'It's Arthur Gore,' he whispered. 'Exactly his sort of prank.' He cuddled her next to him in the cooling water as he called unconvincingly: 'Bugger off, Gore.'

'Don't you dare use that sort of language in this house, young man. This is Lilian Watson speaking and I shall be reporting you both to your university authorities.'

This time Peter looked to Samantha for guidance. She had no idea what to do. Either it actually was Gore, a gifted mimic who was playing Professor Van Helsing in *Dracula*, or else they were in so deep they couldn't get much deeper. So she shouted out: 'If you really are Lilian Watson, roll your glass eye under the door.'

Dracula had started life three months previously as a May Week extravaganza in Cambridge. In the heady end-of-term atmosphere it had proved popular with the graduating students although less so with the theatre critic of the university magazine, *Varsity*. 'It is hard to know,' he wrote, 'whether Mr Winston intended this show to be appallingly obvious or obviously appalling. Either intention is a crime of equal magnitude and the fact that he has already stated that he expected to get it in the neck from the critics is indicative of his enfeebled sense of pun. The least offensive elements are the tunes which he has shamelessly pirated from polyglot sources; why didn't he steal a few old jokes while he was out on his grave-robbing expeditions? As an amateur actor he would be well advised to keep his performance for the tennis court – at least in the Varsity Match he wasn't obliged to sing.'

Grace had come to the closing night in Cambridge – bravely supporting herself with a metal crutch – and had offered her son equally brave support as well. She was proud of Peter: an upper second in law, a show of his own and a tennis Blue. The fact that he was returning for a post-graduate year in order to become captain of tennis, rather than for more academic reasons, seemed acceptable to her as long as the recently enlarged cheques kept coming from Boston.

She just wanted to see him happy. Happiness was something that she had not managed to achieve for most of her own life, which she now measured in months rather than years although she had never mentioned this to her son. The cancer had spread so omnivorously through her lower body that the surgeon had abandoned all attempts to arrest it. Dr Weghofer's past-life therapy had proved no more successful. Grace had often thought that if she really believed in it, it might have worked. But she didn't and it didn't.

That night's performance of *Dracula*, the first in Edinburgh, seemed powered by some exotic new form of electricity. Nobody in the cast was able to look anyone else in the eye for fear of convulsing in giggles. So the whole thing took on the dramatic sweep of a thirties production at the Old Vic with people delivering their dialogue to some unidentifiable point in the mid-distance beyond the footlights. It added a new and unexplored dimension to the romp, quickened the pace and highlighted the humour as never before. The merriment in the company communicated itself to the audience and at the points where their laughter reached a crescendo this, in turn, reinfected the cast who glanced at each other, corpsed and found themselves barely able to continue. Unexpected characters crept into the piece such as Connie Lingus, Professor Van Helsing's serving wench, and a bowler-hatted porter who introduced himself as Blow, a distant cousin of James Bond's old adversary Odd Job. New lyrics such as 'I gather Lilian's by the door again' and 'Come into the bath tub, Maud,' mysteriously interpolated themselves in the score and Lucy's every appearance was inevitably greeted by the chorus of 'I'm forever blowing bubbles.'

Word of the incident had evidently crept out. Both Peter and Samantha had felt an obligation to explain to the rest of the company their precipitate exit from Log's Lodging House and, as Peter was to discover, Samantha had described it in somewhat more detail than he. The very words 'Log's Lodging' took on a new connotation for the Cambridge crowd and could no longer be mentioned without a snigger.

Count Dracula walked tall that night, emboldened by the knowledge that his derring-do off the stage seemed almost to mirror the aplomb of his deadly bite on it. For the first time in his life Peter experienced the undiluted power of holding an audience in the palm of his hand. Even after he had died of daylight and lay in his open coffin, he sensed the house had an appetite for more and rose from the grave to conduct them in an encore of 'Raindrops keep falling on the dead.' Snatches of the song could be heard echoing down the dank stairways that descended from the Royal Mile as satisfied customers made their way home.

'Why did you tell people . . . you know . . . everything?' He guided Samantha by the arm as they negotiated the slippery cobbles leading towards the Fringe Club.

'Oh, I don't know.' She shrugged her shoulders. 'It just makes the joke so much better. Besides, I want to be remembered in Cambridge after I'm gone and notoriety seems as good a way as any.'

'But what about Hadow? I mean, he's bound to hear.'

She stopped and turned towards him. The murky sodium street lights came alive in her piercing blue eyes. 'Do you really want to know about Hadow?'

Peter paused for a moment, ever the actor. 'No,' he replied.

'Good.'

'But I want to know about us.'

This time she was unable to look at him. 'Why can't we discuss that at the end of the run. Why complicate things now?'

Her words chilled him more than the damp Edinburgh night air. 'I must know.'

'Well,' she kept her eyes averted. 'You're going to Portugal to tennis camp.'

'And you're coming out,' he added quickly, 'for the last weekend.'

'That's what I wanted to discuss,' she replied evasively. 'Not a good idea. My father's given me an air ticket, Peter. I was going to tell you. Round the world. After three years cooped up in Cambridge it's not a bad place to go.'

'When?'

'Two weeks after we finish here.'

'And for how long?'

'I dunno. A year. Maybe less.'

'But what about us?' He tried not to sound as if he were pleading but he knew he was.

She gazed wistfully up at the illuminated castle, proudly standing sentinel over the silent city. 'When I was a little girl, my parents brought me to the Caledonian Hotel and my father insisted that we had a suite where you could see Edinburgh Castle. I suppose I was six or maybe seven at the time and I pretended I was a princess living in there all on my own. And now I'm twenty-one and I know a bit more about life and I don't pretend that any longer. You've made me happy, happier than I could have imagined over the past years, but I don't pretend that a relationship that's been right for my life as a student will be right for all my life – all our lives. If you'd thought hard about it, you'd agree. Things change. So it's good for me to go away and good for you to find out what Cambridge is like next term without me. And if we discover in years to come that we guessed right first time – you know Plato said of the perfect relationship that in the beginning it was one and then the man and woman split apart and they have to find that other part, the perfect soul mate – well, let's get together, yeah, yeah, yeah.'

'You seem to have worked everything out.'

'Come on,' said Samantha. 'We should join the others. I need a quadruple something.'

As they walked into the smoky throng of the Fringe Club they could distinctly hear someone at the bar loudly repeating the punchline of a story . . . 'And she yelled out of the lavatory: "Roll your bleeding glass eye under the fucking door, you fat Scottish git." '

Peter Winston was still in an emotionally subdued state as he embarked for Portugal. He knew Samantha too well to believe that there was any chance of changing her mind. Besides, there was nothing really to change her mind about. She was merely going to travel for a year and when she came back they would see how things stood then. The only point that she, somewhat hurtfully, had emphasised was that during this time their relationship would be in limbo. Both would be free to do as they pleased.

He reserved his bitterness for her father who had calculatedly presented her with the round-the-world ticket. Nigel Bergen had never warmed to him since that first encounter at Wimbledon. The words 'rich girls don't marry poor boys, Jay Gatsby,' rose like an unspoken bubble above his head on any occasion that Peter had collected Samantha from their Holland Park house. Doubtless Nigel had peppered his daughter's international path with letters of introduction to the sons of the wealthy and well-connected from Hong Kong to New York. The least her father expected from her three years at Cambridge was the acquisition of a man of better fortune.

Grace was having to attend the hospital for regular treatments and Peter tried to use this as an excuse to delay his departure until the same day as Samantha. But his mother refused to let him stay, pointing out that he might jeopardise his position as next year's captain if he failed to turn up at the training camp on time. He then levelled with her as to the true reason. Grace was sympathetic but firm: if Peter were to marry and spend his life with the only girlfriend he had ever had, he would also spend his life wondering what it would be like with someone else. This interregnum was a perfect opportunity for him to find out. It was also, she didn't tell him, the perfect opportunity to have Peter to herself for the last months of her own life.

Samantha had actually turned up at Gatwick to bid a surprise farewell. Whether this had been a final gesture or fresh grounds for hope was something that he chewed over as he tried to ingest his Leeman Air curried chicken, thirty thousand feet above the Bay of Biscay. The Cambridge team were, for the most part, tall men, and the seats of the charter flight were pushed as closely together as greed would allow. As the quarter bottles of rosé went down, their complaints became more raucous. Cecil Parke pressed the bell and summoned the stewardess to see if she had a saw in order to amputate his partner's legs as he had lost all feeling in them. When it was found that the girl had little sense of humour she remained constantly in demand, with Arthur Beamish asking if she was quite sure they were going in the right direction and Sidney Smith insisting that the travel agent had promised them that there would be a vomitarium on board which, after eating the Leeman Air curried chicken, they wanted to visit.

As Peter and the rest of his team emerged from the customs hall at Faro Airport, young women in folklorique Portuguese frocks handed them fresh carnations wrapped in invitations to The Big One Parque Aquatico (Free Bar-b-que, Wednesdays and Sundays) and offers of cheap massages and reduced price rounds at the new Vale do Gringo golf course. The reception area resembled the Chicago Futures Market as brightly caparisoned tour guides and resort representatives waved stickers and clip-boards to try and assemble the British punters who would be under their care for the next fortnight.

A man named only Hank – at least he never yielded any further name – who styled himself head of public relations at the Don Brown International Tennis Centre had promised that either he or even the eponymous Don would be there to greet them. There was no need for Hank to describe himself, he had insisted in a thick Australian accent, he would recognise them. But so far he hadn't. Peter scanned the young men in their crushed pink or striped saffron blazers for someone who could possibly be a Hank – the possession of a bush hat with corks hanging from it would be a conclusive clue and even someone swinging a tennis racquet would offer an outside one – but that Sunday evening Faro Airport appeared to be deficient in the Hank department to the tune of one.

Sidney Smith, the Old Etonian team secretary who had made the arrangements, spied an attractive girl in a magenta mini-dress who was counting the candidates for Quinta do Apollo – the resort which contained Don Brown's camp – and went to ask her in faultless Portuguese whether she knew a Hank.

'What on 'erf you goin' there for?' she replied in not quite faultless English. 'You must be barkin' mad. It's a rest home for Australian piss artists.'

'Whatever it may be,' said Sidney, 'it remains our destination to which we were promised transportation.'

'Who's we?' she demanded, intrigued by his lyrical phraseology.

'Why, this merry band,' he answered, indicating the team members each with a sky-blue tennis bag.

She surveyed them for a moment. 'You a bunch of poofs or somefing?'

'I daresay some of us are,' Smith responded wearily, 'but we may have to wait until the end of the holiday to discover which.'

She looked at him suspiciously. 'If you lot behave yourselves, you can sit at the back of my coach. The police took away the Don Brown mini-bus last month – weren't properly insured and it didn't work properly neither. But I don't want you annoying none of my customers, okay?'

'That seems a fair bargain,' Sidney solemnly assured her. 'I'll see if the lads can restrain themselves on this occasion.'

Unlike the villas and apartment blocks and the unlovely Guadiana Hotel which decorated the upper slopes of Quinta do Apollo and were fashioned in stone and mock marble and Portuguese plaster, the Don Brown International Tennis Centre consisted of a cluster of primitive wooden huts surrounding half a dozen dirt tennis courts. Viewed from afar it looked not unlike an American mining community from the previous century or even a small fishing village, with only a low range of sand dunes separating it from the pounding Atlantic.

Conditions inside the huts, as the Cambridge team were immediately to discover, were equally primitive. They were furnished largely with tightly packed bunks that appeared to have been acquired from a defunct boarding school or possibly a refugee camp. The rest of the furniture – such as there was – seemed to bear the marks of battle, as if it had been used to defend the place in a state of siege, with scratched tables, broken-backed cupboards and three-legged chairs.

'Just the basic necessities,' said Barry, without a hint of apology, as he noticed the crestfallen expressions of the new arrivals in the faint twilight. 'Youse won't be spending much time in your dorms. You'll be out on the courts or down on the beach or having a few relaxatives at Don's Bar.'

Hank, it seemed, was no more; the authorities had decided that his working papers, like those of the minibus, were not in order. So apart from the local Portuguese – or Pork and Cheese, as Barry jocularly referred to them – who came in daily, the permanent staff consisted of Barry, Barry and Shirley who, evidently, combined the skills of tennis coaching with those of cooking, maintenance and general administration.

But not the drinks. These were under the sole administration of the great Don himself in the bar that bore his name. Nobody entering the place could doubt their host's enthusiasm for tennis: racquets and tournament posters and pictures of players adorned the walls, and behind the bar was a jumble shop of trophies and mementoes and framed press cuttings. An antique gramophone with a store of 78 rpm records formed the centrepiece and, when suitably moved by emotion and alcohol, the landlord would put on barely recognisable arias from *Manon Lescaut* sung by a diva whose voice sounded as cracked as the disc. It was Don's claim to fame as a tennis player that he had once been the travelling reserve on an Australian Davis Cup team in the days of the legendary Harry Hopman. But now his travelling days were over and his legless nights were frequent. A still strong thatch of blond hair, bleached nearly white by the powerful Algarve sun, crowned his square reddened face, and a pint of chilled lager rested sempiternally in his chunky right hand.

On the first evening he traditionally gave his introductory talk to the strains of the strained Puccini as sung by Dame Nellie Melba, a woman who was famous – Don pointed out – for being the aunt of the former Australian champion, Gerald Patterson. The lecture proved to be neither an analysis of modern tactics, nor even his philosophy for winning, but a paean of praise to the ancient glories of Australian tennis.

'Cambridge boys, eh?' he nodded as if the news had come as a surprise to him, although they had booked six months ago and appeared to be the only current residents. The team's initial apprehension at their spartan surroundings had been mitigated by Barry's lavish barbecue of steaks and sardines, washed down by a limitless supply of the local Apollo wine. This, combined with what they had already consumed on the plane, had elevated their spirits considerably as they had been ushered into the lair of the proprietor.

'This silken scarf was once worn by a Cambridge boy.' Don lifted it down from a hook at the back of the bar where it had been reposing like a religious relic. 'Belonged to Anthony Wilding. Came from Christchurch, as a matter of fact, in New Zealand. How do you know when a New Zealander's been rummaging in your fridge.'

The question was abruptly directed at Sidney Smith who shrugged his shoulders in surprise.

'By the love-bites in the leg of lamb,' Don explained with a gurgle of sorts, taking a further sup of lager. 'But that was at a time when Australasia played as one team in the Davis Cup. Wilding was a tall guy with fine fair hair and beautiful blue eyes. He'd put this scarf round his neck and ride on his motorcycle throughout Europe, staying at the homes of kings and princes. Studied law at your place and won Wimbledon in 1910, 1911, 1912, and 1913. Why didn't he win it in 1914? Any takers?'

'There was no Wimbledon in 1914.' It was Charles Dixon who ventured the answer. 'The war.'

'Wrong,' declared Don. 'He lost the championship to Norman Brookes, the first Australian to win the title, first left-hander too. You're right about the war, though. Wilding lost his life in that a few months later. Killed by a shell at Neuve Chapelle. Now this,' the barman carefully replaced the scarf and took down a white peaked hat from the next hook, 'once belonged to Sir Norman. He always wore a hat and very often a tie as well when he played tennis. Great all rounder. In the year they held the Australian Croquet Championships in Melbourne he challenged the winner to a match immediately after the final and beat him – although he'd never played the game in his life before.'

Peter attempted a surreptitious glance at his watch. There were nearly eighty more years of Australian tennis to go and even one of Don's bunks was beginning to look more welcoming than his anecdotes.

'That's one of his mallets on the wall behind you.' Brown was pointing straight over Peter's shoulder. 'And beside that is a rare artifact indeed. Could you just hand it over to me, young fella.'

Peter sprang unsteadily to his feet and did as he was bid.

'A free pint of anything you want to anyone who can put a name on this,' Don demanded, waving the curiously shaped racquet above his head.

'An Aboriginal lesbian-detector.' The suggestion came from Arthur Beamish who had consumed enough not to be in fear of offending his host.

'Close, but wrong,' laughed Don. 'This is the Flat Top Cressy Wizard. The unique style of racquet pioneered by . . .'

'I know.' Cecil Parke sprang from his seat. 'Jack Crawford. First man to win the Australian Championships three times in succession. I think he married a great aunt of mine or something.'

'We are in the presence of royalty,' the landlord acknowledged. 'A relation of the legendary Gentleman Jack. When Crawford won Wimbledon in 1933 he beat a Japanese player in the semis called Jiro Satoh who jumped off the boat on the way home because he knew he'd let down the Emperor. Their Davis Cup team lost its best player, though.'

For a moment Don Brown lost himself in his own thoughts. He was beginning to become more than a little maudlin as the midnight hour approached. 'That was when players had a sense of honour and obligation to the national flag. Now they've had to abolish the Davis Cup because nobody's interested any longer. They'd rather play exhibition matches in Illinois. All they want is sponsorship and dollars . . . dollars and sponsorship . . . it's a relief that Hoppy isn't alive to see this sad day. Twenty-one times he led his country in the Davis Cup, sixteen times he emerged victorious. And you Poms wouldn't even give the poor bastard a knighthood . . . I dunno . . .'

He lapsed into a ruminative form of coma.

'We should get off to bed,' Peter remarked thankfully.

'Yep, better get an early night.' Don Brown's slurred voice followed the departing team. 'You've got an international match first thing tomorrow: Great Britain versus Australia.'

He had not been joking. The full Australian Federation Cup team descended on the Don Brown International Tennis Centre the following day and Barry, Barry and Shirley had drawn up an elaborate pattern of matches with both teams playing each other at singles and doubles in the morning with reverse singles in the afternoon. The outcome was a narrow victory for the British, with Cambridge triumphing over Australia by eleven matches to nine.

A party on the beach had been arranged for the evening with the

Barrys lugging the barbecue over the dunes to the firmer sand left by the receding tide. Don Brown, who had only surfaced to urge on his nation in the afternoon matches, had loaded a selection of wines, beers and spirits into a battered Landrover which had become stuck in the soft sandhills. So he enlisted some of the sturdier players as slave-labour to push him to the beach.

'If you're training in Don's camp,' Peter enquired of the opposing captain, 'how come you're not staying there as well? There's plenty of room.'

'Some of us have been here before,' came the knowing reply, 'and I don't think anybody voluntarily sleeps in those bunks a second time. The girls would mutiny if they were forced to. So it's better for us to come down during the day and stay up at the Guadiana Hotel. It may not look much from the outside but one of its virtues is that you don't have to listen to lectures on the glories of Harry Hopman every evening.'

Peter laughed loudly; she had delivered the line with a poker player's face. 'What made you come here in the first place?'

'A bit of sun and sea. Most of the girls have had a tough summer in Europe so it's a good place to get together and sort out a team for Frankfurt. The Davis Cup boys always used to come here. I think Don's pretty pissed that they don't play that any longer.'

'I think you're right,' Peter agreed. 'But did he really play it? I mean, was he really a travelling reserve?'

'Luckily the record books don't record the reserves,' she smiled. 'Actually I'm not the one to ask, you should talk to Bush Baby. Her dad played Davis Cup.' She looked around the gathering. 'Maybe she's not here, she didn't make today's team. No, that's her coming now.'

A bottle of sparkling Dão in his hand, Peter walked unsteadily onto the softer sand to greet the arriving Australian. She was worth meeting: clad in shorts and a singlet, her tanned body was the stuff of swimwear adverts and her dark hair curled alluringly under her chin. The captain had been right about her eyes.

'Christ,' she exclaimed, when she saw Peter. 'What are you doing here?'

'Playing for Cambridge,' he responded obviously.

'I never knew.' She came up to him and gave him a kiss. 'I like the hair.'

He was mystified. 'Thank you.'

'And the accent. They obviously teach that there as well. I know I should have kept in touch but my game hasn't been going too well and my parents have been shitting on me.'

'I'm sorry,' he was more confused than ever. 'I hope you don't mind me asking, I've had a bit to drink, but have we met?'

She stood back and stared at him, her bush-baby eyes wide as the Pacific Rim. 'James, right?'

He shook his head. 'Peter.'

Her hand flew to her mouth. 'Oh God, how embarrassing. It's me who should be sorry. There was this guy who was at tennis camp in Florida who was . . . well, you.'

'My Doppelgänger.' Peter offered her a glass of Dão. 'Well, I wish I was him. Then I would have met you sooner.'

She took it from him, glancing at his hand. 'Your finger . . . how long?'

'From birth,' he acknowledged.

'Can I do something?' Phoebe stepped towards him and, pushing the hair away from his forehead, traced her finger around the very faint red mark.

'Apparently it was quite prominent when I was a baby,' he said.

'Your brother's goes the other way,' she replied.

· Thirty-One ·

'When's he due?'

Eamonn Quinn fished an old-fashioned fob-watch out of his waistcoat pocket, flicked open the gold lid and examined it for the sixth or seventh time that afternoon. Despite the summer heat that had refused to leave as the calendar ordained on Labor Day but had lingered into September, he was wearing his winter uniform of a thick chalk-striped three-piece suit with his familiar cream shirt crumpled at the collar and emerald green tie.

'Depends on the traffic.' Dawson Silver glanced down from his study window at Marlborough Street below, as if that might be a pointer to the conditions in the Callahan Tunnel. 'I should have gone to meet him at the airport.'

'Prudence first, sentiment second,' his lawyer counselled. 'What if he came off the plane waving a writ? You've no idea what his state of mind is going to be. He might have all of Scotland Yard trailing behind him.'

'Do you think so?' Dawson turned back from the window, clearly worried.

'I'm joking,' Quinn explained. 'Relax. Are you sure Doherty has been told what he looks like? He's not one of life's brightest creatures, you know.'

'Moses said he looked the same as James.'

'Has Hoffman seen him?'

'Nobody's seen him,' Dawson turned towards him in exasperation. 'And nobody would have seen him if that fucking Phoebe hadn't managed to interfere.'

'It was going to happen sooner or later.' Quinn pulled a document out of his briefcase and started to thumb through it.

'Later would have been better. Or never. Better never than late. What if he brings his mother with him? What then?'

The lawyer looked up from his paperwork. 'Did Moses say she was coming? You didn't tell me.'

'All Moses said,' Silver repeated patiently, 'was that the kid wanted to see me and he'd be on today's Virgin flight. I've had Mary make up a room but I don't even know whether he wants to stay or sue.' He shook his head in angered exasperation. 'Fucking Phoebe, fucking Phoebe, fucking Phoebe. Why couldn't she just let it pass . . . shut up . . . do nothing? She's on the phone to Hoffman in the middle of the night she's so goddam keen to tell him.'

'You could have procrastinated,' Quinn suggested. 'Laughed the matter off. Told him it was nonsense. It might have gone away – for a bit, at least.'

'Moses seemed to know. He denied it, but I had the feeling he'd spoken to Edmund Michaels and that guy just can't wait to get his hands on Peter to start his goddam tests. I hope the kid tells him to fuck off.'

'Let's worry about you and forget about Michaels.' Dawson traced his pen along the paragraphs of the contract which he had spread on the desk. 'This looks like a case that's going to have to be decided by the court. There's no precedent for it. In strict American law you remain liable for education and maintenance of your child up to eighteen. I've no idea how much that might be.'

'Don't worry, I've worked it out,' Silver replied bitterly. 'Seven hundred and seventy-five thousand dollars if you include compound interest.'

'Have you got that much?' Quinn enquired.

'Not without selling this house and, as you should know, it's not mine to sell.'

'Exactly. So you should stop tormenting yourself with those figures. People who live by the calculator tend to die by the calculator.'

The seventy-year-old actuary was not amused.

'Look,' Quinn went on. 'For starters, he's likely to settle. So you can reckon half a million if we don't go to court, maybe less. But that's in America. Don't forget she signed this contract in Britain so it's open to interpretation under English law. If you've got no money over there, the state looks after you. Even up to university. Not only that but Grace Winston in fact broke the contract there . . .'

'She didn't break it,' Dawson looked accusingly at his lawyer. 'She found a loophole.'

'But you did make an honest offer to take care of both . . .'

The large man fell silent as the internal phone on Silver's desk sliced into his flustered explanation.

Dawson lifted the receiver. 'Yes, Mary. Is he alone? . . . Good, show him up. Straight away.'

This was the encounter he had lived in dread of for so long. How much did the boy know? Had his mother told him that but for the Indian kid snatching him from the car, Peter might well have been brought up an American citizen? Had Grace Winston worked out for herself exactly how Quinn had stitched her up in the negligence case so that she would be vulnerable to the surrogacy offer? Had she poisoned the boy's mind against Dawson, as she had probably every right to do? Had Peter, perhaps, come here to kill him?

There was the lightest tap on the door. Before Silver had time to answer, it swiftly opened and a young man stepped into the room. Dressed smartly in an open-necked white shirt, navy blazer and correctly creased grey flannels, he was – with the exception of his neatly trimmed hair – the mirror image of James from top to toe.

Both the Americans rose to their feet. Dawson extended his hand. 'Peter,' his voice, dry to begin with, nearly died of drought as he noticed the missing top of the middle finger in the hand that met his own, 'it's good of you to come.'

'It all came as rather a surprise to me,' admitted the Englishman, sensing the suppressed emotion in this ageing, bald man with thick pebble spectacles whom he presumed to be his father.

'This is Eamonn Quinn. Perhaps your mother might have mentioned him. An old family friend. Actually knew her before I did.'

'No,' Peter took the lawyer's hand. 'She never did. But that could be because I haven't mentioned anything to her. Could I sit down for a moment . . . I'm feeling a bit wobbly.'

'Here,' Dawson ushered him into a studded leather chair by the empty fireplace. 'I must get Mary to turn the air-conditioning up.

It's not much of a match against this sort of humidity, I'm afraid. Would you like a drink?'

'No, I'm fine,' the Englishman smiled. 'It's just I'd been rehearsing this moment all the way over on the plane and I didn't know for a split second there whether it was real or I was still rehearsing it.'

'It's real,' Dawson assured him, staring through his half-shuttered eyes at his second son. 'As real as you are.'

'You said you hadn't mentioned anything to your mother.' Loophole Quinn was never slow to get to the heart of the matter. 'Does she even know you're here?'

'No. She's not well. I didn't want to cause her any extra anxiety. After Phoebe Carter told me about James, Maurice Hoffman confirmed all the details over the telephone. When he sent me the ticket I sensed they weren't pulling my leg. And I presume that if that photograph on the desk isn't of me, it must be of my brother. Extraordinary.'

Dawson nodded, patting it paternally.

'You say Moses sent the ticket?' Quinn inclined his head inquisitorially.

'Is that his name? Yes, very kind. Virgin Upper Class – you even get your own telly. Mr Hoffman's coming to Boston tomorrow. He said I might qualify for some tennis scholarship, although I doubt it.'

Silver had fallen very silent and just sat in the chair opposite the boy and peered at him. Cambridge. The young man was so smart and well-spoken and companionable in every way. This was the son he would have settled for. 'I can't . . . I can't . . .' he gestured with his hand in front of him in a stuttering motion. 'It's just as if James had gone off to some finishing school in Europe and come back with a new haircut and a posh accent. Will you look at him, Eamonn.'

Quinn was fearful that his client might be so overcome with emotion that he would let slip something injudicious. 'It's his twin all right,' he agreed, 'no doubt about that.'

'Not the prisoner of Zenda,' ventured the Englishman, but the remark was lost on the older men. 'By the way, I was rather hoping James might be here. Moses said . . .'

'He was,' Silver hastily assured him. 'And he'll be back. Got a little nervous and went off to hit some balls at the Beacon Indoor.'

'I can sympathise. It's not easy, not for any of us.'

'I'll get Doherty to drive you up there. It won't take five minutes.'
Dawson never took his eyes off the boy for one moment as he spoke.

'He'll be here for some time,' Quinn pointed out. 'And you, too, have a little catching up to do. I mean, how's your mother, Peter? Does she speak fondly of Dawson.'

'As I said, she's not at all well. In fact I don't think she's prepared to let on how ill she is. Grace has always been sort of secretive that way. For instance she's never actually mentioned your name – Dawson. She just said I had an American dad and that she met him when she was here for the marathon. And that I would meet him when the time was right. I'm afraid I've rather pre-empted her.'

'She was a fine woman, Peter,' Dawson sat back in some relief as he began his story, 'and she had this terrible accident . . .'

It was already dark when Doherty dropped Peter off outside the Beacon Indoor Tennis Club. The chauffeur indicated James's BMW motorbike parked in the street by the entrance. He must still be here.

Whether it was the onset of jet-lag or the amount of information that had alternately been fed into and drained out of his brain in the past hour, Peter felt emotionally exhausted as he followed Doherty up the iron fire escape to the viewing balcony above the three courts. He would dearly love to postpone this moment, to have a sound night's sleep and put everything the two men had told him into perspective so that he could come face to face with his twin when he was better adjusted to the prospect. But as the chauffeur abandoned him on an otherwise empty balustrade, he knew that he had no choice.

Instead of a sense of relief, or even joy, at being reunited with a long-lost parent, his prevailing feeling after meeting Dawson was one of loss. Too many years had passed for there to be any hope of them forming other than the most formal of relationships. Some things could never be recaptured and childhood was at the top of the list. The blood of an American father might course through his veins, but it would never reach his heart. His feeling of profound disquiet at this new-found knowledge was augmented by a deepening guilt about the way he had deceived Grace. He had made up a story about the university requiring him to go to Harvard to discuss a tennis fixture, and she had accepted it with such innocence and shared pleasure at the prospect of the trip that the betrayal now haunted him like a besetting sin. Debating with himself whether to compound the fiction and maybe never acknowledge to her that he had met his father or his brother, he climbed the final steps to the viewing area.

And there he was. Peter spotted him immediately although the two courts nearer to him were also occupied. But the striking blond hair, swept back by a chequered band, would have drawn anybody's attention to the rangy, well-built player on court three. From the evening that Phoebe had told him about James, he had tried to imagine what this experience would be like and now he knew. It was disturbingly familiar. He had been here before, standing on a balcony, watching himself play tennis. Bali Bhava, Bali Bhava. The first time had been during that game at Wimbledon with Nigel Bergen but it had not been the only time. On many occasions when a match seemed as if it was slipping away, he would invoke his mantra as he sat by the net and frequently, but not always, achieve an out-of-body experience that would guide him through the next game.

He had never revealed this to anybody else. Even if they understood, and that was fairly unlikely, they would probably regard it as a mystical form of cheating. But now he was confused. Now as he looked down and saw himself – albeit a blond self – taking on this black man and angling volleys to either side of the court, he began to wonder if this hadn't always been the case. That in some equally inexplicable way he had managed to transport his unknown twin from wherever he was to watch over him and an unspoken communication between them had guided him through the game.

He prayed inwardly that James would not look up and catch his eye, although it would be hard for him to discern anybody in the unlit gantry. However the American's concentration was on the game. Peter noted how much more aggressive than him his brother was. When the tiniest chink of opportunity opened for him to take the net he would charge in and stoutly defend it like Horatio holding the bridge.

After twenty minutes, maybe more, James's partner came forward to congratulate him as he put away a final smash. The other courts were vacant now and the two men gathered their belongings and began to make their way to the locker room which Peter realised must be directly under where he was standing.

The Englishman felt a gnawing nausea in his stomach as the players approached. Should he try and attract James's attention or just go down and wait by his motorbike for him while he got changed? His instinct was to opt for the latter course, but his brother removed the need for any decision from him.

'Go on ahead, Lucius,' he said, tapping the other player on the shoulder with his racquet, 'give you your revenge at the weekend. Going to hit some serves.'

James then put his tennis bag down on the vacant number one court and stood for several seconds with his back to the balcony. When he sensed that the coast was clear he called out quietly but distinctly: 'Why don't you come down and have a hit. I've laid out some clothes and sneakers for you in the end cubicle by the showers. Figured you'd probably be the same size as me.'

'Exactly the same size.' Dr Edmund Michaels entered the measurement in his red report book with satisfaction. 'Six feet one and a half, and a hundred and fifty-five pounds. I'm too old to handle metrification. You can get dressed now.'

Peter was glad to retrieve his shirt from the back of the chair and put it on again. Despite the continuing heatwave, there was something cold and uncomfortable about the makeshift Castor Street surgery. But Moses Hoffman had insisted on a complete medical check-up before he could commit himself to a scholarship.

'We just need to assess your eyesight,' the doctor went on, 'although from what I hear about your session with Mo yesterday, you don't have too much difficulty following a moving ball. Take a look at that newspaper photograph at the bottom of the notice board. I bet you a dollar you can't read the caption underneath.'

Narrowing his eyes so that they became mere slits beneath his furrowed forehead, Peter was determined to take the money. 'Grace Winston . . .' he began and then swivelled his head towards Michaels in amazement. 'It's my mother.'

The doctor seemed nonplussed. 'Sure. That's why I chose it. You can take a look in a moment. But read it from there first.'

'Grace Winston, aged 30, from London England,' he read on,

'is taken to hospital with a suspected ruptured pelvis and broken leg.'

'Quite incredible.' Michaels made a further note in his book. 'If eyesight were rated like the intellect you and your brother would both be in the genius category. It's hereditary.'

'Really?' Peter moved over to inspect the faded cutting. 'Are you sure? My father told me he's got this terrible retinitis disease and my mother maintains she's never been able to see very well since the day this happened.'

'Her eyesight was fine before. That's what counts.'

'How do you know?' Peter's suspicions deepened. 'And how come you've got this on your wall.'

'Didn't Dawson tell you?'

'Tell me what? All he said was that he and my mother had a brief affair but it didn't work out. They never intended to have a child, let alone twins.'

Edmund Michaels closed his book slowly and punctiliously and then commenced tapping it with his pen in a seemingly absent-minded fashion. 'You're an intelligent man, a Cambridge graduate and you have a right to know more than that. Am I able to rely on your total discretion? Not even James is fully aware of what I am about to tell you.'

Although desperate to know, Peter had no desire to give a verbal promise that he might one day break, so he merely nodded his head.

The doctor settled on a stool by the empty work surface. 'There was no affair between Dawson Silver and your mother. He wanted a child; he was estranged from his wife. Grace Winston, as you know, was an athlete and an educated woman and, as you evidently don't know, agreed to be the surrogate mother. I performed the operation. I even did my first check-up on you in this very laboratory. We call it preimplantation diagnosis: it's possible to remove a single cell from an early embryo, grow it and screen it for chromosomal damage. I could tell you were a boy from the Y chromosomes. It's continually amazed me how the Catholic Church still insists on the virgin birth, even though you need male sperm for Y chromosomes. Dawson wanted a son, for reasons I won't go into, and we could have inserted the correct gene to give him that if it hadn't been happening already. In fact I could have cleaned up any genetic problems, things like dwarfism, but you'll be glad to hear there weren't any. Today I could probably have popped in a dose of Interleukin—4 and given you immunity against cancer.'

Peter wondered whether Michaels was aware of his mother's present condition but decided against mentioning it. 'I thought that was still awaiting approval,' he said instead.

'Good God,' Michaels waved his hand dismissively, 'if we scientists hung around till everything was approved, medicine would never move forward. It's possible to tell you when you're going to die even before you're born if we diagnose a gene that'll cause cancer in middle age. The fact that you were twins took me slightly by surprise, although I always knew there was an increased possibility.'

'Who was born first? James or me?' The question presented itself from nowhere in Peter's mind and he let it slip without thinking.

'Let's find out.' Edmund Michaels, encouraged by his interest, opened his file once more. 'The boy, subsequently called James, preceded the infant Peter by two minutes. Both by Caesarean section. So that makes you the younger. That's what it says here, anyway. Have they abolished primogeniture over in Britain?'

'Yes, except in families with titles.' As he uttered these words Peter instinctively thought of Samantha and wondered where she was now — and with whom.

'Cheer up. You'd be okay in Japan, they consider the twin born second as the elder. And not so long ago if you'd been born in an Aboriginal or Eskimo community you'd have been killed. Primitive people always thought that twins came from an evil spirit. In a lot of African tribes they believed that two babies could only be produced by two fathers. So the adulterous mothers would be banished to a distant village for life. Gives a whole new meaning to the expression twin town.'

The Englishman essayed a laugh, half-hoping to soften the doctor up for an indiscretion of his own. 'How far do your medical records on me and my mother go,' he asked, indicating the red book.

'Not as far as I would like.' Michaels was not going to give away any more than he intended. 'British medics tend to treat personal details like state secrets, even between fellow doctors. In fact there are a few details you might be able to fill in for me.'

Peter couldn't help but admire the American's aplomb in turning things around. 'Like what?'

'For instance, did you remember your twin?'

'How could I remember him? He was about a week old when he was taken to America.'

'Memory begins in the foetus after six months,' the doctor explained. 'It's been demonstrated that twins are aware of each other for their last three months in the womb. If one dies in childbirth, the other often grows up with an inexplicable sense of loss. James, when he was a child in Florida, used to do drawings for me and he'd think they were finished but they would be incomplete. The missing bit was you. Ever do anything like that?'

Peter slowly shook his head. 'No, not that I can recall. I'd have to ask my mother.'

'What about your fantasies? Did you ever sense that someone was missing, ever have an invisible friend? Some kids do.'

Of course, Peter thought, Charlie. Long gone but not forgotten, especially by Grace who used to tease her son about the way he made her hold open doors or squeeze up on the sofa to accommodate Charlie. But Charlie was not someone he was about to share with Dr Edmund Michaels, at least not at the moment. The man was becoming over-intrusive. Peter felt he had given away too much already. 'I can't think of anything like that. I guess I must be very different from James.'

'On the contrary, you are more alike than you know.' Michaels slipped off his seat and went over to a dresser by the wall. Pulling open a drawer, he started to search through a mess of papers. 'The extraordinary thing is that monozygotic twins such as you and James who have been reared apart are in some traits more alike than twins reared together. They discovered this first in a survey of Finnish twins and since then a lot of other countries have pooled their knowledge in the Minnesota Study. Here it is.'

He pulled out a transparent folder stuffed with photocopied papers which he offered to Peter. 'You can keep this, I've another one back at the hospital. What it establishes, in effect, is the overwhelming dominance of the genes over the environment. Parents can affect their children's rate of learning but they have relatively little influence on the ultimate level attained. And you'll see, in matters of personality and temperament and occupational and leisure-time interests, monozygotic twins reared apart are about as similar as those reared together. Explains why you and James are both keen on tennis, for instance. Have a read and let me know what you think.'

Peter accepted the file as much as an excuse to bring this tutorial to an end as through any desire further to help the doctor with his enquiries. He retrieved his jacket from the back of the door to indicate his intention of leaving. As he did so his eye was ineluctably drawn to the forlorn figure of his mother being borne away on a stretcher. He owed her a phone call. There were several pictures of James taken at various ages of development on the noticeboard with equivalently sized gaps beside them, suggesting Michaels was waiting for something to fill them – or had removed some that were there.

'Your mother was a brave woman, Peter.'

He swung indignantly round to face the doctor. 'She's not dead yet.'

'I didn't mean that. I meant then. I rang a guy I know at WNTV – they've still got footage of all the marathons they ever covered in their archive. So he copied me a tape of the 1975 race. Thought maybe you'd like to have a look at that, as well.'

Edmund Michaels dug deep into the pocket of the white laboratory coat which had been hanging under Peter's jacket and handed him a compact parcel, wrapped like a box of chocolates.

'There's nobody here, I'm afraid,' Mary Doherty apologised as she answered the door at Marlborough Street, managing to make it sound as if it were somehow her fault. 'Mr Silver said he'd be back at seven and I've no idea where Mr James is. He went off on his motor cycle in a track suit, but then he wears that all the time. Would you like a cup of tea?'

'Love one,' said Peter, thankful to get in out of the heat. 'I'm exhausted.'

'Are you finding your way round Boston all right?' The house-keeper felt obliged to engage the guest in conversation since there was nobody else to do so. Besides, he was more than a guest; he was a son of the house.

'Almost. I think I got out of that transit train too early. I had to walk across the Common. But if I hadn't, I'd never have seen those Swan Boats. I actually went for a ride. I love that sign where you get on — "Open Every Day Except Rainy and Windy Days". Made me feel like a child again, sitting behind the noble head and splendid red beak and just gliding along.'

'Yes, Mr Peter,' Mary's face seemed to reflect none of his enthusiasm, almost hinting he had committed some forbidden act of truancy. 'You should have gotten off at Arlington Street.'

He chose to ignore her subdued expression. 'Somebody loaned me this tape. I doubt if it'll work in England. Is there a video I could use anywhere?'

'I'm sure your father wouldn't mind you watching it on the one in his study. I'll get Joe to show you how it works.'

'Please don't bother.' Peter made for the stairs. 'I'm quite good at trial and error.'

'I'll bring up your tea when it's ready,' she called after him.

In fact the Panasonic was very similar to the one in the Junior Common Room at Selwyn College. The only problem was finding the correct television channel to watch the tape on — no easy task with more than sixty to choose from. Eventually he discovered it — seven.

Peter scrutinised the early shots of the mass of runners assembled at the start for a glimpse of his mother. Although he thought he saw a man in a Badger vest move through the frame, it seemed a near-impossible task. He remembered Grace saying that the accident happened towards the end of the race so he spun the tape fast-forward, stopping at intervals to check.

Mrs Doherty came in with a pot of tea and some scones which, to judge from their appetising aroma, had recently been baked.

'I'm looking at the marathon,' he explained. 'My mother, you know.'

'That was a bad business,' the housekeeper commented as she closed the door.

And there she was — doggedly determined in her Badger vest, running alongside the camera car, running as if her life depended on it. And there she wasn't. In a split second she stumbled and fell as somebody screamed and the camera went out of focus as it searched for her and the truck came to a swerving halt.

He coated a scone with raspberry jam, bit greedily into it and rewound the tape to watch the accident again. There was a morbid fascination in being able to observe his mother's flirtation with death nearly a quarter of a century after it happened, comforted by the knowledge that she was alive if not well.

God, she was trying. It was almost as if she was out to win the bloody marathon, yet it had been evident from the earlier shots that there were quite a few women well in front of her. Again she fell and again the camera fell out of focus.

But he sensed there was something wrong. Something very wrong. Peter wound the tape back once more and then edged the picture forward, frame by frame. It was her expression, her final expression before she fell. She was no longer trying, she was no longer out to beat the world. She was out to leave it.

He froze the picture on his mother's face and moved forwards on his knees towards the television set to examine the shot more closely. It was there for anyone to see, but expecially him. A child can read its mother's face like a weather-vane. All hope had drained from Grace's, all fight, just a final sigh of despair. And now when he ran the picture slowly forward it all became horribly clear: she had dived. Nothing had made her fall under that vehicle save her own volition. She had tried to kill herself.

He drained his tea, feeling sick at what he had uncovered. He couldn't bear to look at it again. For a while he just sat on Dawson's study floor in silent shock and then his hand went out to the phone on the fireside table. 'Operator, I want to make a call to London, England.'

Peter had no idea what he was going to say when he got through. It was hardly the time to come clean about any of the things that had happened in the past three days in Boston. He merely wanted to talk to her, to hear her voice, to tell her that he loved her.

But it was Nevis who answered. This was most unusual – the calls were only routed upstairs when Nevis was out and Grace was spending the day there preparing the house for some reception.

'It's Peter,' he said. 'I'm ringing from America. Is everything okay?'

'I wish I could tell you that it was.' From across the Atlantic, the photographer's voice came flat and empty. 'You'd better come home. As soon as you can.'

· *Thirty-Two* ·

Peter cast an eye along the crush of faces assembled behind the lengthy railing of the arrivals hall at Gatwick. Not that he was himself expecting anybody to meet him; more to see if the law of coincidences offered up anyone he knew. But, to his surprise, there was Nevis, clad in a mock-tropical beige suit topped by the trademark white cravat that matched his well-coiffed hair.

For a moment Peter wondered what he was doing there. Had he come to meet some exotic new companion from the Orient? Evidently not. As he caught sight of Peter a look of relief came across his face, only to be chased away by one of concern.

The worst thought of all immediately assailed the younger man: Grace was dead. She had probably died as he sat with Dawson Silver, betraying her trust. This was to be his punishment, the burden that would henceforth accompany him until he reached his own grave.

'I thought you might welcome a lift to the hospital.' Nevis took the baggage trolley from him as if Peter himself were too infirm to be able to push it himself.

Hospital — the very word was a cause for hope. 'She's all right then?' he cautiously enquired.

'Not all right,' Nevis said solemnly, 'but alive.'

The M25 had yet to assume its unintended function as London's orbital car park at that time of the morning and the green pastures of Sussex looked dewy fresh and very English compared to the arid, end-of-season fields of Massachusetts.

'Carcinoma of the pancreas,' Nevis enunciated the words with precision. 'She's known for some time. To begin with they tried a form of radiation therapy but eventually . . . you know.'

'But I thought it was to do with her bile duct.' Peter seemed intent on trying to argue his mother well again. 'And they arrested it.'

'One arrest doesn't stop a crime wave. I suspect if the doctors had paid less attention to that they might have spotted the greater evil earlier on. Cancer's a cunning character, you know, capable of mounting a fake assault to hide the real onslaught elsewhere. It's the devil's horseman.'

'They can do things now,' Peter was trying to reassure himself. 'Genes and things.'

Nevis looked across from the steering wheel of the venerable Bentley to see how serious he was. 'Not with your mother. It's too late. You know that.'

'I don't know anything. Just the bile duct, that's all. She only ever told me about her illnesses when she got better. "I think I've had the 'flu for the last couple of days but it's much better now". That would be the first I would hear of it.'

The traffic was beginning to thicken slightly as Nevis signalled left to take the slip road for the A3 into London. 'She only informed me a few weeks ago. Wanted to know if she was covered by any employer's insurance but unfortunately not. She asked me not to tell you, said it was your special summer. Your mother's proud of you, Peter, rightly so. You're lucky to be able to make your peace with her. It's not given to every child.'

The very thought of making his peace or coming to terms with a final farewell was more than he could accommodate. 'How long has she got?' he asked limply.

'How should I know?' came the crisp reply. 'I'm not a doctor and even they don't know. No one consults us about whether we want to be born or when we want to die.'

'She did.' Peter felt the need to confide in someone and Nevis was the nearest. 'She didn't consult anyone, but when she was young and vigorous and healthy – before I was born – she tried to kill herself.'

'How do you know?'

'She told me,' he lied. 'I think it might have been because of someone she loved. I'm not sure of the exact reason.'

'It's certainly the best reason,' said the older man.

They drove on in silence, the morning commuter traffic accompanying them in increasing clusters until it fully clogged their progress as the highway headed up to the Wimbledon roundabout. When they came to a halt, Nevis reached across to the glove compartment and removed a paper bag with what appeared to be a bottle of medicine in it. He handed it to Peter.

'I want you to forget what I'm about to tell you,' he began mysteriously. 'This conversation never took place. Your mother is in pain and there is more pain to come. Okay, they give her drugs to alleviate it but what's the point? You say she once tried to kill herself so she obviously affirms the right to be determinist about her own life.'

'What is this?' Peter looked at the bottle in horror. 'Poison?'

'The reverse of poison.' Nevis was calmly emphatic. 'An elixir that can cure all ills. It has been tested. Two friends. One of them even managed to describe the early part of his passing before he lost consciousness. It was as if he could command time, he said, his parents – long dead – came back to help him on his way and all manner of relatives and friends and other people, some yet to be born, assembled in this endless room and wished him well. "This is the happiest I have ever been." Those were his last words.'

'What's in it?' Peter was fearful of even touching the outside of the bottle. The substance looked milky-grey and cloudy as if it consisted of male semen.

'I don't honestly know exactly. Nembutal, temazepam, diazepam, chlordiazepoxide, alcohol, a concentrated dosage of anti-depressants. It's necessary to eat some bread to help it down, and drink all of it. Mind you, there was a chap came back. He'd drunk most of it but his system was too strong. Said the experience was wonderful, better than those pot and Pomerol parties we used to have.'

The photographer gave a grim laugh at the thought of it as the car crossed Putney Bridge. To their left, they passed the Coronation Arch that marked the entrance to Bishop's Park and the hallowed turf of the Fulham and Gibraltar Lawn Tennis Club within.

'Don't be upset if she doesn't recognise you. We had hoped to keep her as lucid as possible until you got here but unfortunately the pain had other thoughts. So we've had to turn up the dosage. She goes in and out of sleep and, to her, the definition between the two states tends to be somewhat blurred. For the best, really.'

The sister tucked the sheets securely round Grace, more as a gesture of comfort than through any need for tidiness, and patted her gently on the forehead with her hand.

'There's a good girl,' she said, as if addressing a child, and then turned to Peter. 'I'll leave you two alone now. If you need any help, there's that button by the head of the bed.'

'What if . . . ' Peter found it hard to find the words. 'How will I know. . . ?'

'You'll know all right,' the sister smiled. 'But I don't think she's going to leave us just yet. She's been waiting for you to come home. And your brother.'

The woman was out of the room before Peter could ask her to explain more. Did Grace know that he had been to Boston and met James? He had made the details of his intended journey as vague as possible, indicating that he would be spending most of his time in New York. He contemplated her, propped up in bed with a tube attached to her nose, a saline drip nurturing one arm and blood slowly being fed into the other. She was only fifty-three but she looked much older, her hair grey and uncared for against the white strictly starched pillow and her face strained and world-weary.

Would it have been better if she had died when she intended? At least then she would have been spared the torment of bringing up half a child. All his life, he realised, she must have looked at him and wondered where his brother was. He had been a constant reminder of what she had lost and yet she had never once as much as hinted at it. Peter had told James that their mother was dying and suggested that he might come and say goodbye. But his sole response was: 'I didn't even get the chance to say hello.' It was understandable. Some acts of compassion could cause more pain than comfort.

'If you had to choose between being a tennis player or an actor, which would it be?' Grace had opened her eyes and was looking at him. It was as if they were in the middle of a conversation, that he had been there all the time.

'I'd be an actor,' he replied. 'More creative. I like spotlights shining on me and I don't think I'd attract many with my tennis.'

'But you liked Portugal,' she went on. 'For a while then I thought we were all there together – you, me and James. And the two of you dug castles in the sand while I lay back with my book and the sun. And it was so warm. Blissful.'

She drifted off again, an expression of contentment settling on her face in contemplation of her thoughts. It was the first time she had ever mentioned his brother's name in his hearing. Perhaps he had no need to say where he had been and whom he had seen. Perhaps unspoken thoughts were a more honest medium of communication than spoken half-truths.

'I want you to keep up your tennis, though. Promise me that.' She had come round again.

'I promise.'

'You can make so many friends through a sport like that. Meet girls, too. Although I daresay you can meet enough of those as an actor. Not the same sort, though.'

'No. There's room in life for both. Besides, I'll probably end up a lawyer. That's what I'm studying to be.'

'Don't do that. A lawyer performs good deeds for whoever is prepared to pay him and tries to do down whoever isn't. I was cheated by a lawyer once. But in the end I cheated him. I got you.'

She tried to lift her hand but she was too weak. Instead he leant across and kissed her on the forehead. 'And I've got you, mother. I want you to stay with me. I don't want you to go.'

'We all have to go. It's what makes us equal in the end. Think how awful it would be if the rich didn't die, but just sat on earth getting richer and richer. Nietzsche said that God is Dead but they misheard him. What he meant was God is Death. The equaliser.'

Peter was amazed at how clear and well-spoken her thoughts were, as if the drugs were endowing her with restored lucidity. At the same time he could see that every effort to speak stole a little more life from her.

'I'd better go,' he said. 'Make sure the flat is all right. Is there anything you need. Slippers? Books?'

'No, thank you. It's all here. This is a wonderful place. Everything is here. People to look after you and change you and bathe you. They make you feel so good. It's heaven.'

He stood up. 'I'll be back then. Tomorrow. At about the same time.'

'Tomorrow and tomorrow and tomorrow.'

Always the teacher, he thought, right up to the end. He could feel Nevis's bottle in his jacket pocket pressing against his hip. Grace had no need of it now. But as he put his hand against the door of the small white cubicle some demon deep within would not let him depart without him uttering a final truth, whether she took it in or not.

'Mother, I've seen James. I've been to Boston and I've seen him. He's all right. Big and strong and well.'

'Be sure and look after him now,' she replied, as calmly as if he had told her that tea was ready. 'Always remember you're the older brother.'

The service took place in the chapel of the crematorium. There seemed little sense in taking over an entire church for so few people and, besides, Grace had had little time for religion while she was alive.

Nevis read a lesson and so did Peter and they sang 'By cool Siloam's shady rill'. The young vicar who came with the crematorium said some nice things about her – that she had been a fine athlete and a dutiful mother and a good woman. And that was the final piece of punctuation in Grace Winston's life.

Peter had tried to contact Samantha but she was evidently somewhere in India. He half-wondered if her father might have come, but the family didn't even send a wreath. However an expensive one arrived from the local florists with a card that simply read 'Dawson and James', as if it were the name of some firm of solicitors. Tom Hall was there, still a teacher at Parsons Primary and still forgetting to take off his bicycle clips. And Ken Worple from the Fulham and Gibraltar. Several of his university friends had said they would attend but he persuaded them not to, insisting that it was just family.

Half a dozen neighbours from along the Talgarth Road and the other side of Baron's Court Tube made up the numbers, plus the usual strangers who tend to appear at funeral services and then disappear without any explanation. Perhaps they just enjoy them, Peter thought.

At first he assumed the cadaverous man with thinning hair in the brown corduroy jacket was one of those, but he warily came up to Peter in the garden of remembrance afterwards and introduced himself as Lenny, a friend of his mother's from her marathon days.

'Is there anything you want to ask me about yourself?' he enquired, awkwardly and somewhat mysteriously.

Peter eyed him apprehensively. 'I don't think there is. Our family is quite reconciled now. I've just been over with my father and brother in Boston.'

'Oh, that's a relief,' he said. 'My wife had been keeping this letter for years that your mother had wanted you to have if anything happened to her. But when we moved down to Devon it somehow got lost.'

'Well, so many things get lost in life,' Peter replied, 'ending up with life itself.'

'True,' he readily agreed. 'Better be getting back. Trains, you know. I'll tell Alice I've met you.'

The other stranger was more noticeable: a portly Pakistani gentleman who looked to be in his forties. He had waited patiently while Peter spoke to Lenny.

'Ranesh Patel,' he said, holding out a well-manicured hand. 'I knew your mother when I was a little boy and I wanted to be a swimmer. But now this.' He padded his ample but expensively suited belly.

'Patel,' the name rang a bell with Peter. 'Newsagent, confectioner and grocer. My mother would talk about you. Rylston Road, right?'

'My father's shop.' Ranesh nodded. 'Very good customer, your mother.'

'And you were very good. She even used to talk about the spirit of Ranesh that saw her through her darkest days.'

'Oh, I don't know about that.' The man was clearly embarrassed. 'But you are all right now, yes?'

He formulated the question as if Peter had been unwell, but this was hardly the occasion to probe further. 'I'm fine,' he replied, 'in the circumstances.'

'Your mother,' Ranesh smiled. 'Always liked to run. Named you after a runner – Jim Peters. Did you know that?'

'Yes.' Peter tried to sound as casual as possible. 'Always wondered why she didn't call me Jim, though.'

'You were James but you became Peter. It's complicated.' Ranesh reached in his pocket. 'Here, take my card. When you have got over your grief we will meet and I think I can explain.'

Peter accepted it, mystified. 'Thank you. One thing, though. My mother, when she was dying, said I was the first born. Do you know?'

'You were the first,' Ranesh assured him, making towards his Mercedes. 'Ring me.'

'I will,' Peter promised. He glanced down at the card as the car pulled away. 'Run a video from Video-Ran' it said at the top. There were many branches; Ranesh had evidently done rather well.

He looked round for the vicar to thank him and say goodbye but the noise of a taxi drawing up on the far side of the chapel captured his attention. His blood-pressure multiplied; it was the sound he had secretly been waiting for throughout the service. Sam. She had heard and she had come back from India. Samantha knew how much he needed her. Now she would stay with him, now they would be together.

Peter broke into an undignified run, swerving through the rose bushes of the garden of remembrance, pushing past the two remaining mourners, to get to her and welcome her home in his arms.

A woman in a dark raincoat with a black scarf over her head had just paid off the cab which was pulling away. She turned at the sound of Peter's footsteps on the gravel path.

'Hi. Sorry I'm late. Don't know London. Sorry about your mum, too,' The bush-baby eyes were deep with sympathy.

· Thirty-Three ·

'With a point for the set, why not go for the net?'

Mo's doggerel pumped through his brain like a rampant virus. If ever he got to the end of this match, Winston resolved that he would undergo a period of intensive therapy to have it completely extirpated. But his instinct made him listen all the same. Shimizu had served short and he picked up the return much earlier than usual, barely before it left the service court. He directed it deep towards the Japanese backhand, at the same time launching himself forward into an attack position. Shimizu's eye was diverted by the unexpected manoeuvre but he still made solid contact with the ball and found a cross-court angle of punishing velocity.

Winston dived. There was no time to make a stroke. He merely twisted his body and speared the racquet blindly in front of him throwing himself forward as desperately as if he were trying to push a child out of the path of an oncoming car.

He must have connected. The noise from the crowd said it all. He even dared to risk a glance up at the players' box and the sight of his sightless father clutching his coach told him what he wanted to know. The third set was his.

At the very rear of the north end of the stadium, in the back row of section 56, Tom Hall poured out some ginger beer for the three chosen pupils of Parsons Primary who had been lucky enough to accompany him to the final. 'That's where sportsmanship gets you,' he informed them.

In the members' enclosure on the left-hand side of the Royal Box, which itself had risen from its usual torpor into a form of modulated enthusiasm, Nigel Bergen removed a twenty-pound note from a calf-skin wallet in his inside pocket and handed it over to his neighbour.

And at the bar of the Don Brown International Tennis Centre at Quinta do Apollo in Portugal, the television set was toasted by a smiling crowd of brick-red Britons who had just been subjected to a relentless week of both tennis instruction and alcohol induction. 'Not bad for a pommie poofta,' yelled Don as he once again replenished his new two-pint lager pot.

· Thirty-Four ·

'Remember that the loser of a match usually plays just as well as the winner allows him. Never forget that the primary object in match tennis is to break up the other man's game. Where two players are equal physically and in stroke power, the determining factor is the mental viewpoint. Luck, so-called, is often grasping the psychological value of a break in the game and turning it to your own account. Few people realise that the science of missing shots is as important as that of making them. At times, a miss by an inch is of more value than a return that is killed by your opponent. Let me show you.'

Moses Hoffman put down the battered green book that he had been referring to and started to search for a piece of chalk in the tobacco tin in front of him. On the blackboard behind he had already written the words 'Mo's Satellite Squad' underlined three times in emphatic yellow. And before him sat the elite six – four young men and two girls – who were going to attempt an assault on the satellite circuit the following year. The Winston twins stayed deliberately apart, both of them had an aversion to being paired or compared in any way. In addition to his emphatically different hairstyle, James had gone overboard in gaudy outfits in the latest Dayglo colours – vermilion and aquamarine and orange – which made him look like a surfer. Peter preferred to stick to college sweaters and traditional white tennis clothes.

He had not returned to Cambridge at the end of September as he had planned. Already doubts had crept in with the death of Grace: amateur tennis, amateur theatricals and academic law seemed luxuries he was in less of a position to enjoy now. There was a growing imperative to get a job. Nevis had kindly offered him the free use of the basement flat until Christmas, but Peter knew that the photographer really needed another live-in housekeeper to look after him in his semi-retirement. His immediate future had been decided for him by two air-mail letters which arrived simultaneously on the Saturday morning of the week after his mother had died. He had opened the unknown one with the Florida postmark first. It was from Moses Hoffman, offering him a full scholarship to Osprey Academy for a year. In ink at the bottom of the somewhat formal letter, Mo had sent his sincere sympathy and suggested that this might be a good way for him to get over his grief. The writer of the second letter had also expressed his condolences but, at the same time, seemed to have found a uniquely brutal way of doing so. The vice-president of customer relations at the Narragansett Bank of Boston – the cigar-store Indian was still its insignia – was constrained to advise Peter Winston that under the terms of the WTT Trust Fund, his mother's death meant the cessation of payments. There wasn't even a final cheque.

So he found himself, this clear November morning, as a member of Mo's Satellite Squad in the primitive surroundings of Osprey Academy, a place still bearing the lack of luxury bequeathed it by the Third Florida Infantry Division. It was a world away from the rust brickwork and climbing ivy of the Old Court at Selwyn College, Cambridge. The other two men in the class were both Californians, graduates of Stanford University where they played more professional tennis than the professionals. Of the girls, Vanessa Cowan was a fourteen-year-old black New Yorker whose parents had been given jobs by Moses, her mother as a receptionist and her father as a driver, so that they could watch their dream come true – or not.

And then there was Phoebe. She had come back to Talgarth Road with Peter and Nevis and a few of the neighbours after the funeral but had been unable to stay for long since she was due to eat dinner with her parents that evening at the Churchill Hotel. She had made no mention then of returning to Osprey and it had come as a surprise to Peter to find her there when he arrived. Phoebe explained that, after failing to be selected for the final Australian Federation Cup team, she had thought it best to come back to Florida to work on her game.

'Let's suppose your opponent has drawn you here' – Mo chalked a yellow cross on the blackboard which already carried the permanent markings of a doubles tennis court. 'You go for it, you get to it, you drive it hard and fast down the sideline but you miss by an inch. Now is that better than scooping it back up to the other guy who by now has advanced to the net? Jim.'

James Winston straightened himself up in his desk. 'It's always better to put the ball in play,' he shrugged. 'Once you're out you're out and you've lost the point.'

'That's blinkered short-term thinking.' The coach waved the chalk at him dismissively. 'Forty-nine times out of fifty your opponent's going to kill the ball and grow in confidence. All you are is winded. But if you go for the line, here' – he jabbed the chalk emphatically into the board – 'then you've gained something. Not the point, you lose that either way. But the other guy's surprised and a bit shaken. He realises how nearly it could have gone in and he's more than a little wary that you're likely to try that shot again.'

Peter raised a finger. 'But what if you are the other guy?'

'You are always the other guy, Peter.' Moses fixed him with a penetrating stare. He looked back at the green book on his desk. 'Tennis psychology is nothing more than understanding the workings of your opponent's mind. First you must study your own mental processes. You react differently in different moods and under different conditions. So you must realise the effect on your game of the resulting irritation, pleasure, confusion or whatever form your reaction takes. A person who can control his own mental processes stands an excellent chance of reading those of another – the human mind works along definite lines of thought and can be studied. Then you can set out to destroy him mentally.'

'Come on, junior, move in on the ball. The net's yours, you take it,' James Winston yelled, adding under his breath, 'if you can.'

Peter felt hot, bothered and frustrated. It was bad enough being beaten by his brother – quite easily on most days – but to be coached and patronised by him was bordering on the offensive. James had been apprised of the full details of their birth and separation, at least in the version favoured by their father. Having learnt that he was the first-born, he subsequently referred to his younger brother as 'junior' or, even more playfully and less popularly, 'June'.

It had been at the back of Mo's mind to train the two boys as a doubles team – after all Tim and Tom Gullikson had done pretty well, making it to the Wimbledon final in 1983 – but it was apparent, almost from the start, that this was not to be. To begin with they did not have the Gulliksons' good fortune of being a left-hander and a right-hander, but also, not having been coached together in their formative years, they had markedly different games from each other. It was Jim's natural instinct to step in and hit everything, whereas Peter operated a more formulated strategy from the baseline.

However, in their first few weeks together at Osprey, Moses observed something remarkable emerge which was the exact opposite of team-work. They managed to bring out the very best in each other as opponents, as well as the very worst in each other. Whenever Mo matched them in a practice set they both raised their game infinitely above the standard they achieved when playing anybody else, succeeding somehow in transcending their natural abilities. Whether it was simply some symbiotic sensitivity which enabled each to read the other's shots or whether it was the darker complexity of twenty-one years' accumulated resentment for the experiences they considered the other might have stolen, the coach deliberately chose not to investigate. He feared that if he were to discover, it might destroy this fragile fission.

'Oh, curses.' James slipped as he was trying to put away his volley and the ball shot off the tip of his racquet, landing at the feet of the blonde girl in denim who had been video-taping the game. Expertly keeping the camera rolling, she kicked the tennis ball back onto the court.

'Thanks, Brandi,' he called. 'Did you get that shot? I must remember how not to play it.'

'Wait a minute.' Peter had failed to notice her before and now came forward and rested his hands on the net. 'Do I know you?'

'Hi, I'm Brandi.' She made it sound as if she were a Playboy bunny and even bobbed slightly while keeping the camera running all the time.

'Do you think you could turn that off for a moment?' Peter was not in the best of moods since he had lost the first three straight games and was further annoyed that nobody had bothered to consult him about videoing the work-out.

Brandi obliged, lowering the camera with a sheepish smile.

'I've seen you before, haven't I?' he insisted. 'You were at Fenners, in England, during the Varsity Match. I assumed you were the girlfriend of one of the Oxford players.'

'Wasn't me, hon,' she replied evasively. 'Never been to England. Nor to Fenway, not even Boston Fenway.'

'Fenners,' he corrected her. 'But we have met. You're very familiar.'

'So are you,' she teased, casting a glance at James. 'Cute, too. But there are a lot of blonde ladies in the world and they all can't be the same person.'

'But I distinctly remember . . .'

'Could we play on?' James was building up a head of steam as he stalked the court at the far end. 'If you have to spin a line to women, could you do it after the game? You might have time then to come up with something more original than the old "Haven't I seen you somewhere before" routine.'

Peter, embarrassed, returned to the baseline to serve and Brandi de Soto took the opportunity to pack up her equipment and leave.

Phoebe Carter looked up from the mound of sand she had been shaping. 'How did you know I was here?'

'Telepathy,' said Peter, squatting down beside her. 'And Vanessa. She said you went to this beach most evenings at sunset so I thought I'd borrow a bicycle and come and spoil it for you.'

'No, you won't do that.' She patted a place for him on the sand. 'Come and share it with me. It's the nearest I get to home. The Gulf of Mexico joins up with the Pacific through the Panama Canal and the Pacific flows all the way to Sydney. I used to cycle out here when I was a teenager and I felt homesick.'

'Do you feel homesick now?'

'A bit. How about you?'

'A bit, too.'

'It wouldn't be natural if we didn't,' she said. 'Although this is your brother's home. He grew up on these beaches. Siesta Key's the next one up from Casey. Osprey's more of a home to him than Boston. Ever talk about that?'

Peter dug both his hands deep into the sand. 'We don't talk about anything much. We're very different. He can't grieve for my mother – his mother – and I can't really regard Dawson as a father. You can't find a father at twenty-one, you're over the legal age of father-finding.'

'What can you find at twenty-one?' She was aware that it was a leading question.

'A new backhand, I suppose. I don't know. I know what you can lose, though.'

'A mother?'

'A mother and a lover. Both at the end of one short summer. I suppose you can lose yourself as well.'

'So I, to find a mother and a brother, in quest of them, unhappy, lose myself.'

'Very good,' Peter congratulated her. '*The Comedy of Errors*. How did you know that?'

'We do have Shakespeare in Sydney,' she retorted tartly. 'And here, too, as a matter of fact. We performed it as a Christmas play.'

'And you were Adriana?' asked Peter.

'No, Luciana, her sister. She's much more manipulative,' Phoebe's eyes gleamed mischievously. 'She gets her man in the end.'

'A year.' Edmund Michaels glanced at the report in front of him once more for confirmation. 'Two at the most. Not more than two, I'm afraid.'

'And then what?'

'Then it goes completely. Darkness. Memories of things. Sounds that will be much more evocative and smells that much sweeter.'

'Forget the fine phrases, can't you do something?' Dawson raised his voice more in sorrow than anger. 'You always know the latest fucking discovery. There must be something.'

'There will be. You're just a little too early, that's all. You've seen your son, though, your other son.'

'What is it with you and those two?' Dawson demanded scornfully. 'All this measuring and files and photographs. Why can't you leave the boys alone? They don't need help – I do.'

'Can't you understand?' The doctor paused while he lit a cigarette. 'Your help – or help for people who follow you – will come from them. The most perfect human template for medical research is identical twins. And those that have been raised apart – sheer joy. How do you think we can accurately test for happiness, stress, neurosis, depression? Is it brought about by our environment or is it within us all the time, part of our genetic code? Only twins can tell us.'

There was a time when the actuary would have been interested in such experiments, but not any longer. 'I don't want them wasting their time in that tennis camp, Edmund. It was all right when James was young. But now they should be doing something with their lives.'

'I believe you underestimate them. Moses thinks they have barely touched on their potential.'

'He's bullshitting you. All this scholarship business. I don't know where he finds the funds.'

'He sent me a tape.' Edmund Michaels swung slowly round to the television set behind him. 'Want to take a look? Move your chair in.'

The cassette was already in the machine. Michaels pressed the play button and Dawson put on his spectacles and peered forward as the recognisable figure of James, with a chequered headband and multi-coloured kit, took on the white-shirted Peter. He was increasingly impressed by what he could see.

'Not bad,' he agreed. 'Why don't they form a doubles team?'

'I recommended that,' said the doctor. 'But Moses thinks they're not really compatible, in temperament or style. There's something of the tortoise and the hare in them, very intriguing. Peter is prepared to extend his opponent all day on court in order to win, by boredom if necessary. Whereas James is like an unsuccessful doctor.'

'In what way?' Silver stepped into it.

'He doesn't have any patients.'

The actuary formed an expression mid-way between a grimace and a grin. 'Why don't they form a fucking relay team, then?' he suggested.

Michaels exhaled reflectively. Part of the pleasure he got from cigarettes was to watch the smoke snake away, imagining the molecules and particles and atoms that were struggling to guide it.

· Thirty-Five ·

At first Dawson Silver imagined that the intrusive sound of ringing was part of his dream. He had become a crippled and confused Charles Laughton scampering round the gargoyles of Notre-Dame shouting 'The bells, the bells.'

But it was the phone. At four o'clock in the morning? His fingers confirmed the time as they traced the position of the hands on a new clock for the partially sighted beside his bed. It must be overseas, he assumed. But it wasn't. It was Moses.

'What's wrong?' He was surprised that one could be so asleep and then suddenly awake.

'James,' came the blunt reply.

'Dead?' Ever since Peter had set foot in America nearly a year ago Dawson had harboured the nagging fear that the Englishman had somehow come to replace James.

'No, he's fine. Well, hardly fine. He's in the custody of the Venice police. We've got a local lawyer whose trying to get bail but they're playing it pretty tough.'

'What's the problem? What has he done?' Dawson was annoyed that the coach seemed to be beating about the bush. 'Drunken driving? Did he steal something? Hit somebody? Is this a fucking quiz game, Moses?'

'No, not a game.' The coach's voice on the other end of the line was flat and feint. 'He was caught in a car with someone, just by Nokomis Public Beach.'

Dawson's heart sank. He had known, of course he had known. But this was America. This was 1999. This was the land of the free and nowhere else in the world had people a more guaranteed right to be gay.

'So what's the problem?' He tried to sound casual, in part to persuade himself that it was small and surmountable.

'The problem,' said Moses, 'is the other person. It was a child, thirteen – maybe twelve.'

'Ten?'

Eamonn Quinn picked up the copy of the *Orlando Sentinel* which was on top of Hoffman's desk.

'Surely they've got that wrong?'

'I wish they had,' Moses agreed. 'I wish they'd got everything wrong. But even Jim's statement to the police makes less than happy reading. Ten-year-old boys are meant to be in bed alone at two o'clock in the morning, not sitting in an automobile with an older man admiring the moonlight on Nokomis Beach.'

'Read me it, Eamonn. Read me the story. Don't spare me anything.' Dawson Silver sat hunched and exhausted in the corner of the room, the strong sun filtered by the half-closed Venetian blinds and the cup of coffee by his side untouched. He had arrived in Osprey with Quinn the previous night, having waited for the lawyer to complete his day in court.

Quinn pushed his half-moon spectacles back up the bridge of his nose and leant forward, placing a hefty hand on either side of the papers in front of him. ' "Tennis player arraigned by Venice police", is the headline. Then it goes on: "James Winston, aged twenty-two, a professional tennis player, was arrested by Venice police early on Thursday morning and subsequently charged with lewd and lascivious behaviour with a minor. It is believed that an under-age boy, whom police have as yet not named, was in the car with Winston, who, when cautioned, stated: 'We were doing nothing wrong.' James Winston, who gave his address as Osprey Academy in Sarasota County reached the last sixteen of the Fort Myers Challenger Tournament in June." '

'What's that got to do with it?' Moses interrupted angrily. The coach felt deeply apprehensive and not a little guilty. The good name of the academy was going to be dragged through the mud. At the same time he had always had a suspicion that this might happen but he had never believed it actually would.

'That helps to make it news,' Quinn replied. 'And I daresay when they go through the cuttings from the sports pages and find James has a twin brother that will make it news again. Especially when this thing comes to trial.'

'There were a couple of reporters sniffing round here earlier,' Hoffman informed them. 'I told them to get lost.'

'What are we going to do?' Dawson Silver, distraught and distressed, anxiously scanned the faces of the other two men for help. 'Can you get him off, Eamonn? You've got to.'

The heavily built lawyer picked up a yellow legal pad and placed it on top of the papers. 'Things don't look at all good,' he began. 'For some reason the police have thrown the book at him. Hit him with a 228 felony whereas they could have reduced the charge to contributing to the delinquency of a minor. It sounds very much as if they'd seen him there before, maybe even cautioned him. Have you any knowledge of that, Moses?'

The coach shook his head. 'I don't know what Jim does with his private life. Okay, there was the relationship with Borogon but that guy was a Christian pervert. Jim's a loner. Ever since he bought that Packard he used to go off someplace after dinner. Nobody here went with him, though.'

'But even if the police had seen him before, that's surely circumstantial evidence.' Dawson pleaded with his attorney. 'It's a first offence, nobody goes to jail on a first offence.'

Eamonn Quinn looked down at the legal pad and scanned to the bottom of the page. 'I'm afraid he'll go to jail all right, Dawson. According to Stonehill, the local guy Moses engaged to apply for bail, James's statement to the police alone is enough for that. And the kid's parents are hopping mad. This isn't some vagrant from a makeshift trailer park. This is a child from a good home whom James met on the beach earlier that day. In fact he's very lucky not to be charged with abduction. If the kid's statement stitches him up and the prosecution can prove that not only was the boy sexually molested but has also suffered lasting psychological damage – and you only need a pair of tame shrinks to stick that one on – we're looking at anything up to five years.'

'I won't have it.' Dawson rose to his feet and grabbed the newspaper nearest to him, tearing the front page into shreds and scattering them across the office floor. 'This is my son. We all know him. He is a good boy. You, above all, Eamonn, remember the pain I went through to bring him here and give him a decent start. We used to go together to watch the clowns in Venice when he was a child. He always said he wanted to be a clown. But not this. This is not right. Not jail. Not James. Don't you understand, my eyes. Even now I can only see him with difficulty. When they release him I won't be able to see anybody. I don't want to watch my son fade from my life through the bars of a prison.'

'I agree. We can't let him go in.' Eamonn Quinn brought his hand down on the table with the authority of a judge's gavel. 'He cannot go to jail. It will be terrible for James inside. Sexual offenders, especially those who have been involved with children, tend to serve an additional sentence – and a pretty harsh one – at the hands of their fellow inmates. I don't know that he'd survive that.'

'So, how do you get him off? Do you fix the jury?' Moses had heard tell of the forensic powers of Loophole Quinn.

'It can't be done.' The lawyer was not offended by the suggestion but dismissed it with a flick of his hand. 'This case cannot come to court. The only course left to him is to jump bail and take refuge in some country where there's no extradition. Given time and exceptional circumstances, we should be able to find a way of plea bargaining him back after a few years. Not soon.'

'Like where?' Dawson seemed appalled at the idea. 'Afghanistan? India? Peru?'

The lawyer shook his head thoughtfully. 'A few Latin American states are safe for the moment but as soon as they sign some trade agreement with Congress there's usually a clause in there agreeing to extradition. The best bet may be France – that guy Polanski, remember, they've never touched him. But there's a problem getting James there. He could double his trouble if he's stopped at immigration. False passports, all that.'

'I don't think there is a problem.' Moses Hoffman's eyes lit up as the plan dawned on him. 'All he needs to do to get a passport is to have his hair cut.'

· Thirty-Six ·

'The tennis racquet is a lethal weapon, it can kill. If you engaged in a duel of racquets — forget about the balls — with a Samurai warrior and he brought his down just here you would die immediately.'

Takeiichi Harada indicated the spot on Peter's neck with his own shining Excalibur Plus. 'No time to cry out, nothing. Dead. Well, you must do the same with your volley. A volley must never return from the grave.'

Peter Winston rather liked Harada, he appealed to the dramatic in him. The Japanese-American instructor was jokingly known as 'imperial aggression' at Osprey; students were sent to him when they were on a losing streak to try and rediscover their killer instinct. Not for Harada the wishy-washy mind control exercises of the usual sports psychologists. He advocated all-out attack, fearless and ruthless. The idea was to annihilate your opponent without mercy. If you lost a few points or games because you found yourself vulnerable during the onslaught, Harada dismissed them merely as casualties of war.

'The net attack is the heavy artillery of tennis,' he insisted. 'It is supposed to crush all defence. The volley must be hit straight — the shortest distance between two points, do not waste time trying freakish curving volleys. And it must be regarded as a point-winning shot at all times. Even more so the overhead smash. This is the Big Bertha of tennis. Remember that, the long-range terror that should always score. The average overhead shot that is missed is netted. So you hit deep. Only twenty-five per cent of the time is the error that your smash goes out, more than **seventy**-five per cent of mistakes on smash consist of putting the ball into the net.'

Peter was self-consciously aware of the fact that the lesson was being observed from afar. His scholarship was up for renewal and that morning Dr Edmund Michaels had arrived from Boston to carry out his medical. The doctor and Moses were in hushed conversation some distance from the court. Although he was unable to hear what they were saying, the older men were only too able to follow Harada's barked orders.

'The trouble with you, Pete Winston, is that you have fallen in love. You love the poetry of the game, the low swing of the forehand here, the graceful follow-through of the backhand here' – the instructor demonstrated the offending shots as he spoke – 'but nobody gives any points for style at tennis. It is not like dressage, you know, with the horses. Too much you are making an exhibition for the crowd with too few winners. Now Jim Winston, he don't give a fuck what he look like. Attack, attack, attack. Okay, so he's susceptible at the back. So I hope he works on that – wherever he may be.'

'Where is he?' Michaels breathed the words into Hoffman's ear as loudly as he dared. 'I call Silver – he won't return my calls. I call Quinn – he says somewhere in Europe. It's more than a month now. The press has lost interest and so has the Bureau. They've got better things to do with their time than worry about people who fiddle with little boys.'

The coach was embarrassed. 'I told you on the phone, I can't tell you.'

'I thought you told me you couldn't tell me on the phone. Why do you think I'm here?'

'To give Peter Winston his medical check-up. He thinks so, too.'

'Come off it.' Michaels gave vocal vent to his frustration. 'What am I going to do? Fail the kid so that I stop paying for his tuition? I need them both, Moses. The whole point is to be able to compare their progress.'

'Well, Peter Winston isn't making much progress at the moment.' The coach awkwardly adjusted the peak of his black cap to block out more of the sun. 'We put him in a couple of Satellites and he did nothing.'

The doctor knew that it was time to work on Hoffman from a different angle.

'Have you ever wondered,' he asked, seemingly out of the blue, 'why some of the world's most celebrated artists – Leonardo da Vinci, Raphael, Michelangelo – produced their greatest works during exactly the same period?'

'Now you come to mention it,' replied the coach, 'no.'

'The Italian Renaissance, the Flemish Renaissance,' Michaels continued, 'the pattern repeats itself. Why were there so many exceptional English poets at the end of the sixteenth century, German musicians at the end of the eighteenth? Think about it, the two outstanding composers of opera – Verdi and Wagner – born in exactly the same year. Doesn't the evidence point very precisely to where so-called genius comes from?'

'It's the same in tennis.' Moses had got the message. 'Competition between comrades – surest way to create a champion. All those British brothers. Even the first woman to win Wimbledon beat her sister in the final. The French Musketeers were at each others' throats the whole time. Hopman and the Australians. Borg and the subsequent Swedes . . .'

Michaels intervened. 'There would have been no Big Bill without Little Bill, am I right?'

'Probably,' Moses conceded. 'All through the twenties they met nearly every year in the final of the Open. Poor old Johnston.'

'Poor old Winston.' The doctor indicated the Englishman sweating it out on the court. 'He can only raise his game when he practises against his brother.'

'So it seems.'

'Don't you see?' Edmund Michaels intertwined his right hand with his left in order to demonstrate his point. 'They even wrestled in the womb, before they were born. Twins have even been known – especially boys – to try and kill each other at that stage. These two have to work together, they're nothing without each other. But together they can bring out the genius within them. Now, where's James? You clam up on me and all bets are off.'

Moses Hoffman chewed his tongue as he watched Peter jocularly pretend to chop Harada with his racquet as the instructor brought the lesson to an end.

'Paris,' he said guardedly. 'Only you didn't hear it from me.'

*

James Winston took a step forward and watched both his sides stretch out with such distortion that he became wider than he was tall. His long legs were cut off so that they appeared to become cloven hooves and his head lost its shield-like shape and mutated into some gasping gargoyle. It wasn't pretty but it was better than being him. He had already made a few preliminary enquiries about plastic surgery. His hand went into his pocket to feel the card he had been given. It was some guy named Gobert on the Rue du Docteur Finlay. He had taken a walk past the place – it lay in the lee of the Eiffel Tower – but had been unable to summon up the nerve to go ring the bell.

A party of schoolchildren had come in and surrounded him. They were all laughing and pointing. To begin with, in his paranoid state, he thought that he was the object of their mirth. But, to his considerable relief, he soon realised they were laughing at themselves and each other.

Nevertheless he decided to get out. He felt slightly foolish being the only adult in the small hall of mirrors but he could never enter the Jardin d'Acclimatation without being drawn to them. They reminded him of happier days: of Violet, of Venice when he was a child, of the crazy clowns at the Ringling Brothers Barnum and Bailey Circus. The Jardin, just by the Porte Maillot at the opposite end of the Bois de Boulogne from the Stade Roland Garros, provided him with a lonely escape most afternoons into a world he wished he had never left. It had elephants and monkeys, the dragon dipper and merry-go-rounds, whipped ice-creams and doorstep-sized pizzas.

He handed over his ten francs and stepped into his favourite go-kart, number eighty-eight, revving the engine to warm it up until the attendant blew the whistle. It had neither the pace nor the elegance of Simon's car, as he had always called it, but it usually seemed to have the edge over the others here. On this cloudy Wednesday, however, the advantage was irrelevant as James was the only one on the track. He navigated through the figure of eight with economy, hugging the corners and crossing the straight at the optimum point. As he did so, with no competitors to worry about, his thoughts switched to the boy he was born to be. He wondered if Simon would have failed his father as ignominiously as he had.

Probably not. Probably he would have become a professor or something by now.

There was only one other table occupied at the outside café where he took his lunch. He watched the couple surreptitiously as he spooned in his soup. Why did French men behave in such an effeminate way when they were with women, always giggling, touching, chattering on about nothing as far as he could follow? Turning his attention to the *Herald Tribune* he saw that the Orlando Magic had lost again and now sat squarely on the bottom of the table. What had happened to Dr Bob's Magic — it seemed to have disappeared. First Dr Bob himself, then the tragedy of Magic Johnson and now the basketball team. His eye was caught by an advertisement for EuroDisneyland; you could get to the Magic Kingdom on the RER. He determined to go there the following week and see if that would sprinkle a little magic dust on him.

He always liked to look at the bears after lunch. They often copulated before they had their afternoon nap. At least the male bear would try to copulate and his mate tried to run away, which resulted in a sort of mobile hump with the she-bear running round the perimeter of the pool with him stuck onto her like an excrescence, trotting anxiously on his small legs. James presumed it was a her. It reminded him of the joke one-eyed Mike had told him about two dogs on the lawn outside a church and a small boy asking the priest what they were doing and getting the reply 'the little dog has gone blind and the one behind is pushing it to the vet's.' This afternoon, however, neither bear seemed prepared for such antics as they lay on separate sides of the pool and eyed each other watchfully.

'Don't you think we're being rather silly?'

He turned round to see to whom the remark was being addressed. It was the girl from the restaurant, with the pale skin and neat features. Her boyfriend was still lurking furtively by the café, some twenty-five yards away, and there was nobody else around. So James could only assume the remark was being addressed at him.

'I said, don't you think we're being rather silly.' She repeated it to reinforce the fact.

'I'm afraid I don't follow.' She must be mad, James thought. English and mad.

'Listen, there's no sense putting on an American accent. You can't go through life acting all the time. You were glancing often enough at my fiancé so you may as well be introduced. Maurice.' She beckoned to the man behind her who came obediently forward.

'I wrote to you at Talgarth Road and telephoned, but they said you had gone away,' she continued under her breath, giving James no opportunity to reply. 'This is Maurice Germot, from the banking family. Peter Winston, old friend of mine from Cambridge. The tennis player, I told you about him.'

James took the proffered hand: 'I'm afraid, er, there's a confusion of identity. You see, I'm not even English. I come from the United States – Florida, or rather, Boston.'

'Oh dear,' Samantha's hands flew to her mouth. 'How embarrassing. You're so like him. I am frightfully sorry.'

'Paris.'

'How the hell do you know?' Dawson demanded.

'Hoffman told me. He even gave me the exact address.'

Dr Michaels sat opposite him in the small office in Boston's Prudential Tower where Dawson Silver still put in one day a week, just to look after his old clients. His sight had stabilised of late, although he now carried a white stick when he was outside. There had been a couple of scares when crossing the road. But the doctor had not come to talk about his well-being.

'I think Peter should go there to join him. I have a plan. Moses is in agreement.'

'What business is it of yours? Or of some bum tennis coach? They're my sons.' The actuary gave full vent to his anger at this interference and at Hoffman's betrayal of his trust.

'It's time you knew what business it is of mine.' Dr Michaels opened his leather medical case and from underneath the stethescope drew out some bank statements which he passed across to Dawson. 'I supported your son. All the way through his childhood in England, right the way through university. If you don't believe the figures in front of you, call the manager of the Narragansett Bank. He'll confirm it.'

Dawson lifted a substantial square magnifying glass from the blotter on his desk and carefully cast his eye over the document. 'So you did. Goes back more than twenty years. Why did you do it, Edmund? No reason to doubt you. WTT Trust, why'd you call it that?'

'World Team Tennis,' the doctor explained. 'I was an investor in that in the mid-seventies. It's the same account.'

'Lost a lot of money, too, I should imagine.' Silver continued to peruse the figures. 'Looks to me you spent nearly half a million dollars on the boy. Where did you get it all from? The old guy Steigenberger leave you a windfall?'

Michaels, riled by his patronising approach, hastily responded by putting more of his cards on the table than he had intended. 'There is no Horst Steigenberger. Never was. It's the name of a hotel in Berlin. The Castor Street laboratories belong to me. And we earn some good royalties from drug companies as a result of our research. Not that I'm obliged to explain any of that to you.'

Silver pushed away the bank statements and carefully set his magnifying glass down on top of them. 'I think you do need to explain, Edmund. Not your money, but what you're doing with my son. You and Hoffman. That scholarship's another fiction, I presume?'

The doctor nodded. 'What you don't realise, Dawson, is the potential these boys have. Moses thinks they could be champions. Not just some diddley town tournament but Grand Slam stuff. Six weeks ago you were saying to him that you feared your last sight of James would be through bars. What I'm offering you here today is the opportunity to sit in the competitors' box and watch your son raise a major trophy over his head. Some parents would voluntarily go blind for such a chance in a lifetime.'

'It'll never happen at Flushing Meadow. He'd just have to step on court for the cops to take him away.'

'We know that.' Michaels was excited by the fact that he had managed to fan his imagination. 'It will have to be Europe.'

'I see. There's that French tournament, James watched it on television. He said he'd never bother with it, too slow.'

'Roland Garros,' the doctor put in helpfully. 'Exactly. We'll need to use it for some qualifying points but, as Moses says, clay is for cuckolds. No, if you're going to aim high, you may as well aim for the highest.'

'Wimbledon.' An image of old ivy and immaculately mown lawns manifested itself before the ageing American's eyes as he said the word.

'Yes,' smiled Michaels, as if congratulating a medical student on getting the correct answer.

'Which boy?' asked Dawson, still digesting the idea.

'Both.'

· *Thirty-Seven* ·

'Make love to me again.'

Peter cautiously opened one eye to remind himself she was really there, that he had not just dreamt her into his bed. The antique four-poster was real enough, he stretched out a hand and patted the solid French oak by his head. The room looked more like a museum than anything intended for modern habitation; ornate tapestries with hunting scenes hung on either side of the double doors and the paintings above the chimney-piece were crowded with cupids and angels. A huge stained-glass window, bearing a Virgin and Child, endowed the room with a consecrated air. On the opposite wall, two smaller latticed windows with clear glass and Norman arches looked out onto endless flat green fields that glistened with the dawn dew.

'You said that we were going to make love all night but you fell asleep.'

'You fell asleep first,' he protested.

'I was only feigning it,' she replied. 'Like my orgasms.'

He reached across the bed and took hold of a handful of the long dark hair spread over the pillow and gave it a sharp tug.

'Ow, what was that for?' She rolled over to face him, her deep bush-baby eyes as wide as a summer sky and the delicate white lace of her nightdress offsetting the Pacific brown of her arms and shoulders.

'For faking orgasms.'

'I lied about the faking,' said Phoebe. 'Is that a double bluff? Good Lord, is that a Virgin? I was too pissed last night to notice. You mean we did it in front of a Virgin?'

'She can't have been a Virgin,' Peter solemnly informed her. 'You can only create a male child with Y chromosomes and those are only found in a man's sperm.'

Phoebe was suspicious. 'What have you been studying here – religion? I thought you'd come to France for non-stop tennis?'

'Non-stop sex,' he replied, pulling her towards him and attempting to slide the nightdress off her shoulders at the same time. 'Actually it was the famous Dr Michaels who told me that, a man who can tell a Jean from a Jim. He's due in tonight.'

'Careful, you'll rip it,' she protested. 'Chantilly lace, don't you think that's appropriate. I bought it as a Christmas present for myself in Back Bay, Sydney, when I got your call. Just the stuff for the Big Bopper.'

'Who's he?'

'You,' she chided. 'You must have heard of him, a golden oldie. "Chantilly lace and a pretty face and a . . ." I can't remember the rest. He died in the plane crash with Buddy Holly.'

'Ah, you're so much older than me.' Peter teased. 'I only go back as far as Kylie Minogue.'

'Watch it,' she warned scraping her fingers down his chest. 'But Chantilly lace does come from here, doesn't it? You must have seen it in the shops and things?'

'The only things I've seen since we've been here are horses. There are more of them in Chantilly than humans and what humans there are look like horses. There's even a horse museum, would you believe?'

'What about girls?'

'Girl horses, yes.' He knew what she was getting at. 'Girls, no.'

'Even with this sexy four-poster to bring them back to.'

'I carry a postcard of it in my wallet all the time, but it never seems to do the trick.'

'What about the one from Cambridge?' Phoebe pressed her inquisition even harder as she spread her fingers menacingly across his paddle stomach.

'Strange you should mention her. She's in France. Or was. She spotted James in some Paris park before Mo and I came over. Even introduced him to her banker boyfriend.'

'Did Jim say who he was?'

'Are you crazy? And that was before Mo drew up the rule-book.

Apart from training runs, only one of us is allowed out in public at a time, while the other stays in this gilded palace like the man in the iron mask.'

'Why did you come?' asked Phoebe. 'I told you you should have gone back to Cambridge. It would have been so much more normal than the crazy life you live in this place. You'd have found the money. My father could have helped you. Why are you here, Peter?'

'To win Wimbledon,' he replied.

She looked at him as if he had lost his mind. But she loved him. So she merely enquired: 'Are things any better between you and Jim?'

'Not really. I mean, professionally they're fine. But we don't have too much personal contact. I give him an hour's English pronunciation each day but even that's not really necessary any longer. He sounds more like me than I do. We pulled a cracker on Christmas Day. Apart from that it's been quiet. I'm surprised Mo let a noisy girl like you come and stay. You must be one of his favourites.'

'I want to be noisy.' Phoebe slipped her Chantilly lace nightdress down to her waist and pressed her hardening breasts into his stomach. 'I want to scream and scream like some Cathar martyr who's being tortured to death. Got any rope?'

When eventually she came down to breakfast, Moses Hoffman was the only one still there. An incongruously small figure in what looked like a giant's kitchen with its outsize griddles and ovens, he was finishing a croissant and the special edition of *Time* magazine that lay by his plate.

'I told you on the phone you'd sleep well,' he grinned, getting up to give her a hug. 'The ghosts never bother you in that little room under the stairs. Was everything all right?'

'Fine,' she replied. 'I just couldn't find the plug for the bath. That's the trouble with these Holiday Inns, the staff will keep taking the bathplugs home.'

'There aren't any staff,' he said. 'Too many tongues. A local woman comes in for a couple of hours every morning while we're at practice and cleans the place and prepares some food – she's doing something special for tonight. She knows there are two other guys here but she doesn't get to see them. You'll come as a bit of a shock to her. There is no plug, by the way, just a handle you turn by the side of the bath.'

'I discovered that eventually.' Phoebe sat down on the bench beside him, freshly dressed in a cream tracksuit with her dark hair caught back in a bun. 'Are they playing already?'

He poured some coffee into what looked like a small bowl and passed it across to her. 'They go for a run first.'

'Don't people recognise them – I mean, see that they're twins?'

'I doubt it. They're usually out by the grass gallops where the race horses train. Not many people there. You wouldn't recognise twin jockeys with their caps and goggles. The boys keep on the move, they're both in hats and Pete wears glasses. You obviously got in too late last night to see Jim.'

'Yes, we stopped for a meal on the way from the airport.' She wondered if they had done anything wrong. 'What about him?'

'He looks like a hippy, didn't Pete say? Hair longer than yours – only not dyed this time – and a scraggly beard to match. It'll have to come off if I need him for the Challengers.'

Phoebe held the bowl of coffee up to her lips and fixed Hoffman with her most innocent expression. 'What's the game plan, Moses? Peter wouldn't tell me. He said you wouldn't, either. But I know you better.'

She didn't have to explain any further. The coach remembered only too well the amounts of money her father had given to Osprey. Besides, Phoebe was like a daugher to him. She had virtually grown up at the academy. Unknown to her, he had been aware of her feelings for Peter almost before she was. And he had watched her fail to read the warning signs in her pursuit of James. What could be a more appropriate antidote to such a scything rebuff than a heterosexual twin brother? The coach had sensed how much Peter had missed her during the isolated winter. It was even beginning to harm his game so it had been at his suggestion that she had been invited over.

'It would be better that you didn't know,' he warned. 'Better for you, easier for us.'

'Nothing that's easy is worth going for.' She covered his hand with hers and squeezed it. 'You taught us that.'

He laughed. 'Okay. But I don't think Jim should be aware that you know. I suspect he already felt a little resentful at you coming, although he still regards you as his friend. Which is more than can be said for the two of them. Michaels has all these reports on the behaviour of twins – but some of the authors should try spending the winter in an old French mansion with a pair. Dinner here ain't like the David Letterman Show, you know. But it should be better tonight.'

'Do you think Peter coming to America caused James to do what he did?' Phoebe eyed him earnestly. 'It was the one thing that used to prevent me getting to sleep back in Sydney, especially on the hot summer nights. I'd lie in my room and just replay it over.' She paused as she did so now. 'I brought him back for me, you know that.'

Moses bowed his head sagely. 'Some things are destined to happen and we can't do a whole lot about them. I guess Jim was letting off a cry for attention, taking risks he wouldn't normally take. But his life was going in that direction anyway. There'd been a guy at Osprey, after you left, although it didn't work out. Who knows?'

Phoebe looked at the coach, crouched and vulnerable, a little walnut of a man in his shiny black wrapping. 'So what are you going to do?' she asked.

'We're going for Wimbledon,' he replied quietly. 'It's more open than usual this year – Garland, Jarvis, Drew, Willford – all good but they all have their weak points. We have a little computer we sometimes play with in the evenings that lets us analyse them.'

'What about Shimizu?' Phoebe knew the international game nearly as intimately as he did.

'He's different. And he's going to be really hungry for that third title. Still, even the yen occasionally has a bad day. They say his stamina isn't his strong point. What you have to understand, Phoebe' – the coach turned over two outsize French sugar-lumps in front of him – 'is that the Winston boys are different now from what you saw in Osprey. They're world class. Quite apart from my training, Michaels has worked out a highly complicated medical programme – some of it I don't understand, like turning creatine phosphate into adenosine triphosphate which they then use in twenty-second bursts instead of carbohydrate. That way you don't build up any lactate in the muscles, so you don't get tired. And there's more besides.'

'But they've still got to qualify,' she pointed out unnecessarily. 'And Peter isn't even on the computer at the moment. You can't be hoping for an English wild card, they don't give them to Cambridge captains any longer — especially those who fail to go back to university.'

'That's why we're here. We need computer points. We're going to play the Challengers at Bergerac and hopefully Cannes. A place in the semis at either or both should be enough to get us into the French qualifying.'

She clicked her fingers as she understood. 'And if you get through to the second week at Roland Garros the British are bound to give Peter a wild card to the All England. That's the plan, isn't it?'

Moses nodded.

'You're using them both. They're interchangeable.' Phoebe was on her feet with excitement, having rumbled the plan. 'Peter — the baseliner — will play the clay courts here in France and then Jim will see how far he can volley his way at Wimbledon.'

'In principle, you're on the right track,' the coach agreed. 'Only their games have changed. They've learnt strokes from each other without knowing it, more from bitter competition than any fraternal sharing. I can choose who will be Peter Winston on any given day.'

'And what about Jim?' Phoebe was still standing up. 'What's the line on him?'

'That's the province of Dawson Silver and Michaels. You can ask the doctor tonight. He's promising a thousand-dollar bottle of wine for the occasion. A boating accident was one plan. Somewhere off the coast of Africa. Let's not talk about it.'

He got up from the table and picked up a pair of tennis racquets that were resting against the wall. 'Do you want to come and have a look? It's just across the courtyard.'

'Who owns this place?' she asked. 'They must be loaded. It's tremendously posh to have your own inside clay court.'

'The Auberts — racing people. Everybody here is. The strange thing is it's not actually modern. They used to play *jeu de paume* in it — you know, with the hand. The French still called it that even after they started using racquets. There's a plaque on the wall says King Henri the Second played there, doesn't give the score though.'

'When we have matched our rackets to these balls,' Phoebe quoted, 'we will in France, by God's grace, play a set shall strike his father's crown into the hazard.'

Moses opened the kitchen door and the cold December blast caused them both to shiver. 'Who said that?' he asked.

'Henry the Fifth,' she smiled, slipping her arm into his as they stepped outside. 'The English Henry. The French sent him some tennis balls to upset him.'

'It was their game,' said Moses. 'They gave it its name. The players used to call out *"tenez"* as a warning before they served. Even the scoring's theirs. Love is just a corruption of *l'oeuf*, because an egg looks like a zero.'

'Love is a corruption of many things,' she suggested wistfully as he opened the door at the end of the indoor court where she could see Peter, in his glasses, knocking up.

'And when they had reached forty-all,' Moses went on, 'The French would call out *"à deux"* – quick way of saying you have to win two consecutive points to decide it.'

'Which was corrupted into deuce – or twins,' Phoebe yelled at the top of her voice.

Peter saw her and smiled and waved his racquet. James had his back to her and swivelled round abruptly. He looked like a Himalayan mountaineer. His tangled dark brown hair settled on his shoulders and his matted beard ran down to his chest.

'Phoebe,' he cried and clambered over the low partition to greet her. He put his arms around her in a bear-like hug and, somewhat to her surprise, the tears just cascaded down his cheeks and moistened his moustache.

'Come.' He didn't want the others to see his state. 'Come and see the *pièce de résistance*.'

Taking her by the hand, he led her through a wooden door opposite the main entrance. And there, in the middle of what was clearly once an indoor riding school, lay a perfect grass tennis court, verdant and smooth and serene.

'The only one in the world – my private meadow,' announced James. 'All through the winter I've gambolled on it, but when the big gamble comes around in June a lot of people are going to be extremely surprised.'

'What's so special about this stuff, anyway?' James drunkenly held up the bottle beside a candle so that he could read the label. 'Château Pétrus, 1959. Don't the French churn it out by the gallon?'

'Not that one,' Edmund Michaels insisted defensively. 'I'm not even sure they have any left. I had to smuggle it into the country – just like you.'

'Ha, fucking, ha.' The younger man was not amused. 'I hope you don't mind me saying this but it tasted kinda musty, rather like truffles. Haven't you left it a bit late?'

'On the contrary, we're drinking it about forty minutes too early.' The doctor glanced at his wrist-watch to confirm the point. 'And it's meant to have a bouquet of truffles.'

'I thought it was divine,' Phoebe reassured him. 'Rich with spicy splendour. I've heard my father talk about Pétrus, not that he ever offered to share a bottle with me.'

'There was a French player called Petra,' Moses never let the conversation stray too far from the game. 'Born in Vietnam and wounded in the Second World War. They were going to amputate his leg but a German doctor managed to save it in a prison camp. Did a pretty good job, too, considering his patient went on to win the first Wimbledon after the war.'

'It's the same name as yours, Peter,' Phoebe responded enthusiastically. '*Tu es Petrus et super hanc Petram aedificabo meam ecclesiam.*'

'If that's French, it's a bit out of date,' James eyed her aggressively.

'Latin,' she corrected him. 'You can see it in Rome. In St Peters, just above the Bernini pillars. You are Peter and on this rock I will build my church.'

'I wonder if Petra let the Kraut have his player's tickets,' James sourly stubbed out his cigarette.

'Doubt it,' Moses took the proposal at its face value. 'Germans weren't too popular in London in 1946. Yvon Petra, played like you, Jim – big serve, big smash. Big upset. He beat your Ozzie number one seed, Phoebe, in the semis – Dinny Pails. Sounds like a school meal, doesn't he? Dinny got stuck on the London metro and was twenty minutes late for the match. The British were more upset about the fact that he kept the Queen waiting than anything else.'

'Was Petra gay?' James enquired waspishly.

'Okay, we're into trivia.' Peter was anxious to defuse his brother's bitter mood. He indicated the empty bottle in front of him. 'For the last spoonful of Chantilly cream on your apple tart, who won Wimbledon in 1959? Dr Michaels, you first.'

Edmund adjusted his bow-tie feeling, correctly, that he was an amateur in a den of professionals. Nevertheless he was anxious not to make a fool of himself. 'Budge Patty?' he suggested tentatively.

'You're about ten years out,' Hoffman informed him kindly. 'I'm pretty certain it was Lew Hoad.'

'No.' Peter was delighted to have caught out the coach.

'I know.' James mimicked his brother's English accent. 'It was Phoebe's pin-up, Mr Reginald Laver.'

She punched him playfully, rising to the bait. 'Rod. And you're wrong. The Rocket won Wimbledon in '61 and '62 and again in '68 and '69 and he would have won it for the five years in-between, which would have made him champion for nine years in succession, if he hadn't turned professional. That would have made him even more indisputably the greatest player who ever lived.'

'Well, who was it then?' James came back at her.

'Doesn't matter if it wasn't Laver. Neale Fraser, I suppose.'

'You're all wrong.' Peter was ecstatic. 'The cream is mine. It was the only time he entered and the only Peruvian ever to win. Alejandro Olmedo.'

'Very impressive, Peter.' Moses pushed the bowl across to him. 'Been doing your homework?'

'No.' Peter was flushed with wine and happiness at the sight of Phoebe sitting opposite him. 'I learnt it at her terrible training camp. There is no person in the world that drunken Don Brown hates more than Alex Olmedo. Peruvian bastard, he used to scream. You see' – he could hardly speak, so amusing was the memory of it – 'he was the member of the American team who single-handedly put an end to Australia's winning Davis Cup run masterminded by Don's guru, Harry Hopman. But Olmedo wasn't even an American. So after Don had had his tenth pint of the amber liquid he used to go around yelling: "They should have sent the fucking cup to Peru." '

The story and his laughter infected everyone at the table. Phoebe wiped the tears from her eyes with a napkin. She was looking forward to her return to the four-poster but she was damned if Peter was going to get away with a slight on her idol. 'It didn't put an end to our run. We won it back the following year and held it for the next three years thanks to the arrival on the team of the greatest player of all time, the legendary . . .'

'Rod Laver,' chorused the rest.

'I don't want to be a spectre at the feast,' Mo interjected. 'But he wasn't.'

'Well, if he wasn't, who was?' Phoebe shot back.

Moses Hoffman found himself at the end of a resentful stare from the beautiful Australian, inquisitive looks from the two brothers and an anxious glance from Dr Michaels. But he was denied an opportunity even to open his mouth and answer. Without warning, the sky outside was suddenly illuminated with rockets and flares as if war had been declared and the bells rang out, loud and joyous and clear, as if it had simultaneously ended.

Phoebe ran to the French windows and threw them wide open. Shouts of *'bonne année'*, *'un nouveau Siècle fantastique'* and *'à l'an deux mille'* arose from the crowded square as the church bell commenced the solemn beat of midnight.

The others came across to join her.

'No need to decide on any resolutions,' Edmund Michaels smiled as he kissed Phoebe. 'I think we all have the same one.'

'Almost the same,' said James Winston.

· Thirty-Eight ·

Bergerac had been bad, very bad. Worse than that, it had been disastrous. Peter Winston stood on the balcony outside his bedroom, his hair soaking and his towelling dressing gown sodden from the relentless rain that was stair-rodding its way into the widening puddles on the grey courts of the Hotel Montfleury in Cannes.

It was the weather that had done for him at Bergerac, although there was little comfort to be found in that. All the clay court practice that he and James had put in during the winter months had been on the smaller indoor court at Chantilly. But the early April tournament had been played in a capricious, swirling wind that switched without signal from breeze to hurricane. He had been lucky to get through the first round, it was only his height and reach that saved him. The opposing Frenchman had been short, probably less that five foot six, and on more than one occasion the ball had simply blown over his head. Even then, Winston had considered himself fortunate to run out a 7–5 winner in the deciding set.

A seventeen-year-old schoolboy had harshly settled his fate in the second round. Max Decugis had been educated in England but returned to his native country fully equipped to deal with both the local weather and his rangy opponent. He and the wind blew Peter off the court, 6–4, 6–4. At the post mortem back in Chantilly Moses had feared this was the end of the plan, jokingly referred to since New Year's Eve as 'Operation Olmedo'. Hoffman had only managed to secure him a place in the Bergerac Challenger because he had coached the children of the tournament director at Osprey and had thereby been guaranteed a wild card. But he had no such strings to pull at Cannes.

Their training had resumed in an icy atmosphere with James carrying his silent resentment around him like an invisible shroud. Phoebe had left early in the New Year for America to continue her assault on the women's circuit there and Edmund Michaels had rapidly returned to Boston, having confidently made a reservation at the Ritz Hotel in Paris for the last week in May and the first in June – the dates of the French Championship.

Dawson Silver kept in regular contact by telephone. His failing sight had prevented him from travelling to Europe but he was scheduled to go into hospital in the middle of June for a new operation that offered the promise of dramatic improvements. He was also fearful that the FBI would follow him if he so much as set foot on an international flight. It had been a big enough problem getting James out of the country over the border to Canada.

Loophole Quinn had duly arranged the drowning. Clothes belonging to James Winston – even a jacket with his name stitched inside – had been washed up on the beach at Puerto Escondido in Mexico, north of the border with Guatemala. Two local fishermen testified to the American investigator that a young man answering Winston's description had hired the sail-boat from them that was found empty and abandoned further down the coast. Whether or not the FBI believed them did not affect the eagerly received dollars that Quinn's emissary had left in the trunk of an ancient Ford Pinto, dumped by their boat.

It had made a brief story on the inside page of the *Boston Globe*. That, and Dawson Silver's statement through his lawyer, saying he would continue to believe that his son was alive until there was positive identification of a dead body. The Sisters of Rathlin had made an unannounced visit to Marlborough Street to express their condolences and to promise that their intercessions would be for the soul of the departed. Dawson wondered if they hadn't really come to size up the house.

For a client to lose one son by drowning was a misfortune, an elderly and cynical judge mentioned to Quinn at a Boston Law Society dinner, but to lose two bordered on carelessness. Although the attorney affected to be deeply offended by the slur, he acknowledged to himself that it might have been more prudent to have chosen a different death – but a burning building would have been less easy to arrange.

'What do we do after Wimbledon, win or lose?' Dawson would continually ask him. The lawyer pointed out that the position then greatly depended on Peter. If he were to acknowledge that James had played every match, in France and England, then the revelation that this superb athlete – a quarter-finalist or whatever he achieved – was in fact the missing James Winston, could surely only help accommodate his rehabilitation in the United States. Community service coaching kids would be the worst he could expect. And if Peter were not to co-operate? This was not an eventuality that Quinn was prepared to speculate on, although he sometimes feared for the Englishman's safety.

Peter knew absolutely nothing of this as he stood, drenched to the skin, on his Montfleury hotel balcony. The bad weather had paradoxically proved to be the plan's salvation. Several of the better players had pulled out of this Challenger because of the rain delay which meant that they might miss a more lucrative exhibition tournament the following week in Milan. As a result Mo's gamble in coming to Cannes anyway had initially paid off with a wild card entry. But success of any sort seemed so far away to Peter that he had already made up his mind to contact Tom Hall and see if there was a teaching post vacant at Parsons Primary.

Hoffman had warned him to be wary of Brandi de Soto. The moment the *Globe* article about James appeared she had turned up at Edmund Michaels' Beacon Hill consulting room raging like a rabid terrier. Why hadn't she been informed first? Why had he deceived her? His protestations that he didn't even know that James was in Mexico went ignored. Brandi knew he knew. She could have done a portfolio of James in exile – lonely shots of the man and the sky and the beach. It would have been worth a fortune. And even if she just got the first pictures of the fishermen and the washed up clothes, *Snap!* would have paid her twenty-five thousand dollars. Michaels had duly written her a cheque for ten thousand but as she stormed out, more vexed than she had stormed in, he doubted if this would keep her shutter closed for long. So in a letter to Moses he had merely told him to inform the boys that she was no longer on their side.

There was an authoritative knock at his bedroom door. Peter went inside to answer it, dripping his way across the carpet. It could only be Moses. The coach looked at him in some surprise. 'Did I get you out of the shower? Do you usually take one in your dressing gown?'

Peter ushered him in. 'I was taking it outside. I thought this time I'd acclimatise myself to the local conditions.'

'I think we should be all right tomorrow.' Mo put the bag of clean tennis clothes down on the bed. 'When it rains on the Riviera it does so in cycles of four days. All the locals up at Vence say that.'

'What's the villa like?' Peter enquired, not without envy.

'Pretty but spartan. There's a pool that Jim could exercise in if the owners had been bothered to fill it. Looks like nature's going to do it for them.'

'Even if it does stop raining' – Peter indicated the pools on the courts outside – 'how long before they can start?'

'Straight away. I've been down to the Carlton Club, they've had the covers on the whole time. You should be in action tomorrow morning.' Moses sat down on the bed, pushed back his cap and pulled some folded sheets of paper out of his tracksuit pocket. 'Listen, they've sent me the faxes on this guy Mallory you're playing in the first round. Read them and study them. He's from Provo, Utah. Hot. All America honours at UCLA. Reached the NCAA semi-finals. Got to the quarter-finals at Schenectady. And a good record in the Challengers. Big serve and volley boy. Might remind you of Jim. But there is one salient difference.'

Peter took the papers from him. 'Really? What?'

Moses lay back on the bed and put his hands behind his head. 'He's probably never seen a clay court in his life except on television. You're on your home ground, Peter, and this is almost as famous an American graveyard as the ones in Normandy.'

'Why can't you get me a draw against somebody on the way down instead of the way up?' Peter muttered as he sifted through the sheets on Mallory. But gradually he took in the coach's remark. 'What do you mean, graveyard? Here in Cannes?'

'Down there at the Carlton. February 1926. The great grudge match. Helen Wills, hard hitter, only twenty-one but three times US National Champion and an Olympic gold medallist. She came to

· 344 ·

the Riviera to clean up but instead she came up against Suzanne Lenglen who was twenty-seven and had never been beaten in France. Wore a salmon pink bandeau – bit like Jim. She used to have a sip from a silver brandy flask every time she changed ends. Despite that she was uncannily accurate; she could finesse a rally to perfection. Wiped out Wills in the first set – it took the American that long to get used to the clay. Helen went 3–1 up in the next but then she got nervous and started to trade groundstrokes. Just remember that, Peter, play your own game.'

'I think I've heard of her,' he said, 'but I can't remember from where. Did she win?'

'Won twice, as a matter of fact. Wills pulverised a waist-high forehand at match point, 6–5, 40–15. There was a call of "out" and the place went wild as the umpire awarded game, set and match to Lenglen. But then this idiot linesman, Lord Charles Hope, pushed his way through all the people on the court and said he hadn't made the call, it was someone behind him, and the ball was in. So the umpire, Commander Hillyard, who – would you believe? – had addressed the French crowd in English throughout the game, instructed them to resume the match. Lenglen was close to collapse. Served what was thought to be only the sixth double-fault of her entire career but she made it. 8–6. Would never have held on for a third set.'

'Six double-faults? In her whole career?' Peter was sceptical. 'Who was doing the counting?'

'What counted was that she never lost,' his coach replied. 'When you want to put yourself in trouble, just throw up the ball and serve a double.'

The weather changed the following day and so did Peter Winston's fortune. Every serve, every stroke, every single tactic that he had practised with his brother under Moses Hoffman's tutelage during the long winter months at Chantilly came to his aid. Mallory was never in the match and found himself swept away 6–3, 6–3 before he even had a chance to enjoy the sunshine of the Côte d'Azur. Because of the three days lost to rain, Winston was asked if he would consider playing his second round match that afternoon. Moses counselled against it – there was too much at stake. But Peter insisted that he was on a roll, like a punter at a casino who finds himself in a charmed time zone just a few minutes ahead of the present and therefore able to win and win again because he has a mystic window into the immediate future.

Moses relented and so did Manuel Alonso of Spain who was no match for Winston's pinpoint rallying and went down having won only four games. Peter sensed somehow he had found a spiritual home at the Carlton Club. Although his match was only being watched by his coach and Alonso's mother and two off-duty ball-girls – unlike the one nearly seventy-five years previously which, he had learned at lunch from Mo, had been graced by King Manoel of Portugal, Prince George of Greece, Grand Duke Michael of Russia, the Duke of Westminster and the Rajah and Ranee of Pudukota – he felt at one with the legendary Lenglen. He could see the spin of the ball as it twisted towards him and the red clay felt like a friendly trampoline beneath his feet as he sprung across the court. But he had no need of a snifter of brandy to experience the intoxication of victory.

The match against Serge Jacob, a ranked French player, the following afternoon was not as sweet. Here was a veteran who had not advanced to the net in years and was prepared to slog it out from the baseline until the sun had dipped beneath the Mediterranean. But Peter was prepared to slog it out, too. He had rehearsed this situation often enough in Chantilly – 'if he just wants to return the ball, show him that you're the sturdier wall' – and in the final set Jacob's stamina began to sink at four games all and the Englishman found he merely had to keep moving him from one side of the court to the other in order to clinch the two concluding games.

Only one round now stood between Peter and the semi-final and only one player: Max Decugis, his conqueror at Bergerac. The match was even more crucial than the final for both players since the last four at Cannes were automatically guaranteed places in 'les qualifications' for Roland Garros.

Moses had jumped for joy as Peter put away the winning backhand against Jacob. He arranged to send a car to the Montfleury to pick him up and bring him to the villa near Vence so that they all could have a modest celebration. The coach had persuaded the proprietor of the Colombe d'Or restaurant of the virtues of takeaway meals – in fact Moses had lied to the woman that he had an elderly relative who had come all the way from America to eat there only to be housebound with phlebitis – and the chef had prepared a stunning cold collation that Peter's driver was instructed to collect on the way.

At the sound of the car arriving Moses jogged up the pathway of the small villa to greet him and repeat his congratulations. It was a pink, stucco Hansel and Gretel building, at the end of a quiet track in a garden dense with pine trees. At the front, yellow roses twined up two pillars to a little balcony above the door. Hoffman dismissed the driver, telling him to be back by ten and helped Peter, still high with hope after his triple victories, carry the food into the house.

But the moment he caught sight of his brother through the kitchen window he divined exactly what was going to happen. He even managed to marvel that so much information could pass through the human mind in such infinitesimal time. Peter knew he would not be returning to his hotel that night, nor indeed would he ever be going back to Cannes – at least not on this trip.

It was a warm evening and James was sitting outside by the pool at the back of the house. He was clad in tennis shorts and a T-shirt and his right foot and his head were responding to the beat of rock music, unheard by anyone but him as he listened through his personal earphones. But this was not the James that Peter had seen every day for the past six months, not the shaggy monster who had pounded a million balls back at him morning, noon and night.

The person he was looking at now was him.

Absorbed by the music, James did not notice his arrival. So Peter rounded venomously on Moses who was unpacking the food for supper.

'Congratulations on the hair-cut,' he said bitterly. 'I wondered why you needed those Polaroids of me. Who was the barber?'

'I was,' Moses admitted sheepishly. 'I couldn't trust anybody else, you know that.'

'You could have trusted me,' Peter yelled at him. 'You could have told me.'

'When?' demanded Moses, biting back. 'And where? In front of all those officials at the Carlton Club? Some of them can understand English, you know.'

'You could have told me when I beat Freddie Mallory, you could have told me when I beat Manuel Alonso, you could have told me when I beat Serge Jacob.' Peter angrily itemised the names on his fingers. 'Or have you forgotten that it was me who won his way to the last eight?'

'Calm down,' Moses ordered him. 'Sit down and calm down. I didn't know who we'd be up against until I left the club this evening. Otherwise it might have been different. There was no guarantee that Decugis would make it through to face us. He could have been beaten.'

'And he could have been beaten by me tomorrow,' Peter went on. 'My game's a hundred times better than it was at Bergerac. Why have you lost faith? Why should this schoolboy upset our system?'

'This is our system.' Mo handed him a glass of rosé wine in the hope of temporary appeasement. 'It was never intended that you should play every match here, nor Jim every match if we get to England. Horses for courses, just like Chantilly. You know that. Decugis has to be dominated from the very first game. He can't be worked from the back like Jacob. Remember, the player who ultimately impresses his tennis personality on the other will win because . . .'

'. . . because by doing so he forces the recognition of impending defeat upon his opponent. I know, I know.' Peter mocked the coach's Californian growl. 'So what now? James goes back to my hotel after supper and I stay here and do the sweating?'

'I think Jim may be sweating a little, too,' Hoffman pointed out. 'Just try and relax. You've done well, Pete. But don't forget this is a team effort.'

'Hi, June.'

Both men looked up. James was leaning casually against the door, a cigarette in his mouth and his earphones lowered to his neck. The tape must have come to an end.

'How do you like my hair-cut?'

'Fuck you,' Peter yelled at him, storming out of the kitchen.

James Winston won easily. The frustration and fury that had been pent up in him since Chantilly was released on the unfortunate Decugis who had worked out a strategy with his coach based on his

Bergerac victory, only to find it thrown to the four winds by the hurricane that attacked him from the opening serve.

Moses immediately brought the good news to Vence and he and Peter set out in the rented Peugeot to drive back to Chantilly through the night. The less time the two brothers spent in the same area the safer. It had been agreed that James would tank his match the following day. Already the local papers were beginning to take notice of the promising English player. Now that their place in the Paris qualifying was assured, Mo's policy was to minimise publicity and retain as low a profile as possible.

James, however, felt the need to celebrate. Not just his victory but the end of the isolation and self-denying loneliness of the past six months. He had rather enjoyed the first public outing of his English accent during the brief interview at the end of the game and decided to give it a watering at the bar of the Carlton Hotel.

Although he had never been much of a drinker – so much of his life had been spent in strict training for tennis – he had always harboured a desire to line up a row of cocktails on a bar the way confident men in trilby hats did in black-and-white movies on television. The barman at the Carlton was happy to oblige and even went so far as to suggest that probably a dry martini was the correct concoction for such an enterprise.

'Trying to drown your sorrows, *m'sieu*?' he enquired very correctly.

'No, actually,' replied James, still employing an accent as dry as the drinks. 'I managed to do that in Mexico.'

He downed the first glass straight away. 'This one's for Edmund Michaels the demon doctor,' he said to himself as the chilled vodka numbed his stomach like a local anaesthetic and then spread pleasingly to his brain. He pointed to the remaining five and named them one by one: 'This one's for Loophole Quinn, who really drowned my sorrows, this one's for Moses who led us to the promised land, this one's for Aunt Violet for watching over me, this one's for one-eyed Mike and Mary-Louise – they'll have to share – and *The Greatest Show on Earth*, and this one,' he ruminatively fingered the stalk of the final elegant glass, 'this one's for Dad – the father the better, the better the father.'

He had no clear idea how long he actually took to consume them all but he hoped he had left a decent interval between each one. What he did know was that when he had finished the world was a far nicer place: he loved it and he felt that at last it loved him.

The barman, happy with his hundred franc tip, gave him directions on how to walk up to the Hôtel Montfleury – although he suggested a taxi might be more sensible – and James, gathering up his bag and racquets, essayed a less than steady passage along the Rue du Canada. On the far side of the Rue d'Antibes some young men were drinking outside a bar and waved to him to join them. But, despite the six martinis and the sexual frustration they had helped liberate in him, a sixth sense of self-preservation told him to head for home.

'There is a young woman, taken your key,' the female receptionist at the Montfleury apologised as he approached the counter. 'Miss Carter. She said she was your fiancée.'

'Oh, yes, yes, that's quite all right,' James replied, surprised at both his sang-froid and his accent which now came automatically.

'I'll give you another one,' the woman said. 'She thought she might fall asleep – jet lag, from America.'

His mind remained numb as he ascended the stairs and walked carefully along the corridor, tracing a passage on the wall with his finger as he went. He opened the unfamiliar door with difficulty and with stealth. From the subdued light in the hall he could see her. She had thrown off the sheets and covers and lay naked face down on the bed like a corpse, her billowing hair running half-way down her well-formed back.

He didn't turn on the light but slipped into the bathroom and urinated as quietly as he could against the inside of the bowl. Letting his trousers fall to the floor, he removed the rest of his clothes and stood naked in front of the basin as he washed himself.

Phoebe seemed still asleep as he lay down beside her. She stirred slightly, but kept her head buried in the pillow. 'Don't wake me yet, I'm in a lovely dream. But you really won. I read it in the *Times* and I came on the plane. How was today?'

'I managed to get through. It went quite well.' His English understatement matched his accent.

'You're good,' she mumbled from her slumber, 'so good. Do you know, I'm wet just dreaming about you.'

She arched her back ever so slightly and taking his penis, which hardened obediently in her hand, guided him into her from behind.

'If only you knew how wonderful that feels,' she murmured. 'Now, slowly.'

But her advice was of little use. James could control himself no longer. He simply closed his eyes and exploded inside her.

· Thirty-Nine ·

Edmund Michaels decided to give in to the waiter. After all there was a potential cause for celebration and if Ernest Hemingway's creativity had extended to inventing the Bloody Mary at the Ritz Hotel in Paris, as the man had insisted, then this was surely the only place in the world where it might be considered permissible to have one with breakfast. Besides, if you called it brunch it became entirely permissible and at a quarter past ten, with the dining room empty except for him, Michaels duly designated the meal Saturday brunch.

The first cigarette of the day had a savour that would be unmatched by any that followed – it sent a signal to his system that the hour had dawned for him to become alert and alive. As he eagerly opened the *Herald Tribune* that lay neatly folded by his plate, it was with a sense of triumphant accomplishment, as if everything had come into place with the precision of a perfectly timed laboratory experiment.

Turning rapaciously to the inside back page which was wholly devoted to the French Championships at Roland Garros, his eye immediately alighted on a small head and shoulders photograph of his protégé with a box round a brief capsule report. 'Peter Winston, aged 23, who faces Pat Wood, 21, in the third round this afternoon for a place in the last sixteen. It is the first time the two players have met and the experienced Australian looks likely to eliminate the only remaining Englishman from the tournament. Winston, a qualifier, had the good fortune later to be given a walkover when Humber Morpurgo of Italy, the eleventh seed, retired with an aggravated groin injury. But the dogged rallying of Wood, a quarter-finalist here in 1999, may prove too much for the former Cambridge Blue whose winter training in Florida and Portugal has given his professional career such a solid start.'

Solid start, he thought, patronising prick. The waiter arrived with a cut-glass half-carafe of what appeared innocuous tomato juice and a basket of warm croissants which gave off an ambrosial aroma. Michaels looked at the photograph again: he had no idea whether it was James or Peter. In fact Moses had played a little game with him, not revealing which brother he had chosen to confront Boussus in the second round and the doctor had only guessed right because he assumed Peter would be the first choice on clay. This afternoon, however, he knew the coach intended to use James for a surprise pre-emptive strike on the Australian. It was Mo's contention that Jim could beat any player in the world over one set and Wood had a poor reputation for coming back from behind.

Michaels had telephoned Dawson Silver in Boston the previous night to give a first-hand report on 'Operation Olmedo' so far. He had felt like a wartime resistance fighter, speaking in an equine circumlocution that would prevent any Ritz hotel operator or FBI phone tapper from being able to ascertain the exact meaning. Yes, both horses were still quartered in the same stables and were in peak condition. And both had now hit top form in the morning canters with little to choose between them. Most probably Longboat would be running this afternoon. Initial soundings with the English authorities confirmed that a win would constrain them to accept the three-year-old for their Derby.

The pure aesthetic pleasure of the Place Vendôme, its perfect Corinthian pilasters counterpointed by the mischievous Bacchanalian faces carved on the top of the arches, compounded the doctor's sense of well-being as he stepped out of the Ritz Hotel into this sunny Saturday. Before him, in the centre of the square, was the bronze replica of the Trajan's column in Rome and on top of that the noblest Roman of them all, Emperor Napoleon, keeping a watchful eye over this city so much of which he had largely recreated as a monument to himself.

'As I walk along the Bois de Boulogne with an independent air.' As he hummed the line to himself, Michaels wondered if whoever had penned those words had indeed been on his way to the tennis at

Roland Garros. The tournament was held at the southern extremity of the park, just by the Porte d'Auteuil, one of the gates to the city. The doctor had fallen in love with the place during his past week there. He adored the Frenchness of it all, especially the fact that no one other than a Frenchman had won the championship for the first twenty-five years of its existence because no one other than a Frenchman had been allowed to enter. And there was a wonderfully Gallic paradox in the thought that the only Grand Slam tournament named after a person as opposed to a place was dedicated to the memory, not of a famous tennis player, but of an aviator who had been shot down in the First World War and had, in fact, been much keener on rugby football. He especially liked the style of the people who went there. Not the beer-bellied, hot-dog munching, whooping types who descended on Flushing Meadow, but elegant men and women, dressed as if they had been commanded to come by engraved invitations.

And the tournament itself was defined by its clientele with stylish canvas boutiques attended by expensively groomed girls selling equally expensive sports apparel and equipment. Even before he had fully digested his bacon and eggs breakfast, his mouth watered at the thought of the succulent ice cream he would purchase from the Mediterranean maiden in the green apron who kept the spotless stall by the gate.

Michaels was early for his meeting with Moses and he lingered by the windows of the impossibly priced art dealers and jewellers on the Rue de la Paix as he idled towards the Métro station at the Opéra. This was by far the easiest way to get to Roland Garros, involving only one change at the exotically named La Motte Picquet station. It was while eyeing a Lautrec lithograph done for *L'Escarmouche* magazine in a gallery window that he became instinctively aware of someone eyeing him. The street was sparsely peopled but no single face immediately offered itself as the observer. However he was certain he was not mistaken. He quickened his pace towards the Place de l'Opéra in the hope of drawing him out. The moment he reached the end of the street he identified the person who had been spying on him, in a doorway on the other side of the road, hurriedly unscrewing a long lens from a camera and stuffing it into a case. Brandi de Soto.

While she was concerned with this, the American girl failed to notice that her prey was now her pursuer. Michaels set off through the traffic, not knowing quite what he would do when he caught up with her but instantly aware that his photograph must be part of a picture story destined for *Snap!* magazine – a story that could be terminally devastating to their scheme.

She caught sight of him immediately and began to run, cutting across the Place de l'Opéra with a reckless disregard for the traffic which screeched and swerved in order to avoid this khaki-clad figure with her safari shorts and heavy camera bag. Nevertheless she could still outpace the seventy-five year old man who chased after her with no more caution for his own safety than she. Even if he didn't catch her at least he could warn Mo and the others, he told himself, as the insistent words 'walked along the Bois de Boulogne' drilled themselves into his subconscious like a toothache.

It was a Volvo that hit him, just as he saw her sprint up the steps of the Opera House. The car was not travelling particularly fast but the two tons of solid Swedish metal thudded into his knees, throwing him up over the windscreen, bouncing him off the roof and depositing him in its wake. The driver stopped at once, as did the following vehicles. People rushed towards the inert figure sprawled in the square, relieved to find he was still breathing. Dr Michaels wasn't dead but neither was he conscious.

Brandi was wholly unaware of what had happened. She had heard the growing commotion in the street behind her but she assumed that this was merely the motorists reacting to Michaels' hot pursuit. Nevertheless she was petrified and perspiring as she ducked into the doorway of her destination: the *New York Times* bureau in the Rue Scribe. Daphne, a girl who had studied journalism and communications with her at Notre Dame, had promised to leave a press pass for the tennis at reception. The envelope was there and Brandi made for the ladies' lavatory on the first floor. She entered a cubicle and sat down, unable to stop herself from shaking.

The doctor was right in his assumption: Brandi had managed to persuade *Snap!* that there was a remote possibility James Winston was still alive. So the features editor, somewhat reluctantly, had agreed to pay her expenses to attend the middle weekend of the French Open Championships in the hope that his brother might lead her to the missing man. She couldn't find out where he was staying but she discovered that Michaels was at the Ritz and had deliberately staked out the hotel entrance that morning, suspecting that he might be a useful lead. Now he knew that she was on the trail, things were going to be a great deal more difficult.

She waited half an hour until she estimated the coast might be clear, then cautiously made her way to the Boulevard Haussmann where she hailed a taxi for the tennis. The traffic was backed up all along the Avenue de la Porte d'Auteuil so the driver, without a great deal of gallantry, suggested she should get out and walk. A more helpful policeman looked at her ticket and directed her along the Allée Suzanne Lenglen to the correct entrance.

Still fearful of being spotted by Michaels, or Moses, or Peter Winston, she worked out that her safest sanctuary would be the Centre de Presse on the south side of the Court Central. To her immense relief, her pass obtained her admission. She climbed the stairs to the second floor – deliberately swinging two cameras from her neck to make her look like an old hand – and found herself in a large room that reminded her of a NASA control centre for a space shot. Some journalists were conversing, either on the phone or to each other, and drinking coffee from small paper cups; others were already attacking their portable computers like crazed pianists, although play had barely begun; and one or two were sitting with earphones on in front of the twin television monitors at each allotted desk.

Brandi sought out the one for the *New York Times* – she knew from Daphne that their correspondent would be arriving late as he was only interested in the third singles on the Centre Court. Settling herself down in his place she began tentatively to work out the system. The top TV monitor was carrying live coverage of the TF1 transmission of the match on Court One but the picture on the lower one could be switched by pressing any of the bank of buttons to her left. She put on the earphones and punched her way through them: Antenne 2, FR 3, Canal-Plus, B Sky B, three channels of statistics about the players, results of matches played and current scores on all the games in progress, closed circuits to both interview rooms, messages, even a screen for your computer should you need it and fixed cameras on every single one of the outside courts with open microphones so that you could hear the umpires calling the score.

'Pretty good, eh?' The Australian voice came from behind her. The man had obviously been observing her experiment with the system.

'It's incredible,' she agreed. 'You don't need to leave your desk all day.'

'Quite a few journos don't,' came the laconic reply. 'They go screen crazy. But we all need a break. There's a bar downstairs a nice girl like you could cheer up no end.'

'I'd love to,' she exclaimed, happy to have found a friend. 'After the Pat Wood match, perhaps we could have a drink.'

He glanced down at the order of play in his hand. 'They're third on number eight. Well, Woodie won't take long. I'll look out for you then.'

Brandi offered him every tooth available as a confirming smile and swung back to her new toy. Not only was it incredib ;, it solved her problem as well. She had feared going out to court eight as she would undoubtedly have been spotted by Michaels. Not that there was anything he could do – she hadn't committed a crime – but she knew from experience there was a twisted streak to the man that it was worth avoiding. The Winston–Wood match was of insufficient interest to merit prope; television coverage but she would be able to monitor it from here. She glanced at her watch. It was improbable that they would be on court for some time – a ladies singles had only just commenced on number eight – so Brandi flicked back to the cartoon on Canal-Plus.

When it finished she went for a stroll round the press centre, noting where the bar was in the basement and picking up the sheets of statistics and player biographies that were on offer. On her return to the desk she once more punched her way through the channels. Many of the outside courts were empty with the exception of number fourteen. She glanced at it for a moment. To her amazement and annoyance it looked as if the Winston–Wood match had already commenced on that very court. How stupid of her. She immediately switched through to the order of play but there the game remained, still scheduled for number eight. However flipping back to fourteen everything was explained: it was Peter Winston all right but he was merely warming up with Moses. She recognised the coach clearly as he came back towards the fixed camera to collect the balls. And she could hear him, too. 'When in doubt, lead trumps,' he shouted at Peter, although she had no idea what he meant.

'You're going to have to demoralise him in the first two sets or else we switch.' Hoffman's voice became much more distinct as they approached the umpire's chair to put down their racquets. 'Don't bitch about it – we're taking a gamble as it is.'

'Listen, I'm cool. It's that schmuck gets all uptight. Hey, there's no way Wood's going to punch me out, man.'

Brandi's immediate feeling was one of relief that her face was pressed so closely to the screen that nobody nearby could read her expression. She knew that voice only too well. It was exactly how he used to converse with Ashley and Lucius in Newton Lower Falls Park so that he could be one of the boys – one of the young boys. That was James Winston out there – whatever the hairstyle, whatever the programme said – there was no mistaking him. No mistaking him at all.

And she remained equally convinced it was James when she watched him slump into his chair two and a quarter hours later on Court Eight as he trailed Wood by a set and three games to four. The way he ran the ice-cold can of Coke down either cheek to cool his face was an all too familiar motion. Before they got up to change ends, he reached in his bag and unwrapped a new Goffi tennis shirt. Stripping to the waist he took off the one he was wearing, damp with sweat and soiled with sand from a fall, and changed into the fresh one. It didn't help him any; he lost his next serve and then the set.

Brandi was about to go and get herself a Coke from the machine outside the press room, when she noticed James approach the umpire. Unfortunately the official switched the microphone off so she was unable to check his accent again but it was clear he was asking to leave the court. The umpire pointed to his watch, indicating the time permitted, and Winston sprinted off through the gap in the rows of spectator seats.

She got up from her chair and saw that her Australian acquaintance of that morning was back at his monitor two rows behind her, so she made her way over to him. 'I see Wood's doing well,' she mentioned as casually as she could.

'Got the second, has he?' the man asked. 'I'd better go down soon and order up our drinks. I haven't been watching. Everyone's following Shimizu on the Centre – it's a better game, you should take a look.'

'I will,' she promised. 'Tell me something, though, Winston's just spoken to the umpire and gone off the court. Is that allowed?'

'Probably gone for a pee, love.' He put his hands behind his head, happy to dispense his expertise. 'The days of going for a snort of coke are over. They used to send an official with you at the time when that was the fashion. Now you can take a gin and tonic on court and swill it down if you want to. People say there was some Froggy woman used to drink brandy between games but I suspect that's one of those stories that's repeated so often if finally becomes fact.'

'I'm Brandi,' she told him.

'Do people take you after dinner?' he smiled. 'Sorry, just joking.'

'That's all right,' she replied. 'It has been said before – like the story.'

She went back to her monitor to continue watching the game. Winston was enjoying a renewed lease of life. The competitor who had returned to Court Eight, still in his fresh white shirt, played like a new man. Against an accurate all-court attack, Pat Wood seemed to have used up his supply of winners and failed to gain more than four games in any of the three remaining sets, eventually going down, 4–6, 3–6, 6–4, 6–2, 6–1.

Brandi remained on tenterhooks as she waited for the player to come and occupy the empty green chair in the light grey interview room. She turned up the volume on her earphones to the maximum the moment he sat down. It was Winston all right, his short hair still wet from a quick shower and his striped tracksuit top distorting the monitor. The only journalists who had bothered to go down to attend it were the British, relieved that a fellow countryman had made it to the second week. Some years they didn't even make it to the first week.

'Peter, in the first two sets Pat was bringing you in and passing you fairly easily. Did you feel he was manipulating your game?'

'I wouldn't say that. He was playing jolly well and my eye was somewhere over the Eiffel Tower.'

There was polite laughter. Brandi was confused, wondering how she could have been so mistaken earlier on. This was undoubtedly Peter. Either that or James had undergone some pretty expensive elocution since last they met.

'It seemed your game improved fairly dramatically after you went to the lavatory. How did you feel about that?'

Winston scratched the side of his cheek. 'I felt relieved.'

More laughter. Moses had instructed them both to be brief and pithy during this obligatory cross-examination.

Brandi could restrain herself no longer. She tore off the head set and made hasty tracks for the interview room on the floor below. People were just beginning to filter out as she turned the corner. Thankfully they were heading downstairs. She could see Winston, in good-humoured conversation with an earnest little man in a blue blazer and spectacles. She debated whether she should risk following him now or wait by the gates later?

But her mind was made up for her by the well-tanned hand that descended on her left shoulder. 'Whisky, was it?'

'Brandi,' she corrected him.

'And Esau was an hairy man,' said Peter, feeling he was back at Cambridge as he spread the theatrical glue across his upper lip and cheeks and chin. The smell of the mixture was redolent of something much more carefree than the red-hot clay of Roland Garros. In the subdued light at the back of the boutique, it was hard to see how much of his face he had covered. He took the Dracula beard out of his make-up box and patted it into position with the heavy moustache fitting neatly on top of his mouth. 'Rain drops keep falling on the dead,' he sang softly to himself.

'What was that?' James Winston was sitting cramped up in the corner of the Desrosiers tent which had been vacated by the sales staff some time ago. He removed an earphone and the sound of post-modern rock thudded out.

'Just a song at twilight,' Peter assured him.

'It's dark now, has been for more than an hour.' James looked irritably at his watch. 'What the fuck can Mo be up to?'

'I told you. Still trying to track down Edmund. He rang the Ritz from the changing room and they promised to call back on that number.' Peter lifted the matted dark wig from his tennis bag and settled it on his head. 'I think this is more you than me. I've never really been enough of a rebel.'

'You look an idiot,' James sneered. 'And Hoffman's an idiot, too. There was no need to take me off. I had Wood's number. By the time you got to play him his game had gone.'

The sound of footsteps on the concrete outside caused both men to freeze. Peter nervously adjusted his beard into place and James immediately snapped off his cassette player. But it was Moses. He seemed subdued, considering the achievements of the day, and offered no apology for keeping them waiting.

'There isn't any sense in trying to sneak out of this place, it will only draw attention to us,' he said. 'Let's make believe we've been celebrating a bit and taking a look round.'

Roland Garros by night was a ghost of its daytime self. The crowds and players and officials had long since departed, but a handful of handymen and cleaners were still at work preparing the place for the following day. A light rain had begun to fall, almost as if it had been ordered up to help them wash the club clean.

The moment Moses Hoffman and the Winstons rounded the high coliseum-like wall of Number One Court they ran into a uniformed night watchman with a Staffordshire bull terrier.

'Excuse me, *messieurs*, may I see your credentials?'

It was irritating how the French were always able to spot foreigners, even before they spoke. Moses pulled out his official pass from around his neck and the other two followed suit.

'We had a win today,' the coach explained. 'A win and then some beers.'

The man smiled understandingly. 'But the stadium is closing. You must leave now or you will spend the night inside, like me.'

'I know,' Moses agreed. 'But, on our way out, would it be all right if we just stopped at the Square of the Musketeers? Tonight we need to pay our respects.'

'Take your time, *m'sieu*.' The guard's attitude changed reverentially. 'I will make sure you are not disturbed.'

Moses thanked him and led the way across to the courtyard that separated the Number One and Centre courts. It shone like marble in the moonlight and the figures of four men stood sentinel in each corner, noble and immortal.

James stretched out a hand into the night air. 'Raindrops keep falling on the dead,' he observed.

Moses ignored the remark. 'I've mentioned the Musketeers before, but now is the time to meet them. The four greatest players France has ever produced, all born within ten years of each other. And that was the very reason for their success. Just as it will be for you two. Their rivalry raised their game way above the reach of any other player in the world – except one.'

He fondly patted the statue next to him. 'Jean Borotra, always known as the bounding Basque. The beret was his trademark. That plus a bunch of tricks – great showman and faker. He didn't have one conventional shot except his overhead but the swiftest eye and fastest feet in the game. Won all the Slams, in fact he was the only Frenchman ever to win Australia. Played in the Davis Cup when he was forty-nine years old and at Wimbledon when he was sixty, can you believe that?'

He indicated the man to his right. 'Jacques Brugnon. Toto Brugnon, they called him, the oldest Musketeer. The most finished doubles player in the annals of tennis – what we hoped for you two at one stage – although he did win the singles here in '21. Made sure the French remained undefeated in the Davis Cup six successive years. And for six years before that he and Lenglen won the mixed. Four doubles titles at Wimbledon and he was still playing there when he was fifty-three. These guys didn't know when age had beaten them.'

'Maybe you can beat age,' Peter suggested.

'Maybe.' The coach continued diagonally across to the statue closest to the Centre Court. He pointed to the man's face. 'The crocodile – René Lacoste. Look at the nose. He never thought he was as talented as the other three so he used to keep notes on every game he played and analysed his opponents. An entirely scientific approach. He invented the ball-machine and people used to wonder if they were playing him or it. The cold-blooded approach paid off, though. Couple of Wimbledon titles and two more here. First foreigner ever to win the US Championships. Then he beat us again in the sportswear stakes – that little aligator keeps on snapping up the market.'

The rain began to thicken and Moses turned up the collar of his black tracksuit as he made his urgent way over to the final figure in the corner. He seemed agitated and anxious to leave. The main exit was just around the side of the Centre Court. He came to a halt, one hand gripping his bag and the other equally clenched as if he were carrying a further burden within him. He deliberately kept his back to the boys, both of whom were beginning to feel extremely ill at ease, as if they were somehow being accused of not coming up to the standards of the four Frenchmen.

'Henri Cochet – the genius of French tennis. His game was a perfect blend of attack and defence and when his technique proved insufficient he threw it to the winds and called on an inspirational creativeness that defied analysis. Never beaten in the Davis Cup for six years in succession. And won the French five times.'

Moses stood very silently for some time, not turning, just looking steadily up at the statue. When he spoke again there was a catch in his throat as if he were still in mourning for the man. 'But despite all those victories he will be better remembered as the person who prevented the first French title and the seventh consecutive championship of the United States by the greatest tennis player who ever lived.'

James and Peter Winston stood uncomfortably side by side, both wondering what had come over the little man. Moses, normally so tight-lipped in praise and sparing in sentiment, seemed to be close to breaking down.

It was Peter who severed the silence. 'Who was that? Rod Laver?'

The coach turned very slowly and stared at them, tears pouring from his eyes.

'Don't you know? Don't you really know?'

The twins remained in mute embarrassment, both worried that a score of security men would bear down on them at any moment and Operation Olmedo, on the eve of its final stage, would be aborted by its emotional architect.

'Don't you really know?' Mo repeated, struggling to regain his composure. 'It was Big Bill. Bill Tilden. William Tatem Tilden. There has never been another player like him, not these four, not anybody since. Nor anybody yet to come.' His gaze moved compassionately from brother to silent brother. 'And don't you know who he was? Have you no idea?'

'*M'sieu*, I think they are about to lock the gate.' It was the helpful guard with the bull terrier shouting from across the quadrangle. 'It's late.'

'Perhaps too late,' whispered Moses as he dropped his bag and went across to the twins and put his arms around them and just held them, helpless in the rain.

'He was your father.'

· Forty ·

Brandi had long ago abandoned her vigil at the main entrance to Roland Garros and only a pair of policemen observed the clean-cut tennis player, his small coach and their hirsute companion cross the road towards the Bois de Boulogne. James took an instinctive initiative. He knew the park from his lone weeks in Paris and led them north up the Rue d'Auteuil aux Lacs. In the early nineteen nineties the two thousand acre wood was closed after dark, less because of the activities of the ladies of the night than the gentlemen. What the Parisians used to refer to as the Boys from Brazil – flamboyant male prostitutes, transsexuals and even surgically reconstructed transvestites all from South America – would ply a profitable night-time trade in the park. But President Lang had cleared all that up and now a controlled number of good-time girls were able to resume their ancient calling.

'He was gay, wasn't he?' James didn't bother to turn his head as he threw back the accusation at Mo.

'Yep,' the coach agreed. 'The first major sportsman to come out of the closet. Well, to be caught in the closet anyway.'

'And he was dead.' Peter remained mystified. 'I thought he died during the war.'

'Later than that. 5 June 1953 to be precise.'

'So how. . . ?' Peter began but he found the question impossible to formulate. The rain had eased off to the occasional drop and the newly washed sycamores and horse chestnuts and pines purified the night air. The smell entered his memory by stealth and he was back aged seven in Bishop's Park with Grace, strolling along the chestnut-strewn towpath. The mystery of her mistake that had puzzled him intermittently since then now became transparently clear. Jim Peters – she said he had been named after the marathon runner Jim Peters. Why didn't you call me Jim, he had asked and she had offered no satisfactory answer. But there was the answer, walking in front of him. She must have been delirious on her deathbed. James must have been her first child and her first choice and she must have given away the son she loved more. He had wondered why he hated his brother so much and at last he knew.

'Michaels.' Mo had no need for him to complete the question. 'In that Castor Street surgery. He collected sperm – students mainly but quite a number of grown-up guys, a few of them prominent, who were flattered into donating their seed to posterity. Big Bill was down on his luck those last years in Los Angeles and Edmund's thousand dollars was probably very welcome.'

'Does my father know?' James had turned and was walking backwards in front of them, looking angrily uncertain and betrayed.

'He couldn't have known. He'd been dead for twenty-three years when you were conceived,' Moses joked. But he could see from their expressions that neither boy was in the mood for levity. 'No, Dawson doesn't know. Nothing. And I don't think he ever should.'

'And my mother?' Peter no longer knew what to believe, his entire life seemed to be scrambled into confusion.

'Nope, not her neither.' Hoffman shook his head. 'Michaels set them both up. He'd been biding his time for this particular opportunity and when Dawson was persuaded that Grace – the ideal person: a graduate, an athlete and an Englishwoman – was better than any of the professional American surrogate mothers, he donated his sperm to Michaels and Michaels donated Bill Tilden's sperm to your mother. Simple as that. And it took.'

'How long have you known?' James shot him an accusing glance.

'That time I came up to Boston. When I met you out in the park. It was so obvious straight away, I pretty well kicked myself for not noticing years ago. You're more than a chip off the old block, both of you.' He gazed at each twin in turn, James smouldering with resentment, Peter much more reserved behind his heavy beard. 'You're the exact image of your father down to your missing finger tips.'

'But we can sue.' James viciously smacked away a fallen cone with his tennis racquet. 'I think my father should be told. He fucking well paid the money to have a child of his own. And I also think Dr Edmund Michaels is in some pretty deep trouble.'

'Deeper than you know.' The coach transferred his tennis bag from his left hand to his right. 'Michaels was hit by a car when he left his hotel this morning. They took him to the best place in Paris, the Salpêtrière Hospital I think it is. Anyway the guy I spoke to said it was the top spot for neurology. Freud studied there. Edmund would have been pretty interested if he had regained consciousness. But he didn't. They drilled two little holes in the front of his skull but it was only a gesture. He died just after nine-thirty this evening. I'll go tomorrow and make some arrangements. I don't expect you two to come.'

'Poor shit,' was James's sole comment.

'WTT Trust Fund' – it came to Peter in a flash – 'William Tatem Tilden. The cheques my mother got.'

'They came from Edmund,' Moses nodded, 'just like you.'

The three of them committed themselves to their private thoughts as they continued through the park, past the padlocked gates of the Racing Club de France – the home of the élite in French tennis. The coach indicated the building. 'Tilden used to play there. Queen's Club – near you, Peter – used him as a ringer, made him an honorary Englishman. So he used to play for Great Britain in games against the French. Long running feud with Borotra. He couldn't stand the guy.' Five hundred yards further on there was a small clearing in front of the Pavillon Royal where an unauthorised catering wagon was dispensing drinks and baguettes to sundry down-and-outs and the crudely clad ladies of the night. Without bothering to ask the boys, Moses went up to the counter and ordered three coffees.

'Don't you want to know about Big Bill?' he enquired quietly as he handed a plastic cup to each of them.

'If he was so goddam good,' James's resentment broke stridently through to the surface, 'how come he never won Paris? There's a list of champions in the programme but I didn't see his name there.'

'He could have, if he'd wanted to.' Moses took two towels out of his bag and spread them on the damp bench by the Lac Inférieur. 'In the 1927 final he was two sets to one up against Lacoste and the Frenchman collapsed in the heat. The day belonged to Tilden – he would have been the first foreign champion – but he refused to claim it. He was prepared to wait more than half an hour while they took René away and gave him injections for his cramps. And then he had championship point, 13–12, 40–30 in the fifth set, and he aced him. Lacoste again conceded defeat and came to shake his hand. But Henri Cochet, who was doing a line, called the ball out and they had to play the point again. Tilden never managed to pull himself back after that. So he lost. But it was Lacoste who collapsed at the end of the match. Maybe Bill didn't particularly want to win it anyway. I think it haunted Cochet till his dying day. He later said that all he ever learnt about tennis he learnt from Big Bill.'

'How can you not bother to win a Grand Slam?' James was contemptuous.

'It's hard to explain but Tilden wasn't really like other people. Not like them at all.' Moses paused as he gazed across the dark and placid waters of the lake at the urgent lights of Paris in the distance. 'In many ways he wasn't really of this world. It was never even intended that he should be born. His parents already had a family, a complete family. His father was fairly well-off, a Philadelphia big-wig. William Tatem Tilden – happily married to Linie and settled for life. But then the diphtheria epidemic of 1884 came to Germantown and killed all their three kids in less than two weeks. They actually had a daughter – Williamina Tatem Tilden – and she was the first to go. Only seventeen months old. When they got over their grief they decided to start a substitute family. There was a boy, Herbert, and ten years after Williamina Tatem died William Tatem was born to take her place. Too late in many ways. His father wasn't interested and his mother fell ill, so he grew up with his aunt Mary and his cousin Selena. They would always call him Junior or June and he always called Selena, Twin – funny that.'

'The tennis,' James perched himself on the arm of the bench and lit up a cigarette, 'where did the tennis come from?'

Moses shrugged. 'It came from inside. When he was nearly your age he was nothing, he couldn't even make his college team. His mother had passed away when he was a teenager, and then his father while he was a student. So he just dropped out of formal education and lost himself in the game. There's no doubt about it: tennis saved him. In a sort of strange way he had nowhere else to go.

Nobody coached him, he coached kids at Germantown Academy and he seemed to learn tennis from his own teaching. Took him all the way to the National Finals in 1918 and '19 but he didn't have a decent backhand and couldn't even get a set off Billy Johnston.'

'Little Bill?' asked James.

'California's finest – Little Bill. The best there was until then. But Big Bill took off for Providence, Rhode Island, and worked all winter on his backhand in an indoor court and when he went to Wimbledon for the first time the following summer nobody could beat him. Nobody in the world. The first American to win there. He came back to Forest Hills in September 1920 to face Little Bill again in the final. And the strangest thing happened. Death always seemed to be keeping an eye on the life of Bill Tilden. At two sets all a plane swooped over the court carrying some photographers and it spluttered and crashed in the next-door field. Everybody there knew the guys must have been killed. But the umpire told Tilden and Billy Johnston to play on to prevent a stampede out of the stadium. It was no longer a question of tennis, it became a matter of total concentration and emotion. Two men died and Big Bill won, became the champion of the world. Unbeatable at Forest Hills for the next five years, top ranked in America for the next ten. With Little Bill he brought the Davis Cup back to the States and we held on to it for a record seven years. And now they don't even bother to contest the thing.'

'But he didn't dominate Wimbledon.' Peter had seated himself on a towel beside the coach.

'He didn't try. He defended his title in '21 and then he stayed away and let the others have a look in. Little Bill, Lacoste, Cochet, Borotra all won. But when people started to say Tilden was over the hill, he came back to claim his crown. Took him three years but he did it in 1930, ten years after he first won it, only person to have done that. He was thirty-seven, the oldest man to have played through the tournament and won. Great favourite with the crowd. Used to applaud his opponent's good shots with a shout of "peach".'

'Why did he quit?' James seemed to have calmed down somewhat and took up a position on the arm of the bench.

'He'd made his point so he turned pro. But you've got to understand, Bill Tilden was entirely different from any other professional. He knew that the public wanted a show. He'd written Broadway plays, appeared on the stage as a professional actor – *Clarence, The Children's Hour, Dracula.* Always got terrible reviews but he understood the entertainment business. It's all there in his books. No player has ever written so much philosophy about tennis. He loved to quote P.T. Barnum – you know, the guy with the circus – "you can't fool all of the people all of the time". Big gestures on the court. Used to stare out linesmen, argue with umpires, but then win back public sympathy by throwing the next point if his opponent got an unfair call. His favourite trick was to take five balls in one hand and end a match with four aces and then throw the fifth ball away. He packed people in to see him as a pro. Even when he was in his fifties it was reckoned he could take anyone in the world over one set.'

'So what went wrong?' Peter asked.

'He did.' Mo's clipped reply seemed to anticipate the question.

'I'm getting cold.' James stubbed out his cigarette and got up from his end of the bench. 'Can we walk?'

Nothing more was said as they made their way towards the speeding lights of the traffic on the Allée de Longchamp, still heading for the Porte Maillot and the Arc de Triomphe beyond. 'You want to party?' a girl in hot pants asked James as they waited to cross. But she received no reply.

'He liked to party,' Moses resumed as he followed James up a narrow path tunnelled with trees and carpeted with damp leaves on the far side of the main road. 'At least he liked to be seen with celebrities. He lived his last years in Los Angeles and began by hanging out with the likes of Errol Flynn and Greta Garbo and Douglas Fairbanks. In his field he had been as big a star as they were. He was the centre of attraction at Charlie Chaplin's tennis parties. He even signed a movie contract himself although the films never amounted to much. Don't forget this was the man the sportswriters of America voted the greatest athlete of the first half of the twentieth century – greater than Babe Ruth, greater than Bobby Jones, greater than Jack Dempsey. This was a man who walked with kings. Do you realise George VI – when he was Duke of York – actually sent his car for Tilden so that he could play him at singles on the court at

Buckingham Palace? Bill thought it would be a push-over but the Duke took five games off him. He'd played Wimbledon himself, though.'

They were walking in single file now, like an army patrol, trying to avoid the soaking branches that attempted to assault them from either side. James had taken a determined lead as if intent on reaching a fixed destination by an assigned time. Peter was in the rear, bearing the brunt of the backlash of spray.

'So what went wrong?' he asked again.

Mo heard him all right but the back of his head offered no physical signal that he had done so. 'I doubt if Bill Tilden was the first teacher in the world to prefer his pupils to his male contemporaries or some suffocating wife and family. And I doubt if he'll be the last. He always had protégés, young boys he would coach for free. He would feed them, take them on vacation, drive them to school. He even made Vinnie Richards his doubles partner in the US Open when the boy was only fifteen. But then he was caught by the cops – he must have been about fifty-three – with some kid in a car on Sunset Boulevard. He was pretty well incriminated by his own statement. "Fooling around" was what he thought he was doing but the judge thought differently and put him away for a year. He served his sentence like a man – took it better than some of his line calls – but, of course, that was the end of him. Nobody wanted to know after that. My dad used to tell me about Soviet politicians in the time of Stalin who weren't just done away with – their name was erased as if they'd never existed. Well that happened to Bill. Dunlop took his name off their racquets, people at tournaments turned their backs on him, the celebrity set dropped him like a leper. All except Chaplin; he was probably up there the day he died.'

'Are we in any way' – Peter was diffident over the question – 'you know, like him.'

'A bit,' Mo smiled. 'Same shape, same chin. Incredible eyesight. Used to chain smoke. "Peach" and "curses" – those were his two favourite words on court.'

'And the finger?' Peter held his up.

Mo nodded. 'Yep. Same with him.'

They could go no further. A tall wrought-iron fence barred their way. James half-heartedly tried the heavy gate which the path led up to but it was securely locked. There were few trees on the other side of the fence but a more ordered environment with swings and slides for children dimly discernible in the occluded moonlight. Without warning a bellowing roar came out of nowhere, a terrifying sound that was neither human nor that of any domestic animal.

'What the fuck. . . ?' Moses grabbed the railing as if in protection. 'They don't have tigers and lions in the Bois de Boulogne.'

'As a matter of fact, they do.' James divulged the information with a superior smile, but his composed demeanour was sufficient to set the minds of the other two at rest.

'How did he die?' Peter pressed his head against the railings trying to see deeper into the gloom.

'Like he lived,' said Moses. 'He spent the day giving a couple of lessons, Chaplin let him use the court for that. Tilden was broke, he was desperate for a few dollars and luckily there were some people who hadn't ostracised him, probably they'd never heard of him. He was so desperate that he was prepared to face all the insults and being ignored and he entered the US Pro Championships in Cleveland to try and make a bit of money. So at the end of that day he went home and packed his kit and lay down on his bed before leaving. And he never got up again. He was only sixty. They said it was his heart and they were right, it had been broken to bits. A few people turned up at the funeral but no one from the American tennis authorities. They didn't so much as send a wreath. And then his ashes were taken back to Philadelphia, to be buried with those brothers and sisters who never had the chance to do as much as Big Bill.'

The howl came again, but calmer and more contented this time as if the beast were settling down to sleep.

'When I die,' James said after a while, 'I'd like my ashes to be scattered here, in the Jardin d'Acclimatation. This is the only place I've felt at peace since I left the States. There are children here, and parents, and lions and bears and happiness.'

'My mother used to talk about this park,' Peter remembered. 'They ran the Olympic marathon through the Bois de Boulogne in 1900 and the man who was out in front – it always made her smile, he was called Ernst Fast – actually lost his way in the woods and lost the race.'

'Like our father,' said James.

'He wasted his life.' Peter felt an inexplicable anger within him. 'He had everything, everything he could want and then he threw it away.'

'You're wrong,' Moses corrected him. 'He didn't have everything. William Tilden wasn't gay in any conventional sense, he never had proper sex with a soul in his life. All the time he was reaching out, all the time he would tell anyone who would listen to him: the one thing he really wanted in this life was a son.'

· Forty-One ·

The rains came late to Wimbledon in the summer of the 114th Lawn Tennis Championship. The first week had been an anachronism of cloudless days, as if the year 2000 had ushered in a millennium of Mediterranean weather, with the temperature making a regular daily trip into the eighties and many of the outside courts becoming distinctly browned off.

But on the Wednesday of the second week a heavenly hose was borne in by the Atlantic westerlies and the place was awash like a steady ship in a heavy sea. Not that it greatly troubled anybody. The Pimms went down and the souvenir sales soared. The British often gain added pleasure from adversity and in the public tents new friendships were forged as tennis fans had the chance to look at the people beside them instead of blinkeredly staring into a stadium.

In the privileged world of prestige corporate hospitality the rain was a positive boon. No longer were the guests faced with that tricky moment when they felt obliged to leave their two-hundred-pound lunch and check their wine glass at the marquee gate in order to go and pretend to be interested in a prolonged duel between two dour Dutchmen of whom they had never heard. Instead they could remain at the laden table and watch replays of tennis highlights on the television monitors and, more importantly, watch their glasses being filled and refilled with unceasing champagne. And whatever worry their hosts might have about the increased entertainment costs was a mere blip on the balance sheet compared to the now wholly captive audience who could be fed seductive titbits about the advertising agency or bank or computer company between the smoked salmon and the profiteroles.

Even the press was pleased. A wet day at Wimbledon always provided a good picture opportunity – a pair of lovers under an umbrella, a stately woman in a silly hat made from a newspaper or an obliging duck reflected in a puddle on the Centre Court cover. It gave the journalists a breather, a reason to offload some of the feature articles that had been commissioned but never used by over-eager sports editors and, most important of all, a chance to catch up with the creative task of accounting for their expenses.

The forecast running up to the weekend was for more settled weather so the order of play committee was able to rest easy, confident in the knowledge that the tournament was ahead of schedule. Already they were having to programme too many mixed doubles to fill up the matches on the show courts and this was a frequent cause of crowd discontent, especially among people who had paid a thousand pounds for a pair of tickets on the black market in the expectation of watching big names throughout the afternoon.

And the added advantage, as more than one tennis correspondent pointed out, was that the British presence in the men's singles would be extended by an extra day. Following his triumphal entry into the second week in Paris – which itself was followed by an orchestrated exit in straight sets – Peter Winston had, indeed, been granted a wild card to the All England Club. Not only that but he had confounded his critics by carving his way through four rounds to the last eight and a chance to play Penn Landry, the sixth seed, for a place in the semi-finals.

Or rather James had. His refusal to let any emotional reaction to Hoffman's revelations about William Tilden surface that night in front of his brother had merely been an exercise in self-control. The moment they were free of Roland Garros the following Monday he immediately took the train east to EuroDisneyland in order to resubmit himself to the Magic. It was there, it was all-American and all around him. He was now gripped by the certainty of his divine mission, just as divine as the moonwalker Col. James B. Irwin and his search for Noah's Ark, to replicate the achievement of his father eighty years before: to go to Wimbledon and win. In their resumed training at Chantilly he had become inspired, infused with hatred at the thought of having to share Big Bill with this insipid Englishman and dealing death blows to every ball that came his way.

So it had been at Wimbledon. Experienced opponents who had taken little notice of the new boy in Paris found their game plans shot to pieces by a player who commanded the net like an artillery captain. Only in the last round had James faltered, letting a Finnish player take him to a fifth set and just slipping through on his mental tenacity rather than his exhausted tennis talent. But his spark had renewed itself at the press conference after the match, as he fired off snappy one-line replies in his flawless English accent, even presuming to remark that he 'hadn't had so much fun since Fenners'.

But it was Peter Winston whom Moses had selected to play when the weather finally let up, pointing out that he was more suited to what could be a slippery court if the covers kept coming on and off. In fact, the coach sensed that James was beginning to burn himself out and needed both some recuperation and a renewed incentive to bring him back to his peak. Peter had been no less formidable at Chantilly, lacking only the ultimate anger that had been high octane in James's motivation.

They had sequestered themselves outside an unvisited village called Wheeler End in Buckinghamshire for the duration of the championships. Eamonn Quinn had secured a month's lease on a forbidding manor house with a well-tended grass court. The electric gates and walled garden offered them almost the same measure of privacy as they had enjoyed in France. Nevis had read about Peter's accomplishments in the paper and had written to him care of the All England Club enclosing a key for the basement flat at 145 Talgarth Road, suggesting that since it was currently unoccupied and close to The Queen's Club where many of the players practised, he might like to make use of it during Wimbledon. Mo saw this as a more controllable front address than a hotel. Accordingly the mail was sent there and it was decided that it might deter any speculation as to his whereabouts if Peter were to spend the night in his old home after his match on Wednesday.

Quinn had flown in to work with Moses on the final details. Joe and Mary Doherty were brought over from Boston to look after the house and the housekeeping, thereby dispensing with the need for local labour. They had another task as well. Dawson Silver's operation had not been a success. On the contrary, it had deprived him of what sight had still remained to him. He was now completely blind and wholly reliant on the Dohertys to be his eyes and guide him. In addition, he remained more than ever in the dark about the true paternity of the twins.

Dawson had not gone up to London for Peter's match, using the probability that it would be postponed as a reason to excuse himself. In fact he still found it hard to relate to this English son and his loyalty to James had been redoubled by his enforced exile.

So Peter sat alone, under the awning of the players' balcony overlooking Number Two Court, waiting for a break in the rain. He was already in his tracksuit and tennis clothes as Mo had made it a policy to avoid the changing room. He had not been to Wimbledon since his game against Nigel Bergen and his encounter with Jonathan Birdwood nine years ago – Peter wonderd if the old man was still alive – but Moses had guided him through maps of the club with military precision so that he would appear to be reasonably familiar with the place. Fortunately James had already established a reputation for remoteness and taciturnity so it was unlikely that he would be obliged to pick up any unfinished conversations.

Instead he glanced through the pages of the Competitor's Guide which was presented to every qualifier. Complimentary hair dressing was on offer to players – but for ladies only – and some West End theatres were even giving away free tickets. Tickets for the tournament, however, were less easy: every player was allowed a daily pass for his or her coach, wife, husband or – as the Wimbledon management so tactfully put it – 'sweetheart'. And you could have two if your parents were coming. Peter wondered if the Wimbledon authorities had cancelled his father's automatic membership of the club as a former champion following his disgrace and jail sentence. The money was better today than in Big Bill's time: a hundred and twenty pounds per diem living allowance and half a million pounds if you happened to win the Gentlemen's Singles. The Prize Money Office was just along to his left – known to the players as Terminal Five since after you had been to collect your cheque it was inevitably followed by a trip to Heathrow Airport.

'Looks like we're going to get a bit of action after all.' Mo had slipped into the chair beside him, distinctive as one of death's outriders in his night-black outfit and matching cap with its predatory peak and moniker 'Mo' embedded in yellow satin. 'The radar says the rain should lift within the next half-hour. They're going to make a start at six. Suits us: bad light, uncertain surface. Landry won't feel so comfortable.'

A bolt of adrenalin assaulted Peter's system, as if he were a paratrooper about to embark on his first drop. He got up immediately and started to assemble his racquets. 'Shouldn't I go to the changing room? Won't they be looking for me?'

'There'll be time,' Mo assured him. 'There's something I need to show you first. It's on the far side of the Centre Court.'

They went up the steps to the west of Number One Court where huddled groups were still standing in the hope of the Landry–Winston match finally getting under way and crossed the rain-washed North Concourse past the area where the television trucks were corralled like wagons in a western. 'Nine minutes minimum for the press interview, two minutes for television,' Peter remembered from the Competitor's Guide.

Moses led him down beneath the well-appointed Debenture Holders' lounge to the eastern entry to the Centre Court, just at the point where an extended electronic notice-board gave prospective details of the day's play and would have given the results if there had been any. There they turned into the bunker-like underbelly of the stadium, the concrete gloom alleviated only by the aperture of light from the court itself, still wearing its damp green cover.

'That's where you come out,' Mo whispered. 'It's directly opposite the umpire's chair. Pretend to be looking at the exchange rates in the window of that bank. Now just to the left – you can see the symbol – is the single lavatory for the disabled. You don't have to remember where it is. On the day Lucius will be waiting for you. He'll be in the uniform of a corporal in the British air force and he'll have a key. My signals will be the same as Paris. The zipper means stay there and slow it up, a sustained tug on the cap for come off as soon as you can.'

'Moses, do we have to go through all this now? We may never get there.' The tension that had attacked Peter's body like a virus throughout the day had begun to take on the properties of paralysis. 'Let's do one thing at a fucking time, all right?'

'Sure.' The coach put a steadying arm on his shoulder. 'I'll take you up to the dressing room.'

'I know the way,' Peter retorted fiercely. 'I'm going to be on my own out there, I'd rather be on my own while I wait.'

'Go on ahead. No problem. Good luck.'

'Thanks,' said Peter, remorsefully offering him a half-embrace.

'And don't forget,' Moses called after him. 'When the grass is wet and the court is greener, bring him up to the net and take him to the cleaner.'

Dawson Silver could not bear to remain in the house with James any longer. He now wished he had gone to Wimbledon to attend the game rather than endure the embittered commentary that his son was providing for him. Fully changed and brandishing an accusing racquet, James, alternating between his English and American accents, poured emetic abuse on his brother as he saw him lose the first set by three games to six.

'He's a wimp and a cunt. Hoffman is seriously mentally deranged putting that crock of shit up against Landry. They're handing him the goddam match on a plate. There's no attack. What does Pete expect him to do – take out a white handkerchief and surrender. What a fucking dickhead.'

Dawson felt his way to the kitchen where he knew Mary Doherty was also watching the game on a portable television.

'I'd like to go outside for a bit,' he said. 'Would you come with me, Mary?'

Although the rain had stopped for the moment at Wimbledon it was still blessing Buckinghamshire with a muzzy drizzle. Dawson and Mary walked far out across Lane End Common, looking for all the world like an elderly married couple, as she took his arm to make sure he remained on the path and avoided any clumps of grass or potholes that lay in the way.

'Bigger than Boston Common, Mr Silver,' she observed quietly. 'And not so well maintained.'

'Commons aren't meant to be maintained,' he corrected her. 'When they are, they become parks. They're just meant to belong to everybody. Even the ducks on the pond.'

'Well, there are no ponds here,' she replied. 'No swan-boats either. Though I think Simon would like it. There's a great fallen oak that he could be clambering all over and they've put a slide at one end with a sandpit.'

'He's too old for all that now.' Dawson, without thinking, referred to his son in the present. 'Surf boards and go-karts. Still likes the swan-boats, though. He'll always like the swan-boats – wherever he is.'

She said nothing more as the two of them, each seeking sanctuary in their individual time warp, worked their way down the hill towards the Dog and Duck pub, already jovial with regulars.

The phone kept ringing in the Wheeler End mansion.

'Joe, Mary, can you pick that up?' James yelled from in front of the television. Peter had just levelled the match at one set all. The bell continued to ring.

'Can you get the fucking phone?'

But there was nobody in the house except him – Joe Doherty had driven Quinn to the tournament. Realising this, James went to answer it himself.

'Yea, whaddya want?' In his haste he forgot to assume his English accent.

'You,' said Brandi de Soto. 'I know you're alive and I know what you're up to. But we can work together. Trust me.'

'Is it dark yet?' asked Dawson.

'It's nearly night,' Mary replied. 'The sun finally showed itself at twilight. Just in time to say goodbye for the day.'

'And are we far from home?'

'Not too bad. Twenty minutes. Maybe less.'

'I need to get there.' He became agitated. 'I need to know.'

'I brought a little radio.' She reached in her bag and fished it out. 'I thought you might be wanting it. Although I fear we've missed the news.'

'Turn it on,' he insisted. 'Turn it on anyway.'

The correct tones of the BBC announcer cut into the darkening landscape as if nothing had changed in the country since the twenties.

'The main points of the news again. The government has decided that the Hong Kong refugees cannot be moved from their present accommodation on the Isle of Wight. In America the President has said that the matter must now be urgently referred to the United Nations. And, at Wimbledon, a British player has reached the semi-finals of the men's singles for the first time since Roger Taylor in 1973.'

'. . . but, of course, Roger Taylor had the benefit of a situation where seventy-nine players – including thirteen seeds – had withdrawn from the tournament owing to the strike by the Association of Tennis Professionals. That was because Nikki Pilic of Yugoslavia had been refused entry because of his failure to play in the Davis Cup for his country – when there was a Davis Cup. Peter Winston, thank you for talking to us and good luck against Charles Garland on Friday.'

Peter inclined his head in acknowledgement as the avuncular television presenter went on to deal with the rest of the delayed day's results. A floor manager scurried forward and unclipped the lavalier microphone from the lining of his jacket.

'I've asked them to get you an official Wimbledon car to Fulham.' Moses was at his side as he left the studio. 'There shouldn't be much delay, there's hardly anybody left. If you go to the main entrance hall they'll be waiting for you.'

'Aren't you coming?' Peter was surprised. 'I thought we were going to practise at Queen's in the morning.'

'I've been thinking about that. There's too much interest in you. The car will be there at eleven tomorrow to collect you. Have a couple of beers – you've earned them.'

Peter experienced a perverse sense of rejection as he waited with the homegoing officials in the hall. Even the congratulations from nearly everyone he encountered were insufficient to compensate for what he knew to be a betrayal by Moses. That he should switch back his allegiance to James before this victory had even had time to sink in seemed both unfair and insensitive.

But he did not harbour the grudge for long. As usual with every move by Mo there was some covert motive.

'Any chance of a ride?' The voice came from the stairs behind him.

'It depends on where you're going,' he replied without needing to turn.

'Anywhere you are.'

He began to undress her the moment they reached the bottom of the basement steps, struggling with the key in the lock with one hand and unbuttoning the top of her skirt with the other.

'I'll cry rape,' she warned.

'You'll be right,' he cried, dumping their bags in the hall and pulling her in after him. 'Rape and pillage.'

'I've always wondered what pillage was,' she remarked.

'You're about to find out.' Peter lifted her up like a virgin bride and carried her into the bedroom. 'Where on earth have you been? I've spent a thousand pounds on phone calls in the past two months —New York, Sydney, Florida, Frankfurt.'

'I'm here now, that's all that matters isn't it?'

He slid her out of her skirt onto the bed, threw the skirt to the floor and himself beside her. As he kissed her, his tongue ferreting into her mouth with frustration, his hands reached up the inside of her shirt and he drew himself away only for long enough to slip it over her head. He licked the perspiration from her neck, excited as a hound greeting a long-lost owner, and moved his mouth down to her fuller than ever breasts and sucked on them insatiably. Tracing a route down her tanned stomach with his lips, he tore back her pants with his teeth and entered her with his tongue, licking and loving her till he ached.

'Is that what pillage is?' asked Phoebe. 'I hope you're going to take your clothes off, too, so that I can have some.'

'Why didn't you come when you said you would?' he demanded as they lay back later.

'I did. Precisely. Are you accusing me of faking it?'

'You know what I mean.' He gave her hair a tight tug. 'Paris. I waited and waited. And there's been a room ready for you at Wheeler End since last week. Everybody's there. Too many everybodies.'

'Lots of reasons. I've kept in touch with Moses. He advised it might be better to let you guys settle in. And I didn't terribly feel like turning up at a tournament that wouldn't let me in – didn't even get accepted for the qualifying. And other things.'

'This used to be my mother's room.' Peter was only half-listening to her as he looked at her body, long and dark and delicious. 'There's something terribly iniquitous about making love on your mother's bed. Not that *she* ever did – not to my knowledge. She would go to bed early and watch the telly. Telly was her sex or, to be more precise, Telly Savalas. Her idea of heaven was reruns of Kojak.'

'What a very limited view of heaven. I hope it's better than that.'

'I hope it isn't any worse,' he replied, stretching out to turn on the bedside light.

'Don't do that.' Phoebe stayed his hand. 'Not yet.'

'Is anything wrong?' He could tell at once from the anxiety in her voice.

'Yes.' There was a tightness in her tone he had never heard before.

'Somebody else?' He had sensed it lingering on the unspoken periphery of the last transatlantic phone conversation they had managed to have. Just like Samantha. History was about to repeat itself.

'Yes.'

'Are you going to tell me who it is?'

'It's a baby. I'm pregnant, Peter.'

The passing traffic threw torches of light across the ceiling as it raced out of the city, anxious to find quieter harbours on the tributaries of the M4. He had no need to calculate. They hadn't made love since January in Chantilly. The nauseous sensation that came upon him was immediate and consuming.

'Anyone I know?'

Phoebe sat up and clutched a pillow to her stomach as if she were already great with child. 'I was going to wait until after Wimbledon but I couldn't bear to let you touch me again without knowing the truth and I need you as much as I need my next breath. You are inside me, Peter. Your blood is mingled with my blood, your genes are in my foetus, my child will look like you.'

• Forty-Two •

'Tie-break.'

The words came both as a conviction and as an acquittal to Winston. He should have evened the match by winning the fourth set much earlier but his determination to adhere to Mo's game plan and keep the Japanese player on court for as long as possible had caused him to slacken his control.

'Shimizu to serve.'

At least he had succeeded in that aspect of the strategy: according to the digital clock on the scoreboard they had now been playing for three hours and thirty-eight minutes. The Japanese was beginning to show the occasional sign of tiredness, especially going up for his overheads.

'One–love, Shimizu.'

What would Big Bill do here, he wondered. His father had never had to concern himself with tie-breaks; the seven–six set had only been part of the game for the past twenty years. No longer could there be scores like the legendary Gonzales–Pasarell encounter: twenty-two–twenty-four, one–six, sixteen–fourteen, six–three, eleven–nine, a match which went on for two days.

'One–all.'

Mo had told him how Tilden helped to get Gonzales's career on the road by forcing the Los Angeles Tennis Club to lift the ban they had placed on the young Pancho because he was a Mexican–American.

'Two–one, Shimizu.'

Just before they had left Chantilly, the coach had given each of them a copy of what he called the old testament: *Match Play and the Spin of the Ball* by William T. Tilden 2nd. It had been written by their father seventy-five years ago but still remained the fundamental work on lawn tennis. When John Newcombe, the last amateur to win Wimbledon in 1967, was asked how he managed it, he simply replied: 'By reading Bill Tilden's book.'

'Two–all.'

'A chain is as strong as its weakest link, a player is as strong as his weakest stroke.' Tilden made his points in print with the same forceful fluency as he did on court. Shimizu had stayed back after his second serve so Winston angled a stop-volley which the Japanese player, always slightly slow in anticipating the short ball, failed to reach.

'Three–two, Winston.'

The tie-break was a time for daring. Big Bill had always insisted that the crucial points in any game were the third and the fourth. But here every point was crucial – the elegant breathing space of the old French scoring system gave way to the new American brutality of Jimmy Van Alen's more sudden death.

'Three–all.'

As in the interval at an opera, everyone in the crowd seemed to need to say something in order to provide a temporary alleviation of the electric atmosphere. The only people who could not avail themselves of that relief, as they changed ends, were the players themselves. Shimizu grabbed a towel and wiped his hands and forehead. At last, Winston noted, he was starting to perspire.

'Quiet please.'

They had studied tie-breaks at Osprey; Moses always insisted they were the crucial test of courage and concentration. In the evenings he would often run the Borg–McEnroe tie-break of 1980 which he maintained was the greatest twenty minutes of tennis ever played. Borg had five Championship points in that time, all of which McEnroe attacked and saved. The American gained the set, lost the match but won the war. It was the moment, Mo said, when Borg realised his Wimbledon dominance was over. The Swede, champion five times in succession, later retired at the age of only twenty-six – just a year younger than Tilden had been when he won for the first time.

'Four–three, Winston.'

'There is no attack without defence,' wrote Big Bill, 'no defence without attack.' The German genius whom Mo pointed to as the most perfect exponent of defence into attack because of the way he prepared his approaches with vicious preliminary bombardment had astounded the crowd here fifteen years previously. Boris Becker was the only unseeded player ever to win Wimbledon and also the youngest. He was seventeen – exactly twenty years younger than Tilden had been when he won for the last time.

'Five–three, Winston.'

Becker had won a tie-break in each of the last five rounds of the 1985 championship, proof – Mo pointed out – of the incalculable mental value of capturing a set that way. 'You win by forcing the recognition of defeat on your opponent' Tilden had written. But if Shimizu was recognising it, he certainly wasn't showing it.

'Six–three, Winston.'

The cheering and applause reverberated around the stadium as if it were championship point, and not just an opportunity to square the match. But there was a sense at Wimbledon that sultry Sunday afternoon that possibly the great wait was going to be lifted off the back of British tennis. It had been sixty-four years since Perry had completed his hat trick; maybe there was only another set to go.

'Six–four, Winston.'

The general pained groan that greeted the second electronic peep from the infallible Cyclops by the service line anticipated both the umpire's score and the linesman's call of 'out'. A double-fault at set point – Winston began to wonder if destiny had somehow decreed that the game belonged to Shimizu. He had, however, another chance to serve for the set and he intended to become more than a match for destiny.

To the mystification of those who were knowledgeable in the crowd, he took up a position with both toes fronting the baseline. Gripping his racquet like a club, he threw the ball up low and brushed across it from right to left, snapping his wrist as he did so. It curved, much slower than his usual serve, from left to right towards Shimizu and then bounced high and sharply to the right. The Japanese player merely stood and watched as the ball looped over his left shoulder. He had never seen a reverse twist before; indeed, Winston had never served one before. He had only read about the technique in his father's book.

Wimbledon went wild. Two sets all. The odds between the number one seed and the outsider were now evened by both men's fatigue and the extreme mental pressure put on Shimizu by losing the third and fourth sets. Ten years previously Stefan Edberg had managed to recover from this position, but before that one had to look back forty-four years as far as the wounded Yvon Petra in the first tournament after the Second World War for a similar recovery.

Peter Winston had other more troubled things on his mind as he slumped with his towel over his head. Like a relay runner, he had covered his allotted territory. Even better, he had successfully managed to turn it into the marathon that Moses had hoped for. His mother would have been proud of him. The short-breathed chesty exhalations coming from Shimizu on the other side of the umpire's chair underlined his accomplishment. His brother had gone over on his ankle while winning the four-set semi-final against Garland the previous Friday, but a pain-killing injection would certainly hold up for the ultimate showdown. Even Peter acknowledged that on his present form, James could probably take a set off any player in the world. And he was going to have to.

Or was he? Peter pushed the towel further back on his head, not so that his eyes could be seen but sufficient to permit him to look up towards Moses. As expected, the coach was pulling at the peak of his cap so frenetically that it was in danger of separating in his hand. Dawson, erect and anxious, was plying him with constant questions. Phoebe sat slightly apart from them, her bush-baby eyes, broodingly dark and downcast, fearing to meet his own. She knew that it was time for him to change places with his brother.

Why should he? Why the fuck should he? Why should he hand the Wimbledon title to the deviant who had impregnated her? He utterly believed Phoebe's account of what had happened, every word of it. In some small merciful way he was relieved that his brother hadn't buggered her. She had sworn Peter to secrecy for life or, she vowed, she would return to Sydney and never see him again. He couldn't have borne that. He couldn't conceive of any form of existence without her. And what she had conceived was his in flesh and blood, his mother's grandchild – and his father's. Nobody but them would ever know the truth, not even James. Especially not James. So he could stay in his disabled lavatory and fuck himself.

Even if Peter were to lose the final set, he would at least have the satisfaction of depriving his brother of it. He pulled the towel tighter over his brow. Bali Bhava, Bali Bhava, Bhava Bhava, Bali Bali.

'What's he doing? Has he gone off yet? What's happening?' Dawson brushed the side of Mo's head with his as he breathed conspiratorially into his ear. Even if the Japanese behind them could speak English they would be unable to hear a word.

'It's fine,' Moses lied. 'Everything's fine.'

'They're applauding them coming out again. Has James made it in time?'

'No problem. He's there. Looking good.'

'Have they exchanged shirts and shorts? The hair's okay, is it? He looks like he's been through four sets?'

'Yep, he sure does.'

Dawson settled back, reassured. 'Well, let's stick it to the Nip,' he announced, a little too loudly.

Something had gone terribly wrong. No matter how hard Peter tried there was no way he could attain any form of separation from self. Perhaps his mental fatigue had exhausted the resources of his spirit. Perhaps he had allowed himself too short a time for meditation. Perhaps the power had simply left him. Not only was he unable to achieve the advantage that this overview usually gave him but the fact that he was concerned about it completely distracted him. He lost the first game of the final set to love.

Even as he chanted to himself at the next changeover he knew it was no use. The fearful sight of Loophole Quinn, burstingly reddened and radiating hatred like a heat-seeking missile from across the court hardly helped. He didn't dare cast a glance at Moses for fear that the coach would cast a stone back at him. Or have him arrested. Perhaps he would denounce the whole fraud to the authorities and Peter would be pulled shamefully from the court.

The second game fell from his grasp as easily as the first and with it his hopes of the tournament. It was only when he was going through the motions of bouncing the ball in preparation to serve for the next that the reason came to him with unclouded clarity – the transcendent essence of the whole Bali Bhava thing. It was so obvious. It must always have been entirely dependent on his brother's spirit being free, even before he knew he had a brother. But Peter was unable to call on the twin powers of someone locked up in a lavatory and emanating an antagonistic aura. He had alienated his spiritual resources; he would have to rely on his human ones. So he drew back his racquet like a bow and let fly an ace.

At first he thought it was just him sweating. He brushed the moisture from his brow with his wristband. Next he feared he was beginning to bleed. The liquid on his cheek was warm and runny. He wiped it with the sleeve of his shirt but it wasn't blood. A drop hit him below his eye, then another on his forearm. Looking up, he could see they were coming more densely now, spitting their way out of the skies. It was starting to rain.

The sight of the tournament referee below the Royal Box – a mobile phone pressed to his ear – confirmed the fact even before the odd umbrella was opened in the exposed part of the crowd. The match was about to be stopped. They were going to go off. There was no way Peter could prevent the switch now. In his desperation he served another double and made his way to the net three games down.

The umpire covered his microphone as he spoke to them. 'I'm afraid we'll have to stop for a moment. Shouldn't be too long. Give you a chance to get a change of togs.'

'I don't want to come off,' Peter remonstrated with him. 'Look, it's clearing. We can play this out.'

'You can play with yourself.' Shimizu was already zipping up the cover of his racquet.

'Ladies and gentlemen,' the umpire had opened his microphone to address the crowd, 'play is temporarily suspended. We are advised this is just a passing shower so would you kindly remain in your seats as the delay is likely to be a very short one. Thank you.'

Shimizu, without waiting for Winston, had gathered his bag and was striding towards the changing room. Peter was caught. There was no way he could face Mo's fury, however communicated. And the thought occurred to him that maybe he had also alienated Phoebe by his action. Certainly she had expressed no facial pleasure nor encouragement during this final set.

Still with his racquet in his hand, he ran across the court, clambered the low fence and dashed up the aisle past Quinn who sat immobilised in anger. At the top of the steps Lucius appeared as if from nowhere, immaculately clad in his RAF uniform, and led him to the lavatory which he unlocked with due deference. It had been used before by Centre Court players in such emergencies.

James was in there waiting, wearing his Goffi tennis clothes, sitting on the covered toilet seat watching a portable television. He immediately tore the headphones from his ears and advanced on Peter.

'You English mother-fucking termite. I saw your face. Going for glory, you couldn't let it go. Well fate thought different. Hurry up and take your clothes off.'

Obediently and without speaking, Peter did as he was instructed, placing his soaking shirt on the wash-basin and stepping out of his shorts.

'Grace chose me, did you know that? Brandi de Soto has tracked down the nanny who took us from the hospital. You're not the son she wanted — you're a mix-up. And when I've finished with Shimizu I'm going to fuck you good and proper. Just as I fucked Phoebe Carter.'

Peter stood helplessly in his jock-strap and tennis shoes as he watched his brother pull on his damp garments.

'Not only fucked her but made her pregnant as well. Brandi sent Carter to her gynaecologist in New York and she has him eating out of her cunt — literally. I've seen photo-statted proof. That child is never going to be yours.'

James made a final farewell gesture with the missing finger of his right hand and turned to check himself in the mirror before leaving. 'Thanks for handing him three games, June. I really needed that.'

Peter looked at him and listened and still could say nothing. His brain was fused and his mind was frozen into one single supposition. The man in front of him was dead already. He had drowned off Puerto Escondido in Mexico. You could not murder a dead man.

The downward stroke from his Excalibur Plus was just as effective as Takeiichi Harada had said it would be. There was no need for a second one.

• Forty-Three •

There was no stopping him now. No impediment between him and victory. Not the weather. Not the score. Not Shimizu. Winston had never experienced such certainty nor such power in his life before.

When he had returned to the court the men were already rolling back the covers. The rain had departed as rapidly as it had arrived and, for the first time that Sunday, the air savoured of freshness – as if the passing shower had somehow cleansed the afternoon.

Every ball flew to the centre of his racquet, every shot that was targeted on the line hit the chalk with computer perfection, every time he asked for an ace he was rewarded with an ace. The burden of the game passed to his opponent as Winston found himself in possession of an increasing and seemingly infinite source of energy.

He even felt obliged to rein back on some of his new-found magic, lest this tryst with perfection should arouse the suspicions of the spectators. Not that he needed to have worried. They loved it. They were trying to nourish him with their own energy and enthusiasm, just as the crowd in Vancouver had tried to will Jim Peters round the stadium and past the line half a century ago.

But he shut them out, deliberately, and listened to his own internal support system. He knew he had forced the recognition of defeat on his opponent. Shimizu knew it, too. Winston could tell from his expression at the changeovers. It was more a glint of bewilderment than anything else. Shimizu was aware that nothing he could summon up would alter the course of the final now. But he didn't intend to jump off the boat on the way home like the self-sacrificial Jiro Satoh who feared he had let down his Emperor. On the contrary Zenzo Shimizu had won Wimbledon twice before and the impending defeat quickened his resolve to play in the Australian Open for the first time the following January and next year become the first Japanese to win the Grand Slam.

Nevertheless he was surprised and mystified by many of his opponent's shots, as if the English player had acquired an entire new vocabulary of strokes during the break. Initially Winston was bewildered by himself, wondering if it was really he who was out there, hitting the ball as he never had in his life before. But he knew better than to question it. 'When your game's on song, don't ask what's wrong.' Mo's rhyming advice had rarely been more relevant.

But as he stood poised, ready to serve for the championship, 5–4, 40–30, the real reason dawned on him like a personal epiphany. He had deliberately stopped himself from wondering whether James had merely been knocked out or was in a coma or worse. Peter hadn't had time to check his breathing. But he knew. His brother was dead. He could sense the death with his own body, not in a negative way but a positive one. James was within him now. The egg that had split in their mother's womb had become one again. Shimizu didn't know it but he was playing two men.

And the powers of Big Bill, the greatest tennis player who ever lived, were no longer divided into two but reunited in this glorious moment. Peter decided to put them to the test: he would end the match with an ace. It was what his father would have wanted.

As the ball cracked off the service line, and a puff of chalk coughed into the air, it ignited the stadium which rose with a roar. Fifteen thousand throats, thirty-thousand hands, every one vociferous in sending the signal to the world that at last an Englishman had won Wimbledon.

Peter fell to his knees and kissed the grass, like a crusader king returning to his native heath and offering votive thanks for his victory. As he raised his eyes from the ground he could see Moses and Dawson clasped in an embrace as if they were lovers who had been reunited after a lifetime apart. But, standing beside them, Phoebe beat her hands together in a joyless and automatic fashion, the tears flowing unrestrainedly down her face.

She knew.

• Forty-Four •

'Why do they keep offering me cups of tea?' Peter wondered. 'Is there bromide in them – like they used to give to soldiers to suppress their sexual urges? Or is there something worse?'

Nevertheless he accepted the mug graciously; it would have seemed impolite not to do so. But he declined the currant cake. The room was quite modern really, freshly painted with a bunk bed that seemed Swedish in design and a neat formica-topped table with two folding chairs. Nowhere to sit down and relax, though.

The officer was back at the door moments after he had finished locking it. 'Your brief,' was all he said.

Eamonn Quinn had never been called a brief before and visualised himself as a sort of Charles Laughton figure in *Witness for the Prosecution*. He had always harboured a clandestine desire to sport a legal wig and gown. As it was, he was still clad in the same lime green summer suit from the day before.

'How are they treating you?' he asked, settling himself at the table.

'They've hardly had time to treat me,' Peter replied with a dash of sarcasm – he had not asked for Quinn to come. 'Except for repeated attempts to drown me in tea.'

'You're a bit of celebrity. I expect they don't have too many of those in High Wycombe police station.'

The lawyer reached down into his bag and retrieved two newspapers. 'Only the rags, I'm afraid. I guess you'll get to see the serious stuff sooner or later. Lucky they didn't find the body any earlier, you've still got some pretty nice headlines to show your grandchildren. The evening papers may not be so flattering.'

Peter glanced at them; in a curious way they seemed to be about somebody else. In the best tradition of British tabloid journalism at its most celebratory both front pages consisted of a single photograph and a single exclamation. In one Peter was pictured receiving the Wimbledon trophy from the king with the quotation 'For you, your Majesty!' in large type above, although he couldn't recall uttering the phrase. The other merely had him with the cup above his head and the words 'At Last!' underneath.

'I think you'd be interested in this account of the match as well,' the lawyer added, sliding a single sheet of yellow legal paper across to him.

Peter picked it up. He recognised the handwriting as Quinn's own. 'This cell is undoubtedly bugged,' it began. 'You still have about twenty hours under the Police and Criminal Evidence Act before they are obliged to take you in front of a magistrate. Bail will then be impossible. But there is an option that just might give us an outside chance. If you were to insist you are, in fact, James Winston and not Peter Winston, then we can request to have you extradited to the United States to face the section 228 felony charges there. Once we start operating under the American system of justice and given the notoriety of the case . . .'

Lifting the sheet with both hands Peter crumpled it into a yellow ball and bounced it across the table back to Quinn. 'I'm not interested. I've signed a confession. They've found the body. That's an end to it. I have no wish to be James Winston.'

'For Christ's sake, quiet.' The lawyer indicated with his hand across his mouth.

'It's all right, Mr Quinn. They don't bug police cells over here. The evidence wouldn't be admissible in court, anyway.'

'Listen, boyo.' Eamonn objected to being patronised. 'You need all the help you can get, right now. It's not just the courts that are going to try you – there's more television and journalists outside this place than there were at Watergate. If the true facts start coming out, a lot of innocent people are going to be hurt – Moses, your father, me even.'

'My father is beyond hurt,' Peter answered enigmatically. 'Don't worry. I'm not going to implicate anybody. I did it and I'll pay for it. The only person who might make a mess of things is that girl Brandi. She was beside the court with a camera.'

'Ah, that's all right.' Quinn looked slightly relieved. 'James was just beginning to do a deal with her. She was looking for a lot of money. But we have enough tape recordings of her asking for it to make sure that Miss de Soto will dance to our tune for the foreseeable future.'

'How's Dawson?' Peter had not intended to ask the question but, faced with Quinn, found it emerged virtually of its own volition.

'He's gone down to Wimbledon to be with his boy. They actually have a morgue there, you know. He was saying an average of one point three people die during the tournament every year. Not normally the players, though.'

Peter managed a twitch of a smile.

'I hope you don't mind me saying so,' the lawyer went on, 'but Dawson never quite saw you as his son.'

'I can understand that,' Peter replied. 'Could I borrow your pad?'

'Sure.' Eamonn pushed his legal notebook across to him and removed a thick fountain pen from his inside pocket.

'It was good of you to come.' He began to scribble furiously as if he were rushing to finish a Cambridge tripos. 'I don't want you to represent me but I would like to see Moses if he would like to see me. And I wonder if you could get this note to Phoebe as soon as you can.'

'No problem.' The lawyer accepted the folded piece of paper and slipped it behind the large yellow handkerchief that flourished from his breast pocket. 'Your first wish is granted. Mo's outside. Been waiting to see you. The custody officer's been very reasonable about visitors. And I'll drop this at Talgarth Road on my way to identify the body.'

'I thought Dawson . . .' Peter began, but then realised his mistake.

Eamonn Quinn got up and stretched out a hand. 'Your mother was a fine woman. She was wronged and then things came right.' The lawyer seemed to be on the brink of a confession but he was merely on the brink of leaving. 'Maybe it's a good thing she didn't live to see them go wrong again.'

He kept his head turned from Peter as he tapped on the window of the door to attract the police officer's attention.

Moses Hoffman was admitted as the lawyer left. Gone were the tracksuit and cap; instead he wore a sombre dark blue blazer and black tie. Peter could not recall ever seeing him dressed so smartly, even on New Year's Eve. He had dreaded this meeting more than any other since he had walked into the police station at four o'clock that morning to give himself up.

But Moses unhesitatingly put his arms around him, his head only reaching as far Peter's chest, and hugged him tenaciously, as if stopping himself from being swept away by a flood.

'I came to apologise,' he murmured choking.

'You?' Peter trembled in amazement.

'I should never have done it. There was always a price going to be paid. God knows, I didn't expect this one, though.'

Peter's legs had lost their power to support him and he lowered himself to the bed. 'You mean our father. That was hardly your fault. Surely Michaels was the one to blame if anybody . . .'

'Not that.' Moses produced an already-used pink tissue from his sleeve and cleared his nose as he leant back against the wall. 'Well, partly that. As soon as I knew you were Big Bill's boys nothing could stop me. No, I should never have set you against each other. It's the formula for great champions but . . . well, it was too much pressure for you two. You were fighting for something more than tennis – and that was fatal.'

'Yes,' Peter grimly agreed. 'But you won, Mo. You won Wimbledon.'

'What was it like?' The coach's eyes came to life. 'I've always wondered – all my life. Every tennis player has.'

Peter lay back on his bed. 'I never intended to kill him, you've got to understand that. Just to stun him, just to stop him. But when I realised what I might have done, I also realised I could do anything. If you have the power over life and death you are no longer part of this planet, you are in some superior way in control of it. From the moment I came back on court there wasn't a chance of me being beaten by Shimizu. Loss was no longer part of the equation. It's not easy to explain.'

'You played like Jim. Do you realise that? Only better.'

'I felt like Jim. I felt him within me. I knew we had become one again.'

Moses said nothing but merely studied the elongated frame lying back on the narrow bed, with his feet hanging over the end. He wondered if he had deprived this young man of his sanity.

'You know,' Peter sat up with a smile. 'I've been spending my time thinking up a sort of a play, maybe a black comedy, about you arriving here to see me today. And you come in that door and I cry: "Moses, Moses, what should I do?" and you reply: "Well, you should grip the racquet a little higher up the handle and move your weight to the balls of your feet . . ." '

Mo kept looking at him, impassive yet amazed. The boy had gone mad. Yet he wanted to humour him. 'Peter,' he said, 'there's no such thing as a tennis joke, at least not that I've heard. There was just one, I remember seeing it in the *New Yorker* in the sixties.' He sat down at the table where Quinn had left his pad and took out a ball-point pen. 'You can't tell it – it has to be visual. It was when Polish jokes were all the rage. You see, these are the results of the semi-finals of the Davis Cup, when there was a Davis Cup.'

He wrote it on the paper in front of him:

UNITED STATES	
AUSTRALIA	UNITED STATES
POLAND	
BYE	BYE

Peter laughed, more out of relief that he still retained a relationship with his coach than from any mirth he could summon up. The sound caused the flap in the door to be pushed aside.

'Your time's up, sir, I'm afraid. I've allowed you more than you were allotted.'

Moses put his pen back in his pocket and, as he did so, removed a thin pamphlet which he pressed into Peter's palm. 'Your father's niece, Miriam Ambrose, was a bit of a writer. I suppose it runs in the family. This was her memory of Big Bill. I thought it might be of some comfort.'

Peter held him again as they stood by the now open door. 'I've always meant to ask you, Mo, did you ever meet him?'

The coach was outside in the hallway before he answered. 'I did more than meet him. I played against him once. It was a sort of a fun tournament at the Beverly Wilshire Hotel.'

'What was he like?'

'He had a gift from God.'

Peter had little idea of the passage of time. There was no window in the cell and when he had thrown on his tracksuit and trainers in the middle of the night he had forgotten his watch and his wallet. How he had actually managed to drive the few miles to Wycombe in his turbulent state remained a mystery to him.

So when the officer opened the door bearing a plate of shepherd's pie and a glass of milk he had no idea whether it was lunch or dinner.

'What's the time?' he enquired.

'Past five, Mr Winston, time for tea.'

'Did a woman come? A girl. To see me?'

'She's been here for some time. We had to bring her in round the back, with that crowd outside. Kindly volunteered a statement to the custody officer. Should help to tie up a few ends before you meet the magistrate.'

'Can I see her?'

'They weren't going to let you, not until you've been formally charged. But the boss has done a deal. If Miss Carter is prepared to make a statement of sorts to that media mob, maybe some of them will find they've got homes to go to. So he's given you five minutes. Do you want to have your tea first?'

'No, bring her now. I must see her now.'

He wished there was a mirror in the room to find out how he looked. He felt his face, it was rough and unshaven. In the small lavatory at the rear of the cell he splashed himself with cold water and patted down the back of his head where he had been lying on the bed.

Even with empty eyes that could cry no more and a complexion that had been drained by distress, Phoebe looked enduringly beautiful and entirely tender in an environment that was deliberately stark and unwelcoming.

'They said there should be no physical contact,' were her first words.

'Did you want there to be?' he responded hopefully.

'I wanted nothing else.'

She assumed a stiff and slightly formal position on one of the chairs as the policeman closed the door.

'How are you?' she asked.

'Guilty but insane,' he replied.

'I didn't know about your ulcer.' Her tone took on a motherly air, as if she were anxious to divert the conversation from anything that really mattered. 'Nevis gave me your medicine. He said you should take it right away.'

Peter interposed his body between the window of the door and the position where Phoebe was sitting. He quickly consumed most of the glass of milk in his hand and gratefully accepted the bottle she had taken out of her bag. Holding it in front of him, he replenished the glass and then downed the lot in one go.

He handed the empty bottle back to her. 'Thanks. The cops said they'd send out for some stuff but it really needs a prescription and, as you might imagine, today's been a bit fraught.'

'I can't imagine.' Phoebe bit hard on her lip. 'I can't imagine any of it, Peter. I can't imagine Jim is dead or you are here. Just tell me it's not true.'

'Do you mind if I eat some shepherd's pie?' he asked, taking the plate from the table to his bed. 'It helps to settle the stomach.'

'Answer me.' Phoebe looked at him sitting there, that broad athletic frame and long limbs crouched into the huddled position of a broken refugee as he spooned his mashed potato into him.

'James knew about the baby.' Peter couldn't bring himself to look at her. 'Worse still, he was intending to make an issue of it. Our life was going to be untenable.'

'What do you think it is now?' She regretted saying the words the moment she spoke, but she meant them.

'Worth a wait.' Peter mopped up the gravy at the sides of his plate with a piece of white bread. 'But maybe not to you.'

The life came back into her bush-baby eyes as she gazed at him with calm compassion and undiverted love. 'I'll wait. I don't understand myself and I don't understand you but I'll wait. Who else would look after you?'

'Oh, my God,' he said, and the tears misted the vision of her from his eyes.

'Sorry again, sir, pressure from upstairs.' The officer automatically cleared away the plate and the spoon from the bed. 'Did you think of any statement? It's not essential.'

Peter promptly stood up and cleared his face with his cuff. He glanced across at Phoebe who had risen, as well. 'Just say that things are not always as they appear to be. That's all.'

'Are we allowed to kiss?' Phoebe asked as she walked to the door.

'No,' the policeman responded with a wink.

He had to steady himself on her shoulders as he bent down and kissed each eye and then the tip of her nose and then her lips, softly at first and then soldering them with love and gratitude and remorse.

'Are you all right?' she asked anxiously.

'Fine now. Are you?' He patted her stomach. 'How's my boy Bill?'

'What if he's a girl?' Phoebe managed a gulping grin.

'We'll still call him Bill,' he smiled. 'Williamina Winston. Good strong name.'

'You be strong, now.' Her lips brushed his cheek for a final time and she was gone.

In fact, he had rarely felt better in his life. The sense of well-being seemed to emanate upwards from his toes and inform his entire system. He staggered a little as he sat on the bed and then remembered the small book that Moses had brought for him. It was there, on the edge of the table. He would read himself to sleep. He bent down to take off his sneakers: left shoe first, some superstitions never change.

There was only one thin pillow so he folded it in two and propped it behind his head. He had pulled the brown blanket up over him; despite the fact that it was a July evening it had grown very cold. There must be damp, he supposed, in the concrete walls of the station basement. Builders always said that once it was there it was impossible to eradicate.

As soon as he had settled down to read, however, he scarcely noticed it. *My Father's Brother* by Miriam Ambrose. Peter smiled to himself: Miriam would be surprised to learn that he was her cousin. Her father, Mo had said, had died at the age of only twenty-nine, two months after his own father. It had been his death that had propelled William Tilden into tennis.

'In essence, none of us really begin on the date of our birth, the forces that contrive us having long been present,' she wrote, 'nor do we exactly complete ourselves at the hour of our death, leaving, as we do, lingering impressions that fade slowly from people's minds. Something of Uncle Bill was evolving in our predecessors from a time nobody can pinpoint, and his having moved through our midst stimulated emotions and reactions in us that are still engaging. His fame accentuated his ramifications, reminding others who never even saw him in life of things he did; so his passage has not yet reached its end . . .'

There seemed to be no divide between the moment when he finished reading and when he woke up but he assumed it must have been quite some time as the room was filled with welcome daylight. And the bed had become a lot more comfortable. At first he thought it must be Phoebe who lay in his arms, the collar of her cream flannel shirt nuzzling against his chin and her legs in long white trousers foetally tucked into her stomach. But it wasn't. It was James, tightly asleep.

'Come on, now. It's nearly noon. The dew dried long ago and most of them are knocking up already. You're going to miss all the fun.' It was their father, in his baggy college sweater despite the warmth of the weather and with his two familiar wooden racquets tucked under one arm. He drew back the curtains and the glorious morning flowed in.

From the steps outside the scene was laid on a well-kept garden lawn. There was a bright warm sun overhead and just sufficient breeze whispering through the trees and stirring the petals to prevent the day being sultry.

The extensive Victorian house seemed to be surrounded by courts. Two games of men's doubles were beginning on the pair directly below them on the far side of the flower beds, multi-coloured with camelias and chrysanthemums, peonies and poppies, that sloped down from the upper path.

'Let's take a look,' said Bill, leading them down the steps. He indicated the man furthest to the right who was about to serve. He was wearing a flat white hat and a striped tie. 'Sir Norman Brookes – first Australian to win Wimbledon and the finest tennis intellect in the world. Makes him the most brilliant strategist around. And that guy in the silk scarf with those beautiful blue eyes and golden hair is Anthony Wilding. Cambridge man, like yourself, Peter.'

'Didn't he die in the First War?' His son was anxious to impress with his knowledge. 'Killed by a shell at Neuve Chapelle on the Western Front.'

'Very good.' They were in earshot of the players now but nobody seemed to be paying them any attention. 'So who are the others? James, do you know?'

His brother remained silent – as he had since they awoke – and merely shook his head.

'You can spot them by their sizes. Big Do and Little Do. Dominated Wimbledon for a decade. Reggie Doherty won it for four years, then Laurie won it for five years. Probably the best doubles pair there ever was, won Wimbledon eight times together. Learnt their tennis at Fenners, too.'

They moved on to the adjoining court where a man in long white trousers was leaping high to sweep away a practice overhead.

'Nice shot, Toto,' Tilden congratulated him, but again the player took no notice. 'Jacques Brugnon,' he explained, turning to the boys. 'One of the most perfect partners whether it was he and Suzanne or he and any man. Didn't really have the artistic temperament for singles. Singles is a creative game but doubles is largely a question of geometry. Some players can do both. Look at Cochet, there. Five French titles. He's the guy who put an end to my luck at Forest Hills.'

'He also stopped you winning the French Championship,' Peter was indignant at the sight of the man. 'Have you forgiven him?'

'You mean the line call?' the older man laughed. 'You've got to accept life's calls, Peter. They seem important at the time, but what's time?'

Winston looked up at him and could tell from the ruminative expression on his face, his heavy jaw securely set, that there was a tinge of remorse in what he said. So he changed the subject. 'Where are the other two – the other Musketeers, Lacoste and Borotra?'

'Oh, they're in the changing room,' his father replied. 'They'll be along when they're needed. Now see that little chap on the other side, Billy Johnston. If ever I had a friend it was Bill. He would have stood by me. Gave up the game when he was thirty and life gave up on him when he was still too young. Maybe he should have played on but he wasn't interested if it wasn't first-class. Do you know I'm not sure he ever loved it enough. That's Dick Williams warming up with him, but he's only keeping my place for me.'

Williams had seen them arrive and came across to where they were standing. He looked the boys up and down. 'Couple more of your protégés, Bill?'

Tilden rested his racquets against the chair by the side of the court in order to remove his sweater. 'No, Dick, not protégés. These are my sons.'

He turned back to Peter and James as he strode onto the court. 'Go and take a look at the Cup. Dwight's up there with it, just by the porch. Pretty significant anniversary, a hundred years and all that. He must be a proud guy, proud as me.'

James followed his father's wishes and set off for the steps where the trophy was glistening in the sun. As he looked up above the building he could see a castellated spire beckoning him and he broke his silence for the first time that day. 'The Magic Kingdom,' he exclaimed.

But Peter wanted to watch the game. There were several other spectators gathered under the cool shade of a tree on a grassy mound just beyond the court, so he strolled across to join them. He was made most welcome. A motherly woman offered him a bowl of strawberries and cream and a man in a blazer with a military bearing stood up and poured him a drink from a pitcher.

'Iced claret,' he explained, as he handed him a glass mug, 'ideal for an intelligent and appreciative enjoyment of the game.'

Peter thanked him and settled himself on the tartan rug with the others.

'This is a good place to be,' he said.

'Oh yes,' the man replied. 'An afternoon spent at lawn tennis is a highly Christian and beneficient pastime.'

· Forty-Five ·

Phoebe could barely believe her eyes. The woman was actually pouring herself a glass of brandy. She must think that she was at a cocktail party rather than participating in a tennis match. Indeed her salmon pink bandeau and flowing frock would have been more appropriate in such a milieu.

Her sturdy, snub-nosed American opponent, a short woman with carefree curls, seemed oblivious to the act. She had declined to sit down at the change of ends – implying somehow that chairs were for cissies – and was already striding towards the baseline.

But somebody had to do something about it and since Phoebe found herself in the umpire's chair she guessed it must be up to her.

She covered the microphone with one hand and leaned down towards the toper. 'I'm sorry. No alcoholic beverages are permitted on court.'

The woman looked up in mute incomprehension, offering a crooked-tooth smile as if she were somehow being congratulated.

Of course, she couldn't understand. What was the French for brandy? How absurd. They made the bloody stuff and yet Phoebe had no idea. She just stared stupidly at the woman who responded by holding up her glass and offering her a drink.

'Take this, it will help to clear your head.'

'No, I won't.' Phoebe pushed away the paper cup, spilling the contents on the bedclothes. She opened her eyes and offered the nurse an apologetic smile. 'I'm sorry. A dream.'

'A happy one, I hope.' The woman dabbed her brow in a motherly fashion. She was quite old for a nurse, probably one of the part-time staff at Sydney's Royal Hospital for Women.

'Tennis.'

'Well, that comes as no surprise. You were watching the Flinders Park final on the television when Mr Bennetts put you under. That Shitzu man won the match in Melbourne while your little girls were coming into the world.'

'Are they safe? Can I see them? I feel such a fraud having them this way.'

'I don't think you had any other option.' The nurse started to remove the damp blanket from the bed. 'We'll just tidy you up and then I'll go and get them. They're even more beautiful than they looked on the scanner. Have you thought of any names yet? Mr Bennetts was asking.'

'Oh, do bring them,' Phoebe pleaded. 'I can't wait another moment. One's going to be called Mo.'

'Mo,' the nurse repeated in her unhurried fashion. 'Is that short for anything?'

'No, just Mo. Maybe she'll turn it into something longer when she grows up. And the other's Petra.'

'Petra. That's an unusual name. Does that mean anything?'

Phoebe gazed at her through the lingering haze of the anaesthetic. 'It means everything – a rock on which to build a church.'

'Petra and Mo. Sounds like a good combination.' The older woman made her way to the door.

'Are they all right? I mean healthy. Ten tiny fingers, ten tiny toes. Everything in order?'

'For premature babies, they're wonderful.' The nurse turned and, smiling sympathetically, pointed to the knuckle of the forefinger of her right hand. 'It didn't show up in the scan but there's just a little bit missing from their . . .'

'I know,' said Phoebe.

A Selected List of Fiction Available from Mandarin

While every effort is made to keep prices low, it is sometimes necessary to increase prices at short notice. Mandarin Paperbacks reserves the right to show new retail prices on covers which may differ from those previously advertised in the text or elsewhere.

The prices shown below were correct at the time of going to press.

☐	7493 1352 8	**The Queen and I**	Sue Townsend	£4.99
☐	7493 0540 1	**The Liar**	Stephen Fry	£4.99
☐	7493 1132 0	**Arrivals and Departures**	Lesley Thomas	£4.99
☐	7493 0381 6	**Loves and Journeys of Revolving Jones**	Leslie Thomas	£4.99
☐	7493 0942 3	**Silence of the Lambs**	Thomas Harris	£4.99
☐	7493 0946 6	**The Godfather**	Mario Puzo	£4.99
☐	7493 1561 X	**Fear of Flying**	Erica Jong	£4.99
☐	7493 1221 1	**The Power of One**	Bryce Courtney	£4.99
☐	7493 0576 2	**Tandia**	Bryce Courtney	£5.99
☐	7493 0563 0	**Kill the Lights**	Simon Williams	£4.99
☐	7493 1319 6	**Air and Angels**	Susan Hill	£4.99
☐	7493 1477 X	**The Name of the Rose**	Umberto Eco	£4.99
☐	7493 0896 6	**The Stand-in**	Deborah Moggach	£4.99
☐	7493 0581 9	**Daddy's Girls**	Zoe Fairbairns	£4.99

All these books are available at your bookshop or newsagent, or can be ordered direct from the address below. Just tick the titles you want and fill in the form below.

Cash Sales Department, PO Box 5, Rushden, Northants NN10 6YX.
Fax: 0933 410321 : Phone 0933 410511.

Please send cheque, payable to 'Reed Book Services Ltd.', or postal order for purchase price quoted and allow the following for postage and packing:

£1.00 for the first book, 50p for the second; **FREE POSTAGE AND PACKING FOR THREE BOOKS OR MORE PER ORDER.**

NAME (Block letters) ....

ADDRESS ....

....

☐ I enclose my remittance for ....

☐ I wish to pay by Access/Visa Card Number

Expiry Date

Signature ....

Please quote our reference: MAND